Sherlock Holmes
and

The Adventure
of the Ruby Elephants

Christopher James

Paperback ISBN 9781780928210
ePub ISBN 978-1-78092-822-7
PDF ISBN 978-1-78092-823-4

Published in the UK by MX Publishing
335 Princess Park Manor, Royal Drive,
London, N11 3GX
www.mxpublishing.co.uk
Cover design by www.staunch.com

For my father

The valley in which I found myself was deep and narrow and surrounded by mountains which towered into the clouds. As I wandered about, seeking anxiously for some means of escaping this trap, I observed the ground was strewn with diamonds, some of them of an astonishing size. I wandered up and down the valley, kicking the diamonds contemptuously out of my path, for I thought they were vain things indeed to a man in my situation. At last, overcome by weariness, I sat down upon a rock but I had hardly closed my eyes when I was startled by something which fell from the ground with a thud close beside me.

It was a huge piece of fresh meat and as I stared at it, several more pieces rolled over the cliffs in different places. I had always thought that the stories the sailors told of the famous valley of diamonds, and of the cunning way which some of the merchants had devised for getting at the precious stones were mere travellers' tales, but now I perceived that they were surely true.

These lumps of meat, falling with so much force upon the diamonds, were sure to take some of the precious stones with them when the eagles pounced on the meat and carried it off to their nests to feed their hungry broods. Then the merchants, scaring away the parent birds with shouts and outcries, would secure their treasures. I chose the piece of meat which seemed most suited to my purpose and with the aid of my turban, bound it firmly to my back; this done, I laid down upon my face and awaited the coming of the eagles.

From The Arabian Nights: The Second Voyage of Sinbad the Sailor, property of Dr. John. H. Watson M.D.

1

ONE

The Fugitive

In the long history of my association with Sherlock Holmes there has rarely been a case of more singular interest than that of the Ruby Elephants. Leafing through my notes I am reminded that there were a number of features which also mark it as one of the most disconcerting we have yet encountered. For unlike many of our exploits it was not merely one problem, but a series of puzzles that were interlinked in the most peculiar fashion. And yet despite its complexity I am quite certain that it elicited the most brilliant of all of Holmes' feats of deduction. My friend, I know, disapproves of my rating of his cases in this way. However, he knows that it is for my own private amusement and need for order and for this he is prepared to turn a blind eye.

It was a morning in mid July when the summer heat was beginning to impose itself on our rooms at 221b Baker Street.
'Do you see this simple length of wire?' Holmes asked, holding a nondescript bit of steel up to the light. I glanced up from my newspaper. 'In two years time it will make a man a million pounds. In five years it will make him ten million.'
'Don't be absurd,' I muttered.
'I have never been more serious in my life' my friend insisted.
'Then will he use it to pick a lock at the Tower of London?'
'Nothing of the kind!' Holmes was clearly in a playful mood. 'Shall I show you?'
'By all means,' I sighed. 'My practice is somewhat sluggish of late and I'd very much like to know how to conjure pounds and shillings from thin air.' He furrowed his brow and began to manipulate the wire, bending it back on itself until it resembled something like a hair clip. He studied it again, rearranged an angle or two, then cast it onto the coffee table in triumph. It skittered across the polished wood and onto our bear skin rug. I picked it up and examined it.
'I fail to see how it has increased in value,' I confessed.
'And that, my dear Watson, is why you are not a millionaire. You are a man of inestimable qualities, but you lack the essential gift of

imagination.' Holmes lit a cigarette, drew on it, then left it smoking in the ashtray. 'Now you are aware,' he went on, 'that I have a somewhat haphazard filing system.' I surveyed the sea of papers around our feet and swamping every available surface.

'I am,' I confirmed.

'This,' he said, holding up the folded wire, 'is of more use than a score of clerks and a hundred filing cabinets.'

He picked up a handful of papers from his feet.

'The notes,' he announced, 'from that curious case of the Laughing Earl.'

'A ghoulish affair,' I remarked.

'And yet one you have not committed to paper, I note,' said Holmes with a slightly peevish air.

'I was under the impression that you put little stock in the written records I make of our adventures?'

'No matter,' he said, brushing this aside. 'Pay attention.' He tapped the sheaf of paper into alignment on the table top, then with a little cough and the air of a practiced showman, he picked up the wire between thumb and forefinger, fixed it neatly at the top of the pages and secured all five sheets together. I stared at Holmes. 'Rather wonderful, isn't it?' he marveled, looking inordinately pleased with himself.

'A million pounds?' I repeated, incredulous.

'If every man in Britain bought a hundred for a shilling,' Holmes calculated, 'it will not take long for our inventor to amass his fortune.'

'Remarkable,' I said, examining the bent wire it in the palm of my hand.

'Simplicity itself,' said Holmes.

My friend and I were enjoying our renewed acquaintance. Mary, my wife of a year, was spending a fortnight in Bath with her friend Louise, taking in the architecture and spa with excursions to Stonehenge and the great cathedral at Wells. Although she had originally mooted the idea as a second honeymoon, I politely suggested she may enjoy it more with her close friend and confidante. At a loose end, I therefore took the opportunity once again to enjoy the company of my friend Sherlock Holmes. I knew

3

that despite his chronic untidiness and irregular habits, some novel amusement and adventure would soon come our way. My timing, as it turned out, was impeccable.

'I note you have spent some time in Bath before,' Holmes remarked.

'I don't recall mentioning that to you,' I said. 'How could you possibly know?'

'Elementary,' Holmes laughed. 'Two years ago I heard you singing a song quietly to yourself. It was about a farm boy who worked in an orchard. The refrain made reference to 'The Rose Coloured Fruit and the Rose Coloured Sky.' I looked it up in an anthology of popular songs and discovered that it had its roots in the Bath area. Rather more prosaically, I later found a sketch of the Royal Crescent on your desk. I remember admiring it for the draughtsmanship, my admiration only slightly diminished when I saw that it was copied from an ink pot you were using, which also carried the legend: 'A souvenir from Bath Spa.'

I shook my head. 'Your memory is as impressive as your ability to absorb the smallest details.'

'You will have heard me say something of the sort before, Watson, but it is so often the merest trifle that is key to all.'

'Quite. But you are perfectly correct. I have had my fill of the delights of Bath. Despite its charms, I could not face another dose of its gentility just yet. I am willing to risk that a separation so soon after our nuptials will not have any negative consequence on our affections. In fact,' I mused, 'I am willing to wager that our ardour will be keener on her return.'

Holmes however appeared to have lost interest in our discussion, instead turning his attention to an experiment he was conducting on his acid stained tabletop. He was busy emptying a liquid from one glass vessel into another, delighting when the second solution appeared to change colour.

'A breakthrough, Watson,' he cried, 'a veritable breakthrough!'

An hour later, Holmes and I were in our familiar positions, he balancing two quantities of an unknown powder on a set of brass scales while I was engrossed in a novel with the sensational title: Return to Doom Island. Being unacquainted with the first visit, I was struggling to find my bearings. Presently, I heard a commotion down in the street. Laying aside my book for the third time that morning, I strolled to the window.

An exodus of Baker Street appeared to be underway. Women were holding their bonnets to their heads and fleeing at speed. Men clutched their bowlers and sprinted like Olympians down the centre of the road. Boys scrambled over each other, kicking up clouds of dust, caps flying as they raced towards the Marylebone Road.

'I say, there's an awful hullabaloo out there.'

'I imagine it's the first day of the sales,' my friend remarked.

'It seems terribly strange,' I said. 'I've never seen anything quite like it.'

I lifted the window and attempted to hail a policeman. Failing in that endeavour, I leaned a little further out, scanning the roof tops for signs of fire or smoke.

'Would you care for a stroll, Holmes?' I enquired, drawing myself back in.

Holmes sprinkled a pinch of powder into one of the scales and smiled in childish delight as they balanced perfectly.

'Really, Watson, I am very close to a discovery in a field so new it barely has a name. However I am also willing to confess that my experiment is somewhat unstable. It is quite possible that if the two powders were to make each others' acquaintance, then a considerable portion of Baker Street would disappear from the map. That really would cause a commotion.'

'Are you at least not a little curious?' I ventured, knowing that Holmes' curiosity would shame any self respecting feline.

'Well,' Holmes wavered, 'perhaps I have reached a natural break in my work and could benefit from a little air.'

Collecting our hats and a hastily compiled packet of cheese and walnut sandwiches from Mrs Hudson, we spilled into the street and the joined the throng.

I collared a lad who was lagging behind the others.

'What's all the excitement?' I demanded.

He looked at me as if I had recently returned from Mars.

'It's Juno, mister, he's on the loose!'

I stopped short and was almost immediately bowled over by a pair of fishmongers who were sprinting in their aprons as if in pursuit of a particularly fleet-footed shoplifter who had stuffed a mackerel inside his overcoat. I looked back for sign of Holmes and for a moment believed he may have been flattened in the stampede. Instead I found him at my shoulder.

'Any news, Watson?' he enquired.

'A Juno, it seems, is on the loose.'

For once Holmes looked as perplexed as I.

I seized another lad, whom I recognised as the son of a local milk carrier, Frank Smith.

'You!' I cried, 'young Smith.'

'Yes, doctor?' he managed, without breaking his stride.

'Who or what is Juno?'

'The zoo!' he shouted, bafflingly. 'The zoo!'

'Ye gods!' cried Holmes, who had evidently divined more from this exchange than me. 'Watson, there's an elephant on the run!'

My friend entered lustily into the chase, dodging and passing other pedestrians with an athleticism I had not seen since my days playing Rugby Union in Blackheath.

By the time we reached Marylebone Road, it appeared the whole of London was giving chase. Most seemed in thrall to a kind of involuntary hysteria, waving hats, umbrellas and rolled up newspapers as if they were attempting to drive the elephant back into its enclosure by sheer dint of numbers and noise. In fact it was entirely unclear whether we are running *towards* or *away* from the elephant. Already I had heard three or four different stories, ranging from a keeper who had taken leave of his senses to tales of a break-out staged by every animal in the zoo. Eventually, in the scrum, I spotted a constable who, with his arms outstretched, was attempting to hold back the crowd – although he may as well have been attempting to hold back the Atlantic Ocean.

'Mr Holmes!' he explained, recognising my friend. 'At last someone with a bit of common sense. What's to be done?'

'Where is the beast?' Holmes demanded.

'On the corner of Tottenham Court Road. We've got it surrounded, but it's made an awful mess of SW4.'

'Constable, I am very much obliged,' my friend said, clapping him on the shoulder. 'We'll see what we can do. Look lively Watson!' We hurtled through the crowd as if charging the Welsh at Cardiff Arms Park. More than once I saw a man thrown up into the sky, only to disappear again among the sea of hats. It was as if the government had fallen and the crowd was baying for the blood of the king. 'This is most dangerous, Watson,' Holmes shouted, using his stick to carve a path through the mob. My friend, it seemed, was as caught up in the hysteria as the next man.

After a further five minutes of jostling, we finally clapped eyes on the wonder: a magnificent female, murky brown, not so different in colour to the Thames itself, and towering a full ten feet above the crowd. Out of the elephant house it looked for all the world like a dinosaur sent to terrorize the West End. It was an Asian elephant that until today had spent its life perambulating the leafy walkways of the Zoological Gardens. Its howdah, in pink and gold, was still in situ on its back, although it had slipped to one side in the excitement.

Yet despite its fearsome size and the hysteria of the mob, it was very much minding its own business, gently tugging at the branches from a plane tree, scooping leaves and nuts into its mouth with its miraculous snout.

Holmes slowed to a walk. 'Perhaps I have not told you Watson,' he imparted with a faraway look in his eye, 'that I have some experience in the art and practice of elephant training.' I confirmed my ignorance of this fact. 'Indeed I spent a profitable summer as a young man in Assam where the wild elephants roam like cattle in the foothills of the Himalayas. I made the acquaintance of a local mahout, who allowed me to shadow him while he went about his extraordinary work, taming the beasts into submission. It is not a profession, I assure you, for the faint hearted, and more than once I saw an elephant toss his would-be master through the air as you or I might flick a fly from the back of our hands.' This did not reassure me in the least of Holmes' powers in this field although it was now clear his course of action was set.

'It was a moment of madness, Mr Holmes,' another constable

explained as we approached. It never ceased to amaze me how each and every policeman seemed not only to know Holmes, but treat him as a trusted friend. 'One minute she's giving a bank manager and his family a ride through the zoo, gentle giant that she is. The next, she shakes them off, takes a left turn and makes her way through the fence. She trod down the iron railings as if they were balsa wood. The sergeant has sent for rifles. It's a terrible business, but there's nothing else to be done.'

'The banker and his family,' Holmes enquired. 'Are they badly hurt?'

'No, not at all, just a few bumps and bruises,' the constable assured him, 'but there's no telling what she'll do next.' The pillbox lying on its side and a hansom splintered to firewood were sufficient evidence of this.

Holmes detained an excitable passer-by with a steadying hand on the arm. He was a squat gentleman, with whom by chance my friend was distantly acquainted.

'Ah, Crabtree!' Holmes said. 'I might have known you'd be here; still questing for adventure, eh? Would you mind very much if I was to take a loan of your umbrella?' Such is the authority of Holmes in such a moment, the man readily complied.

Armed therefore with little more than a brolly and the hazy memory of summer holiday in the 1870s, Holmes advanced on the beast with the stealth of a trained keeper. I kept at his shoulder, but was quite ready to beat a tactical retreat.

'It's all about trust and reward, Watson.' Holmes assured me, fishing an apple from his pocket. 'Think of her as an overgrown lapdog, and you yourself would be able to master her in minutes. This,' he said, waving the umbrella, 'is what the mahout called an ankus, used to persuade the most obstinate of elephant.'

Juno sensed the approach of a new and different kind of foe, and curtailed her lunch, stepping from the pavement onto the road to face Holmes.

'Good girl,' said Holmes in a low voice I had not heard before, proffering the piece of fruit, before switching to words in the native tongue of its homeland, which I took to be a branch of Bengali.

For a moment I was uncertain if the elephant was going to charge my friend for his audacity, insolence, poor grammar or a combination of the three. But to the admiration of the spellbound crowd, the animal accepted the gift and allowed Holmes to guide her with the help of his impromptu ankus back in the direction of Regent's Park. As we left him, Holmes patted the elephant's side and examined for a moment a bloodied patch on its flank.

'My my,' he said, 'you have been in the wars.'

'Probably a scrape with a railing or broken branch,' I ventured.

'Yes of course,' said Holmes.

TWO

The Jeweller

Once more, Holmes and I found ourselves in the comfort of our armchairs, the morning papers spread open on our laps.

'This is nothing short of a disaster, Watson,' my friend moaned. 'A trifling matter blown up into a proper stink. The inspector assured me there would be no publicity and that that my name would be kept out of the papers.'

'Oh, come, Holmes, it was hardly his fault. Half of London and all of Fleet Street were witness to your 'elephant whispering'. This bubble around was entirely unavoidable.' My friend continued to glower at the headlines.

When Mrs Hudson appeared at the door, therefore, with a card on a silver platter, it was something of a welcome distraction. 'A Mr Wenceslas Chatburn, of Queen Street's Jewellers,' she announced. Holmes hesitated.

'Do you think he's buying or selling, Watson?' he asked.

Mrs Hudson cleared her throat before I had time to respond.

'He appears to be in considerable distress,' she elucidated, 'and says it is a matter of the gravest urgency.'

Mr Chatburn appeared at the door like an apparition, holding his hat in trembling hands. He was pale faced, with rheumy eyes, with an aspect so resembling Jacob Marley that a monocle dropped from my eye. The likeness was uncanny in every respect with the exception of the chains. On closer inspection, however, these were present too. I noted not one but two pocket watches hidden in the folds of his waistcoat. The glittering rivulets spanned his midriff like the chains on Tower Bridge. His dark suit was of an older style and unfashionable cut, suggesting a man from another age; a spectre from the past.

'Perhaps, Mr Holmes,' he began falteringly, 'you do not remember me.' Holmes looked inscrutable. 'It was I who attended to the broken lid of your golden snuff box, some time ago. We exchanged a few words at the time about Wedgwood.' An uncomfortable silence fell upon the room. 'It is possible of course,' he added, trailing off, 'that the encounter was more memorable for me that it was for you.'

'On the contrary,' announced Holmes at last, advancing on the man with his hand outstretched. 'I remember our intercourse with nothing but positive associations, not to mention your superior work on the snuff box. However what is troubling me, is my difficulty reconciling the man standing before me, with the hearty, ruddy faced jeweller with whom I bandied in March of 1887. But tell, me why did you come via The Strand, and not Pall Mall, which would be infinitely the most straightforward route?' Our visitor appeared dumbfounded.

'Why,' he said, perplexed by Holmes' apparent intimate knowledge of his morning's journey. 'There was an accident involving a hansom and an omnibus, and a constable took it upon himself to close the road. But how could you possibly know? The incident took place not ten minutes ago.'

'It is absurdly simple,' said Holmes, lowering his eyes. 'A ticket stub from the Princess Theatre is attached to the sole of your shoe, which must have been acquired during your detour.'

'Yes of course,' Mr Chatburn confirmed, 'I stopped to buy a newspaper on The Strand, only a few yards from the theatre. Mr Holmes, I see your powers of deduction are as keen as ever.' His eyes clouded over again as he remembered the business at hand.

I invited him to sit.

'Now perhaps you will be good enough,' my friend began, 'to furnish us with the details of the problem. Please be as full and as frank as possible in your account.'

Mr Chatburn laid his hands flat on his knees and composed himself.

'As a jeweller,' he began, 'one would expect from time to time to encounter some of London's more unsavoury elements. I was aware of that when I entered the business. For the aspiring burglar, he is a pane of glass away from a prize that will lift him from the gutter into a world of comfort and ease. On my side of the window, I am a pane of glass away from a ruinous robbery or even a fatal blow to the back of the head. That is a risk we run.'

'Naturally,' said Holmes.

'Of course we take every conceivable precaution. Everything of value is transported to the safe at night; our shutters are virtually impregnable and the local constables display the highest degree of vigilance.'

Holmes narrowed his eyes, pressed his palms together and allowed his fingers to dance with the very slightest impatience. The jeweller quickened his narrative.

'And so it was this morning that I opened the shop as usual, sat at my desk to begin the business of the day when I discovered a note had been placed in the centre of the desk addressed to me.'

He handed over the note, which contained only a single line:

MELA SHIKAR

'Was anything taken?' I asked.

'Not a thing,' Mr Chatburn assured me.

'And what do the police have to say about this?' Holmes enquired.

'I have not yet troubled them,' the jeweller confessed. 'As I said, there has been no robbery.'

'And your staff,' Holmes pressed. 'Are they partial to practical jokes of this nature?'

My two staff have have never displayed the least tendency towards this kind of behaviour. They are both sober, respectable men who value their position above all things. This would be an absurd whimsy and entirely out of character.'

'I am not a linguist,' Holmes said, 'but perhaps it would have been more instructive if you had visited a library before your arrival here. It is merely an instinct, but I would not be surprised if they words were not Assamese in origin.'

'Mr Holmes, I am more impressed than ever.'

'Having spent time on the Indian sub-continent, I am familiar with the phrase,' Chatburn revealed. 'It refers to the way elephants are caught in the wild. A lasso is thrown by the rider of one elephant and its great bulk is used to secure the other.'

'How extraordinary,' I ventured.

'And entirely logical,' Holmes added, 'given their Brobdingnagian size. But can you think of any possible inference?'

'No I can't,' Mr Chatburn assured us.

'Do you have any idea how your intruder may have gained access to your premises?'

'None at all. I hold the only set of keys and there is no sign of a break in.'

'If I had a guinea for every time I heard those words, Mr Chatburn, I would be sitting at this very moment in a small café bar in Florence reading the works of Mr William Shakespeare and enjoying a glass of something cold and invigorating. Well, it's a fine day for an excursion Watson, what would you say if we joined Mr Chatburn in Queen Street?'

Soon we were confined in a hanson cab, hurtling down Baker Street, a glossy brown mare bearing us swiftly onto Wigmore Street. We took a smart turn at Goodge Street, galloped through Bloomsbury before being deposited in Drury Lane just as the matinee crowds were exiting the theatres.

'It's been an age since we took in a play, Holmes,' I remarked.

'They're staging a splendid production of The Jaws of Death at the Britannia and I hear that The Mystery of the Gladstone Bag at the Pavilion is absolutely capital.'

'Do you not find our own adventures dramatic enough?' Holmes asked, peering at a man in a pince-nez and a large black beard standing outside a public house.

It is sometimes refreshing not being at the very epicentre of the drama,' I ventured.

'I hold the world but as the world Watson,' Holmes mused. 'A stage where every man must play his part.'

The shop reflected its owner: perhaps a little too sober and austere to truly excite the potential purchaser of an engagement ring. There were tall, narrow windows, each lit by an overhanging lantern painted in black. It had more of the air of a funeral parlour than the place a rash young man would conceive a romantic notion and suddenly commit himself to married life. One had the impression that if such a customer appeared, Mr Chatburn would do his best to dissuade him of the merits of his scheme, selling him the item only with the utmost reluctance.

Mr Wenceslas Chatburn led us into the shop. Holmes inspected the locks, both front and back while I applied the same test to the windows. They were the strongest I had seen and would have secured even the most cunning and resolute of Her Majesty's guests at Wormwood Scrubs. The place was a dragon's lair of riches: precious stones winked at every turn. In one cabinet I found a fabulous menagerie containing a dragonfly encrusted with sapphires, a diamond studded bumblebee and a monkey with emeralds for eyes. There was a musty air; it was more of a museum than a shop.

'Tell me,' Holmes suddenly asked. 'When did you lose your tie pin?' Chatburn was caught entirely off guard.
'My tie pin?'
'Yes,' my friend persisted. 'We have met on two occasions and on both you were wearing the same pin: a fine ruby elephant. What's more I can see the outline on your tie left by its absence.'
'Mr Holmes,' Chatburn said hurriedly. 'I am a jeweller with a hundred different tie pins. I wear some for a week, some for a day and some days none at all. You will allow a dull man such as I the indulgence of some small variety.' It seemed to me a valid point and Holmes let the matter rest.

We followed the jeweller on a dour journey through the upper floors, gloomy havens with couches hidden beneath dustsheets, paintings turned to the walls and dark paper peeling from the walls. A smell of damp hung about the place.
'You will note that the windows are as secure here as on the ground floor,' Chatburn assured us.
'And the roof?' enquired Holmes. 'Is there an attic?'
'There is, although it is of no consequence. It is barely visited.'
'All the same,' my friend insisted. 'If we neglect one aspect then most likely that will be where the answer lies.'

We allowed our eyes to accustom to the gloom. At the top of the stairs, Holmes stared at the jeweller, as if spending a moment with the man's most intimate thoughts.

Climbing into the attic was like travelling from London directly into another continent by means of some secret trapdoor. What lay before

14

us appeared to be a room in the palace of the Viceroy of India. Holmes asked for another light to be passed up and led the way into the upper chamber. On the floor I could see a magnificent rug of intricate design. There were rows of tall backed chairs in dark wood that lined the sides of the room and at intervals there were cabinets filled with porcelain bowls, jugs painted with Punjabi patterns, intricate gold candlesticks and other paraphernalia. At the other end of the room, low couches with soft coloured cushions and a large, forbidding wooden chest carved with the likeness of an ancient palace. Most alarming of all was the row of tiger heads peering into the room as if through high windows. All bared their teeth, wearing their final savage expressions for all eternity.

For once, I believe my friend was lost for words.
'Mr Chatburn, you have surprised us all,' he said finally.
'Do you like it?' Chatburn asked, looking delighted at our startled faces. 'I was a company man in Calcutta and took quite a liking to the place. I was allowed a generous baggage entitlement on my return.'

Holmes scoured the room with an expert eye, carefully inspecting the wall panels and roof, satisfying himself it was secure.
'Is the room used by anyone, except yourself of course?'
'Never,' Chatburn assured us.' It is a place of memories, little more.'
'Then what,' asked Holmes, 'explains the cigar ash in the ashtray? You are not a smoker yourself. What's more, I have counted the remains of two different brands. Mr Chatburn, you will understand that while Watson and I are charmed by your mementos we cannot afford to waste our time. I have half a dozen cases that Scotland Yard have left with Mrs Hudson in the vain hope I will give them half an hour of my attention. This is proving to be a fruitless, and dare I say, exasperating diversion. When we are given half a story, we cannot very well be expected to find the whole truth.' Mr Chatburn moved uneasily to a chair and sat down.
'Mr Holmes, it is clear that I must now tell you everything.'
My friend's eyes gleamed like two pearls in the gloom. I produced a silver cigarette case and the flash of my match lit a fire in the tigers' eyes.

'I would be grateful if you would,' said my friend. 'And be warned, Mr Chatburn, we only have time for the facts.'

'For some five years I was in the employ of the East India Company, valuing and preserving artefacts, including those in the possession of the viceroy himself. You can imagine, Mr Holmes, that I moved in some of the most exclusive circles in India, mixing with some of our most important people. Over that time, certain alliances were formed and I found myself in the company of gentlemen with similar interests – namely polo, pig sticking, fine wines and object d'art. There were eight of us in this affiliation and as time went on, our bond became more intimate. Soon, we were a club, with our own emblem, etiquette and even our own name: The House of the Ruby Elephant.

'For many months, we revelled in our newly established society, with black tie dinners, lectures, expeditions deep into the Punjab. However some half a year after our formation, certain tensions could be observed. Two of our number, Jack Brace, a business man, and Warwick Snitterton, a veterinarian by trade, began vying to lead our small party. Neither would cede their claim and successive votes proved inconclusive – largely because none of the other members felt they wanted or needed such a president. Eventually the dispute was settled when Snitterton left the society after a particularly fearsome argument across the table one evening, swearing he would never return. He was never seen by us again and he left India itself shortly afterwards.

'One by one, we returned to England, meeting informally as the opportunity arose. Soon it was apparent that all remaining members, except Snitterton of course, wanted to meet once again and under our old name. We were reunited one evening in the Carlton Club. I vowed that night that I would provide a fitting venue of my own that would remind us of those heady Indian days. We held our first meeting in the room not two days ago and it was the start of a new era for us. Then this morning I found the note.'

Holmes crushed his cigarette into the ash tray like a man putting paid to a bad habit, not that for a moment did I think he would ever give it up. He smoked enough to fumigate a thousand swarms of bees into a lifetime of slumber. As a medical doctor I have cautioned against his excess and yet he ignores my council. Tobacco in all its forms delights the narcissist in him, the actor in him, and it colours his every thought and deed.

My friend peered intently at the reproduction of a portrait of Warren Hastings, the first British Viceroy of India.

'Well to me it's quite clear who wrote your note,' Holmes declared at last.' Mr Snitterton is the thirteenth fairy who hasn't been invited to the ball.'

'That much I had divined myself,' said Chatburn with some impatience.

'I suggest that you make contact with the man and have it out with him. Failing that, I would inform an officer of the law and ask that they pay him a visit.' Chatburn peered at the ground.

'There is one thing more,' he muttered. 'You were right about the tie pin. It was the only object missing when I opened up this morning. The ruby elephant was the badge of our society. Some of us had them, others did not. There are eight in existence. To us, they are a mark of rank and prestige. As a prominent member, naturally I had one and prized it above all other things. I kept it in the cabinet you saw downstairs. In terms of intrinsic value, it is not worth much more than the other trinkets you see in my shop. It is well made, naturally. But in terms of what it means, it is priceless beyond measure. You must understand, Mr Holmes, that I am an unmarried man and have no family to speak of. The friendship, the indelible bond between men offered by our society, means everything to me. Without the badge I hardly dare show my face.'

'Surely they will understand your circumstances,' I put in.

'Dr Watson, as I made clear, The House of the Ruby Elephant is a society with its own rules and peculiarities. On this point, we are quite strict.' We heard the rain begin to drum on the roof above the attic room.

'Gentlemen,' Chatburn continued, 'this Snitterton is not to be trifled with. When he is on your side, no firmer friend could you desire. But turn him against you and he is the perfect devil of a man. I once heard of a young officer who cheated him at cards. The soldier found himself bound at the wrists and ankles in the mountains alone with no food, water and it was only by a miracle that he was rescued by a passing patrol. Snitterton had no qualms about leaving him to the wolves. Mr Holmes, I believe my life is in danger. This note is a warning.'

'Mr Chatburn,' said Holmes in measured tones. 'Dr Watson and I will return to Baker Street to consider the matter further. It has certain features of singular interest. You will hear from me by midday tomorrow if we wish to take the case.'

The newspapers had not yet arrived. Unusually, Holmes was already up, pipe lit, and wearing his favourite mouse-coloured dressing gown. Lying open on the table was a volume of his famous Index of Biographies and I did not have to look hard at it to see that it was open at the letter S: Snitterton.

'Well,' said Holmes with that customary gleam in his eye. 'I did not hold out much hope of finding our veterinary friend and yet here he is. Born 1835 in Bromley, studied at The Royal Veterinary College in Camden. Specialises in exotic animals. While still a student he saved a leopard and white tiger at London Zoo when all hope had been abandoned.'

'So how does a cow-doctor end up in India?'

'It says here that he received a CBE while only 23; he was offered his own choice of post. He probably chose India to get at close quarters with the big beasts.'

'And what of his human interests?' I enquired.

'Engaged to the Countess of Salisbury. Called off at the last moment. Received a fine while still in Calcutta for threatening behaviour: dangling a man upside down from a tree a few feet above a starving tiger while on a hunting trip.'

'Strikes me as a man with a peculiar sense of humour.'

'Redeems himself by saving the Viceroy's pet elephant which had contracted blue tongue.'

'Another elephant!' I exclaimed.

'Ah,' said Holmes retrieving a pencil from his acid stained tabletop, 'now this is of is singular interest. Returns to England shortly after the death of a servant who was savaged by an Asiatic Lion in the service of the Viceroy. The two matters remain unconnected.'

I picked up the volume and continued to read. 'It says here he has extraordinary powers of observation, medical deduction, superb reactions and an uncanny empathy with animals.'

'Sounds a capital fellow,' said Holmes. 'Now where would we begin to look for him in London?'

I was troubled that night by a strange dream. I was back in uniform in Afghanistan, and found myself, as so many nights before, in the Maiwand Pass during that traumatic battle and retreat of 1880. In the smoke and the chaos, I felt the burning sensation as the Jezail bullet entered, wreaking its terrible havoc on my shoulder, exploding the bone and missing by a hair's width my subclavian artery. I could see Captain Slade and those formidable men of the Royal Horse Artillery as they covered our retreat, knowing full too well that they would soon be overrun.

And yet this time things were different. From my vantage point, across the pack horse upon which Murray, my orderly, had thrown me, I saw the Afghans begin to fall back. I saw a look of horror and fear on the faces as they abandoned their weapons, turned on their heels and fled. Despite the horrible pain I began to laugh at the astounding turn of events. Who or what had intervened in our favour? It was then I heard the trumpeting, the thunder of feet and saw the dust clouds as eight elephants charged the Afghan lines. They were an unnatural hue: a devilish shade of red, with burning white eyes, as if they had stormed straight through the gates of hell.

I found myself being shaken awake. It was with some relief that I saw it was my old friend Sherlock Holmes staring kindly back at me.

'Chasing phantoms again, Watson?'

'Just a dream, old fellow. I am frightfully sorry if I woke you.'

'Not at all,' Holmes assured me. 'I didn't hear a thing.'

'Then what's all this about? What's the time?'

'A quarter to three in the morning,' Holmes informed me, as if this was a perfectly reasonable hour to rouse a man from his bed. I noticed he was fully dressed, his coat hung loosely around his shoulders. From the nutty vapours, I could tell that he had already smoked his first pipe of the day. 'I'm embarking on a small expedition if you would care to join me.'

Five minutes later, I had climbed into some day clothes and splashed cold water on my face.
'I hope this is worth it, Holmes,' I muttered as we tiptoed down the steps to avoid waking our neighbour's cocker spaniel, or worse still, Mrs Hudson.
'You said it was a dull dream,' Holmes countered. 'And anyway, with a bit of luck we'll be back in time for kippers and coffee at seven. I've left a note with Mrs Hudson to have them ready on our return.'

A hansom was waiting for us on the corner. The driver's face was hidden in shadow and he gave no greeting. The minute we were inside, he shook the reins and we were away, flashing like a black phantom down the road. We saw barely a soul, just a solitary drunk performing a slow waltz down Marylebone Road and a single constable on silent patrol. The street lamps flickered like the dreams of a million sleeping Londoners.

We darted along several rat runs and largely kept away from the main streets. At one point we bumped along cobbles and I caught a glimpse of Paddington Street Gardens; however, the unusual choice of route, combined with the darkness of the hour, finally succeeded in throwing my sense of direction.
'Where in heaven's name are we heading?' I demanded of Holmes, but he refused to be drawn.
'Now it is the time of night,' my friend recited, his eyes twinkling, 'that the graves all gaping wide, every one lets forth his sprite, in the church-way paths to glide.'
I was astonished then, to find ourselves once again in Queen Street, pulling up just short of the jeweller's shop we had visited the previous afternoon.

Holmes leapt out of the cab, his cloak flapping like a bat's wings about him. I followed him, taking a moment to drop some coins into the palm of our mysterious driver. Holmes rarely dealt in small change himself as I had learnt to my cost.

'Now Watson, my dear Watson,' whispered Holmes. 'Are you ready once again to trust me with your life?'

'What makes this occasion any different from the others?' I answered.

'Then you must do exactly what I say. This is not a moment for initiative or originality, do you understand?' I was flattered that Holmes believed I was capable of either.

We stood outside the dim, unlit shop a moment, while Holmes scanned the environs left and right for any sign of life. A lamp flickered at the end of the street casting its shadow across the road.

'Right,' he said, satisfying himself we were alone, 'follow me.'

Holmes whipped around to face the wall and placed a hand on the cold, grey stone. Reaching up, he hauled himself a foot off the ground.

'Ready for a little night climbing, Watson?'

I had heard of this form of urban mountaineering, which was said to be practised by athletic gentleman in our more exclusive universities. However, never once had I felt the inclination to try it for myself.

'Come along, Watson,' urged Holmes, 'it's far easier than it looks.'

Soon we were both twelve feet up, sidling along a thin stone ledge. The street appeared to be several miles below. Holmes had attached himself to a drainpipe and was using it as a support to reach the second floor window. I followed suit and joined him, a little breathless, on the window sill. For a moment we stood like two petrified saints high up over the London street. Holmes pressed a finger to his lips then pointed upwards. I rolled my eyes.

My friend stepped out to his left into what appeared to be thin air. However I deduced that he had once again employed the drain pipe, this time to swing himself around the corner of the building. Once again, I did the same, with no real sense of what I would find on the other side. The answer was very little indeed. I found a small protruding brick onto which to plant a foot and another to cling to with my fingertips. There was no sign of Holmes. The night was warm; a slight breeze ruffled my shirt. For a terrible moment I believed he had fallen, characteristically without a sound so as not to place me in jeopardy. Surely not! I searched frantically in the darkness and with a sense of monumental relief recognised my friend's pale, thin features lurking in the shadows.

I joined Holmes in an alcove, making my position safe by lodging myself between the two brick walls. I dimly recollected that in climbing circles, this manoeuvre was called chimneying. We smoked in silence side by side and although I have enjoyed tobacco in more relaxed circumstances, it was given an extra frisson by the inherent danger of our precarious perch. I watched the blue-white smoke coil upwards as if a snake was being charmed from its basket.

We continued our ascent, walking our way up the walls until we were level with the third floor. Suddenly Holmes froze. His hearing, keener than mine, had detected something. Sure enough, there were footsteps approaching and below us I saw a constable on his beat, walking in that particular measured and vigilant sort of manner unique to officers of the law. He was looking to his left and right as part of his natural gait.

Holmes responded by entering a zen-like state. If I did not know better, I would have said that by some miraculous means he had managed to stop his heart beating and his lungs performing their vital work. To my horror, it was at this moment that a coin, which I had held back from the driver of our hansom, in part due to his rather offhand manner, managed to work its way out of my pocket. I heard it drop to the street and land on the pavement with a sound like a dinner gong. The constable stopped immediately. He shot a glance behind him. He performed a slow 360 degree turn and then walked to the source of the noise. The coin gleamed in the moonlight. The constable picked it up and examined it between thumb and forefinger as if he had never seen one before. All he had to do was raise his head and he would find us hanging above him like a pair of ravens roosting in a tower. But luck was on our side. He looked in every direction except up. Pocketing the coin, he had evidently convinced himself that it was his after all.

We were untroubled again until we reach the roof. Here we found that an athletic twist was required to swing ourselves up onto the final stone ledge supporting the guttering. Already I was feeling dizzy from the altitude, the nervous encounter with the constable and the unexplained nature of the visit. However I had been in stranger spots with Holmes and the cards had invariably fallen in our favour. I had no choice but to trust him.

Holmes is a man of extraordinary paradoxes. One moment, he is akin to a convalescing patient, pallid of skin, listless and apparently without energy. He can languish in his armchair, consuming nothing more nourishing that Persian tobacco with the look of a man who has died in his sleep. At other times, he exhibits an extraordinary vitality, no doubt the secret behind his effortless mastery of several branches of martial arts and the marvellous strength that allows him to bend metals and bring men twice his weight to the ground. I have never quizzed him on these contradictory states; however, it is clear that he has hidden reserves that may be drawn upon in extremis. It was from these reserves that Holmes drew to make an extraordinary leap onto the roof. In a moment, my friend was peering down at me, proffering a gloved hand. I accepted gratefully and at last, like two alpine adventurers, we found ourselves at the summit.

There was a narrow indentation in the building that ran from the pavement to the roof: surely just a whimsy of the builder for it appeared to serve no practical purpose. And it was in this that Holmes had lodged himself, his back pressed up against one side, his feet planted on the other and nothing but fresh air beneath him. His arms were folded as if he was seated in an armchair at the Reform Club.
'Care to join me?' invited Holmes.
He proffered another pair of cigarettes and I gratefully accepted one.
'I'm not expecting a lamplighter at this hour,' he said. 'Do you have a flame?'

'Well,' I said, feeling something like Nelson himself standing over London. 'Have I earned an explanation yet, or am I to assume that

London's greatest detective has finally turned to the very devilment which he has hitherto vowed to destroy?'

'Not quite!' Holmes said. 'But your answer is just moments away.'

As fleet as an alley cat, Holmes hopped across the tiles and headed for a small elevated window. I followed him on all fours, a little less keen to risk my life on loose tiles and gravity. I finally caught up with Holmes at the window, which he was attempting to raise.

'As I thought, Watson,' my friend muttered, 'it is quite secure.' For a moment, I felt that Holmes had discovered a flaw in his plan, without caring to admit it to me. 'This leaves just one other possibility.' With a short jump he arrived at the foot of the chimney and pressed his hands to the surface, as if testing for a loose brick.

'Watson,' he hissed, with a triumphant look, 'fortune favours the brave.'

When I finally reached the chimney myself, I found that my friend had once again disappeared. The rooftops of London are a ghostly sight at night; I imagined them dispatching the thoughts of the sleeping masses into the clouds. At once I felt a terrible melancholy and utterly alone. It was strange that this man, so cold in disposition, so cool minded and cerebral in his dealings now proved so indispensable to me. I heard the scraping of bricks and there was a chink of light.

'Will you join me?' a familiar voice enquired. The opening grew wider, and with a little discomfort I managed to squeeze myself through the aperture.

I emerged in the attic room and saw my friend already seated in one of the chairs around the long table, reading by the light of a single candle. It was only once safely inside that I realised that I had clambered directly through the painting of The Viceroy of India. I examined the frame and saw to my astonishment that the canvas was held on an elastic catch and could be rolled back and forward as required. It snapped back into position as soon as I was through.

'Ingenious!' I exclaimed.

'Perfectly simple,' said Holmes. 'An old magician's trick.'

'But how did you know this was the way in? We barely spent a minute here yesterday.'

'Again, this can be explained with the utmost ease,' Holmes replied, laying down his piece of paper. 'To begin with, I noticed on the exterior of the building black scuff marks on the brickwork, which could not explained by anything other than the toe or heel of a gym shoe. It is the safest way to climb the exterior of a building and always favoured by members of the illicit climbing fraternities of our great universities.'

'Yet we didn't wear any such shoes,' I put in.

'Which is precisely why we found it so difficult,' Holmes admitted. 'Besides, I wanted to prove that it was possible without the right footwear, the reasons for which will become clear.'

'And the painting?'

'The painting I had no idea about,' Holmes conceded. 'I merely knew there had to be a means of entry somewhere from the roof. We may well just have arrived through the mouth of that fearsome Bengali Tiger over there on the wall.' It was reassuring to hear that my friend could still surprise himself from time to time.

Given the early hour and the excitement of the morning so far, I felt a strong desire for a cup of cocoa. Holmes appeared to understand the cause of my agitation.

'Not long now Watson,' he said.

'Not long until what?'

'The start of the meeting,' he replied.

THREE

The Meeting

I stared at Holmes in disbelief.

'The meeting is due to begin in ten minutes,' he explained calmly, 'which gives us precisely nine minutes to find somewhere suitable to conceal ourselves and attend the meeting as uninvited guests. I have a copy of the minutes of the last one. Chatburn was careless enough to leave them lying around, which furnished me with the relevant details.'

'But what do we possibly have to gain from such an imposition?'

'I have reason to believe that Chatburn is not telling us everything about The House of the Ruby Elephant or its curious activities.'

I considered the matter, then scanned the room.

'I had pre-selected this trunk for you,' my friend advised, as if I was the prospective purchaser of a delightful new home. 'I believe it to be sufficiently large and well ventilated to prevent suffocation.'

'That is reassuring,' I remarked, 'and what of your accommodation?'

'I will be hidden beneath the cloth of this low table.'

'Let us hope then,' I said with resignation, 'that the chairman keeps the business brisk.'

'Indeed!' Holmes beamed.

The next hour was simultaneously the most uncomfortable and astonishing of my life. While the trunk was roomy enough, as my friend had predicted, it had a peculiar musky smell that I could not quite put my finger on. It was not by any means unbearable, but it made my breathing rather laboured and succeeded in bringing on a headache. My legs were folded beneath me and it was while I was still adjusting their position that I heard the door open and the sound of low muffled voices. I detected the scent of cigar smoke as others entered the room.

Soon a man called his fellow members to order. I will not trouble you with the minutes of the entire meeting, and in this capacity, no doubt the secretary of the society did his job with admirable diligence. However, these would not have captured the strange

26

atmosphere at the start of the gathering, which to my ears were more akin to the beginning of a voodoo ritual than a meeting of professionals. I heard what appeared to be someone humming a low, sustained note like a man attempting to tune a piano without the aid of a tuning fork. The voice was joined by another, at the same pitch. If there had been more musicality to the performance, I might have taken them for a male voice choir warming up for an evening of Monteverdi, which would have made Holmes and me feel very foolish indeed. The sound swelled to a cacophony, making the lock of the trunk rattle. I was almost certain at this point that this was indeed a musical company, and thought for a moment about revealing myself. Surely a fulsome apology and a firm handshake would have sufficed.

It was then that I heard Chatburn declaiming above the racket, in a voice filled with affected mysticism:
'By the two lamps of the sun and moon, and in the blood of Prince Nizam, I declare open this meeting of The House of The Ruby Elephant!' It was rather overdone, I felt, and smacked of amateur dramatics. I knew that Holmes would be similarly scathing about the performance. Then a chill ran through me:
'If there are enemies amongst us, let them show themselves now, or we seek them out and drain them of their God-light.' I shut my eyes, almost expecting the lid of the trunk to be flipped open. I felt entirely protective of my God-light.
'Then let us begin,' Chatburn finished. I expelled the remaining air in my lungs.
'What news of Snitterton?' a voice came in.
'Yes Jack, what news?' came another, rather more prosaically. I puzzled at the name.
'Still at large. But I have taken steps. You will have heard of the great detective, Sherlock Holmes? I have engaged him to seek out Snitterton on our behalf. Where we have failed, Holmes will surely succeed. I provided a simple clue that will send him on a chase across London. Once he delivers him to us, we will finish him.'
'Naturally, Chatburn,' came a voice of authority, we are all concerned that Snitterton is gathering his forces. We have heard that he has sworn vengeance on us all.'

'And yet,' came yet another, 'It is you, Jack, with whom he has his grievance. What say you to squaring up to him, man to man, eh? Get this thing over with.'

'I wish,' said Chatburn wistfully, 'I only wish it was that simple. You heard the curse he placed on our order as he left. No man can lift such a curse, not even I.'

The room broke into a flurry of conversation. I heard the strike of matches and the sloshing of drinks.

'Order, brothers, order,' Chatburn called. 'Mr Smyth, would you care to furnish us with what we know of Snitterton's plans?'

'Of course, Mr Chairman,' came a low voice I had not yet heard. There was the sound of chair legs grinding backwards as he rose to his feet. Some heavy steps worked their way around the room, coming slowly towards me. Clearly this was a man of some size and stature.

'Brothers, this news came to me from an acquaintance, who has neither the wit nor the inclination to lie. Snitterton has formed a society of his own: The Order of the Sapphire Butterfly.'

'Sounds somewhat derivative,' a voice chipped in.

'Think what you will,' rebuked Smyth. 'He has already signaled his intention. No doubt you will have heard of the elephant that escaped from the London Zoological Gardens. I believe the elephant was drugged with a powerful stimulant that sent it mad and out into the streets. With Snitterton's knowledge of animal medicine, such a stunt was easy enough.'

Once more, the room broke into a mutinous fray, before Chatburn called them again to order.

'Brothers, please!' A relative hush descended, before a dissenting voice called out:

'Who will be next? You, Ignatius? How about you, Peaceheart?'

'Gentlemen. Here is my pledge: that before the week is out, Snitterton will be out of the picture for good.'

The meeting proceeded in varying degrees of audibility while my confinement become increasingly uncomfortable. Try as I might, I failed to glean the purpose of the society, precisely what role Chatburn held or the common interest that bound them together. I hoped Holmes had divined something more useful than I.

Just as the blood had drained entirely from the lower half of my legs, the meeting drew to a close. Once more the strange humming filled the room and Chatburn's incantations were every bit as ridiculous as those which began the meeting: 'You who wait for the sun to set on the sea, the rain to fall on the desert, the day to pass in the hills; wait for the hour of the elephant. Hathhee, in the hour of the setting sun we honour and salute thee.'

'We honour and salute thee,' the other members chorused.

The chairs scraped again and the conversation turned to general matters; I heard more than one yawn, excusable given the early hour, and within ten minutes, the last of them had gone. Still I dared not move. Who was to say a house servant or even Chatburn himself would not return to empty the ashtrays?

Presently I heard a light knock on the lid of the trunk and before I had time to panic, the lid lifted to reveal Sherlock Holmes. He peered down at me, folded as I was, like a spider in a matchbox.

'I fancy you are ready to be posted to West Bengal, Dr Watson.'

'I would prefer that to our other exit options,' I replied ruefully, uncoiling myself and testing my weight on a leg.

'A most enlightening meeting, wouldn't you say?'

'I'm not entirely sure, Holmes,' I said honestly. 'In fact I would go as far to say that I am perhaps less enlightened than when we arrived.'

'My dear Watson,' Holmes assured me. 'All will be revealed in a moment. But as for now, there is something else.' Holmes strode to the other side of the room where a large cabinet stood and thick curtains covered much of the dark wood. 'Would it surprise you very much if I told you we are not alone?' With a magician's flourish, he tore down the curtain to reveal the shadowed form of a tall man.

I staggered out of the trunk and shambled a few steps forward. My mind reeled; filled with horror and incomprehension.

'Would you care to step into the light, Mr Snitterton?' my friend invited.

Dutifully, like Frankenstein's monster, the man loomed towards us. Snitterton was a great beast of a man; forty, black bearded with shoulders like Atlas and a livid purple birthmark that pulsed angrily on his neck. He was wearing a rich blue jacket in the military style, with a white silk shirt. He had the curious air of a circus strongman, slightly dandyish and with a fierce intelligence. His eyes blazed like hot coals and his high, wide forehead was red with fury. Like us, he was pearled with sweat from his confinement and he clenched and unclenched his fists as if to mirror his shallow breathing.

'You have made a sorry mistake, Mr Sherlock Holmes,' the man growled. 'You are mixed up in a business beyond your limits and jurisdiction.'

'I am beholden to neither,' Holmes returned curtly.

'I would dare say your ignorant friend Dr Watson here has more sense than you in this matter.' I bristled somewhat at this backhanded compliment, but was more preoccupied by the pins and needles creeping up my legs, denying them of their ability to hold me upright. I crashed forward, unwittingly toppling the giant, who quickly scrambled to his feet.

'First class, Watson!' my friend applauded. 'A magnificent opening salvo.' Holmes adopted a stance I had seen before, something he practised during long evenings at 221b Baker Street, especially when we were without a case. His legs were set akimbo, bent at the knees. His left arm was down in anticipation of a blow from the taller man. Above his head, he held a poker, which he had produced seemingly out of nowhere.

He parried Snitterton's first blow and then slid lithely beneath him so the man rolled over Holmes' back, with barely any contact being made. Once more, Snitterton found himself on the floor.

'Perhaps our friend is unfamiliar with the art of bartitsu,' Holmes chided. Snitterton growled, again picking himself up before hurling himself at Holmes, this time with a revolver in his hand. In an instant, Holmes had sent his cane spinning like a blurred bicycle wheel, which succeeded in knocking the weapon from Snitterton's hand and snapping his fingers at the same time. The fiend emitted a howl like a dog whose paw had been caught beneath a shoe and he reeled backwards - far enough for Holmes to place a jab directly onto his jaw. Snitterton's thoughts now had turned to flight and he glanced at the picture of the Viceroy, clearly aware of what lay behind it.

'Quick, Watson,' my friend urged, 'he's at the twenty two yard line. Bring him down!'

I tackled as best I could, but the feeling had still not entirely returned to my legs. We both watched aghast as Snitterton ran at the painting of Warren Hastings and crashed directly through it, leaving the Viceroy in ribbons. We ran to the empty frame and peered beyond as the morning light filled the room. The roof slates reflected the brilliance and we squinted out beyond them and down onto the cobbles. Either he had slipped to his death or else made a miraculous escape across the rooftops. There was the sound of feet coming up the stairs, no doubt Chatburn come to investigate the commotion.

'I think,' said Holmes, 'that we would be wise to follow suit.' We scrambled through the painting and out, once more into the wilds of London.

'Three nil!' Holmes exclaimed. 'Really my dear Watson, you must do better.' I glared at the great detective, the lid of a cigar box gripped in my hand, before retrieving the champagne cork that had ricocheted off the table into the corner of the room.

It was Holmes' idea to revive our occasional sporting rivalry with a game of ping-pong. We played in the manner my friends and I had pioneered in the officer's mess in Afghanistan; that it is to say, to line up a pile of cheap novels in the centre of the dining room table and wallop a makeshift cork ball over the top. It was generally first class fun, but of late Holmes' game had improved no end and I rather suspected that he had been getting in some private practice.

It was late afternoon by the time Holmes and I had reconvened. After a perilous dash across three rooftops, a leap onto the roof of a Greek restaurant next door and a necessarily speedy descent down the drainpipe at the rear of the premises, we had lost no time returning to 221b Baker Street. After a pair of kippers courtesy of the inestimable Mrs Hudson and a cigar apiece, we found ourselves entirely spent from our morning's exertions. We had therefore opted to retire to bed for a few hours to recover our wits.

I served smartly, only to find the cork back on my side courtesy of a deft backhand slice. Holmes let out a snort of triumph. 'The secret is to examine the behaviour of the ball and in a millisecond, project yourself into the ball's future. You will be there to meet it in precisely the right spot and in precisely the right moment. Quite elementary.' In a mood such as this, Holmes could be unbearable.

I dispatched the ball again in Holmes' direction. 'Take me back to the very start,' I said, as he sent it back with topspin. 'How did you know that access to Chatburn's place could be gained from the roof?' 'At first this threw me,' my friend confessed. 'I saw no obvious ladder or steps and the door to the attic itself from the inside was perfectly secure; three separate locks you will have noticed. On our exit, therefore, I examined the walls again and noticed the tell-tale marks of black rubber plimsolls, the kind favoured by university climbers. I wagered that these belonged to Snitterton, whom we know attended King's College, Cambridge as an undergraduate and no doubt was one of the infamous night climbers.' I retrieved the ball from the floor.
'Do you make that five nil, Watson?'
I grunted my acquiescence.
'That took us, after a little investigation, you will remember, inside the attic room. Chatburn's minutes provided the date, time and venue of the next meeting. If I had found the minutes, then I deduced that the previous intruder had also seen them and planned to eavesdrop in the same way.'
'But weren't we taking a colossal risk being in the same room as this brute?' I asked.
'A small risk perhaps,' admitted Holmes, 'but it was too valuable an opportunity for Snitterton to listen to the society's plans to reveal himself with all of them in the room. '
'He must have breathed an almighty sigh of relief when we chose alternative hiding places.'
'I deliberately steered you away from him, having divined his presence moments after arriving in the attic room. I saw the indentations in the rug leading to the cabinet corroborated by the smell of Dr Cox's Antiseptic and Liniment, an animal medicine.'
'Extraordinary,' I murmured, marveling at my friend's audacity. 'So what have we learnt?'

'A great deal Watson,' Holmes declared as another ball sailed past me.

'I must confess I am rather at a loss,' I admitted 'So much so that I am hardly sure now who our client is.'

Holmes laid down his paddle and retrieved his stash of tobacco from his Persian slipper.

'Let us consider the facts.' He settled himself into his tall backed chair and began to prepare his pipe with delicate expertise, much as a skilled fishmonger might dress a fresh piece of fish. 'Chatburn came to see us on Tuesday morning, fearful of his old associate Snitterton, who it appears has recently returned to England.'

'And he was counterfeiting his distress?'

'I believe that at the time his fear was genuine. However we now know that Chatburn was in fact the rival, going under the name Jack Brace. Chatburn is the name he uses here.'

'Indeed, it is emblazed above his door,' I put in.

'Indeed, Watson.'

'He employed me to find Snitterton in an attempt to remove the threat.'

'The threat to what?'

'To his lives; to all their lives. Snitterton will clearly stop at nothing until he has the eight ruby elephants in his possession.'

'Well we stumbled upon Snitterton sooner than we expected,' I exclaimed. 'It is just a pity we didn't hang on to him. Perhaps we should have interrogated him before throwing him around the room.'

'I fear the circumstances provided me with no other option. And besides, we have all the information we require.'

'Whatever do you mean, Holmes!'

'Well, for one, we have an excellent idea where we shall find Snitterton and his whimsically named Order of the Sapphire Butterfly.'

'Pray tell, Holmes!'

Holmes lay back and puffed triumphantly, rather like Mr Stephenson's Rocket on its voyage along the Liverpool and Manchester Railway.

'Did you notice anything odd about Snitterton's attire?'

'Not in particular,' I said.

'What have I said about observation? You have eyes but you do not see, Watson! The man was festooned with feathers.'

'He is an animal man,' I countered, 'surely that is a satisfactory explanation.'

'His specialtiy, as we know is the big beast, not ducks and chickens.'

'So where do a few feathers lead us?' I asked, reasonably enough.

'Nowhere at all by themselves,' said Holmes. 'But during our scuffle in the attic, Mr Snitterton was careless enough to drop this.' Holmes held up an envelope, with the name 'Fotheringay's Feather Factory' and an address scrawled across the centre in black ink.

'No detective work required, Watson, the postman would find it just as easily as we would. Now what say you to a little self-poison?' He administered two doses of The Dimple, a smoky blend of Scotch whisky of which we were both inordinately fond.

The smoke, I noticed, was beginning to creep across our rooms with the deadly stealth of a boa constrictor, slowly enveloping not only Holmes but everything else too. It curled around my shoulders and neck as if waiting for its moment to strike.

'Would you mind very much,' I asked, 'If I opened the window?'

Holmes shrugged.

'Only if you want us to catch our death.'

'A little close today though, wouldn't you agree Holmes?'

'O, how shall summer's honey breath hold out,' he declaimed, 'against the wreckful siege of battering days.'

'I'm not entirely sure,' I confessed. 'But speaking personally, I feel a trifle confined.'

'There's nothing worse than a confined trifle,' Holmes remarked facetiously. Heaving up the glass frame I inhaled a life giving blast of oxygen.

The streets teemed with the bustling of hundreds of Londoners; a lawyer snapping his fingers to hail a hansom; a drunkard weaving his haphazard way to the corner of Marylebone Road. Their shadows danced at their heels, like accomplices.

'Wait,' Holmes uttered, suddenly starting to his feet. 'Music!' A remarkable transformation was apparent on his features, charging his cheeks with colour. His eyes glinted as they did when finally making headway in a particularly difficult case. Through the maelstrom of birdsong, chatter, the clatter of hooves and the calls of the paperboys and flower girls, I too could pick a melody.

'Paganini, if I'm not very much mistaken.' declared Holmes, joining me at the window. 'Violin Concerto No. 3. Simply majestic.'

Holmes stood with his eyes closed, in a state of utter serenity, as if absorbing a noble gas. Suddenly the practical part of his mind took over.

'Where do you think the sound is coming from?' he demanded. I scanned the rooftops and windows.

'I would say from a westerly direction,' I said, my hands clinging to the bottom sill.

'Look at those flowers down there,' he pointed out. 'Do you see how they are blowing in an easterly direction? I would suggest the sound is coming from somewhere to the east, bouncing off the facade of that not insubstantial town house over there and returning to us for our own private delectation.'

I searched the upper windows to the east and sure enough made out the silhouette of a figure playing a violin behind a curtain of white lace some three floors up from street level.

'I am quite certain it is a woman playing,' Holmes deduced 'from the colour and tone and from the barely perceptible breath between phrases. I would also wager that she studied under the influence of Ignatius Wimpole, from the minute stress she is placing on the final phrase in each bar. She also has a slight injury to her right hand.'

'Remarkable,' I said, 'although I am only sorry we have no way of discovering the accuracy of your speculations.'

'Nonsense,' said Holmes, collecting his hat and cane from the stand. 'We should pay her a visit this very instant.'

Holmes hurried me along Baker Street at an uncomfortable pace, somewhere between a march and a light jog. This was customary when he was seized with an idea. His legs seemed to span continents with each stride. He appeared to be counting flagstones with his cane and presently began to slow down. Finally he stopped in front a dark green door, and delivered two loud raps with the end of his cane. A bonneted servant with a ruddy complexion appeared in the doorway.

'Ms Penelope Braithwaite please,' declared Holmes, 'handing over his card. 'Mr Sherlock Holmes and his associate Dr Watson at her

35

disposal.'

'Astonishing' I said.

'A simple mathematical calculation based on sound, speed and distance,' he explained, suddenly distracted by the haphazard flight of a bumble bee inspecting the flower in the window box. 'Were you aware, Watson,' he said, breaking off and continuing to inspect the insect, 'that a honey bee's wings beat some 200 times a second? This is what produces that pleasing buzzing sound.'

I smiled at my friend. 'And I believed they were simply of a musical disposition.'

'Perfectly inaccurate,' Holmes dismissed as we were finally granted admission.

We were led up a staircase of dark wood carved in the old fashioned style, with a set of amateur watercolours depicting scenes from rural India hung at intervals along the wall. On the third floor we were shown to an elegant parlour. The rooms were decorated in a tasteful, eastern style. A low table was set with a plain vase containing a single orchid; a white upright piano rested against the far wall.

'The two gentlemen to see you,' the housekeeper said, before pulling shut the double doors behind her. Miss Braithwaite was an attractive woman of thirty, with a tangle of strawberry blonde hair and a short pretty nose. By far the most unusual aspect of her appearance, however, was the fact that she was wrapped in a sari of startling turquoise blue. She held both her violin and bow in her left hand and waited, with an expression of vague ennui, for an explanation of our interruption. My friend took the lead.

'Please accept our apologies,' Holmes began, 'but my friend and I have a private detective practice on Baker Street, not one hundred yards from your address.'

'Mr Holmes,' she interjected, 'your fame precedes you. You will credit me firstly with being able to read and secondly a familiarity with the pages of the London press. You are rarely away from them.'

'Quite,' said Holmes. He paused while he joined his fingers and gathered his thoughts, perhaps unused to an interruption of this nature. 'I do wish I were here under happier circumstances. However, as I explained, and as you appear to be aware, I am concerned with cases of the most delicate and difficult nature. These are invariably problems that require concentration of the most intense kind. I sometimes even find it necessary to ask my friend Watson here to refrain from speaking for certain periods. Miss Braithwaite, I will be plain. Your musical practice is a distraction of the most unwelcome nature.'

The woman appeared flabbergasted. 'I am a student of the great Ignatius Wimpole. I am perhaps one of only three violinists of serious note in the whole of London and you appear to be suggesting that I should refrain from practising during daylight hours so you can sit in your armchair and think of ways to increase your wealth and fame. Mr Holmes, I am minded to call an officer of the law and have you both forcibly removed from my property.' She took a step towards us.

'Perhaps,' suggested Holmes coolly, standing his ground. 'It is Mr Wimpole who should explain himself to the police after the incident with your hand.' Miss Braithwaite stopped in her tracks, her expression suddenly clouded with confusion and anxiety. 'Please go, Mr Holmes,' she muttered, and we retreated down the stairs.

The reader may imagine I was left in a state of some perplexity after this interview. However it was not until we were safely back inside the confines of 221b Baker Street that Holmes was willing to explain himself. The bowl of his pipe flashed with flame and he proceeded to breathe life into the tobacco with some expert bellows work.
'Well I wasn't expecting that,' I confessed. Holmes concluded the business of ignition.
'What exactly were you expecting?'
'For you to pay her a compliment. You were quite taken by her performance if I recall correctly. But how the devil did you know her name?'
'Once I knew she was a student of Wimpole,' my friend replied, 'it was all absurdly simple. I happen to know that he takes very few students and recalled reading in the London Spectator that the only woman in this number was Miss Braithwaite.'
'And the injury to the hand?'

'Well that was an educated guess based on the fact that I already knew that she was playing in some pain. I have heard that Wimpole can be something of a brute when his students do not meet his exacting standards. He also has a notorious temper. A violinist of her order would otherwise take the utmost care to avoid such an injury.'

'Still, I believe we made something less than a positive impression.'

Holmes began to pace the floor in a methodical fashion, which I took to mirror the workings of his mind.

'I'm afraid that was a regrettable, but unavoidable consequence. What did you notice about the house?'

'Well,' I said, reflecting. It was furnished in a somewhat bohemian manner, certainly. Not exactly to my tastes, but perfectly suited to someone of an artistic temperament. There appeared to be something exotic about the Indian decor and dress. I also noticed the music open on the stand. As you surmised, it was Paganini's Violin Concerto No. 3. I cannot fault your knowledge of the subject. '

'Very good, Watson.'

'It will not surprise you that I had entirely different reasons for entering the house.'

Naturally, it did.

FOUR

The Order of the Sapphire Butterfly

When I descended for breakfast the following morning, I could find no trace of Holmes. His bed had been slept in but his coat and hat were still hanging on the stand. I asked Mrs Hudson if she had seen him leave. 'Only if he climbed out of the window, doctor,' she assured me, before beseeching me to tackle the kippers before it was too late. I ate in silence, wondering as to the nature of my friend's errand, while scanning the newspaper. I was not surprised to see that there was still talk of Juno's escape from the zoo and our old friend Langdale Pike had written up his column in the most sensational terms.

With no thought for his own safety, and while all of London cowered behind him, Sherlock Holmes approached the beast with a stare like an Indian Fakir. Armed with little more than a brolly and an iron nerve, the detective performed his curious magic, mastering the mighty elephant within moments.

Holmes would be appalled, I thought. Presently Mrs Hudson returned enquiring after the kippers.
'Perfectly done, Mrs Hudson,' I said, although in truth I was too distracted to eat. There were now two dangerous societies in London with which we had become embroiled and despite Holmes' explanations, the matter lay in a confusing state. Once more my mind wandered. I was just weighing up the merits and demerits of a trip around the corner to the lending library to exchange *Escape From The Sinking Island* for *The Octopus with Nine Legs* when there was a knock at the door. Mrs Hudson appeared with a card.
'A Mr Ishmael Bartholomew,' she announced. 'He says that he is a hatter with a shop in Whitechapel and wishes to see Mr Holmes on urgent business.'
'Most peculiar,' I questioned. 'Holmes hasn't said anything about a hat.'
'Perhaps there is some other matter. A personal enquiry maybe?' suggested Mrs Hudson.

'Yes, perhaps,' I said. Holmes had few social callers, outside of his brother and perhaps Pike, especially if he was seeking some juice relating to a current case.

'Yes, please show him in. I'm sure Mr Holmes will return momentarily.'

I rose to greet the visitor, although as it transpired, this was hardly necessary. He was the most terribly stooped man I had ever seen. Old beyond his years, he was deeply lined about the face and wore a clouded pair of spectacles with a broken left lens. The lining of his coat had burst at the seams and his hat was so crumpled that one could be forgiven for thinking that it had been sat upon my our runaway elephant. It seemed a curious calling card for a man in the hat trade.

'I'm afraid Mr Holmes is out,' I explained, 'but you are welcome to wait for him.' I passed over the newspaper and indicated to Mrs Hudson to refresh the pot.

'Oh, don't be afraid, Dr Watson, 'the old man croaked, peering at me in a rather sinister way.

As Mrs Hudson left us, Mr Bartholomew and I spent an awkward moment or two together in silence.

'How would one go about choosing a new hat?' I asked, by way of conversation.

The visitor considered this question as if it was one of life's great imponderables. Even seated, he was stooped and appeared to address his answers to the floor.

'That would depend, Doctor,' he said in his cracked voice. 'It would depend on the occasion, on your personal taste and the fashion of the day.'

'And what would you recommend for me?' I asked, happy to accept this free consultancy.

'You are blessed Doctor,' he offered after some time, 'with a well shaped head, which deserves to be aired, rather than hidden from view.'

'But surely you are doing yourself out of a sale,' I countered.

'Doctor, it is better to tell the truth, even if it is to your cost. Over the long term, truth will always be rewarded.' This seemed remarkably profound for a hat maker from Whitechapel.

'Would you perhaps care to share the nature of your business with Mr Holmes,' I ventured.

'That, my dear Watson,' the man said, looking up and beaming, 'is entirely out of the question.' I stared again at the old man and at once the scales fell from my eyes.

'Holmes!' I exclaimed. 'You are incorrigible!' My friend sat up straight, tore the grey moustache from his lip and discarded the hat.

'You fooled me entirely,' I said, shaking my head with incredulity.

'The mind and the eye are easily deceived; it is less the work of disguise and more the power of persuasion. Now I believe Mrs Hudson still has some kippers warming for me; they are my first priority.'

Holmes tucked into his breakfast with gusto and was now restored to his familiar garb.

'Perhaps you are wondering Watson,' remarked Holmes, forking in mouthfuls of smoked fish 'why I went to the trouble of becoming my own client?'

'Besides a natural tendency for showmanship and a childlike pleasure in dressing up?' 'Well there is, of course, good reason. Just as we infiltrated the House of the Ruby Elephant, it is equally essential that we get closer to the Order of the Sapphire Butterfly, whatever that might transpire to be. Thanks to Mr Snitterton's carelessness, we now know the location of the butterfly house. However, we need an excuse to get inside. I have ruled out a rooftop entry – I fancy Mr Snitterton might be wary of that possible weakness.'

'Then how do you propose to get in?'

'By walking in through the front door,' he said simply. 'I will, in the persona of Mr Bartholomew of Bartholomew's Hatters of Whitechapel, arrive on legitimate business wishing to purchase feathers for a new line of ladies' hats.'

'An audacious entrance,' I admitted.

'On the contrary,' said Holmes, 'It will be perfectly ordinary. We will visit this very afternoon.'

It was not unusual for Holmes to spend many hours in silence. He had for most of the rest of the morning stood in silent vigil over a glass vessel on his chemical table, adding thimblefuls of coloured powder to a mixture that was bubbling gently over a low flame. His concentration was absolute, as if there was not another soul left alive upon the Earth. Neither was it unusual for the atmosphere inside 221b Baker Street to be one that is no longer capable of supporting human life. I loosened my collar and looked longingly at the window, knowing that it was against Holmes strict instructions to open it while he was conducting his experiments. Presently, there was a small explosion, and from the chemical table thick black smoke began to belch from the beaker. As the smoke cleared, I saw Holmes' face like the devil himself igniting the very fires of hell.

'My dear doctor,' he said, appearing to shake himself from his trance. 'Would you be so good as to open the window and share our fumes with the rest of London?'

'A pleasure, Holmes,' I said, flinging open the window and feeling the cool air lapping in. 'I trust your experiment reached a satisfactory conclusion?'

'Dramatic if not entirely satisfactory,' Holmes confessed, 'although it has advanced me in one respect. It has eliminated yet another avenue of enquiry. As I have long said, if you eliminate the impossible, whatever you are left with, however improbable is the truth. Now what say you to a simpler experiment – the infusion of tea leaves in boiling water?'

'That always brings a satisfactory result,' I agreed.

While Mrs Hudson prepared the tea, I did my best to coerce the smoke to the window, wafting it out with yesterday's copy of The Times.

'What the devil were you doing anyway, Holmes? You had the very look of a medieval sorcerer.'

'You are closer than you think in your assumptions,' nodded Holmes. 'I was attempting to make diamonds.'

'Well of course you were,' I laughed. 'Why, if I had left you a little longer, then I would have been able to close my medical practice; you could have wound up your detective work and we could both have retired to Devon to live off sea air and cream teas.'

'What a conventional fantasy, my dear Watson. Would you not wish to visit the mountain monasteries of Tibet, the great lakes of Africa or the Inca ruins of the Americas?'

'Not especially,' I admitted.

'Nor I,' he said. 'There is sometimes a joy in the mundane; the deep peace of the west country, the lavender in the field, the clouds in the sky, the quiet public houses in the quiet streets of English villages; the buzzing of the bees . . . '

He threw himself down in his velvet lined chair and lit his pipe. A white plume rose up and joined the black fumes en route to the window. 'But surely we are city men, Watson,' he countered, equally happy to make the opposing case. 'Would you not miss the fizz in the air, the mighty money men and architects of the Empire walking the streets like the gods of the Earth? And what of the women, Watson? That, as I have said before, is your department. What infinite delights of sophistication and beauty dwell within these ten square miles? Could you turn your back on that so readily?'

'Holmes,' I said. 'You know I am more than happily married. But you make both cases so persuasively I hardly know my own mind.'

Just then we heard the unmistakable strains of a violin.

'Ah,' said Holmes. 'Ms Braithwaite strikes up again. Mozart, this time, I think. Still a little underdone, would you not agree, Watson?'

'It sounds perfectly serviceable to my ears, Holmes,' I put in.

'Perhaps I should be so bold as to give her a lesson from here.'

He leapt from his chair as quickly as he had dropped into it, displaying once again that strange athleticism that he could suddenly summon at will. He seized his fiddle and bow from the shelf, where they were balanced on a freshly printed copy of The Gentle Art of Making Enemies.

He stepped lightly to the window and listened intently for a moment to the music drifting across the rooftops. To my astonishment, he picked up the piece immediately and played either from memory or extemporised brilliantly on the theme. After a minute or so, he stopped and listened again, keeping perfectly still. It appeared that Miss Braithwaite had stopped playing. But then her violin started up again, more strident this time. Holmes gave me a bright eyed look and let her play on for a while longer, before joining in again, the music taking extraordinary leaps and dives as it travelled up and down the scales. I watched him as his slight figure played against the window, his movements as fine and nimble as a cricket balanced on the end of a blade of grass.

This long-distance duet played out for the next five minutes, no doubt much to the bemusement of the passers-by beneath our respective windows. Finally Holmes laid his violin aside.
'Here endeth the lesson, Watson,' he declared. 'Violin Concerto No. 2 in D Major. A work of genius. I am much moved by the idea of genius,' he added more quietly, and there was no need to explain further.

He sipped his fifth cup of tea of the day with immense satisfaction. He was, I noticed, smiling to himself between sips, although I could not tell whether this was because he felt he had in some way bested Miss Braithewaite or because he felt he had impressed her. Knowing something of my friend's cool relations with the fairer sex, I decided it must be the former.

Lunch passed without ceremony and so it was that Holmes and I found ourselves a street away from a large red brick building in the East End of London. Once more Holmes had assumed the persona of Bartholomew the milliner, and in the hansom Holmes disconcerted me somewhat by staying entirely in character throughout the journey. When I asked him for the time he peered at me with rheumy eyes as if I were a stranger on a train. Only as we approached the building did I hear the voice of my inestimable friend: 'Remember, Watson. Be here on the stroke of midnight, wait for the flash in the third floor window. I will come down and let you in.'

I watched Holmes as he turned the corner and became, once again, the ancient milliner, a pronounced limp coupled with a lugubrious manner rendering him every inch the weary tradesman. I considered the career he might have enjoyed on the London stage. He would have been a sensation.

I passed the evening as best I could, laying aside one pot-boiler after another: The Black Shawl, Silver's Revenge, The Unending Storm, but none could sufficiently distract me from the fate of my friend at the plumage factory. Suppose his cover was blown? He would be beyond the reach and protection of the law. We had not even let our old friend Inspector Lestrade in on the case; there were no burly constables waiting in the shadows to bowl in at the first sign of trouble. I wondered whether Holmes had overreached himself this time.

To pass the hours, I decided to walk the majority of the way and marched at soldier's pace through the centre of the city, taking especial notice of the fine bonnets worn by the women of London spilling out of the cafes and theatres, the shops and restaurants. I saw magnificent creations: silk hats decorated with rhinestones and flowers, glittering with sequins. It was admiring these wonders that I almost collided with Miss Penelope Braithwaite. She was wearing a tightly fitted blue silk turban in the modern style with a single green feather as a plume.

'Do look where you're going, won't you?' she reprimanded.
I spluttered my apologies. 'Forgive me, Miss Braithwaite.'
'Doctor Watson!' she exclaimed.
'My mind was somewhere else entirely.'
'And so were your manners,' she snapped, 'but no matter.'
'I am a perfect oaf,' I blushed. 'I'm so terribly sorry. And you must excuse my friend Holmes, too for his outburst at your flat the other day. His manner can be, shall we say, direct?'
'I imagine that he has not got where he has got to today by being anything other than direct.' She adjusted her turban a little and glanced down the street. I was uncertain whether she wanted to continue the interview.
'We have certainly enjoyed your playing these last few days,' I put in. 'No doubt you have heard, Holmes' too?'
'Indeed,' she said. 'For an amateur he has a surprisingly good ear.' I smiled inwardly, certain that my friend would wince at this faint praise.
'Please,' I insisted, 'I must not detain you. You are clearly on an urgent errand.'

'That is true,' she confessed. 'But doctor, the remarkable coincidence is that my destination is 221b Baker Street. I have an urgent matter that I need to discuss with Mr Holmes.' I was taken aback at this startling information, but quickly recovered myself.

'Then perhaps I can save you an unnecessary journey?' I said, 'because Holmes is currently engaged on other business. I imagine tomorrow afternoon would be the earliest he could consider an appointment.' Her face immediately fell into despondency. Her blue, glassy eyes clouded with fear and uncertainty and she narrowed her rose lips.

'Doctor, it is a grave matter.' I was at a loss.

'Then surely an officer of the law should be your first port of call?'

'That is quite impossible,' she said quietly. 'The police cannot be involved at any cost.'

'Surely a few hours will not make so much difference?' She shook her head. 'I am in some danger. I cannot return to my flat and even standing here talking to you I feel is quite unwise.'

'Then you must proceed to Baker Street as you planned,' I said. I scribbled a note on my prescription pad and put it in her hand. 'Hand this to Mrs Hudson and she will make you quite at home until we return.'

'Thank you, doctor,' she said. I nodded, much affected by the woman and her predicament.

That night was exceptionally warm and clear. The moon hung in the sky like a freshly minted shilling. By my pocket watch it was five minutes to midnight. I leaned back against the wall in what shadow I could find. Despite my best efforts to conceal myself however, one or two drunks had lifted their hats to me on their return from The George and Vulture public house on Pitfield Street. Finally at two minutes to twelve, I turned the corner and looked up at the dark shape of the plumage factory looming above me. There was no sign of light save for a weak yellow glow from a window on the ground floor. This, I imagined, was the janitor's room. But as the bells of St Leonard's chimed the hour, sure enough, in a room on the third floor, there were three bright flashes, which I took to be the sign.

Creeping like a burglar up to the door, I crouched down out of the line of sight of the janitor's window. Lurking in such a manner would take some explaining if an officer of the law happened to be passing. The last peal died away and all that could be heard were distant voices and faint clatter of a hansom running a late fare.

Presently, there was the click of a latch. The door opened a fraction and my blood froze as I waited for the man to identify himself. It did not take long for me to recognise the brilliant glint of my friend's eyes and the trace of a smile on his thin lips.
'Watson,' he whispered, 'be quick, for we are not alone this evening.' He pushed the door outwards and I slipped inside.

The corridor had a cold, institutional look about it. The bricks were painted two colours: a pale yellow up to waist height and a horrible blood red from there to the ceiling. Pipes ran along the walls and disappeared around the corner. Holmes, still dressed as the milliner, tugged my arm and hauled me a little way up the corridor, before dragging me backwards with that curious strength of his into a small ground floor room.

Holmes pressed a finger to his lips and almost immediately I heard the sound of footsteps outside the door. As well as being possessed of one of the finest deductive minds I have ever encountered, Holmes also had a highly developed sense of hearing: the sort more readily associated with a piano tuner. Presently I saw him relax.
'The bird has returned to its roost,' he announced, evidently alluding to the janitor scuttling back to his broom cupboard. 'Well, Watson, it has been a remarkable day. The case has seen some singular developments and presented some most interesting points. I am happy to admit that it has succeeded in winning my entire attention.'
'I assume then, that your disguise held out?' I began.
'Indeed it did,' said Holmes. 'On arrival I was taken to an upper room and shown an aviary's worth of feathers. Of course I feigned as much interest as I could, without my mind being the least bit engaged. As expected, the vendors were clearly not interested either. I remarked that the men of the company were not those with whom I normally did business. They were perfectly polite and explained that there had been a company takeover. I then enquired, barely able to

keep a straight face, whether they were expecting any emu feathers to be delivered soon. They told me they were expecting some in shortly. This revealed them to be the charlatans I knew they were and almost certainly part of the criminal gang calling itself the Order of the Sapphire Butterfly. I paid for some feathers which none of us could identify, then told them I would show myself out, explaining I had visited many times before. Presumably not to arouse any suspicions, they agreed and I left the room.'

Holmes and I crept out of the cupboard. My friend sprang up the stairs, as light footed as a fawn and I stumbled after him. It was a marvel to see this apparently aged milliner so sprightly. We edged along a corridor and stopped at a door halfway along. Holmes reached into his waistcoat pocket and produced a key that he had plainly acquired during his afternoon's work. Inside the air smelled of cigars and formaldehyde. Holmes locked the door again. In the gloom I could make out a mass of papers heaped haphazardly on the table. Feathers were scattered everywhere as if there had been a fatal struggle between every bird on Earth. On the far wall was a map of some description, and it was to this that Holmes turned his attention.
'What do you make of it?' breathed Holmes.
'It appears to be a map,' I posited, 'a plan perhaps of some building. A large building.'
'Very good,' Holmes twinkled. 'Now we must work quickly, Watson,'
He handed me paper and charcoal. 'Draw as much as you can as well as you can. It is essential to capture as much detail as possible.'
A poor draftsman, I nevertheless settled down to my challenge while Holmes paced the room searching for other clues. At intervals I heard murmurs of delight as Holmes made discoveries of one kind or another, while I struggled with the plan before me. It was the most confounded work and my charcoal snapped on more than one occasion. The glass in the door suddenly flashed with light.
'Under the table,' Holmes hissed. Folding ourselves beneath it, we let the cloth fall and held our breath.
The light from a lamp spilled across the floor. The carpet of feathers shone with gold and we heard the click of the lock.
'In here,' a man said.

It was deep, commanding voice, which I immediately recognised as Snitterton's. We watched two pairs of boots make their way to a couple of poorly upholstered armchairs not three yards away from our hiding place.

'Cigar?' Snitterton invited.

'Splendid,' replied the other. It was an older voice, but equally well mannered. Through a small tear in the cloth, I could just about see him; he was in his early sixties, I would say, thin lipped, with bright eyes and a startlingly bald head. Tufts of white hair sprouted just above his ears, bordering the bare hill of his cranium. The veterinarian had, I noted, a striking charisma that switched easily between charm and menace.

'So you have three,' the older man said, picking up a conversation that had clearly begun elsewhere.

'Yes, three,' Snitterton confirmed. 'My own, Chatburn's and Peaceheart's.'

'And there are five more.'

'Exactly,' said Snitterton, 'just as I said.'

'Would you mind if I examine them again?'

'If you must,' said Snitterton, 'but it is really not necessary. Each is identical in every way.

'My client is very particular,' the bald man explained. 'And he has been burnt in the past.'

'Are you questioning my integrity?' Snitterton accused him, his tone suddenly cooler.

'Not at all,' the man soothed. 'He has perfect faith in your ability to deliver.'

'That's not exactly the same thing.'

Understandably, perhaps, given the evening's excitement, by the time Holmes and I returned to Baker Street our candles were burning low. We let ourselves in and clambered the stairs thinking of little but a hot bath, a slice of Mrs Hudson's cold meat pie, a smoke and a nap. It was only reaching the top of the stairs that I remembered my encounter with Miss Braithewaite and my instructions to meet us here.

'Well, Watson,' sighed Holmes as he pushed open the door to our sitting room, 'I don't mind admitting I'm deuced tired. Given the choice, I prefer brain work to night-owling, but sometimes we have little choice in the matter.'

'Quite,' I agreed. 'There was just one thing, however. You have a client waiting for you.'

Holmes stopped his tracks. He peered in through the doorway, open not more than two inches.

'If you mean Miss Braithwaite, then I'm not in the least surprised.'

Once again, Holmes confounded me.

'But I haven't mentioned a word,' I started. 'How could you possibly know?'

'Simplicity itself. I caught a slight scent of her perfume on you when you joined me in the feather factory,' he explained. I shook my head in wonderment.

'And besides,' he added, 'I've just seen her umbrella in the doorway.' I closed my eyes.

Ms Braithwaite was sitting reading quietly in my chair. She had the good sense at least not to sit in Holmes' place. She looked up and closed the book as we entered.

'Ah, The Time Machine,' said Holmes. 'A book more in line with Dr Watson's tastes than my own,' he smiled. 'But who wouldn't wish for such a device? The crimes we could undo. The futures we could reinstate.'

'You will forgive the intrusion,' she said, 'but without Dr Watson's invitation I fear that I would have nowhere else to turn.'

'Our evening has been an unusually taxing one,' Holmes explained. You will understand if we delay our interview by a few hours more. You will be perfectly safe here. Please avail yourself of more tea and once you have completed the novel, Dr Watson I know will be pleased to receive a full report on its merits.' Holmes and I then retired to our respective cots and for a few blank, blissful hours, slept the sleep of the dead.

FIVE

The Violin Teacher

I was awoken by the sound of a violin. The piece was not one I recognised, but I knew immediately it was not my friend Sherlock Holmes playing. His was a jerky, somewhat fitful style that mirrored the restless nature of his mind. This was sonorous, mournful music. It was sorrowful, mysterious and entirely intoxicating. I could have lay listening for hours. Eventually I prised myself from my pillow, dressed and joined Holmes and Miss Braithwaite in the sitting room.

'Ah, Watson,' exclaimed Holmes. 'We are in need of a critical ear. Perhaps you are familiar with Tchaikovsky's recent concerto?'

'I confess I am something of a Philistine when it comes to such matters. But it sounds wonderful.'

Miss Braithwaite gave a hesitant smile, then laid her fiddle aside.

'Mr Holmes, Dr Watson, you will forgive me,' she began, 'but as you know, there is an urgent question on which I need your advice.'

'Naturally,' nodded Holmes, 'but before you begin, perhaps you can tell me why you have not attended your lessons this last week?' She stared at him.

'But . . .' she started, 'this is nothing short of wizardry!'

'Nonsense. Living so close, we have become somewhat familiar with your routine. Surely, Watson, you too have noticed that on a Tuesday and Thursday morning we are usually deprived of Miss Braithwaite's talents. This last week we have had the pleasure of hearing you play every morning.'

'That's precisely the reason, I'm here,' she explained. 'I am gravely concerned about the welfare of my teacher, Mr Ignatius Wimpole. Last Tuesday I called as usual at half past nine and received no answer. I spoke to the janitor and Mr Wimpole had not been seen for two days. I returned on Thursday and there was still no trace. On returning to my rooms, I found this note waiting for me.' She handed a folded piece of paper to Holmes, who received it between two long white fingers. He studied it for a few moments.

'Most singular!' he pronounced. He passed the note to me and I scanned it.

Your lessons are now over. I have nothing left to teach you. I wonder in all honesty whether I ever had anything of use to impart in progressing your ambition to be the pre-eminent concert player of the day. You have an unusual gift that would be better developed in the hands of another. Please do not call again and I am sorry we cannot bid farewell in person. Yours, Ignatius.

'A remarkably sad note,' I put in.
'I agree. A very poor way to end things. Do you recognise the handwriting?' asked Holmes.
'Yes, of course,' said Miss Braithwaite. She produced another note and presented it to Holmes. 'I received this two months ago.'

Your playing reminds me of my own. Very proud today. Ignatius.

He compared the two as a master forger might hold up two banknotes to the light.
'Certainly there are similarities,' he said. 'If it was the same author, the longer note was clearly written in a mood of extreme agitation. There are inconsistencies in the letter formations. Did you ask the janitor any more questions?'
'Mr Wimpole's rent is paid some months in advance. The man was unwilling to disclose anything more.'
Presumably you have alerted the police to this disappearance?
'No.'
'Why ever not? This sort of abrupt farewell feels rather ominous don't you think?'
'I agree entirely,' she said. 'Then I received this.'

You have been asking questions. Don't. Our professional relationship is at an end. If you persist, or ask the police to track me down, I will not be responsible for the consequences. Ignatius.

Holmes lay back in his chair.
'A strangely contradictory tone. What do we know of the man? Does he have a wide circle of friends? Does he travel? Has he made enemies?'
Miss Braithwaite was silent.

'There is something more,' she said. 'At my last lesson, Ignatius asked me to marry him.'

'Well,' said Holmes, joining the fingers of each hand and raising them to his lips. 'There is our answer.' Miss Braithwaite remained silent.

'How did he respond,' my friend asked, 'when you said no?'

'Well that's just it. I didn't say no.'

Holmes and I rose to our feet.

'Then what's the meaning of these notes?' I spluttered.

'If I knew that, doctor,' she said blushing, 'I wouldn't be here!'

Holmes had already retrieved his hat and was putting on his coat.

'There's a hansom on the other side of the road,' said Holmes. 'If we are quick we can catch it and be at Wimpole's place in ten minutes.'

We bundled out of the cab, but it was clear we had been pipped at the post. A burly, bearded constable was standing outside the property. Holmes peered at the man.

'Constable Rance, if I'm not mistaken,' he said.

'Mr Holmes,' he nodded.

'You've moved to day duty, I see.'

'It certainly appears that way, Mr Holmes,' he muttered glancing up at the sky.

'And I said that you would never rise in the force,' countered Holmes. 'How wrong I was. Would you be so good as to let us in?'

'I'm afraid not, Mr Holmes. This case is under the supervision of Inspector Tobias Gregson of Scotland Yard and the area is strictly off limits.'

'Then would you be so good as to pass him this note?'

Holmes pressed something into the constable's hand.

'If this is bribery, sir, then you've picked the wrong man.' He stared straight ahead.

'Bribery!' laughed Holmes. 'Constable Rance, you hold in your hand the solution perhaps, to the entire case. If Inspector Gregson discovers you have delayed the delivery of this piece of evidence, I can only think of the consequences for your career.' Rance shifted uneasily.

'Perhaps if you were to wait here a moment,' he said, 'I shall see

whether the inspector will admit you.'
'I am obliged,' said Holmes.
'What did you give him?' said Miss Braithwaite.
'Nothing more than my card,' said Holmes.

Presently Gregson appeared at the door, bounding with energy as ever, almost as tall as the doorway itself. The sun gleamed from his fair hair and his eyes twinkled with the thrill of a new case.
'Sherlock Holmes!' he said, extending a hand. 'You don't waste a minute. You must be able to smell trouble from ten miles. Surely news has not yet reached the wire?'
'What news?' enquired Holmes. Rance narrowed his eyes.
'The violin teacher,' said Gregson. 'Grisly, but it looks like a suicide to me.'
Miss Braithwaite's face drained of colour and she teetered. I caught her just before she made contact with the pavement.
'Splendid save, Watson,' congratulated Holmes. 'I can see why the University of London valued your fielding skills.'

Leaving Miss Braithwaite in the care of Constable Rance, Holmes and I followed Gregson upstairs. We entered through a bright yellow door and found ourselves in a richly decorated room, adorned with plants, pictures and ornate oriental-looking furniture. There was a strong smell of incense and coffee. On the writing desk was a small white elephant. Holmes and I exchanged a glance.

Lying on a caramel coloured rug was the long, slender body of Ignatius Wimpole. His face was a horrible, bloated blue and there was a horrid thin gash across his throat. A deep red stain had formed beneath the wound.
'Poor devil,' I muttered. 'Is this how you found him?'
'The janitor was here first,' explained Gregson. 'He cut him down.'
'Violin strings,' said Holmes, inspecting the wire around the unfortunate teacher's neck. 'What a ghastly exit.'
'Yes, we noticed that,' Gregson put in quickly.
'Have you found the violin yet?' enquired Holmes.
'Still looking.'
'Is that a motive?' I asked

'I doubt it,' said Gregson, 'There was no sign of forced entry.'

'Really?' cried Holmes in disbelief. 'Even though it's a Stradivarius? Good God, man, it could be worth tens of thousands of pounds!'

'For a fiddle?' said Gregson, dismissively. 'There's a note too,' he added, handing over a piece of cream writing paper. Holmes peered at the handwriting carefully then handed it to me.

All the beauty has vanished from the world. The jewel of my eye has been taken from me. Nothing can replace it. All art, all hope, all love has gone. I will go now to the mountain of light. Only there will you find the truth.

'Rather poetic, don't you think,' said Gregson. 'Impressive, given that it wasn't his line of work.' My friend scribbled down the words on a scrap of paper, then appeared absorbed in his own thoughts. He was pacing the apartment like a lion in his cage, his eyes scanning this way and that, as if committing each detail to that photographic memory. He stopped a few feet from the body, stooped down to the floor and inspected a small patch of white powder with the tip of his finger.'

'We've given the place a thorough examination,' Gregson informed him. 'Further work is quite unnecessary, Mr Holmes.'

'Thorough, you say,' repeated Holmes with only the smallest trace of irony.

'Yes, thorough,' confirmed Gregson, barely disguising his irritation.

'Then you won't mind me taking a sample of this white powder for examination?'

'Mr Holmes, you may take powder of any colour you please,' Gregson laughed. 'But on this occasion, I fear your presence here is merely ornamental. It is a suicide. Sometimes,' he said, drawing himself up to his full height and sounding a philosophical note, 'there is no mystery, only tragedy.'

'This janitor,' Holmes said abruptly. 'Do you still have him?'

'I've already given him a grilling. Rance is holding him downstairs.'

'I think we have seen enough,' nodded Holmes, and wrapping the sample of powder in a fold of paper, we wished Gregson good luck and made our exit.

The afternoon sun lit the motes of dust as they drifted through our sitting room. We had found some temporary accommodation for Miss Braithwaite with one of my female patients and Baker Street was ours once more. Holmes sat staring at Wimpole's final note, occasionally twisting it between his fingers as if there was some way of angling it to the light which would suddenly reveal its meaning.

'Confound this thing,' cried Holmes at last, casting it aside. 'I cannot fathom it.'

'Is it not possible,' I suggested, 'that these are merely the words of a heartbroken man? Perhaps there is no riddle.'

'Impossible,' snapped Holmes. 'I will swear this note was written under duress or I will never touch another case. He is attempting to tell us something unbeknown to his captor and executioner.' Holmes sighed, joined his hands as if in prayer and pressed them to his pursed lips. 'There is nothing else for it,' he announced with an air of resignation. 'We will need to consult my brother.'

'Mycroft,' I shouted, 'of course!' And yet, quietly I could not believe my friend was at a loss. It was almost without precedent. Holmes, I think detected my disappointment.

'Watson,' he confided, with an air of solemnity, 'it seems my powers are waning.'

'Nonsense,' I said firmly, 'It shows character to ask for help.'

'You are, Watson,' smiled Holmes, 'a friend of the first order.' He whipped a gold watch from his pocket, glanced at it, then returned it just as swiftly. 'If we are quick,' he said, leaping from his chair, 'it is just possible we may be able to intercept Mycroft as he makes his way between Whitehall and the Diogenes Club.'

'You know his routine to the minute?' I marveled.

'He is as predictable as the two fifteen from London to Brighton. He does not swerve from his beat except on Christmas and holy days. He is a creature of the most unwavering habits.' We seized our hats, raced down the stairs, tumbled out of the front door and into a waiting hansom.

As we neared Charing Cross, Holmes leaned dangerously out of the window. 'There he is,' he cried, right on time.' I peered over his shoulder and sure enough, turning into Cockspur Street was the great, lumbering figure of Mycroft Holmes. Such was his size and bulk, it was as if a walrus had escaped from the zoo and was waddling its way steadily across the city.

So as not to alarm the man, we alighted from the cab and walked the last twenty yards. Given our haste, he could easily believe we were attempting an abduction. Mycroft appeared to have detected our presence however and turned slowly, like a giant suddenly aware of a sound distantly below him.

'Sherlock,' he sighed, on seeing his brother, 'this can only mean unwanted excitement. I note you arrived by hansom and came up past the Red Lion.'
'Mycroft, I cannot help but observe that you enjoyed eggs for breakfast this morning and have changed your brand of cigar. If I'm not very much mistaken, I believe you are now smoking the Gurkha. Rather modern for your tastes, I would have thought?'
'Surely, Sherlock, you can allow a man the capacity to change.'
'Ah, yes, but some things never change, my dear Mycroft. Your appetite for bedtime reading. You stopped at Henderson's for a copy of Mr Jerome's new novel did you not?'
'There you have me,' admitted Mycroft with a small, noble bow of his well made head. He produced a copy of Three Men in a Boat from his pocket.

'My dear Mycroft,' soothed Holmes. 'To business if we may. Forgive us this intrusion; you are a fellow of regular habits. If I could have forewarned you of our interruption I most certainly would have. However I seek your most urgent counsel on a matter of the gravest concern. But where can we talk in private?'
'Surely, my rooms,' Mycroft began, 'would be the logical starting point.'
'No time!' cried Holmes.
'Then perhaps the Diogenes Club?' I put in, recalling that this was Mycroft's principal haunt.
Mycroft and Holmes both peered at me with a mixture of contempt and disapproval.
'You will remember Watson,' scolded Holmes, 'that the Diogenes has particular rules, the salient one being that no one may speak

within its walls, except in the Strangers' Room, which is hardly inviting.

'Then may I suggest the patisserie on the corner?' drawled Mycroft. 'They serve an excellent cream horn and I challenge any man in London to defy their éclair.'

'A capital idea, Mycroft,' proclaimed Holmes. 'Lead on!'

I gazed in wonder at the mountain of pastries before Mycroft. An enormous napkin billowed beneath his chin as he prepared for the task ahead. He gave it a little tug to check it was securely fastened in the same way a yachtsman might check his sail before attempting to circumnavigate the world.

'And how is Her Majesty's Government?' Holmes enquired.

'As a matter of fact,' his brother replied, 'I am engaged in a delicate matter myself, upon which I would value your opinion. We are about to cede a British possession to a foreign power. The flag is to be returned to Great Britain and there are conflicting ideas about what to do with it. The Prime Minister is minded to have it burned and the ashes scattered in the North Sea. The Home Secretary believes it should be kept in The British Museum. The Foreign Secretary is determined to have it made into a suit for him to wear during meetings with governors of British Protectorates who are causing us difficulty.'

Mycroft took a huge bite from the end of an éclair and a great blob of cream dropped to his plate. 'I would be grateful for your own views.'

It was impossible to know whether this was some attempt from Mycroft at humour. His expression was entirely inscrutable and presently he returned his attention to his pastry.

'The matter is simple,' said Holmes at length. 'The flag should be folded carefully and kept in the foreign office until Heligoland is returned to the British Empire. A large piece of éclair shot out of Mycroft's mouth and landed on the next table. His eyes bulged and his cheeks flushed a deep shade of red.

'Need I remind you Sherlock, that this is an entirely secret matter of state! How the devil did you discover the name of the possession?'

'Anyone who reads The Times once a week could make the same educated guess. And besides your splendid new cuff links are

German made; I am guessing they are the gift of a German diplomat who has grown generous in anticipation of its new acquisition. Mycroft recovered himself.

'With a little practice, Sherlock,' he said with a wry smile, 'you will make a passable detective.' He glanced across the half empty café for eavesdroppers. 'Now what is it can do for you?'

Holmes produced a notebook upon which he had scribbled the contents of Wimpole's suicide note. He also outlined the general points of the case: how we had learned from the previous notes that the teacher was infatuated with his brilliant student. My friend also sketched, in some considerable detail, the unpleasant state in which the body was found. Mycroft listened dispassionately to the details, looking for all the world as though he was listening to someone reading a weather report. 'Well,' said Mycroft dabbing cream from his chin, 'there are two possible explanations. Either this is a genuine note, or...'

'Yes?' I urged.

'Or,' he repeated casting me a reproving look, 'he is attempting to communicate with us from beyond the grave.'

'Beyond the grave?' I ejaculated.

A waitress clearing plates at the next table gave a small gasp and a fork clattered to the floor.

'Control yourself, Watson,' urged Holmes. 'Go on, Mycroft, you have interested me exceedingly.'

"'All the beauty has vanished from the world.' Mycroft muttered, reading over the line. 'He has lost something of immeasurable worth. Well, that could be read either way: the loss of the violinist's affections or something else of immeasurable worth. The answer is in the next line. "*The jewel of my eye has been taken from me. Nothing can replace it.*" This could of course be interpreted in the metaphorical sense, but we know he was no poet. So let us suppose for a moment he is not referring to Miss Braithwaite. Let us suppose he is referring to an object; the Stradivarius for instance. "*All art, all hope, all love has gone. I will go now to the mountain of light. Only there will you find the truth.*"' Ah,' professed Mycroft. 'Here is where it becomes more difficult.'

'Yes,' sighted Holmes. 'My own reasoning had taken me to a similar point.'

'Difficult,' said Mycroft, raising a finger, 'but not entirely opaque.'

My friend's eyes gleamed.

'He mentions the word jewel in the previous sentence for a reason. The only jewel I know with that name is the Koh-I-Noor.'

Holmes clapped a hand to his forehead.

'What a glock I have been!' he cried. 'Watson, I have been as gulpy as a schoolgirl. The Koh-I-Noor. It means mountain of light!' I stared at the brilliant brothers and inevitably felt somewhat dim-witted in their company. I was aware of the famous gem, but I remained confused.

'But what possible significance could this have?'

'Unless I am very much mistaken,' said Holmes, summoning the bill, 'someone is planning to steal the diamond. Find the thief and we will find the murderer.'

'But it has not yet been stolen?'

'Rest assured it will be.'

'Then we must also warn the Queen!' I cried.

'There should be no cause for alarm. We must let time do its work!'

SIX

The Confectioner

After a magnificent lunch of sardines and an 1884 vintage claret, Holmes was housed once again in his favourite leather chair. He was absorbed in a periodical from The Royal Institute of Chemistry, while disappearing like a stage magician in a fog of his own tobacco smoke.

'Do you have any fixed views,' my friend enquired, 'on the question of stereochemistry?'

'None at all,' I remarked. 'I am a perfect blank on the subject.'

'Think of it then, as the relative distances between atoms in a molecule. Compare it for example,' he said, tapping the bowl of his pipe gently, 'with the variable distances between you and I, and Mrs Hudson downstairs. Together we make up our household, just as atoms make up a molecule. At any one moment our whereabouts can be plotted on a three dimensional model. We would never inhabit exactly the same coordinates twice.'

'Oh I don't know about that Holmes,' I countered. 'For instance, you are prone to muse at length in your chair, whereas I am likely to be found at the window, pondering the comings and goings of the street, the perambulations of the flower girls and businessmen.'

'Ah, yes,' agreed Holmes. 'An estimable point, but you have not factored in the constant motion of Mrs Hudson, who occupies the same space for little more than a second at any given time.'

'And what is the possible significance?'

'Her movements, as the third in our triumvirate, give the whole an entirely distinct signature.'

'I am not certain I have divined the upshot,' I confessed.

'Nor am I,' my friend conceded, refilling his pipe bowl in much the same way that a squirrel restocks a tree cavity with nuts for the winter. 'And yet the unique signature of any given object, animate or inanimate, at any given moment, would make the work of detection a matter for the chemist rather than the policeman.' The smoke curled above him, as it would a genie newly emerged from his bottle.

'With the exception of yourself, Holmes,' I ventured, 'I have yet to see a scientist leap through a window clutching a Webley Bulldog,'

61

Holmes managed a thin smile then cast the periodical to one side.

Following our scientific exchange, Holmes grew increasingly restless. He paced the room, once or twice took up his violin, drew back the bow and played a desultory bar of some mournful air before laying it down again. Opening a volume from his Index of Biographies, he searched for an entry, then, evidently failing to find his man, snapped it shut again. He made repeated forays to the Persian slipper for tobacco as if he was stoking the hungry firebox of a locomotive on the Great Western Railway.

'Excuse me gentlemen,' said Mrs Hudson. 'I can see you are engaged in important matters.'

Holmes raised an eyebrow.

'A Miss Peaceheart calling for you, doctor,' she said.

Holmes and I exchanged a glance.

'A patient of yours?' asked Holmes.

'Show her in,' I instructed.

A small pretty woman with a white, leonine face appeared in the doorway, dressed in the black and white costume of a shop assistant.

'Oh, doctor,' she stammered, struggling to get her words out. 'You need to come straight away. It's father.'

'Mr Peaceheart. Yes, I remember, the confectioner on Berwick Street. What seems to be the matter?' I asked.

'We're afraid he's losing his mind,' she said.

'What symptoms?' I demanded.

'He's giving away stock, for nothing! Mother's tried to lock the door, but he won't have it!'

'Care to join me, Holmes?' I asked, retrieving my hat. 'From the sounds of it, you will at least receive half a pound of clear gums for your trouble.'

'Certainly,' replied Holmes.

We thumped down Oxford Street in a brougham, Miss Peaceheart anxiously clutching a handkerchief throughout the journey. 'Our family as you know has been away for some time. We only returned to reopen the business last year. He has not been himself,' she explained, 'not by any stretch.'

A crowd was already assembled on the corner of Berwick Street and we drew to a halt beside a group of grubby looking boys in short trousers sitting on the curb with a gleeful look on their faces.

'Chocolate, sir!' one of them cried, his cheeks and chin smeared with the stuff. 'More chocolate than you've ever seen!' Another's pockets were overflowing with fruit pips, bulls' eyes and pear drops. Each boy was in a happy trance, his eyes perfectly glazed over.

Holmes stepped smartly past them and parted the crowd in a masterful manner.

'Doctor coming though!' he cried, 'stand back there!'

It is my positive belief that besides an alternative career as one of the world's greatest villains, Holmes would have been a great commander of men. He had an unswerving belief in his own judgement and an ability to impress his character upon any situation. The scene that greeted us at the shop front was like something directly from the Vaudeville stage.

Mr Peaceheart, a small, slack-cheeked, balding gentleman was standing on a stool with a jar of humbugs under his arm. He was scattering them into the crowd as if feeding the ducks. His wife was attached to one of his legs, partly to prevent him from toppling to the floor and partly in an effort to bring him down from his perch.

'Another jar, Mrs Peaceheart,' he cried. 'Another jar!'

His daughter, whom we had ushered through the crowd with us, looked on, quite bewildered.

'I am not afraid to say,' she confessed, 'that before today, he was one of the meanest men I have ever known. And I say that as his loving daughter!'

'Mr Peaceheart,' I shouted above the throng. 'I'm a doctor! Would you give me a moment?'

'Can't you see, doctor,' he replied, without breaking away from the disposal of his livelihood, 'that I have important work to do?' He hurled an entire jar's worth of pineapple cubes into the air, most of which landed in a sheet held out by some enterprising urchins.

'I'd very much like to speak with you now,' I called back. A handful of Tom Thumb Drops dropped into the brim of my bowler hat while a cloud of sherbet, like dandruff, gathered at my shoulders. The clamour grew more intense and the crowd was plainly beginning to swell as word spread.

'Can't you do something?' his daughter implored.

Holmes, I noticed, was studying the man with a look of great intensity.

'Watson,' he said. 'I am going to make a citizen's arrest.'

'You can't possibly, Holmes,' I called back. 'It's not illegal to give away humbugs!'

'I believe this to be the murderer of Ignatius Wimpole.' I stared at him, astonished.

'On what possible evidence?'

'I'll explain later,' said Holmes and reaching into his pocket, he retrieved his Webley police revolver and fired a shot into the air.

The effect was instantaneous. The crowd, maddened by sugar, dispersed at speed, leaving a trail of liquorice sticks, aniseed balls and black toffees on the streets in its wake.

Mr Peaceheart was left standing on his chair in the doorway like a politician without a crowd.

'But we still have so much left!' he cried.

'Mr Peaceheart,' commanded Holmes. 'Step down from that chair or the next shot will pierce your heart. Watson, would you be so good as to find a police constable? Send word to Inspector Gregson to meet us here.'

Half an hour later, we were inside the shop with the door firmly shut. Gregson was pacing the room, sucking thoughtfully on a rhubarb and custard.

'Perhaps you could tell us, Mr Peaceheart, what you were doing on the evening of the 16th July?'

'He was here with me,' Mrs Peaceheart interjected.

'Is that true, Mr Peaceheart,' Gregson persisted.

'I have no idea,' the stout confectioner muttered, his arms folded.

'Have you ever heard of a man called Ignatius Wimpole?'

I have no idea,' he repeated, then started to laugh.

'Do share the joke,' growled Gregson irritably.

Peaceheart's laugh grew louder, then more shrill, until it was clear he was now sobbing.

'Get a grip, man,' said the inspector, but the shopkeeper was clearly beyond our help and now in a hysterics. 'I think it best,' Gregson said, ushering the wife and daughter to the door, 'that we take your husband into our temporary care for his own safety.'

'What is it you think my husband has done?' she cried.

'I'm sure this is simply a misunderstanding,' I said. 'Now perhaps a cup of tea?'

Holmes was unusually quiet on the way back to Baker Street.

'Did the confectioner look familiar to you?'

'Of course he did,' I admitted, 'he was my patient.'

'When was the last time you saw him?'

'Two years ago?'

'You disappoint me,' said Holmes lightly. 'Well, let's try something else. Did you notice anything unusual about his house?'

'There was a pair of crossed elephant tusks on the wall.'

'Bravo!'

'A little exotic for the back kitchen off a tradesman off Oxford Street, don't you think?'

'Yes, I suppose it is.'

'Now think back to our midnight climbing adventure. It took me a moment, but now I am quite certain. I believe that our Mr Peaceheart was sitting directly to the left of Mr Chatburn at the meeting of the House of the Ruby Elephant.'

'No!'

'I am quite certain.'

I now registered his voice, clearly, as one of the speakers at the meeting of that sinister club.

'I do believe you're right, Holmes.'

'You sound surprised! There is one thing more,' he added. 'He was also one of the men who attempted to sell me the emu feathers in the factory.' I stared at my friend, dumbfounded.

'A double agent!' I cried.

'So it would seem.'

'Then he is working for Snitter . . .

'Or Chatburn . . ' added Holmes.

'But why are you so certain that he is the murderer of Ignatius Wimpole?'

'Do you remember the white powder we found in his apartment?'

'Yes,' I confirmed.

'Lemon sherbert,' said Holmes.

As we turned into Baker Street, I noticed four smartly dressed men standing together on the corner, locked in close discussion. They were wore identical black tail coats, top hats and walking canes.

'What do you make of those gentlemen, Holmes. Lawyers or stockbrokers?'

Holmes peered at them.

'Neither,' he declared. 'I believe they are mercenaries. Private soldiers; former military men, trained at Her Majesty's expense. See how they stand in conference, four square, with their hands clasped behind them like officers before a battle.'

'Really Holmes,' I said, dropping my newspaper to my lap and surveying the pandemonium that was our room. 'It's years since I've seen the rug. Do you think we ought to have a clear out?'

My friend appeared not to have heard me. He was picking his way gingerly across a mine field of correspondence, bundles of notes and towers of old cuttings to the coat scuttle where he kept his cigars.

'What do you say to a good American cigar, Watson? There is a choice of a Kentucky Cardinal or an Uncle Bob's Satisfaction.'

'And what do we have to celebrate?' I demanded. 'We have a dead violinist and a confectioner who has lost his mind. It feels like we're making precious little progress.'

'We're making excellent progress, Watson!'

'Now let me give you the latest in the Tranby Croft affair,' said Holmes raising a white hot piece of charcoal from the fireplace and touching it to the end of his cigar. The case has aroused my curiosity although I believe it has not yet made the papers.

'A colonel has been caught cheating at baccarat at a house party. He had been invited at the invitation of the Prince of Wales himself and was foolish enough to get caught red handed. A pact of secrecy was made to save his honour in exchange for a solemn vow that he would never play again. I was called myself to the house to investigate at the request of the prince himself.'

'Holmes, you are an utter mystery to me,' I said, accepting the repulsive American cigar despite myself. I cannot remember you mentioning this.'

'You will recall I said I had a small matter to attend to in the north?'

'I remember that,' I mused, thinking back. 'I believed that was to assist an inspector in the East Riding of Yorkshire with the Case of the One Legged Vicar.'

'I attended to that at the same time.'

'Holmes, it seems impossible to me that I am your closest confidant and yet I feel I know next to nothing about you. You are a closed book.'

'Watson,' mused Holmes wreathed in a mellow balm of smoke. 'A friend should bear his friend's infirmities.'

I peered at him.

'Is that you or Shakespeare?'

'Cassius,' said Holmes.

'So what did you do?'

'I instructed them to say nothing but continue to play as planned the following evening, stationing observers at discreet angles to the colonel. He was quite clearly seen topping up his stake. It was my suggestion that the colonel should sign a declaration stating that he will never again gamble in polite society, to preserve his reputation, though in my heart I knew it would get out. The prince is greatly troubled by it and I fear he himself will be summoned as a witness.

'Impossible!' I cried.

'Just you wait, Watson.'

SEVEN

The Test

'Mr Mycroft Holmes is waiting for you downstairs,' Mrs Hudson announced.

I lowered my copy of *The Observatory* and glanced over at Holmes. He was holding open *Wright & Ditson's Complete Manual of Boxing* and wore a look of perfect astonishment. An unexpected visit from Mycroft was almost without precedent. My friend dropped the volume and leapt to his feet, evidently assuming the world had tilted on its axis. It was an otherwise ordinary Wednesday in July; a fine bright day, all the more welcome after a spell of prolonged rain.

'Won't you show him up, Mrs Hudson?' asked Holmes with some urgency. 'It is clearly a singular emergency and I cannot imagine why he is delaying at the bottom of the stairs.'

'He is unable to ascend, Mr Holmes,' Mrs Hudson explained.

'Good heavens,' I started. 'Is he injured?'

Her arms were folded and a wry expression was forming on her face.

'Not at all,' explained Mrs Hudson. 'It appears he is impeded with a large hamper.'

'A hamper?' I blurted.

My friend and I bolted down the stairs to be met with a most extraordinary sight.

My previous experience of Mycroft had revealed him to be a high minded man with limited capacity for sociability and almost none for frivolity. And yet, here he was in a cavernous sports jacket hung loosely over his portly frame, a straw boater balanced on his vast cranium and something approaching a smile growing on the nether reaches of his considerable jowls.

'Surely it is too fine a day to spend indoors,' he began. Holmes peered at him with a look of great concern.

'Are you quite well, Mycroft? ' he enquired. 'Surely a Wednesday morning will find you somewhere in the depths of Whitehall poring over matters of state.'

'Ordinarily, yes,' agreed the brother. 'But have you not heard how the test match hangs in the balance?'

'Last I heard, it was not entirely going our way,' I said, still taking in the scene. 'Wasn't Grace out for a duck in our first innings?'

'Alas yes,' said Mycroft dolefully. 'But he is our finest man for a reason. Even though his knees are not what they were, his spirit remains indomitable. Besides his batting average remains near 40, he has recorded a top score of 344 in First Class cricket and has made over seven hundred catches. There is nothing like him. He is in a class of his own; he is our whiskered Hercules.' I could easily see how the statistics that cling to the game would appeal to Mycroft's mathematical mind.

'I have, through a colleague, managed to acquire four tickets to the day's play and a brougham awaits outside.'

'Four tickets?' repeated Holmes, 'are you bringing a friend?'

'Three friends,' said Mycroft solemnly. Sherlock peered into the empty carriage.

'Then where is the fourth?'

'Standing right behind you,' said Mycroft bowing low. Mrs Hudson blushed a deep shade of crimson. 'I have taken the liberty of packing us a small luncheon, so you need not concern yourself with vittles,' the honourable fellow continued. 'Play begins in an hour, so if you would be good enough to move things along, we should be there in good time.'

Thirty minutes later, we were amidst the mighty crowd at the gate. Such was the crush we almost lost each other in the throng of straw hats and parasols.

'There's firty fousand in the grounds!' shouted a programme seller. 'But still plenty of programmes left, so come and get 'em!'

Mycroft and I were at either end of the enormous basket that contained our lunch, although it could easily have accommodated a fully grown man lying at full stretch.

'What exactly have you got in here?' I panted, as my arms elongated under the strain.

'Just a few cold cuts,' muttered Mycroft, eager to take his place. We were soon settled comfortably inside the new pavilion, with its fine terracotta facing and ornate lanterns.

'Splendid seats,' I complemented. He nodded vaguely and was staring hard at the grass.

'The pitch has been rather slow,' he complained, 'but it's drying out nicely, and I dare say we have a chance of making a decent fist of it today.'

Holmes, who had very little interest in cricket, was sitting contentedly with his hands behind his head and his long legs stretched out before him. 'I hope you've brought plenty of reading material,' he remarked to Mrs Hudson, 'these matches do tend to drag.'
'Drag?' she cried, looking up from her programme. 'I have been following the progress avidly. This has all the makings of a nail biter.'

Australia's Barrett was proving something of an obstacle, remaining stubbornly at the crease throughout their second innings, but he failed to find a batting partner to match his form. Lyons and Murdoch had restored some dignity after Turner and Trott went for nought and two respectively, but the middle order and tail enders were all falling cheaply.
'I would watch that fellow Burn,' warned Holmes. 'I watched him while we were filing in; he has a defiant look in his eye and I could tell from the wet grass of his shoes that he was out late practising last night. If there's anyone who's going to give us trouble, it's him.'
'Burn?' I scoffed. 'He'll be lucky to survive his first ball.' Holmes raised his eyebrows and retrieved his boxing book from his jacket pocket.

We soon settled into an agreeable routine of squinting into the mid distance, snoozing and contributing to the sort of polite applause which is the very hallmark of test cricket. Mrs Hudson was absolutely engrossed, sitting forward in her seat and fluttering her programme about her face.
'Did you see that?' she said to Holmes more than once, clutching his arm. At these interruptions, he rolled his eyes and buried his nose further in his book.
Mycroft meanwhile was busying himself with the hamper, which he opened to reveal the sort of provisions that would keep an army marching for three days.

'Heavens above!' I exclaimed when I saw the extent of the man's preparations. 'What have you got there?'

'The bare essentials,' he explained gravely, moving items around carefully the basket. 'We have some cold meat pies, naturally,' he began, counting them off on his fat fingers – 'chicken, beef, lamb, mutton, pork and partridge. With these, we have a selection of pickles, some onions and gherkins; some sauces, including bread sauce, mint jelly and cranberry. I left the mint sauce behind in the interests of weight and economy, but I can't help but feel a certain pang of loss for its absence. We have a variety of breads, freshly baked last night by my inestimable housekeeper. There's butter and cheese of course. Now when it came to the cheese, I was faced with a difficult decision. I kept the Bay Blue, the Blarney Castle, Brie, Cairnsmore and the Double Gloucester. I left out the Feta, the Gippsland Blue and the Lincolnshire Poacher. I took out the Red Windsor, but then put it back in at the last minute. I will let you be the judge of my actions.'

I stared at the bounty laid out before us. 'That sounds ample,' I suggested.

'And then there are the treats,' he continued. 'Fruit pies: raspberry, cherry, strawberry and blueberry. Biscuits naturally . . .'

'Enough!' I shouted.

'Do you have any tea?' asked Mrs Hudson. 'It's awfully warm.' Mycroft looked at her, alarmed. He delved into the deepest recesses of the hamper as Arthur Evans, the archaeologist might peer into a iron age barrow.

'I'm afraid not?' he admitted.

'How about a little water?' He glanced down again.

'No water.' Aghast, he rose to his feet, raising himself to his full regal height. For a moment the sun seemed to disappear and we were cast into darkness.

'Mrs Hudson,' he intoned. 'I have failed you entirely.'

'Sit down, won't you?' a spectator behind us demanded.

'I will not sit down!' Mycroft retorted, red faced.

'How about we all adjourn for some tea?' I said, attempting to diffuse the situation.

'A splendid idea,' agreed Holmes.

'Capital!' agreed the spectator.

Refreshed, we returned in better spirits and England too, appeared revived. Grace had rediscovered his form and was swatting away anything the Australian bowlers could hurl at him. Presently, I became aware of a hubbub at the other end of the pavilion. What appeared to be a blind man was being led down the steps by a number of minders, who together made up an impressive entourage. The entire party were dressed in fashionable clothes and the Lord's officials appeared highly deferential towards them. Most noticeable, apart from the blind gentleman himself and his diamond tipped walking cane, were the four men at the rear of the group in matching striped red and white blazers and gas-pipes, those rather tight fitting trousers that were fashionable at the time. It occurred to me immediately that these men resembled closely the four men lingering on the corner of Baker Street. I gave Holmes a nudge.

'Mmm?' he said, waking from a catnap.

'Russian royalty?' I suggested, pointing towards the group.

He peered at them.

'I don't think so,' he said, sitting up, his curiosity suddenly awakened. 'New money, I would expect. Royalty of any stripe wouldn't join us in the pavilion.'

At lunch, after we had gorged ourselves to capacity, Holmes and I left Mycroft to his second and third helpings in search of a glass of beer. Mrs Hudson appeared to have forgiven Mycroft his transgression over the tea and the two of them were getting along famously.

Outside the pavilion the home crowd was in buoyant mood and the scent of victory was in the air.

'I say, Holmes,' I said, 'there's our blind millionaire.'

Sure enough, there he was being led around the grounds like the Count of Monte Cristo; an acolyte on each side and one to the front and rear. He was a man of sixty five, still vital, with grizzled grey hair, cut close ahead his head. Red capillaries marbled his cheeks and his eyes were a little sunken. He wore a new silk shirt, perfectly white, and a diamond tie pin.

Holmes put himself deliberately in their path.

'Enjoying the match?' he asked cheerfully. 'That man Ferris is a devil with the ball, isn't he?'

'Stand aside,' one of the men in striped blazers said coldly.

'Ah,' said Holmes, mischievously. 'You're with the tourists, then!'

'I won't ask again,' the minder threatened.

I was about to retrieve Holmes from the fray when the blind man himself spoke up.

'Who are you, sir?' he asked. He spoke English with a slight accent.

'My name is Sherlock Holmes,' said my friend. 'When did you return from South Africa?'

'How could you know that?'

'It is my business to know what others do not,' he said simply. 'But I see that you are a Suffolk man,' he continued.

'Michael,' said the blind man. 'We will stay and speak with Mr Holmes a while. Unless he is a fraudster or charlatan, I would hazard that he is possessed of the most remarkable powers. '

'Tell me, Mr Holmes, how does a man from Suffolk reveal himself so easily?'

'Your jacket is a made from a wool to be found only from the town of Lavenham. The unusual arrangement of the three buttons at the cuff is also a trademark of your tailor is it not?'

'Go, on,' he laughed. 'I am finding this most diverting.'

'I think we ought to be getting back,' said the man referred to as Michael. He had a mean look about his face and was as pale and thin lipped as Holmes himself, but without the kindness and keen intelligence in the eyes.

'Nonsense,' scoffed the blind man. 'We have plenty of time.'

'Raphael,' he instructed, 'a cigar for Mr Holmes and his friend here.'

Another man stepped forward, an equally surly fellow with an ugly horizontal scar directly across his chin.

'Ah,' said Holmes, approvingly, 'the mighty Ghurkha! A popular choice in South Africa.'

'Mr Holmes, there seems to be nothing you don't know about me. And I believed that I was keeping a low profile. Well let me test you a little further. As you can see, I am a man of some means. Perhaps you will be able to tell me how I acquired my wealth?' My friend smiled and looked at the man, his clothing, his cane, the patent leather shoes, the gem encrusted chain on his pocket watch. His eyes were concealed entirely by a pair of small, neat, jet black goggles, rendering him somewhat inscrutable.

'I would suggest,' said Holmes at length, 'that you have had some considerable success in the mining industry.' The blind man appeared taken aback. 'Is it gold or gemstones?' Holmes added innocently.

'Have I been set up?' the man demanded, all trace of humour suddenly leaving him. 'Michael?' he barked. 'Where are you? Get me back to my seat. Who let this charlatan get in my way?'

The minder stepped forward and with brutish force, shoved me backwards, knocking the cigar from my lips. I saw it break under the ruffian's foot. My friend's reactions were quicker; he stepped back deftly, setting the man off balance. In an instant, the strange entourage had moved on.

'What a shame,' I said, forlornly, 'a perfectly good cigar.'

'How very singular,' said Holmes. He reached down and picked up a tiny, silver tie pin.

'Whatever is it?' I asked, frowning.

'I believe it's an angel,' my friend said.

EIGHT

The Alchemist

I had just settled down for another trip in *The Time Machine,* when Holmes swept into the room, his cape across his shoulders and hat planted on his head.

'Fancy a little night air, Watson?' I frowned.

'I had planned a quiet evening in the company of Mr Wells,' I admitted.

'I promise more excitement in the next hour than a week spent with your pot-boiler,' Holmes wagered, 'or your money back.'

I closed the book with a sigh, marking my place with a single strand of blonde hair that I had found across the armrest.

'I would warn against any attachment to Miss Braithwaite, Watson,' said Holmes, noticing my keepsake. 'She is an unknown quantity.'

'I am a married man!' I retorted. 'Regardless, Holmes, you would warn against a liaison with any woman.'

'True enough,' he admitted.

It was late on a Sunday evening and couples were returning arm in arm from their perambulations in Regent's Park. Holmes doffed his hat to a passing pair and the woman blushed. It struck me that if Holmes was so inclined, with his commanding aspect and distinctive features, he could have the pick of any girl in London. And yet his preoccupations were elsewhere.

A carriage waited outside and no sooner had I stepped upon the footplate than Holmes slapped the door and we were away.

We turned right onto the Marylebone Road. I glanced up and saw the last of the sun catching the white alabaster gargoyles that perched at the very apex of the four-storey block. The light seemed to quicken them into life, shivering their wings, preparing them for their twilight mischief. Rattling past the gothic splendour of the Old Marylebone Grammar School, Holmes, I noticed was possessed of that familiar twinkle of mischief and anticipation.

'No clue as to our destination, I suppose?' I asked Holmes.

'I'm afraid not,' he smiled.

'Wouldn't it be novel for once, just once,' I protested, 'to know what the future holds.'

'Have more than you know,' my friend intoned, sparking a cigarette into life, 'speak less than you know.'

'Blast you and the Bard,' I muttered and folded my arms.

'Courage, Watson,' said Holmes, 'a miracle awaits on the other side of the river.'

As we crossed the Thames, Holmes hummed a sonata under his breath as if doing a little mental violin practice. It put me in mind, of course, of Miss Braithwaite, and her bewitchingly free spirit. How different she was to Mary. These matters were not straightforward and they were not something I could discuss freely with Holmes. It would be easier discussing cats at Crufts.

The great dog's show, my papers remind me, caused something of a stir that year. Holmes and I had spent an agreeable afternoon at the Royal Agricultural Hall in Islington, inspecting the breeds and speculating about the winners. Holmes took great delight in correctly predicting several, with the caveat that none of them were a patch on Toby, his own mongrel currently in the care of one of his many associates. 'I prize usefulness above intellect and kindness above beauty in all my dealings,' he had told me. It felt like a pointed reference.

Holmes and I sped through Borough, past the bright lights of the old inn at Elephant and Castle and down through Streatham. Our driver was skilled in his trade and we delayed for no man as we thundered through Norbury.

The lights grew fewer and the houses more scarce before we were consumed in all pervading darkness. It was beyond me how the coachman could see the road before him at all. It was only when Holmes muttered the name Purley, did I have any inkling of my geography. Eventually I felt the carriage decelerate and heard the horses' hooves slow to a canter and finally a trot. We appeared to be still on a country road, an indeterminate distance from the nearest dwelling with thick woods on all sides. The moon had crept out from behind a cloud and climbing down from our hansom our shadows were thrown on the trees like the ghosts of long dead highwaymen.

'Ere, Mr 'Olmes,' our driver warned. He was a portly fellow whose face was almost entirely forested in ginger hair, curled in dense ringlets across his jowls. A pair of bright eyes emerged from this forestation. 'Are you sure you don't want me to drive you into the huey? I 'ear there are all sorts of bludgers 'round these parts and there 'ain't too many of those blue bottle friends of yours to help you out. You'll get into a load of beef if you 'ain't too careful.'

'Thank you for your advice, Mr Biggin,' my friend smiled, signalling me to hand over a sovereign, 'but we will take our chances. We look forward to meeting you here at the stroke of midnight.'

'I'll be here, Mr 'Olmes, sir,' he vowed, 'but will you?'

'Never fear, Mr Biggin. The good doctor and I are quite capable of looking after ourselves. A Bulldog and a Wesley are reassuring companions on a night such as this.'

'Be that as it may, but you best be on the lookout for them that play the crooked cross. The King's Head we passed back up the road is a flash house if ever I saw one. If one of them dragsmen saw my growler stopping' on the road he'll 'ave his shiv to our throats before you can say Jack Horner.'

'Mr Biggin,' Holmes said, showing now just a little impatience. 'Your consideration is as expansive as your vocabulary. We shall see you at midnight.' Holmes glanced up the road.

'This way, Watson!' he cried, then hopped the ditch and stepped into the wood.

At first I thought it a kind of madness, stumbling through the pitch dark woodland in the dead of night, tripping over roots and being snared in brambles. I feared that any minute my foot would slip down a foxhole or that I would tumble headlong into ditchwater. The wood was possessed of a terrible silence.

'Holmes?' I called. 'Are you there?'

There was a crack as a badger or deer stepped on a branch then the snuffle of the same woodland animal, followed by the questioning hoot an owl.

'Who? Who?' it asked, then growing in eloquence, added: 'Who do you think you are?'

'Holmes! This really is too much. We could break our necks in here.'
'Nonsense, Watson,' scoffed Holmes, amused by his little joke. 'This is a picnicking spot. In the light of day you would laugh at your foolishness.'
I had forgotten my friend's astonishing power for seeing in the dark. It was as if he was possessed of feline blood. I recalled one of our adventures where he led me through a house in utter darkness, striding forward as if it were bright as day.
'Lord help the honest men of England if ever you turn to crime, Holmes. You would murder us in our beds.'
'Then let us hope it never comes to that,' he said. 'Now, we are not too far off. Do you see that light?

Not only could I perceive a yellowish light through the trees, but also a smell like sulphur burning in my nostrils. I could make out a small stone building in a clearing in the trees. Smoke was bellowing from the chimney. Holmes advanced on the front door of the building and rapped hard with his cane. We heard hissing steam and the throaty roar of a furnace.
Eventually the door fell open an inch or so, producing a beam of red light and a blast of hot, foul air.
'Like the gates of hell themselves,' I muttered. 'You cannot possibly enter, Holmes. I forbid it. Your lungs would burst with your first breath.'
'I have inhaled the foulest smoke from the coarsest tobaccos on Earth; my lungs are accustomed to such punishment. Be brave Watson!'

Inside, the heat was astonishing. I felt my collar dampen and pressed a handkerchief to my mouth. But still I could not see the man or men stoking this furnace. Then, through the smoke, I saw something move, a figure most like a man, but with a strange hood upon his head. I edged closer, following Holmes as he strode forward confident as ever. My breath faltered, not because of the searing heat in my throat, but because of what I saw upon the head of the figure - what appeared to be nothing other, than a pair of horns.
'Holmes!' I yelled, instinctively. I saw him raise a calming hand, then extend it in friendship with the demon. I knew Holmes had

contacts in every strata of society, but never did I dream that his circle extended to the devil himself. The figure waved in my direction as I staggered back towards the door.

I came around lying on a hard, wooden bench looking up at the moon. Holmes was standing over me, proffering a small flask, which I gratefully received.

'The only true medicine for a doctor,' he chortled. 'Now come, Watson, your amateur dramatics have cost us time. We cannot keep our coachman waiting much past midnight or the very sump of London's criminal fraternity will drag him down to their underworld.'

Presently a bright-eyed, middle aged man approached. He was wearing a burnt leather apron and a slightly theatrical moustache twisted to a point at either end. His head was untroubled by hair and sweat dripped from his brow. He wore a pair of enormous gauntlets that covered his arms to the elbows.

'May I present Asslo Wilberforce,' introduced Holmes, perhaps our pre-eminent scientist and certainly our greatest magician.'

'Really Holmes, you flatter me,' said the man. 'Dr Watson, I am little more than a hobbyist.'

'Well, a hobbyist perhaps,' admitted Holmes, 'but one that has produced remarkable results.' I felt the brandy doing its vital work and sat up, scrutinising the fellow.

'Well if you don't walk the boards, Mr Wilberforce' I began, 'then you are wasted talent. Your turn as Mephistopheles was most convincing and your ability to work in that heat is nothing short of miraculous.'

'Which is why I created this patent hood,' he said calmly, 'producing his elephant-like mask, two ventilation tubes sprouting from the top.' I had learned not to be surprised by anyone in Holmes' circle.

'Mr Wilberforce works in a specialised branch of the natural sciences,' Holmes explained. 'I use him from time to time for a second opinion in the matter of forgeries.'

'Bank notes?' I speculated.

'Precious stones,' corrected Holmes. 'But Mr Wilberforce has taken his interest a further stage further. You see, he has, and I will permit you a further gasp of astonishment, perfected a process that facilitates the manufacture of diamonds.'

Wilberforce's face passed into shadow as a cloud crossed the moon. When it re-emerged, I noticed a grin had replaced his previously sanguine expression.

'My dear Holmes,' I cried. 'Is it true?'

'Perfectly.'

'Then this is the end of poverty. The end of every social ill. The beginning of a new age!'

'Quite possibly,' he agreed.

'How many people know about this?'

'Four,' replied Wilberforce. 'Yourself included.'

'Ridiculous!' I cried. 'The Prime Minister must be informed at once.'

'Not so fast, Watson. Think of the repercussions. All diamonds would become worthless. They would become as common as lumps of coal. The fortunes of kings and countries would be reversed at a stroke. There would be anarchy, Watson.' Holmes' eyes glimmered in the silver light. 'Then think on this. Imagine that this wonderful discovery falls into the hands of a master criminal. They use it to bankroll their sinister activities. They could make hundreds of small discrete sales that remain undetected. With their endless resources they would strangle every law abiding nation.' Holmes raised his arms to the moon. 'They would become invincible, Watson!' I stared at him in horror.

'Then we must destroy it, Holmes!' I cried. 'It is a fearsome weapon.'

'Destroy what?' he asked. 'The elements required are common place. Bone oil, lithium and a dash of paraffin. You could buy them in an ironmonger without arousing the least suspicion. No, it is the knowledge that is the value; the intricacies of the process. These exist only in the mind of its creator. I stared at Wilberforce, the bearer of this imaginable burden.

'What is to be done, Holmes?'

He reached into his pocket and withdrew a large object, covered in a piece of black cloth. For a moment I believed it was his Bulldog revolver. He unfolded the edges until it was revealed in all its brilliance in the centre of his palm.

'What you see before you, Watson, is one of the largest diamonds in the world.'

I was seduced entirely; seized with an outrageous greed and a covetous urge to possess it. I was lost in its thrall.

'But it is it a fake,' I spluttered without averting my gaze.

'It is what you see before you,' reasoned Holmes, 'a perfect diamond.'

I arrived at Baker Street at about mid-morning armed with the day's papers, a bag of Cox's Orange Pippins and an ounce of a loose shag tobacco procured from The House of Carreras on Prince's Street. I bundled in, filled with unfathomably good cheer and handed a packet of sugar to Mrs Hudson on my way up the stairs. I felt utterly invigorated, charged with that singular energy found only in the world's greatest metropolis.

'Do you ever feel, Holmes,' I asked him as I put down my parcels and removed my coat, 'that you are part of a sublime mechanism working in perfect harmony with itself?'

Holmes lay slumped in his chair like a man deflated. To his left, lay an emptied syringe, no doubt containing his trade mark seven percent solution. To his right, more worrying still, lay his Bulldog revolver. Opposite on the wall was a trail of bullet holes puncturing the wall around the mirror which now hung at an oblique angle. Plaster coated the carpet and mantelpiece.

'What hope is there,' asked Holmes, turning over a playing card languidly between his fingers. 'when there is no development of any note, no clue worthy of any scrutiny. Where does that leave us, Watson?'

'It leaves us, Holmes,' I replied, 'with time on our hands.' I tossed an apple through the air in Holmes' direction. A second later it was pinned to the wall, stuck through with a pocket knife.

'The world moves on without us, Watson,' sighed Holmes. 'In Italy there is a man sending invisible energies through the air, transmitting messages that can be received and understood miles away. This is sent by telegraphy and entirely without wires. It is a wonder. Meanwhile we sit in our rooms like troglodytes shouting back at the echo of our own voices. Watson, mark me when I say the world is leaving us behind. Baker Street has become a backwater.' Holmes moved a cigarette to his lips and sunk lower still into his chair. I knew Holmes too well to bother him in a mood such as this and removing some of the larger pieces of plaster from the upholstery, I settled quietly into my own chair with a copy of The Times.

No sooner had I glanced at the front page when I started in surprise.

'Really, Watson,' complained Holmes. 'You are an insufferable jack in the box this morning. What is it this time?'

'Chatburn,' I cried. 'We are too late. He's been murdered in his bed.'

'Murdered?' said Holmes, brightening somewhat.

'They have found his bed sheets covered in blood. But the body has vanished.'

'This is a tonic, Watson, a veritable tonic!'

Holmes leapt to his feet and dashed excitedly to the window.

'The game is afoot, Watson, the game is afoot!'

Once again we found ourselves thundering through London towards Queen's Street. Holmes was feverish with excitement twisting his hands together and sitting at the very edge of his seat, a man utterly transformed.

'Faster, I say!' he bellowed, 'leaning out of the window,' haranguing the driver.

I noticed a crowd of children, the boy Wiggins and the rest of the Baker Street Irregulars cheering us on by the side of the road as if we were racing a highwayman.

No sooner had we arrived when my friend sprang from the carriage and bounded past the constable guarding the door. The poor man barely had a chance to lower his arm. By the time I had reached him, he put up no resistance.

'You'll find Inspector Gregson upstairs,' he sighed.

I burst in on a ghastly scene. The room was turned upside down; drawers were upended on the floor, pictures pulled from the walls and at the centre was the poor jeweller's bed. A horrific red stain was expanding there that threatened to engulf all of London.

'Confound it, Holmes,' the inspector cried, 'what an absolute mess.'

Gregson presided over the scene with his usual commanding presence, his arms crossed, a look of distaste and disapproval across his face. A fleck of blood had found its way into his fair hair where he had swept it back.

Holmes was still taking it all in, his eyes darting this way and that.

'Masterful work!' he exclaimed.

'Masterful?' questioned Gregson. 'You have some admiration for these fiends?'

'I wouldn't go that far,' cautioned Holmes. 'They have taken exceeding pains resulting in a most convincing attempt. But the outcome is flawed.'

Gregson looked confused, then irritated at Holmes' remarks.

'This is the scene of a murder, Holmes,' he frowned. 'Not a stage in Drury Lane. If you have nothing useful to offer then I would suggest that you and Doctor Watson leave us to our work. There are certain elements of this case that are beyond dispute. The door to the room was deadlocked from the inside when we arrived. It took two constables and my own shoulder to bring it down. Not only that, the front door of the premises was also double locked and the shutters were closed all night. I have testimony from the local constable to this effect. There is evidence that the windows have not been opened anytime recently – the catches are rusted shut in fact. We have checked the floor for trapdoors and the walls are sound.

'If you would permit me to spend five minutes here,' Holmes replied calmly, 'I will be able to provide you with information of the greatest use to your enquiries.' Gregson glanced at his pocket watch.

'Five minutes,' he repeated. 'And please keep out of our way.'

'Excellent,' said Holmes, then promptly left the room. I busied myself examining the stain and the tears in the mattress where a knife had made several rough incisions. It appeared to have been the most frightful struggle. Presently my friend re-emerged through the wardrobe on the opposite wall.

'Good day inspector,' said Holmes coolly, stepping back into the room. 'I appear to have found an alternative entrance.'

Gregson barely had time to raise his jaw from the ground when Holmes began his appraisal.

'The wardrobe you will see rises to the full height of the room. It provides access, via a ladder, to the upper attic, where you will find an exotically furnished meeting room. From the attic, there is easy access to the roof.'

'Then that is how they dragged away the body,' said Gregson, recovering his wits.

'Impossible,' snapped Holmes. The ladder is inclined at a steep angle and at the top it is necessary for a man to twist and haul himself up with his own strength. It would be quite impossible to expect a dead man to accomplish such a feat.'

'Are you suggesting. . . ' Gregson began.

'Chatburn is alive and if not well, then still breathing London's foul air just the same as you and I.'

'But the bed,' Gregson said. 'A set up? For what possible reason? An insurance scam?'

Holmes sat on the edge of the bed and placed a finger in the blood.

'Well it is certainly human blood,' he said, holding up his fingertip. With the thumb and forefinger of his other hand, he picked up a feather, one of many jettisoned from the exploded pillow and mattress.

'To what bird did this once belong, doctor?' Holmes asked.

'A duck or goose, I expect,' I guessed, examining the brilliant white feather, fluffed at the edges.

'For all your knowledge of our frail human frame, Watson, you are no veterinarian. This in fact, once belonged to swan.'

'Rather exotic for a feather bed,' I remarked.

'Not to mention illegal,' added Gregson, puzzled at this diversion. 'But what possible relevance does this have?'

'I suggest we should be looking for someone with connections in the feather trade.'

I shot Holmes a look.

'A wild conjecture,' said Gregson. 'Now how did you fathom the wardrobe business, Holmes?'

'As I have often reminded my friend Dr Watson, eliminate the impossible and whatever you are left with, however improbable is the truth.' Gregson frowned once again.

'He has no relations and no acquaintances that we can identify beyond his assistants.'

'Well, Inspector,' said Holmes, returning his hat to his head. 'We will leave this puzzle with you. Watson, what say you to a pipe by the river before lunch?'

'A capital idea,' I said.

'Not so fast, Holmes.' said Gregson slowly. Holmes stopped and turned to the man. 'Have you ever met this man Chatburn?' Holmes froze, but betrayed no emotion whatsoever.

'Why do you say that, Inspector?'

'Why not try answering the question, Mr Holmes.'
'Well as a matter of fact, I have,' admitted Holmes. 'He fixed the lid of a snuff box for me and made an excellent job of it too. I shall be at quite a loss the next time I need a small repair. Did you know I have in my possession an emerald tie pin from Queen Victoria herself. It has a small blemish and I was meaning to ask Mr Chatburn's professional opinion before this ghastly business occurred.'
'What sort of man did you take him for?' asked Gregson.
'A serious minded fellow,' said Holmes. 'Disappeared to India for a while, I heard. Now if you don't mind, Inspector, I will obey your wishes and leave you to your investigation. I make that five minutes, don't you Watson?' I produced my pocket watch.
'Exactly right, Holmes,' I corroborated.
'Good day, Inspector,' said Holmes and he vanished around the corner.

Holmes and I found ourselves a bench in Victoria Embankment Gardens in the shadow of Steele's magnificent statue of Robert Burns. My friend glanced up at the poet. 'Morality, thou deadly bane,' he intoned. 'Thy tens of thousands thou has slane.' On either side of us other statues rose like the spectres of great men dead and gone. We watched the barges slug along the murky river laden with girders bound for Tower Bridge which was slowly rising down river like the legs of the Colossus. It was a mellow summer afternoon and Holmes and I clutched glasses of lemonade bought at an extortionate price from a wily vendor in a straw hat. I peered at the river and fancied I could see George Stevenson himself at the prow of the ship being ferried towards his mighty construction. The sun glittered on the water like a scatter of shillings.
'Well, Holmes,' I said, sipping at my concoction. 'Will you tell me what you wouldn't tell Gregson?' My friend peered across the river to the South Bank as if in a trance.
'I fancy you can still hear the voices from The Globe if you listen hard enough,' he said. 'In 1600 it is probable that London thought itself the most modern place on Earth: the very pinnacle of civilisation. And yet they were baiting bears and throwing their lunatics to the wolves.'
'Chatburn,' I said, returning Holmes to the present, 'is he alive?'

'Certainly he's alive,' said my friend, snapping out of his trance.

'Then where?'

'The case has developed a most satisfactory degree of interest,' said Holmes obliquely. 'There are just one or two more features upon which I would like to reach a point of certainty before I draw my conclusions.'

'Really Holmes, you are exasperating!'

'Watson, you know that I am in the business of fact, not speculation.'

'For example,' he continued. 'It is a fact that the man you see there hurrying along the embankment is newly married, has recently joined the police force and is wearing his second best suit. If I am not mistaken, he is on his way to visit his brother to return a sum of money to him, the amount of which I believe to be five pounds.' I stared at the man, who looked to my eyes little different from the scores of others going about their business.

'Explain yourself Holmes. That is an absurd conjecture based on nothing at all.'

'Watson, you offend me!' retorted Holmes. 'My deduction is based on the simplest observations.'

'Such as?' Holmes lit his cigarette and exhaled a ghost.

'He holds in his hands a bouquet of tulips rather than roses; roses are the extravagant purchase of a man who is courting; a man who has everything to gain. Tulips are the affordable flower of domesticity. His ring is a little too tight, causing some discolouration to his ring finger. He has not yet found time to have it adjusted. His shoes are police issue, of a new type provided only just this month to fresh recruits.'

I shook my head. 'And his brother?'

'Like our friend Chatburn, he is carrying two pocket watches. Do you see the double pair of chains and matching jade catches? They are of an identical kind; the variety a father would purchase as a pair and give to his sons as a gift.'

'The pawn value is five pounds. He has picked it up on behalf of his brother and is returning with the sum of money.'

'My dear Holmes,' I shouted. 'That's impossible!'

'Nonsense,' he smiled. 'It is quite elementary.'

'No, Holmes,' I urged. 'That statue, I believe it moved.'

Holmes frowned and looked in the direction I was pointing.

'It is merely a trick of the sun,' he said, 'the ripple of a heat haze.'
'I swear it moved,' I said shaking my head, looking again and seeing nothing untoward.

'Our next port of call will be back at the feather factory,' announced the great detective, nodding slightly to himself as he set himself on his inexorable course towards the truth. It was as if I could hear the minute cogs of his mind whirring beneath his aquiline brow.
'Holmes!' I cried. A shadow swept over us, as if a shawl had been thrown across the sun, swiftly followed by another, as two of the statues became suddenly came to life and descended on us with deadly menace. My friend had already sprung from the bench, pushed me clear and seized the cane of one of our assailants. He assumed the defensive stance I had seen before, most recently in Chatburn's attic but also, memorably in the Adventure of the Silver Thimble, which I have not yet had the opportunity to record. His legs were akimbo, the feet almost at opposite angles to each other. He held his left arm out straight before him; the other was bent above his head, holding the stick aloft.
Before us stood two of the two villains in their sinister dark eye glasses, black frock coats, each wielding a glinting blade.
Holmes glared at them as they bared their teeth like demented hell hounds.
'Perhaps you are unaware of my reputation,' my friend warned, 'as England's foremost practitioner of Bartitsu.' The shorter man, I later learned to be Uriel, laughed at my friend's words.
'Your reputation as England's first detective to be diced in a public park will exceed it,' he hissed. A crowd of onlookers had gathered at a safe distance, although none had mustered the courage to come to our assistance.
'Watson, your coat!' my friend called and before I knew it, he had torn it from my back and hurled it across the face of Michael, the other aggressor.

For a moment, the fiend flailed like a beast caught in a net, fighting to rid himself of his bonds. Holmes wasted no time landing a smart jab to his solar plexus, causing the man to buckle. Uriel rushed at Holmes from the other side and it was only my friend's fleet footwork that prevented him from being skewered on the man's lethal cane. Half hypnotised by my friend's performance, marvelling at how easily Holmes' physical prowess matched his mental agility, it was only now that I remembered I was carrying my service revolver in my pocket. But no sooner had I begun to draw it, when I felt the crack of a stick on the back of my head, a surge of dizzying pain and I crumpled to the ground. In a detached sort of way, I was still able to observe as Holmes skirmished with the other two like a superman, parrying their blows, sweeping them from their feet with his strange techniques and even hurling them through the air and down his back. But even with his extraordinary abilities I knew that the bout would not go our way if it continued with these odds.

'To me!' I heard Holmes shout, and it was with outstanding relief that I saw four constables, every one a giant of a man, bowling towards us from The Strand and throwing themselves manfully into the fight. I saw a gush of blood as one of them received a fearful injury to his arm and yet he did not so much as flinch as he delivered blow after blow to the head of Uriel. Now the villains knew the game was up and exchanging a look, they slipped from the clutches of Holmes and his four defenders and took flight like ravens. They fled with torn capes and broken eye glasses in a cloud of dust kicked up from the edge of the path.

'Bravo!' congratulated Holmes when he saw that we had won the day. The four constables were wheezing and crimson-faced from their exertions, bent double with their hands upon their knees.
'We came as soon as we could, Mr Holmes,' the injured policeman panted, still unaware that his arm was gaping from the Archangels' attack. 'I'm only sorry the blighters got away.'
'You all did splendidly,' said Holmes, 'a credit to the force.' He himself had regained his composure with extraordinary speed. 'But now constable, I insist that my friend, Dr Watson tends to your wound. You are sufficiently recovered from your own scuffle, I trust, Watson?'
'Certainly I am,' I said, rubbing a lump on the back of my head. I tore a piece of shirt and trussed the constable's wound. 'Just a flesh wound,' I assured him. 'No doubt it will smart a bit later this evening

and you may have a souvenir from the day to remind yourself of your valour.'

'No one in London is safe while these men are at large,' Holmes reflected, looking in the direction of their flight. 'But for now, it's brandy all round. Tonight, gentlemen, you are the toast of London.'

NINE

The Concert

Holmes was in his element. From our comfortable box in the second tier of the Royal Albert Hall we watched the evening crowds find their way to their seats, their programmes fluttering like the wings of a thousand butterflies. My friend clutched his own programme as if it were the title deeds to Buckingham Palace.

'Now Watson,' he gushed. 'You know my opinion of this piece, Mozart's Violin Concerto No 5 in A. Not as bombastic as his symphonies, more understated than his horn concertos, it is a sublime delight of infinite subtlety.' I dipped another stick of rhubarb into my pot of sugar.

'I'm sorry, Holmes,' I garbled. 'What was that?'

'Really,' said Holmes, lighting a cigar, a trail of smooth white smoke unfolding from his lips. 'It is so terribly uncouth.'

My friend of course had a fetishist's interest in the violin and would no doubt have been here on any account. However, there was another reason to explain our attendance. It was the first performance by our new friend, Miss Penelope Braithwaite since the mysterious demise of her teacher. We both thought it prudent to attend, but had decided not to announce it, since her nerves were still somewhat frayed. We were therefore to a greater or less extent, incognito. Through my opera glasses I could see Penelope clearly below us in a blue chiffon dress, fidgeting in her seat, flicking the pages of her music backwards and forwards. The conductor, a rotund, genial looking man with an enormous set of grey whiskers, appeared to tumultuous applause. He smiled and pressed his palms together in appreciation.

'A genius,' declared Holmes, applauding as loudly as anyone. A hush soon fell upon the room and the fine strains of the opening bars drifted high into the rafters.

I found the piece pleasant enough, although lacking the drama of Mozart's other compositions, and I soon found myself feeling rather sleepy. My friend, on the other hand, was in a rapture. His eyes were closed, his long chin raised and he appeared to be conducting the music himself, holding a tiny, invisible baton between the thumb and first finger of his left hand.

To pass the time, I scanned the men and women in their rows of seats, peered up at faces in the circle and the gallery, wondering if I was alone in allowing my thoughts to drift. I believed I could spot two or three of my patients: an ageing colonel with a rather severe case of gout. I was impressed he felt able to attend at all. Then there was a station master whose frozen shoulder had dogged him for years to the point he was often unable to raise his whistle to his lips. It was only then that I saw Snitterton in the stalls directly below us. His dark, fulsome whiskers masked much of his face, but the fine high brow and indomitable manner were unmistakable. I glanced across at Holmes but felt that it unfair to disturb his reverie.

'Watson!'
I woke with a start.
'Don't tell me that you nodded off?' sighed Holmes.
'Well,' I began, somewhat blearily. The concert appeared to be over and people were beginning to leave their seats. 'I noticed *you* had your eyes closed.'
'In appreciation!' he said.
'Well I was doing the same,' I countered. Holmes did not look convinced.
'So,' I said, a little more chipper now I knew I was safely on the other side of the interminable piece, 'shall we head back to Baker Street for a nightcap?'
'A nightcap?' smiled Holmes. 'My dear fellow, that was only the end of the first part of the programme. We have so much more to look forward to.' My spirits sagged. 'But at least let me buy you a glass of champagne to tide you over. You may even find you enjoy yourself. "The man that hath no music in himself is fit for treasons, stratagems and spoils. Let no such man be trusted. Mark the music."' Holmes' wisdom from the Bard was becoming something of an irritant.

We made our way through the crowds to the bar, Holmes nodding occasionally to former clients or contacts in his professional circles. For a man with few friends, he was acquainted with a surprisingly large and diverse group of individuals, from archdukes to

91

greengrocers. Suddenly we heard a familiar voice:

'Sherlock Holmes!'

We turned to find Inspector Lestrade behind us, his keen, dark, eyes fixed upon my friend.

'Inspector!' smiled Holmes. 'What a delightful surprise. I never had you down as a music lover.'

'And you are quite right,' Lestrade admitted. 'This is not my cup of tea at all.'

'Then alas, both you and Watson are passing an equally disagreeable evening.' I raised my eyebrows in solidarity. 'But if music has not brought you here,' Holmes went on, his eyes quickening with interest, 'then you must be here on some official business.' He glanced around him. 'I see you have some agents with you. Ten if I am not mistaken.' Lestrade looked astonished, then suspicious. 'How could you possibly know?' he demanded.

'Well, I see three around me now,' pointing out three entirely innocuous looking gentlemen milling around near the bar. Five would be too few for such an important visit and as a man with a sense of neatness and order, you would not have picked an odd number. Ten would be the number you would choose. Am I right?'

'What visit?' I garbled, 'Did I miss something.'

Holmes raised a glass towards Lestrade.

'How is Her Majesty enjoying the concert?'

'Keep your voice down,' pleaded Lestrade, glancing to his left and right. 'Do you want the whole of London to know?' Holmes flashed a congenial smile.

'Confound it, Holmes,' Lestrade added, shaking his head at the great detective, 'is there no secret safe from you? You have a devilish way of tickling out the truth.'

We made our way to a side gallery and Lestrade explained the detail. The Queen was on a low key visit, having developed a taste for Mozart and his violin concertos in particular. However, she was also exhausted by recent commitments, especially her Golden Jubilee celebrations, and felt an ostentatious entrance and exit would prolong the evening unnecessarily and simultaneously shorten the musical programme. She was, however, Lestrade explained, showing signs of restlessness and, he felt sure, would appreciate the diversion of a meeting with one of London's brightest minds.

We were ushered through a pair of plush, green, velvet curtains. Behind these were two footmen standing rigidly still and staring straight ahead. Lestrade stepped forward and opened a door to a second room. I followed him and Holmes through, adjusting my necktie nervously and brushing sugar from the collar.

In the corner of the room was a stout, grey haired woman sitting with a pile of knitting in her lap. At first I took her for a lady in waiting before catching that imperious, unmistakable look. I became quite rooted to the spot. Remembering our manners we gave a low neck bow.

'Gentlemen,' she said, putting her needles to one side. 'Please take a seat. Have you had some refreshment?' Lestrade gave a little cough.

'Yes Ma'am,' he stuttered. 'Thank you for asking. You remember Mr Holmes?'

'Remember?' she cried. 'Mr Holmes, the Empire owes you a debt of honour a hundred times over. How could we forget your innumerable services to the Crown?' Holmes nodded demurely and stepped into the light.

'I see that you are wearing my favourite colour in your tie pin,' she noted. 'It is as if you knew I would be here.'

Holmes smiled his inscrutable smile.

'How are you enjoying the programme, Ma'am?'

'Exceptional,' she pronounced. 'We particularly enjoyed the lead violinist. A Miss Braithwaite I believe?'

'Yes,' I put in, 'she is very fine.'

The Queen peered at me in a most disconcerting way. Clearly some protocol had been breached.

'Yes, a talent to watch,' she agreed at some length. 'Are you fond of this concerto, Dr Watson?

My eyes were drawn to a startling brooch the Queen was wearing. The diamond was simply enormous, a rounded, glistening gem that transfixed me with its glare.

'Dr Watson,' prompted Holmes. 'Her Majesty has asked you a question.'

'Yes,' I cried, without thinking. 'It is nothing short of magnificent!'

'I see you have taken a shine to my brooch, doctor,' she said, following my gaze. 'Well I cannot blame you. For a thousand years it has driven men mad with rage, women wild with jealously, started wars and brought down Empires.'

'A noble stone, Ma'am,' said Holmes. 'Is it not the Koh-I-Noor itself?'

'I see you have an eye for such things, Mr Holmes'

'Is it such a feat to identify the most famous jewel in the world? But I have not seen it for many years,' confessed Holmes. 'I understand your late husband commissioned some vital work to enhance its qualities.'

'He succeeded spectacularly,' I glowed.

'Dr Watson, I am beginning to like you,' said the Queen. I was quite speechless. 'Are you blushing, doctor?' she asked.

She rang a small bell and a man appeared from behind another curtain. He was a handsome Indian, with a fine black beard, a head dress of white and gold cloth, red vest and elegant robes.

'Gentleman,' she said. 'May I present one of the wisest, most gracious men in London: Karim, the Munshi.'

Again, we bowed low. I had heard something of this man, an attendant who had won the favour of the monarch; they had become almost inseparable. There were whispers in court that he was a charlatan and a thief but nothing would stick. The Queen held him in an esteem she had reserved only for the Scotsman, John Brown and of course Prince Albert himself.

'Dr Watson,' she asked calmly, would you like to hold the Koh-I-Noor?' Then she turned to her friend. 'Karim, would you be so good as to remove it from my person?' I glanced at Holmes, who raised his eyebrows.

'Are you sure that's wise, Ma'am?' asked Lestrade to my irritation.

'Is the doctor a known diamond thief?' she asked.

The Indian stepped forward, his eyes on the Queen.

'Of course,' he said softly, in accented English. He struck me as a noble man, with graceful, deliberate actions. He stepped forward and gently unpinned the brooch from her dress without ceremony or a moment's hesitation. I noticed a brief smile pass between them.

'What can you tell us about this stone?' she asked him.

'It is a stone of wonder and enormous power,' he whispered. 'It was cut from the Kollur mine of Andhra Pradesh and was once said to be the eye of a goddess. The other eye is lost to time. It has passed through the hands of many great men and women. It brought great glory and great misfortune. It was once known as the Diamond of Babur, the prize of Akbar and Lodi. It was once in the Peacock Throne of the immortal Shah Jahan, he who built the Taj Mahal.' I listened, enraptured by the Munshi's knowledge, as I felt him place the stone into my hands. Its weight was stupendous; a heat seemed to radiate from within and my heart leapt as if a current of electricity had passed through me.

'You hold in your hands the history of India,' said the Queen.

'May I?' asked Holmes.

'But of course,' she said. 'How could we deny you the thrill too, Mr Holmes?'

He produced a pair of gloves from his pocket and slipped them on. I passed the stone gingerly to him, as if handing over an unstable compound. In an instant, my friend whipped it up to the light.

'A purity beyond measure!' he marvelled as the light burst through its core and exploded. We were for a moment blinded by its brilliance.

The five minute bell sounded.

'Your Majesty,' said Lestrade. 'We cannot detain you any longer.'

'Really,' she said. 'I feel altogether too tired to return to the concert. Really, I am such a Philistine. You will not think ill of me if I were to return home, would you Mr Holmes?'

'Your Majesty has the same freedom as any citizen of England to come and go as she pleases.'

'This,' he said, handing back the brooch to the Indian, 'is a privilege that we will never forget.' He bowed once again. 'As-Salamu Alaykom,' he said, the meaning known only to them.

'Inspector,' added the Queen, a little more severely. 'If you learned Mr Holmes' impeccable manners, I cannot help but feel you would go further.'

Holmes and I hurried back along the gallery towards our box.

'Astonishing,' I said shaking my head. 'I had no idea you and the Queen were on such familiar terms.'

'A women of extraordinary substance,' said Holmes. For a man who did not compliment the fairer sex as a matter of personal policy, this was an incredible statement.

'And what of the diamond?' I asked.

'What of it?' asked Holmes. 'I think it is the most perfectly useless lump of rock I have ever encountered. The dullest mind holds infinitely more fascination for me. Its capacity for cunning, deception, evil and skulduggery has no limits. Its ingenuity increases with its desires and its workings are our most fathomless mystery. A diamond on the other hand, is merely a lump of prehistoric vegetation crushed into existence in the deepest kilns of the Earth. Its value is a construct of the human mind.'

'Bit of a sparkler, all the same, don't you think Holmes?'

'Smoke and mirrors,' scoffed Holmes. 'Albert almost destroyed the stone trying to make it shine. He may as well have tried to polish the sun.'

'Did you know that she would be here this evening?'

'I have a friend inside the palace,' Holmes admitted, 'who overheard a chance remark suggesting as much.'

'And you never thought to tell me?'

'You never asked, my dear Watson.'

The orchestra had barely struck up when I noticed the empty seat below me.

'Snitterton,' I cried. 'Do you see? He hasn't returned.'

Holmes frowned and peered into the empty seat as if the very act of staring would make him materialise.

'Most disconcerting,' he said. 'The reason I chose this box was to keep an eye on him.'

'You knew he would be here?'

'Naturally,' he said.

'Enough!' I whispered. 'I am utterly in the dark. I insist on some clue!'

'There is no time,' said Holmes. 'Mozart will need to wait for another day.'

He rose from his seat, tore his coat from the stand and made for the door.

Holmes and I dashed through the foyer and out into the balmy evening, tailcoats flapping, pursued by an agitated looking Lestrade.

'The diamond!' panted Lestrade. 'Someone has stolen the diamond!'

We skidded to a halt.

'You don't mean to say . . .' I began.

'The particulars, quickly, Lestrade,' demanded Holmes.

'The Queen was returning to her seat. As we turned into the corridor a man with a shrouded face ripped the diamond from her dress. We gave chase but he was too far ahead of us. We have half the force out with his description.'

'This is grave, very grave' muttered Holmes. 'It will be the talk of London.'

Lestrade shook his head. 'This cannot get out,' he said. 'We will be a laughing stock. Her Majesty is beside herself.'

'You must examine the scene, Holmes,' begged Lestrade.

'We have our own urgent business,' said Holmes. 'A man we have been pursuing in an entirely different matter has been sighted.'

'It must wait!' said Lestrade.

'Very well,' said Holmes. 'Watson, you go on ahead. Speak to that driver in the blue coat. I shall meet you back at Baker Street. Here, take my opera glasses.' He stuffed the black leather case into my hands then disappeared back inside with Lestrade.

'You there,' I called to the driver of a hansom who was feeding his horse.

'Did you see a growler leave in a great hurry?'

'And what if I did?'

'Well did you?' I asked. He continued to tend to the animal.

'There's half a crown in it if you did,' I coaxed.

'In which I case, I did,' he concluded, patting the neck of the glossy mare tethered to his cab. I frowned.

'Did you really?'

'Really what?'

'See a carriage leave in a great hurry!' He was becoming exasperating.

''Ere what are you, some sort of jack? A crusher in mufty? I 'ain't no buck cabbie you know. I saw a carriage leave in a hurry, or my name 'aint't Matthew Porter.'

'Do you happen to know what direction it left in?' He narrowed his eyes at me until I had pressed the coin into his hand.

'That way, I reckon,' he said, cocking his head towards Knightsbridge. 'And that 'aint no flam.'

'Then let's go,' I cried. 'You have yourself a fare. Catch him and there's another crown in it for you.'

'Well,' he said, hopping up to his seat, 'so long as you've got the chink, I'll follow the devil through the gates of hell.'

We took Kensington Road at a clip, the Royal Geographical Society flying past on our right, the Serpentine on our left until we arrived at Hyde Park Corner. I leaned my head out of the hansom and called to the driver.

'Any idea which way?' I shouted.

'If I know old Hasker,' Porter replied, 'he'll go straight up Piccadilly.'

We clattered on, speeding past lumbering broughams and omnibuses until finally in the distance I could see another hansom travelling almost as fast as ours.

'There he is!' shouted my driver in triumph.

'Keep your distance,' I yelled back, 'but don't let it out of your sight!'

'Right you are!'

We kept on its tail through the city, swerving between the drinkers and ladybirds, the bobbies and the loafers.

'I don't believe it,' I muttered to myself after we had turned left onto Euston Road, 'I do believe we're heading for Baker Street.'

In fact we travelled directly along it. I glanced into our dimly lit chambers, reflecting on the peace we had enjoyed just a few days earlier. But we didn't stop, whipping into Park Road and only slowing as we reached the cricket ground. Mr Porter and I stopped at a safe distance and after settling up I slipped into the shadows where I could observe the passengers disembarking.

Soon enough, I saw the large, overbearing figure of Snitterton jump down from his carriage, then climb the steps to the front door of a narrow terraced house. The door was open just long enough for me to see that it was none other than Chatburn who had let him in.

'Two sworn enemies under the same roof,' Holmes cried later that evening. 'The game's afoot, Watson, well and truly afoot!' He was pacing our rooms with the agitation of a boxer waiting for a bout to begin. 'The two are in cahoots,' he cried. 'I knew it!' Mrs Hudson appeared at the top of the stairs.

'Ms Penelope Braithwaite is here to see you both. I didn't keep her waiting as I felt sure that you would wish to see her.'

'Quite sensible,' agreed Holmes. A moment later she stepped into the room like a goddess from a cloud.

She wore a free flowing green gown tied loosely at the waist with a white sash. Beneath, she sported a white silk blouse. Her hair was held in place by a silver band, at the centre of which was a single ruby. Her neck was bare.

'You look simply ravishing!' I cried, before I could help myself.

'You like my outfit, Dr Watson?' she asked flirtatiously. 'I have been asked to play at court on Monday next and wanted to try it on ahead of time.

'Well,' I said, 'my advice is to go right ahead and wear it.'

'Do you not think it a trifle daring for the Queen?' asked Holmes a little waspishly.

'I think she likes it when people are themselves.'

'Very well,' said Holmes. 'But on your head be it.'

She rolled her eyes and moved to the couch. Clearing a heap of periodicals, she found a little space to sit down. She glanced around the room.

'Well,' she said. 'Did you enjoy the performance?' I glanced at Holmes.

'How did you know we were there?' I asked, somewhat taken aback.

'Despite your attempt at a low profile, word soon travels when Sherlock Holmes is seen in a crowd. Did you hear the rumour that the Queen herself was there last night?'

'We did,' I muttered, still unable to tear my eyes away from her.

'In answer to your first question,' said Holmes, 'it was a remarkable performance. Please accept my congratulations. There was however a small lapse in the second movement; an unintended glissando perhaps?'

'I knew you would spot that, Mr Holmes,' she said. Mrs Hudson brought in the tea.

'Would you care to join us for lunch?' I asked Miss Braithwaite.' Mrs Hudson is preparing tripe and onions.'

'Alas, it is just a flying visit, Mrs Hudson. But thank you.'

'A pity,' said the venerable woman, 'there will be plenty to go around.'

'Well,' she said, after Mrs Hudson had left us a second time, 'have you had any success in tracking down Wimpole's killer?'

'The trail is warming,' said Holmes peering out of the window.

'And what of the ruby elephants?' she asked.

'What of them?' asked Holmes, abruptly.

'I know they are of interest to you. I heard you and the doctor discussing them and I believe there was one at Wimpole's flat.'

'You didn't mention that before,' said Holmes.

'I never thought to,' she said in a rather blasé fashion, leafing through the London Illustrated News.

'Tell me,' asked Holmes. 'How is your father?'

'Who?' she asked without looking up.

'Your father.'

'Oh, lord knows,' she said. 'I haven't seen him in years.'

'Would it surprise you,' said Holmes, 'if I told you that he was at the performance last night?' She laid down the newspaper.

'Will you repeat that, Mr Holmes?'

'You heard me well enough.'

'Mr Holmes,' she said imperiously, rising from the couch, 'I am late for an appointment and I have nothing more to say to you.'

'Good day, Dr Watson,' she said. 'Thank you for your advice. I shall be wearing this to Buckingham Palace.' She stormed out of the room, down the stairs and slammed the front door behind her.

I collapsed back into my chair and loosened my collar.

'What a woman, Holmes!'

'Indeed!'

'And you are a madman to rile her. What's all this rot about her father? Whoever do you mean?'

'Just a theory I am testing,' he said.

'Well, you're playing a dangerous game.'

'They happen to be the ones I enjoy the most!'

TEN

The Fake

'Well, well,' I said, folding The Times to a manageable size. 'There has been a disturbance at the National Gallery.'

'Go on,' said Holmes.

'The critic and aesthete, Abercrombie Macintosh,' I read aloud, 'was forcibly ejected from the National Gallery on Tuesday afternoon. Macintosh, who was suspected of being drunk, was found disturbing visitors in Room 35 of the gallery. At 2.45pm a constable was called to assist gallery staff and after a short struggle they succeeded in restraining him. Macintosh continued to make claims outside the gallery telling the crowd that the painting The Shrimp Girl, by George Hogarth, and a number of other works in the gallery were fakes. The Director of the Gallery, Sir William Frederick Burton, made the following statement: "We very much regret the incident on Tuesday afternoon and wait in full hope and expectation of an apology from Mr Macintosh, who hitherto was considered a friend of the gallery. We are pleased to confirm that the gallery has no forgeries in its possession and that the painting by Hogarth has been independently verified as an original work by the artist."'

Holmes blew a series of smoke rings into the air.

'Sounds like Abercrombie's been at the absinthe again,' I put in, laying down the paper.

'Do you think?' asked Holmes evenly.

'Well, I would assume Sir William knows his own paintings.'

'Why don't we take a trip down there,' suggested Holmes, 'and see for ourselves?'

This said everything about my friend, Sherlock Holmes. He was never content with a second hand account of anything, even if it came from a supreme authority.

'Even though we are assured to the contrary?'

'My friend,' Holmes said, rising imperiously, his eyes gleaming. 'London is in thrall to a superior criminal mind. Its manifestations are all around us: on the streets, in the galleries and along the corridors of powers. As my friend Mr Shakespeare forewarned: 'Hell is empty and all the devils are here!'

It was unusually busy when we arrived in Trafalgar Square. A large crowd was gathered at the entrance to the National Gallery, which rose up like the Temple of Artemis.

'Whatever Sir William's views are on the matter,' said Holmes, peering through the window of our two seater, 'the scandal has unquestionably been good for business.'

We queued up with the others and filed patiently through the rooms until we were standing before the painting. My appreciation of art is strictly as a layman, but I know what I like when I see it. The portrait was of a vivacious working class woman, a fishmonger's wife, with a large, flat basket balanced on her head, laden with shellfish. Despite her exertions, her expression was hopeful, even happy. Up close, the style appeared somewhat slapdash with streaks of paint seemingly applied at random and yet the overall effect was undeniably impressive.

'If you want my view, Holmes,' I said with a grin, 'except for what's balanced on her head, there's nothing fishy about this painting.' My friend appeared unmoved by this attempt at humour. Instead he was studying the floor immediately beneath the painting, the ceiling and the four corners of the room.

'Surely, Holmes,' I said, your time would be better spent analysing the painting itself.'

'On the contrary, Watson,' my friend explained. 'I am an expert in observation, logic and probability, not fine art.'

'Sherlock Holmes!' addressed a careworn voice with a soft Dublin accent.

We were greeted by the stern face of the director himself, Sir William Frederick Burton. With a snow white beard, high forehead and owlish glasses, he wore the tired look of an artist who had turned, reluctantly, into an administrator.

'My dear Sir William,' said Holmes.

'I would have thought that you of all people,' said Sir William, 'would have been able to resist the cheap sensationalism that has surrounded us this week.'

'I'm afraid not,' my friend replied. 'It is very much our stock in trade. Now how do you account for Macintosh's outburst? He is a

man of impeccable taste and reputation. Do you have a theory?'
'Of course,' said Sir William. 'The bottle. It has been the ruin of some of our greatest minds, from Byron to Shakespeare himself.'
'So you believe his accusation has no basis in fact?'
'None whatsoever. The painting was certified on its acquisition and has been certified again.'
'By the same individual?'
'As it happens, no. But it was a pre-eminent authority.'
'You do not believe there is any way the painting could have been switched during cleaning or loan?'
'Impossible.' he said. 'It has remained in the same place since it was purchased six years ago.' The gallery doors are locked at night. There are twenty guards who patrol the building every evening and an additional guard who stands at each entrance. The roof and basement are both impregnable.'   Holmes nodded thoughtfully.
'Then Sir William, I apologise for questioning your judgement.'

We retired to a bench on Trafalgar Square and luxuriated in the sunshine, smoking in companionable silence.
'It appears there is no crime to solve,' I said at length. 'If you are in need of fresh blood, Holmes, would you not be better off visiting Scotland Yard and asking to see their files of unsolved cases?'
'Did you notice,' he asked, without taking his eyes off Nelson, 'that pair of large vases either side of the door in Room 35?'
'I can't say I did,' I admitted.
'They were Chinese porcelain, five feet tall, each with four carved lion's paws emerging from a round wooden base. On the top of the lid was a stylised ceramic lion.'
'Perhaps I did,' I mused. 'But what of them?'
'It struck me that with a little discomfort a man might be able to squeeze inside and hide himself there.'
'A fanciful notion!' I laughed.
'Yes, it is rather,' said Holmes. 'But would you not agree that it is also possible?'
'At a pinch,' I said.
'Why don't we hear,' my friend concluded, 'what the great aesthete has to say for himself.'

We arrived outside Abercrombie Macintosh's Kensington flat early that same evening. The day had softened into balmy night and a full moon irradiated the white stucco front of the building. A lamplighter was making his way slowly along the street as if fixing the stars to the sky. A demure lady housekeeper with a long suffering look answered the door and we presented our cards. 'You will be aware that Mr Macintosh has been under some considerable stress,' she said quietly, perhaps mistaking us for the police. 'Do not press him too hard.'

We were led to a spacious upstairs room, where on a green upholstered chaise-longue the great man lay in a pile of purple robes. He glanced over at us then rose to his feet.
'My dear Sirs,' he exclaimed. 'Forgive me! How long have you languished there?'
'We have only just arrived,' I stated.

He cut an extraordinary figure. He wore a pointed goatee with a long moustache; his brown hair was parted into two silky curtains that entirely hid his ears. His robes were somewhere between a dressing gown and a magician's outfit. It was impossible to say whether this was all for our benefit or whether he usually spent a mid week evening wearing such attire.
He glided over to a drinks cabinet then handed us tooth mugs of a greenish liquid that could only be absinthe.
'Do you have any wine?' asked Holmes.
'No,' he replied curtly.
'Have you had a pleasant day?' I asked in earnest.
'Any day above ground is a good day,' he replied. 'Isn't that so, Mr Holmes?'
'Quite,' my friend replied. 'Now Mr Macintosh.'
'Abercrombie, please,' he said with a winning smile, returning to his couch. His swung his legs high, then crossed them at the ankles. 'Now I am certain you know I am telling the truth.'

The room was quite as eccentric as the man himself. A stuffed owl sprang from the wall by the fireplace with outstretched wings. Two gold dishes that looked Aztec in origin flanked an enormous mirror with an intricate gilt frame. The mantelpiece was lined with an exotic crimson fabric with red tassels that hung loosely over the edges. An icon of the Madonna and child was placed high up above us while below our feet was a large, colourful Persian rug. The green panelled walls were almost entirely obscured by works of art of varying sizes. Incense burned furiously giving the whole place the air of a Moroccan bazaar.

'As a matter of fact,' Holmes nodded. 'I have a theory, which I would be happy to outline. However first I need to know for certain that the painting is a forgery.'

'A forgery?' cried Macintosh. 'That is too good a word for it. I have visited The Shrimp Girl once a week for almost a year. When I saw it on Tuesday last, it was like returning home to find your wife replaced by an impostor.'

'I wouldn't know about that,' said Holmes.

'And neither would I,' returned Macintosh archly.

'The delicacy of the flesh tone, the lightness of touch around the eyes; the finely balanced absurdity of the composition – all are missing.' He swallowed sunk a half glass of absinthe then brought the empty tumbler down emphatically onto the table. He rummaged in the deep pockets of his gown.

'Where are those infernal things?' he muttered to himself.

'Are you looking for this,' I asked handing him a silver cigarette case.

'Mr dear doctor,' he said with gratitude. 'I can see now why you are in the business of saving lives. Won't you help yourself? You too Mr Holmes.' We took a moment to enjoy his choice Turkish tobacco.

'Then it is a fake,' my friend concluded.

'It is indeed,' said Macintosh in a dense cloud of smoke. 'Art is not a reflection of life; it is mirror of the soul. I have stared into this mirror and found nothing there.'

Macintosh's housekeeper appeared at the door.

'The soup is ready,' she announced.

'We have already dined, thank you,' advised Holmes.

'I would be indebted,' said the aesthete, 'if you were to try just a little of this. It is a rare delicacy; a once in a lifetime experience.'

Three bowls of a steaming, clear broth were produced and we sat with them on our laps.

'Will you give us an inkling,' I asked, 'as to its ingredients?'

'Taste it, my friends!' Macintosh cried. 'What is life if not an adventure?'

I raised a spoon tentatively to my lips. The taste was somewhat elusive. It was somewhere between French onion soup and a light lamb broth.

'Not bad at all,' I said, taking another spoonful. 'Are you going to let us into the secret? Is it Lamb?'

'Mammoth,' smiled Macintosh.

I spluttered into my napkin.

'I acquired a Mammoth's femur on the Portobello Road. Rather than add another ornament to my collection, I thought it would be more amusing to put it to some practical use. Consider it a culinary form of time travel.'

'A singular flavour,' complimented Holmes, sipping thoughtfully. I, meanwhile, had decided my own culinary adventure was over.

'So tell me,' said Macintosh, returning to the matter in hand, 'how do you intend to expose this foul play?'

An hour later Crabtree stood outside Macintosh's door. It was the same man, I recalled, who had leant Holmes his brolly during the incident of the runaway elephant. He bore every resemblance in his stature and manner to a mole. In fact, his twitching and squinting became more pronounced the closer he came to us.

'Let me introduce my friend, Crabtree,' said Holmes. 'You will no doubt be acquainted with his optician's practice in Jermyn Street and his particular interest in the art of the monocle.'

'Delighted to make your acquaintance,' said Macintosh. 'You will know, Mr Crabtree, like every great artist, that to reveal its true beauty, the world must be viewed through a lens.'

Crabtree was a small neat man, cleanly shaven with the unusual affectation of a pair of monocles suspended on lengths of string from his buttonhole. He clearly believed that the promotional value of such a gimmick outweighed the obvious inconvenience of having to insert each one carefully into the eye socket. You might say he was his own shop window.

'At the risk of pointing out the obvious,' said Macintosh studying the man, 'would it not be easier to wear a pair of spectacles?'

'Spectacles,' Crabtree repeated, as if repelled by the very mention of the word. 'That would be a different proposition entirely.'

'Entirely different?' questioned Macintosh. 'Are they not simply two monocles with the convenience of a connecting bridge?'

'That would be like saying that by connecting two unicycles you could produce a bicycle. A monocle is more like a glove: each must be individually fitted to the eye - delicate and unique in its own way.'

'You will tell me next that you shop in different places for each trouser leg.'

'I fail to see the connection.'

'As do I!' cried Macintosh.

'You would not think of joining your shoes together,' Crabtree countered, 'so why your eye-glasses?'

'As you wish, as you wish,' said Macintosh, conceding defeat 'you are the expert.'

When I say that Crabtree was small, he was barely five feet. He had no doubt spent the greater part of his adult life convincing people that he was indeed a fully grown adult. This endeavour would have been further hampered by his boyish enthusiasm. Holmes explained that on more than one occasion he had desired more than anything to be embroiled in one of our adventures.

'As you know, I have been waiting,' said Holmes with a masterful air,'for a case that could make use of your singular talents.'

'Oh yes,' said Crabtree eagerly.

'I believe,' my friend said, 'that I have finally found it.'

While waiting for Crabtree we had imbibed a higher than recommended dose of the 'green fairy' and I was entering something of a heightened state. Holmes had furnished Macintosh with the details of his scheme and of the role he intended our diminutive friend to play. The critic was highly sceptical of Holmes' theory, but in the interests of entertainment alone, was prepared to play along.

Now Crabtree was standing before us, Macintosh seemed to warm to the idea. 'Won't you have a drink, dear boy?' he asked and without waiting for an answer sloshed a finger or two of absinthe into a glass and handed it to Crabtree. The man looked at me uncertainly. I hoisted my own glass into the air and grinned.

'Chin, chin!' I cried. Holmes then outlined the plan.

Crabtree peered at us with dismay. 'You want me to spend the night at the National Gallery inside a porcelain vase?'

'That's it,' said Holmes. Crabtree swallowed carefully, glanced at his glass, then nodded.

'Very well,' he said.

'Good man!' I shouted and then charged our glasses for the next toast.

It would be fair to say that we had a slow start the next day. When I finally stumbled into our sitting room it was with a cold compress on my forehead and a stifled groan on my lips. Holmes was brooding in his armchair, holding open a copy of The Times, keeping movement to a minimum. The room was thick with smoke.

From what I recalled of the remainder of the evening, we had celebrated Crabtree's willingness to take part with several more mugs of absinthe. We then made various preparations, none of which I could now remember. I did have a recollection of Macintosh re-enacting an unlikely, but colourful story of how he and Oscar Wilde staged an impromptu performance of Hamlet for the King of Denmark. Wilde had played Hamlet and he Gertrude. This was all before Macintosh had encouraged us to sample some his Lloyds' Cocaine Tooth Drops, which he recommend highly to us, toothache or no. Holmes had required no encouragement to try them out. We had returned home by unfathomable means.

I collapsed into my chair and took several deep breaths. The only bright spot of hope was the smell of eggs cooking downstairs, accompanied by what I suspected to be devilled kidneys. Suddenly breakfast did not seem such a good idea after all.

'Have you any idea what happened to Crabtree?' I asked Holmes after regaining my composure.

'Mm?'

'Crabtree? Did he find his way home?'

'Yes, I expect so. He fell out of the brougham at Wardour Street. That should have been close enough.' We sat for a moment in silence.

'I must confess,' I said, 'that I am in the most astonishing pain.'

'Physician, heal thyself!' muttered Holmes. He held up the newspaper and shook it out in front of him.

'Now, Watson, what do you make of this?' he asked. 'I've just spotted this in the small ads:

Lost: small red glass elephant; of sentimental value only. Reward. Apply to 14 Caledonian Road.'

'Good Lord,' I shouted. 'He's taken to public appeals. Surely this means Snitterton is becoming desperate.'

'Perhaps,' said Holmes, 'and perhaps not. It could of course be a lure. He knows we're on to him. Who knows what is waiting for us at 14 Caledonian Road.'

There was the sound of footsteps on the stairs. Mrs Hudson appeared with a tray laden with breakfast things.

'You don't deserve this,' she tutted, 'not after the racket you made last night. Dr Watson, I had no idea you were possessed of such a fine voice. I heard your rendition of Polly Perkins of Paddington Green before you had even turned into Baker Street.'

'Really, Mrs Hudson,' I began. 'I'm most awfully . . .'

'It's a bit late for that now,' she said. 'Now eat this while it's still hot.'

She poured the tea while Holmes and I tucked into our devilled kidneys.

'Most frightfully good,' I said admiringly, between mouthfuls and sips of tea. Mrs Hudson shook her head, then disappeared back downstairs.

'Do you think we ought to postpone our investigation at the gallery?'

'Postpone?' spluttered Holmes. 'Nonsense.'

'But what of this advertisement?'

'Let him wait a day or so. I can't imagine he will be inundated with callers. No, this evening must proceed as planned. I have a strong inclination, as yet unsupported by fact, that the business at the National Gallery is of some wider significance. Pass the Worcestershire Sauce, Watson.'

At four in the afternoon, Holmes, Crabtree and I found ourselves standing in the long shadows of the Doric columns of the National Gallery. To avoid unwanted attention, Macintosh had stayed away. Perhaps this was just as well given the state we had left him in the previous evening. There was no way of knowing whether he was even out of bed. I rather lamely sipped at a flask of water still not entirely myself from the night's misadventures.

'So, Crabtree,' said Holmes. 'Are you quite clear on the order of events?'

'I have two questions,' he said, glancing anxiously at the mighty stone building, 'possibly three.'

'Throw the spear!' invited Holmes.

'How certain are you that the original thieves will not make a return visit?'

'I'm not certain at all,' said Holmes. 'But while it is not impossible, it is unlikely. After the break in, the gallery will be on a heightened state of alert.'

'If that is the case' said Crabtree, adjusting one of his monocles, 'is it not possible that I will be discovered and detained?' It was a perfectly valid point.

'Of course that remains a possibility,' admitted Holmes.

'This takes me to my last question. If I am discovered, what is there to prevent them arriving at the conclusion that I am the original thief?'

Holmes and I glanced at each other.

'Crabtree, my friend,' Holmes laughed. 'They will never believe it! And besides, we will vouch for you. However my strong suspicion is that they have discounted the possibility of a small person hiding themselves inside a vase as an absurdity. But as we know, simply because something is absurd, does not render it impossible.'

We strode in through the main doors at intervals to avoid suspicion, some ten minutes to closing time, taking special care not to attract the attention of the security guard. Assembling in front of Turner's Dido Building Carthage, we made our final battle plans.

'At two minutes to five,' explained Holmes, 'the warden will leave Room 35 to lock rooms 30 to 34. That will be our cue.'

At three minutes to five, there was only one visitor remaining. He was standing before The Shrimp Girl: a noble faced young man in his middle thirties, with fashionably long hair, a purple tail coat and a slightly sad look about the eyes.

'Astonishing, isn't it?' the man said to no one in particular, leaning forward to inspect the painting, his hands joined behind his back. 'If it's a fake, it is the work of a singularly gifted criminal. I might even say it is an improvement. Constable was never quite sure whether he had finished this work.'

'But never having seen the subject,' I reasoned, 'we will never know whether it is a likeness.' He gave me a long, penetrating look.

'No great artist sees things as they really are,' he said. 'If he did, he would cease to be an artist.'

Presently, the three of us were alone again.

'There's no time to be lost!' urged Holmes in a stage whisper. 'Crabtree - now!'

Sherlock Holmes pressed a set of cards and a small hip flask into the man's hands. I lifted the lid of the vase and together we bundled the diminutive shopkeeper inside, feet first. It was a close fit around Crabtree's waist where he was perhaps a little stouter than we had anticipated, but with a concerted effort we pushed him down through the neck and into the vase itself. Soon, only the top of his head was visible.

'You are quite sure,' he asked Holmes with great seriousness and something of an echo, 'that this is useful to your investigation?'

'Profoundly so,' my friend assured him. I had only just replaced the lid when the guard remerged.

'Gentlemen, please,' he said, frowning. 'The museum is now closed.' He glanced around the room, then back at us. 'If you would be so good as to make your way to exit. Thank you.'

We caught our breath outside on the stone steps. It seems loathsome now, but I could not help but laugh at the thought of Crabtree quivering in his pot. Holmes was watching the Londoners crossing the square.

'Who knows whether our city will still be here in a hundred years,' he mused. 'Did the Romans believe their civilization would ever end?' he asked. 'Not two years before Rome fell, the citizens still believed themselves to be the greatest people on Earth.' He bit the stem of his pipe and looked up at Nelson on his column. I see the barbarians coming up Pall Mall. They will topple the great men of the Empire, pull Nelson from his plinth and drag Wellington from Copenhagen. They will burn our art and raze Parliament to the ground. They will charge across Hyde Park and our Queen will flee to the East.' He appeared to be in something of a trance. I hailed a hansom and we set off in the direction of Baker Street.

I was awoken the next morning by a loud banging on the door.
'Mr Holmes! Mr Holmes!'
I ran in my nightclothes to the sitting room and pulled open the window.
'Wiggins!' I shouted, 'what's the meaning of this infernal racket?' I peered down at the grubby features of the most irregular of the Baker Street Irregulars.
'It's Sir William, sir,' he called back, 'he wants you and Mr Holmes to come down to the National Gallery quick smart! It's kicking up a shine down there and his dander is right up!'
Holmes appeared behind me, tying his dressing gown.
'I won't pretend I understand everything you've said, Wiggins,' my friend said calmly, 'but we will proceed directly.'
'Fank you, Mr Holmes!'
Wiggins lingered expectantly for a moment until I realised he wanted payment for his services. I found a shilling and dropped into his filthy mitt.

A crowd had gathered at the gallery entrance and we were ushered through a corridor of policemen.
At the end of line was our old friend, Inspector Gregson.
'Have you been assigned to every crime in London?' I asked.
'So it would seem,' he said drolly. 'When you gain a reputation for

112

competency,' he added rather immodestly, 'it does rather lead to more than your fair share of the chores.'

'Competency?' Holmes repeated a little scornfully, once out of Gregson's earshot.

Sir William advanced towards us with the hollow look of a ghost. His white face and hair seemed twice as blanched as the day before.

'They have returned,' he said, shaking his head. 'The place was alive with guards last night and yet and yet . . .' He trailed off, his face filled with fear and bewilderment. 'If I didn't know better, I would say that supernatural forces are at work. Gentlemen, we are dealing with an invisible menace.'

Sir William stood aside and we were met with the most astonishing sight.

As far as the eye could see, small cards were attached to the frames of paintings throughout the gallery. On each card was printed a single word: FAKE.

'I cannot begin to explain this,' said Sir William in dismay. 'Not least to my board.'

'Then are you prepared to admit that the painting may have been switched?' asked Holmes.

'Yes,' he said. 'Someone has made us look like fools. We may as well leave the doors wide open at night and put tea and cake out for the thieves. Naturally you will help us and inspect the crime scene, Mr Holmes?'

'Of course,' said Holmes. 'But first are you willing to publicly restore the reputation of Mr Abercrombie Macintosh'

'Yes,' Sir William muttered. 'Yes, very well. There may well be some truth in his observations.'

'Very good,' said Holmes brightly. 'Now perhaps we could begin in Room 35?'

Holmes swept imperiously through the gallery following by a posse consisting of Sir William, Gregson, numerous officers and museum staff until we arrived in front of The Shrimp Girl.

'Would you be so good as to pick up the card, Sir William,' invited Holmes. 'Now please turn it over.'

'Twenty seven of your art works are fakes,' he read aloud. 'They have been stolen, one at a time, under your very nose.'

'But how could they have done such a thing?'

'You might say, by pot luck,' quipped Holmes.

'Whatever do you mean?'

'No less,' said Holmes, 'than by letting the genie out of the bottle.'
He strode over to the vase.

'Genie,' he cried, throwing his arms wide. 'Show thyself!'

At first, there was nothing, then a slight reverberation; the wooden base began to wobble until the whole vase began to dance across the floor.

'Villainy!' Sir William shouted.

Gregson drew his pistol and took aim at the vase, but not before Sir William had thrown himself in the way.

'For God's sake, man,' he yelled. 'It's ninth century!'

The vase continued to teeter until finally it toppled over.

With a superhuman effort Holmes caught hold of the thing. I rushed across and together we restored it to the upright.

'Thank you doctor,' my friend congratulated. 'A small practice such as ours would not be covered for such a breakage.' He surveyed the room of astonished faces, each one agog.

'May I present,' said Holmes, lifting the lid from the vase, 'the bravest man in London, Mr George Crabtree.' There was a groan from inside the pot, followed by the emergence of a tuft of unkempt dark hair, which promptly disappeared again.

'Are you in there, Crabtree?' asked Holmes, taking a peep inside. 'Gentlemen, would you be so good as to lend me a hand?'

Together, four of us lowered the vase to just below the horizontal and gently tipped out the unfortunate Crabtree. He slithered onto the gallery floor and lay there a moment gathering his wits. He was as pale as a condemned prisoner, his hair matted with sweat.

'Quick,' I said, 'fetch some water.'

'The other vase,' Crabtree murmured, 'look inside the other vase.'
With this, he passed out. Holmes frowned, then rushed over to the far corner of the room.

'Don't touch that vase, Holmes!' cried Gregson, warding the great detective away with his revolver. Instead, the inspector cautiously approached the vase himself.

'Jones,' he shouted to his men, 'Biggins. Get behind me and shoot anything that comes out of that pot.'

'Don't shoot the pot!' cried Sir William. He darted forward and in his haste knocked over the vase himself, which wavered, then fell and shattered on the ground into a thousand pieces. Everything was still. Amongst the broken porcelain lay the bloodied body of Wenceslas Chatburn.

ELEVEN

The Leopard

We were used to strange messages arriving at 221b Baker Street, both by telegram and especially in person, but none were as singular as the one that arrived that summer morning in July. There was a scene of considerable excitement in the street as a horse and cart, the sort that would normally transport flour or sugar, stopped outside our rooms.

Holmes was still in his dressing gown stoking his first pipe of the day despite the fact that it was well past eleven. I peered down into street.
'Are you expecting a delivery, Holmes?' I asked.
'None I have requested. I am only waiting for delivery from this infernal boredom.'
'But we are in the middle of a case, are we not?'
'A case with several closed doors. We are awaiting a development.'
'You don't consider the discovery of Chatburn's body a development?'
'Not especially.'

There was a commotion at the bottom of the stairs as Mrs Hudson negotiated with the tradesman, no doubt attempting to persuade him that he had the wrong address.
'Perhaps I should see if I can be of assistance,' I muttered, and trotted down the seventeen steps to settle the matter.

'I swear this is the right drum,' said the driver, a small, leather faced man of fifty with a single eye, glancing with some difficulty either side of the building. 'I've got it written down right here. 221b Baker Street. A right jemmy house it is too,' he said, admiring our handsome lodgings.
'Is there no name?' I asked.
'No name,' confirmed Mrs Hudson, 'just an address.'
'Well,' I said, looking at the large crate, I think we should accept it and take it upstairs.'

'Would you be so good as to lend me a hand?' I asked the driver. 'Mrs Hudson will watch your cart.'

We manhandled the wooden crate off the vehicle and up the stairs. It was not as heavy as I expected and it was soon in situ beside the rug in the sitting room under Holmes' disapproving gaze. I tipped the man and my friend and I were left alone with the foreign object.

'I hope you know what you're doing,' said Holmes. 'I have more enemies in London than a hanging judge. How do you know that thing is not stuffed with dynamite?'
'I don't,' I mused, 'but it made a curious sort of tinny noise as we hauled it up the stairs.'
'All the same,' said Holmes. 'I think I will take a stroll while you prise it open.' He selected a couple of papers, his golden snuff box and the Persian slipper that contained his tobacco. 'I don't wish to alarm you, Watson, but perhaps we ought to say our goodbyes in case we don't get another chance.' I looked at my friend for a sign that he was pulling my leg, but did not detect any irony.
'Very well,' I said, extending a hand. 'But I think you're being absurd, Holmes.'
'It has been a distinct pleasure,' said Holmes, receiving my hand and giving it a brisk, firm shake. 'I shall see you on the other side.'
He disappeared through the door without so much as a backwards glance and presently I could hear him and Mrs Hudson on the street outside in conversation about the weather.

Using an iron rod I had found beneath the sink, I took a deep breath, shut my eyes then pulled up the first plank from the packing case. I was still alive. I worked at another and then another until I had a clear view into the container. It appeared to be some sort of mechanical contraption in several parts, the most distinctive being a brass trumpet shaped device. I laughed out loud.
'A phonograph!' I shouted.
I ran to the window.
'A phonograph, Holmes!' I called. 'Come on up and take a look.'

It took some time to assemble the components. Holmes watched with interest, susceptible as he was to new inventions, and keenly awaited the finished article.

'I think that will do it,' I said, tightening the last bolt.

'A wonder of the age,' marveled Holmes. 'Now let us see what it has to say.' He stepped forward as if he was used to operating such a thing every day. He released a catch, fiddled with a button and began to slowly turn the handle.

'Greetings Mr Sherlock Holmes,' a thin, distant voice began. I started at the sound. 'Greetings to you too, Dr Watson.'

'Wizardry!' I cried.

'My name is Duleep Singh, the rightful owner of the Koh-I-Noor.' Holmes and I exchanged a glance. The recording was rudimentary, but the voice was that of a middle aged Indian, one known to us as the last Maharajah of the Punjab, now a country gentleman who ruled a more modest kingdom on the Norfolk/Suffolk border. He was famous for his love of shooting, dinner parties and French wine.

'The diamond known as the Koh-I-Noor was taken by your countrymen from my father when the Punjab became part of your great empire. For many years, as you may know, I have been a friend of the British and a guest of your great Queen. I have no argument with your country. In many ways I am now more British than the British. I have worn your clothes, eaten your food and shot your game. But as I grow old, I feel the call of my home and my religion. I long to gaze into the hills at Shivalik, watch the sun set on the Sukhna Lake and kneel at the temple of Chanti. But most of all, now I know I must right a final wrong. Mr Holmes, I seek the return of the diamond that belonged to my father the Maharajah, Ranjit Singh. It must return with me to the Punjab where the natural order of things can be restored and the stone returned to its people. As a loyal subject Mr Holmes, I do not expect you to help me in this enterprise. I would forgive you if you were to report me immediately to your government.

'But I appeal to you now, as one noble man to another, to help me in this matter. I have received word that others are pursuing the diamond and that the Queen herself may be in danger. I have heard from my friends that there is a man hell bent on obtaining the diamond for himself and who will stop at nothing until he holds it in his hands. His name is Warwick Snitterton and there is no more fearsome man alive in all of England.

'Mr Holmes, do what you can to stop him. Find him before he finds the diamond. The police will not help solve a crime that has not yet been committed. To help you, I have placed an object on the roof of St John's Lodge, in Regent's Park that I believe will be useful in your efforts. You are a man of immense powers. I place this matter into your hands and now only providence knows our destiny.'

There was the sound of static and hiss and it was clear that the contraption was still running. 'How do you stop it?' we heard Singh ask. 'The lever, there,' a voice returned. 'Yes,' Singh replied, 'yes, of course.' There was a click and the recording ceased.

'Marvelous,' cried Holmes, 'quite marvelous!'
'Enough about the machine,' I said, rising to my feet, 'what does this mean for our case?'
'The case has developed a pleasing level of complication,' my friend returned.
'Then Chatburn was right about Snitterton? He is a monster, intent on obtaining these Indian diamonds. He must be stopped Holmes!'
'Of course,' replied Holmes. 'But in any case, the Maharajah has announced himself as another interested party and provided a name with which we are familiar. He has also provided a tantalizing clue.'
'My brain has begun to ache with all this,' I confessed.
'Then let us seek some refreshment in Regent's Park, my dear Watson, and retrieve this clue. It may yet provide the key to it all. And if we fail to find anything they serve splendid lemonade by the boat house which will provide ample compensation.'

'There is a small question,' I put in, as Holmes and I walked briskly towards the park in the brilliant morning sunshine. 'The Maharajah mentioned that his clue was on the roof of St John's Lodge.'
'You are quite right,' my friend replied. 'I heard the very same thing.' We stepped through Clarence Gate and made our way across

the bridge.

'Is the house not occupied by the marquis of something or other?'

'Quite possibly,' agreed Holmes.

'And do you not think he would object to the pair of us clambering about on his roof?'

'Again, quite possibly!' Holmes repeated. We walked a few steps in silence and I wondered for a moment at the banality of my existence had I never met this exasperating and extraordinary man. We took a detour north, missing the house entirely.

'I have the makings of a plan,' said Holmes, 'but it will require a degree of audacity. Would you prefer to sit this one out, Watson?'

'Never!' I declared.

'Splendid,' said Holmes, 'then follow me.'

We advanced on the park keeper's lodging at the edge of the Zoological Gardens and Holmes rapped smartly on the door with the end of his cane. A tall, gangly looking man answered the door, initially with a rather severe looking expression, the reason for which was obvious. He was holding in his hands the apparatus with which to make tea and we had plainly interrupted his tea break. It was possible that he was approaching fifty and his hair was receding, but his eyes were as wide and optimistic as those of a boy. His eyebrows leapt at the sight of Holmes.

'So close a neighbour and so rare a visit!' he exclaimed.

'The fault is all mine,' said Holmes bowing low.

'I haven't yet had a chance to thank you in person for your assistance over the little embarrassment of our runaway elephant. You will be pleased to know we have had words with Her Hugeness and she has given me her word not to repeat the stunt.'

'Watson, may I present one of the great men of London: Mr Nicholas Kibble, the Head Keeper at London Zoo.'

'The pleasure is all mine,' I replied removing my hat. 'However do you keep them all from devouring each other?' I asked, rather foolishly.

'With iron bars and regular meals,' he replied smartly. 'Now what can I do for you gentlemen?'

'May we come in?' asked Holmes.

'Naturally,' said Kibble. 'Please excuse the mess.'

His office was compact and colourful. One wall was lined entirely with shelves laden with books on every conceivable topic relating to the beasts in his charge. Against another were the skulls of some of his former tenants, each accompanied by an affectionate nickname. A pair of skulls that conceivably could have once belonged to a pair of lions or tigers were endearingly labelled: 'Samson and Delilah.' His desk was a mountain of paperwork and as a measure of the international nature of his correspondence, there were envelopes with postmarks from around the world. Kibble continued with his tea-making chores and fetched two extra cups and saucers from a small cupboard.

'Now,' said Holmes, sparking his pipe into life, 'you will remember The Adventure of the Empty Giraffe House?'

'How could I forget?' said Kibble. 'Your help was invaluable in that most delicate of cases.'

'It is another, alas, that Watson has not yet written up for posterity,' bemoaned Holmes, a little unfairly. 'However, due to its singular nature, I cannot blame him, for it would defy credulity.'

'Yes,' agreed the keeper. 'For a giraffe to disappear and reappear again in the same place after three days is the work of a stage magician not a criminal. You have never fully explained it to me to this day.'

'Well,' said Holmes. 'Perhaps I will provide a fuller account on another occasion, but the point is this. In the matter of Juno, I suspect foul play.'

'Impossible!' Kibble replied, bring his tea cup clattering to the table.

'My man in the elephant house is one of the best we have. He is still overcome with guilt over the matter but his honour is beyond question. It was a freak of the elephant's own nature.'

'Be that as it may,' replied Holmes, calmly. 'It is my belief that a toxin was administered to the elephant which caused a momentary bout of madness.'

'Who would have access to such a medicine?'

'A man used to dealing with wild beasts; an expert in his field. We have such a man under our watch.'

'Who is this man?' demanded Kibble, feeling a creeping insinuation.

121

'His name is Snitterton,' replied Holmes.

'Snitterton?' he shouted. 'Warwick Snitterton? If it is the same fellow, I knew him as a young man. A more talented veterinarian I have yet to meet. He had a sixth sense for an animal's ailment and a Midas touch when it came to administering the remedy. He saved Princess, our snow leopard and Sinbad, our white tiger when I had told him to leave them in peace.'

'Can you think of any grudge he may have held towards you?'

'None,' replied Kibble. 'He was a fine man. A little arrogant perhaps, and one who did not suffer fools gladly, but no more so than any man keen to make his way in the world. Tomfoolery such as this would not be in his nature.'

'He has returned from India and is at large in London. However, we believe he is close at hand and it is our desire to question him over the matter.'

'I still refuse to entertain the idea,' said Kibble sipping at his tea, 'but I acknowledge at least that he would be capable of administering such a dose. But the question remains, how can I help you?'

'We simply require two park keepers' uniforms,' my friend explained, 'one in my size, the other to fit Dr Watson.'

'An odd request,' said Kibble, dabbing tea from his lips, 'but if you believe it will help that is easy enough to arrange.'

'And one more thing,' asked Holmes. 'What is the name of your rarest bird?'

Ten minutes later Holmes and I were outside the grand front entrance of St John's Lodge dressed in matching blazers and bowlers. Holmes was clutching a butterfly net while I was holding a pail and hooked stick. My friend had rung the bell and we waited rather anxiously for a response.

'Play a straight bat, Watson,' my friend advised.

A tall venerable fellow, clearly the butler, answered the door. His hair was a thick white as if his head had been dipped in cream. In contrast, his cheeks were a livid raspberry, giving the overall impression of a flavoursome iced dessert. He appeared to have difficulty making us out, squinting into the midday sun.

'Yes?' he drawled.

'We are from the Zoological Gardens,' explained Holmes. 'A Ruby-

Throated Hummingbird has escaped from the aviary and has been spotted on the roof on the Lodge. I appreciate it's an awful imposition, but would you mind if we go up and retrieve it?'

'A ruby . . what?' the butler began.

'A Ruby-Throated Hummingbird,' my friend repeated taking a step forward into the hall.

A more magnificent porch could not be imagined outside royal circles. Large oil paintings adorned the walls; magnificent tiles were laid underfoot and gold dripped from every fitting.

'Is it this way?' Holmes asked, taking the first of the wide luxuriantly carpeted stairs without waiting for an answer. 'My name is Mr Stanley. I don't think we'll be more than ten minutes. Once these things come down to roost, they don't fly off again for hours. We're not expecting any fun and games are we Livingstone?'

'None at all,' I confirmed and followed Holmes up to the first floor.

'Do mind the vase at the top of the stairs!' the butler called, his mind, slowly engaging.

'We shall!' my friend yelled back.

We climbed flight after flight. It seemed impossible that we had not yet reached the roof. As we passed a miniature version of Michelangelo's David, however, Holmes pointed out a small door which we found unlocked. It led outside to a narrow set of winding iron steps.

'This way, Watson!' he called.

We clambered out onto the roof.

'Have you fathomed,' I panted as I followed him up the staircase, 'how the Maharajah managed to plant the item on the roof in the first place?'

'Of course, Watson. He is a man who moves in the most fashionable circles. It would be easy enough for him to slip away during a little soiree for a little night air.'

'Holmes,' I said, catching his arm. 'Wait.' My friend paused mid step. 'Is it not possible that this is a trap?' There was a moment's hesitation.

'Anything is possible until it is proved otherwise, Watson. But I have taken what precautions I can.' This failed to reassure me.

The roof was divided into a number of rectangular spaces, each with raised ironwork at the centre and handsome white balustrades at the front and sides. A small ornamental tower rose from the rear of the lodge.

'What are we looking for, exactly?' I asked, scanning the rooftop.

'For anything and everything,' said Holmes.

We split up and methodically searched the roof for anything out of the ordinary. I found a pair of empty wine glasses left behind after some midnight tryst and a gentleman's comb. Neither of these things struck me as items of any importance. Holmes himself came back empty handed.

'Think Watson,' urged Holmes. 'What are we really looking for?'

'Over here,' I cried. Tucked inside a small alcove was a small, black tin box.

'Bravo, Watson!' cried Holmes.

Holmes knelt down and examined the tin, which I identified immediately as an ammunition case, routinely used by the British in Afghanistan.

'Well, well,' my friend began, 'what will we find inside Pandora's Box?' A pair of gulls swooped over our head in the direction of the Zoological Gardens.

'You may never find out, Mr Stanley. Get to your feet.'

We rose slowly to find the butler standing at the top of the stairs, holding a pistol.

'No luck!' called Holmes. 'It must have flown off before we got here. There'll be hell to pay when we report this.'

'Do you take me for an imbecile?'

'Certainly not, sir,' said Holmes. 'You are the Marquis of Bute.'

'I have long since been in the habit of opening my own front door,' he said. 'Too many fraudsters have slipped past my dim-witted butler and made off with the family silver. I wanted to catch you red handed. But what the devil do you hope to find on the roof?'

'A magnificent, exotic bird, of course,' replied Holmes. 'You can vouch for our credentials with Mr Kibble, the head keeper himself.'

'A likely story. What have you got there?'

'Nothing but an empty tin. A cigar box perhaps?'

'It seems half of London has been up on this roof in the last week.

Only yesterday a government inspector came around to check the leading. His paperwork appeared to be in order but I followed him up all the same. I frisked him as he left to check he wasn't hiding my heirlooms down a trouser leg.'

'A sensible precaution,' said Holmes.

'I'm afraid I'm going to take the same precaution with you and your colleague.'

'Please go ahead,' my friend said cheerfully.

'But first, the box,' said the marquis. 'Hand it over.'

Holmes passed it to the man, keeping his eyes on the pistol. The hirsute aristocrat flipped open the lid.

'Empty,' sighed the Marquis, failing to disguise his disappointed. 'Now Mr Livingstone, if you wouldn't mind standing still'. He checked us in a fair and respectable manner then sighed.

'It appears,' he said at length, 'that I owe you gentlemen an apology.'

'Not at all,' said Holmes. 'But if you would excuse us, we have a bird to catch.' We left the Marquis alone in his mansion once more, yet another unwitting player in our drama.

'A close call,' I muttered as we walked back into the park, 'but still nothing to show for our efforts.' Holmes looked at me bemused.

'Nothing to show?' he repeated, 'don't talk nonsense, Watson.' He reached into his pocket and produced a small, gleaming artefact. I stopped dead in my tracks.

'A ruby elephant!' I shouted. 'How is this possible?'

'A little diversion and the simplest sleight of hand,' Holmes explained. 'You remember I gestured towards the birds? We all raised our eyes, including the Marquis. This provided ample opportunity to extract the treasure.'

'But what about the search?'

'The easiest switch,' laughed Holmes. 'A child could have done it given five minutes' practice.'

He tossed the elephant into the air in triumph and caught it in the same hand. His eyes gleamed.

'We have another bargaining chip, Watson.' The day was balmy and the sunlight flooded the grass except where large cumulous clouds drifted drowsily over, casting their wide shadows over the strolling couples and solitary gentlemen lost in their private thoughts.

'Now what say you to that long glass of lemonade?' suggested Holmes. 'Surely a little celebration is in order?'

All at once I heard a shriek coming from across the park.

'A leopard!' shouted one gentlemen, dragging his wife after him towards the Hanover Gate.

'Impossible,' I spluttered, staring in disbelief. 'Is there not a moment's peace, Holmes?' Holmes and I peered into the middle distance and it was not difficult to identify the escaped animal. The crowds fled like wildebeest, leaving a trail of parasols, top hats and walking canes in their wake. A couple of policemen made a stand for a few moments in a perfunctory display of bravery before joining the fleeing masses.

'Snitterton's behind this,' warned Holmes, 'you mark my words, Watson.' He turned towards the drinks seller.

'A pair of lemonades if you don't mind,' he said calmly.

The vendor was a thin, nervous character whose eyes were fixed on the hysterical crowd.

'We've just closed,' he mumbled, dropping the wooden lids on his cart, the blood draining from his cheeks. He untied his apron, flung it to the ground then sprinted for the exit. I cleared my throat.

'Do you think perhaps we should make our own excuses?' I ventured.

'For a leopard?' asked Holmes incredulously. 'It's hardly a lion or a tiger. Surely there are enough mongrels in London to satisfy it before it turns on the likes of doctors and detectives. My view is this: that we walk very calmly towards the Zoological Gardens. After all, what fugitive runs towards the prison after a gaol break? If it follows us, then we will be the heroes who returned it to captivity. If it doesn't, then we are perfectly safe.' I nodded, submitting to Holmes' absurd logic.

Against my better judgement, we started in the direction of the Zoological Gardens.

'No need to hurry,' said Holmes, stopping to sniff a flower.

'No hurry?' I spluttered, watching the masses sprinting in the opposite direction. 'I have no intention of ending up as something's lunch.'

'The faster you run, the more of a target you will present,' he explained.

'I'm not sure I agree with that,' I said.

'Well put it like this,' my friend reasoned. 'Your top speed is something like twenty miles per hour. A leopard's is closer to forty. Running, or even hurrying would be an act of sheer futility.'

'It would make me feel better!' I reasoned.

Within five minutes, the park had almost cleared. We heard the clank of chains securing the gates and we were left exposed in an unnervingly large and empty space. I could see the leopard prowling, apparently unable to make up its own mind where to go next.

'Keep your eyes on the gates,' said Holmes peering ahead to the walled gardens, 'and walk without fear.' Despite the advice, I continued to glance back every ten paces or so.

'I hate to tell you, Holmes, but he's now following us.'

'Excellent,' said Holmes. 'We will be the toast of London when we bring it home.'

'What happens if we arrive on the inside of the leopard rather than outside?'

Twenty yards further and the leopard had broken into a canter. Gradually, he appeared to be picking up speed and I could see its muscular frame rippling beneath its fur. He wore the deadly, impassive face of the hunter.

'I'm awfully sorry about this, Holmes,' I said. 'But I think I'm going to run for my life!'

'Only another 200 yards, Watson, hold your nerve.'

Suddenly, from the branches of a tree four black shapes dropped to the ground.

'The Archangels!' I shouted. Each was armed with a sharpened cane. The man I recognised as Raphael also wielded a long pistol, which he aimed in our direction.

'Right,' said Holmes. 'Now is the time to run!' We tore off towards the cricket pitch. A shot rang out and Holmes and I tumbled to the ground, picking ourselves up as they gave chase.

'The leopard is still with us too!' I shouted. 'How grossly unfair.' I thumbed in the direction of the Archangels. 'What's wrong with them?'

'Once a wild animal is set on a course, it is liable to be rather single minded,' Holmes admitted.

'So I see!'

A small pavilion gave us a little temporary shelter. I produced my service revolver and crouched low.

'We are in something of a jam,' I muttered. On one side, the Archangels advanced by degrees in a horrible, stealthy way, seeming to appear and disappear like vampires. The leopard meanwhile stalked us from the other side.

'Stay exactly where you are Watson,' Holmes whispered. 'No matter what happens, don't move so much as an inch.'

I heard two gunshots from another direction entirely. Raphael dropped to the ground, his pistol flying out of his hand. In what seemed like the same moment the leopard buckled, rolled, then lay still on the grass, his tongue lying limp across his fangs. Suddenly the odds on our survival seemed greatly enhanced. I levelled my pistol at the remaining Archangels, but found myself reluctant to shoot. One of them had slung the injured man on his back and the group was retreating into the trees.

'It appears,' remarked Holmes, 'that we have our own guardian angel.'

'My stars, Holmes!' I shouted.

In the far distance, we saw the figure of a man, dark skinned, with a shot gun resting on his shoulder. He hailed us with his other hand. I blinked and then he was gone.

TWELVE

The Roofers

I was dreaming again. This time I was being pursued by a herd of red elephants across Green Park. On the back of each one was a member of the strange order we had infiltrated all those nights ago. I ran to a tree and started to climb until I was level with the riders. They came closer until I realised each man had the same face – Snitterton's. I climbed higher until I was far above the park. The elephants were like pebbles below me. Then I fell. I dropped down from the tree, rushing through the branches but instead of hitting the ground I kept falling and falling.

'Doctor!' I recognised the voice. Mrs Hudson was on the other side of the door.

'What is it?' I shouted sitting bolt upright. I pulled on my dressing gown. 'What time is it?' I asked.

'Past nine,' she said. 'You have a visitor.'

'Two minutes,' I called, mopping my brow. Is Holmes awake?'

'You know better than that, doctor, it's far too early!'

I peered at myself in the looking glass and saw a pale, aging face staring back. Flecks of grey had begun to break through my moustache.

I dressed and walked through. A wily looking character was lounging in the sitting room.

'Well, well,' he said, rising slowly to his feet, 'You must be Dr Watson.'

'And you are?'

'Jeremiah Stubb,' he said, extending a greasy hand. He was tall man with shock of black hair, a door knocker beard, dark shadows around the eyes and a worn suit. On his feet were heavy hobnail boots.

'You are a roofer,' I ventured.

'Why do you say that,' he asked suspiciously.

'There is a deep horizontal groove at the end of each of your boots, as if they have repeatedly knocked against slate. The knees in your trousers are more worn than the rest of your suit, and the gauge sticking out of your pocket, I believe, is used almost exclusively by tradesmen in your line of work.'

''Pon my word,' he said admiringly. 'By the sounds of it you're the brains of the outfit, not Sherlock Holmes.'

'I would not go that far,' I said, a little flattered. 'I have merely observed his methods and occasionally like to try my hand at applying them.'

'Where is he, anyways?'

'You must forgive my friend, Mr Holmes. He is a late riser but I'm sure will be with us presently. In the meantime, perhaps I could take the particulars of your case?'

'Is that normal practice,' he asked, somewhat defensively. 'I had hoped to speak with Holmes himself.'

'He won't mind if we make a start,' I said.

'Well you know him, not me, and I don't want to start no collie-shangles between you.'

'Not at all. Please proceed.'

'Well it's like this,' he began, fishing out his tobacco pouch and rolling papers. 'Work has been in short supply of late and what with my fall last year, I'm not at the top of the list when labour is called for. So what do I do for tin? I started fishing about the house for trinkets and what-have-you, that might fetch a price, when I found these.'

He reached into his pocket and produced a pair of small ruby elephants. I stared at them in disbelief.

'You look like you've seen your grandfather's ghost, doctor. What's the matter?'

'Nothing,' I said. 'Nothing at all.'

'So I'm thinking I've finally found something I can flog that will mean I can carry on feeding my sauce box.'

'Quite possibly,' I said. 'Have you had it valued?'

'Well that's the funny thing,' he said. 'I was about to do just that when I sees this ad in the paper. He produced a rolled up copy of yesterday's Times from his pocket. He carefully unravelled it to show the advertisement in question.'

'Now, tell me that isn't a coincidence?' he said.

'An astonishing coincidence,' I agreed.

'It was too strange for me. It was like someone knew I had it. So I came straight here. There's no one in this city who deals with stranger cases than Sherlock Holmes.'

'You're not wrong!' I said, rising to my feet. 'Now let me see if I can rouse him. I have a feeling this will be of immense interest to him.'

'It most certainly is!' I turned and stared at the man. He held a wig in one hand, a beard in the other and an enormous grin across his face.

'Bravo, Watson,' congratulated Sherlock Holmes. 'A bravado performance! Your observation about the boots was first class.'

'Holmes,' I growled. 'You are insufferable!'

'It seemed a sensible idea to test the disguise before putting it to use,' reasoned Holmes, 'particularly when the stakes are so high.'

'But the second ruby elephant!' I cried. 'Where did you get it?'

'From Wimpole of course,' he said. 'I found what the police and Peaceheart failed to when they scoured the teacher's rooms.'

'But where?'

'The janitor,' said Holmes. 'It was perfectly obvious that the janitor would take the only thing of value. He must have known exactly where to find it. I accused him straight out and he handed it over in exchange for my silence.'

'But why Wimpole?'

'Another member of The House of the Ruby Elephant, Watson. Remember I could see more from my closet that you could from the inside of your wooden chest.' Holmes handed over the elephant and I stared at it. It was perfect in every respect.

'This little fellow and his friends have a lot to answer for,' I mused.

'Now Watson, the bad news for you is that today, you will playing the role of roofer's mate.'

'What?'

Holmes returned to his chair and continued to roll his cigarette.

'You remember the advertisement? Today we will pay a visit to 14 Caledonian Road and discover what fate awaits us. But we will take precautions. I have looked up the property and discovered that it is rented accommodation. What's more, the new tenant only arrived a week ago. We will turn up posing as building contractors, which will be entirely plausible. While there we will attempt to gather as much intelligence as we can. If we do not encounter Snitterton in person, then we will at least be able to interview his agent.'

An hour later I did not recognise myself in the mirror. At half past ten, I walked out of Baker Street with a new name and occupation.

'Mr Huffam,' Holmes said. 'Would you be so good as to summon a growler and instruct the driver to take us to Islington?'

'Delighted,' I replied.

We pulled up some distance from the address. Holmes and I then tramped up to the front door of a respectable looking terrace lugging a bag of tools between us. As was usual when Holmes was incognito he stayed entirely in character throughout the expedition, speaking in a sing-song cockney voice and throwing in snatches of drinking songs. He climbed the stone steps, cleared his throat and rapped twice on the door.

'Readiness is all, Watson,' whispered Holmes.

The door opened an inch.

'Don't you worry,' began Holmes in his broadest Cockney accent. 'We're not on the knock. We're not sellin' nuffin!' It opened a little wider to reveal a respective looking woman with a white apron and a close resemblance to our own Mrs Hudson.

'I should hope not,' she said. 'Please state your business.'

Holmes threw his eyes to heaven. 'Me and my chuckaboo 'ere, are 'ere to see to your roof. Landlord's orders. You've got loose tiles. You're risking life and limb every time you step out the front door. Myself and my associate Mr Huffam are in 'arm's way as we speak.' He produced a scribbled note from his pocket. 'There's the instruction from the landlord, Mr Sackville, right there.' He allowed the lady to glance at it for a moment before returning it to his pocket.

'Would you mind waiting a moment?' she asked politely then closed the door.

'No good,' I whispered. Holmes remained impassive. Then came something that astonished us like nothing else that day. 'Mr Holmes!' we heard her holler, on the other side of the door. 'Dr Watson! Visitors.'

I stared at Holmes in confusion. He raised a hand. 'Hold your nerve,' he hissed.

Once again the door crept open.

'You may come in,' she smiled.

'Very much obliged,' said Holmes, doffing his hat. 'Come along John, shake a leg.' I lugged the bag of tools inside and we were shown up a staircase of seventeen steps. At the top was a broad sitting room that resembled our own in every respect from the two chairs by the fire, the bear's skin rug on the floor, the ceremonial swords to the violin leaning against the wall. I felt faint. Two gentlemen turned to greet us. One was my friend Sherlock Holmes. The other was Dr John Watson. He fixed me with a curious look then turned back to his newspaper.

I have heard it said that it is fatal to meet your doppelganger. It was this thought and this alone that consumed me as we stared at ourselves reclining in our easy chairs.

'What have we here?' asked the other Holmes, rising. He was a tall, gaunt man with dark, receding hair and a superior manner.

My friend appeared entirely unfazed.

'It's your roof,' he said. 'It's in a terrible old state. An hour or two is all we need. I've explained everything to the good lady. Sorry to tramp in the dirt, but are you alright if we 'back slang it'? The only way to get the job done is round the back.'

'And how do we know,' questioned the other Holmes, 'that you aren't a pair of old lurkers planning to rob us at knife point? Those tools look authentic but what if this is an elaborate ruse?'

'Ask me a question about my trade,' my friend challenged him. 'Anything you like.'

'Very well,' he said, selecting a claw hammer from my bag. 'What would you call this?'

'That's a slater's pick, that is,' said Holmes.

'And this?' he asked, picking up some cutters.

'Come along,' taunted Holmes, 'that's hardly going to stretch me, is it? That's a simple old pair of tin snips.'

'It appears,' laughed the other Holmes, 'that we have been far too suspicious. Gentlemen, perhaps we can provide you with some sustenance before you begin your travails?'

'As it happens,' said Holmes, patting his stomach contentedly. 'My friend and I dined like kings not an hour ago. For lunch we had a couple of those bags 'o mystery they sell for tuppence down at Smithfields.'

'Very well,' continued the other Holmes. 'Mrs Hudson will show you to the back garden, where you will find a ladder and good access to the roof. Now if you will excuse us, my friend Watson and I were about to indulge in a hand of Sixty Six. Would you pass me the cards, Watson?'

I was shaking as we passed through the kitchen and into the back yard. Once alone I turned to Holmes who was still entirely unruffled.
'That's higher than I thought,' he said, still in character, rubbing his chin and peering up at the roof. 'We're going to have to watch our step, my friend.' I stared at him.
'Have you lost your mind?' I demanded.
'Stop your carping, Huffam,' he snapped, 'or you won't see no tin from this job. Not a farthing.'

The yard was enclosed on all sides with grimy stone walls, each fifteen feet tall. Moss and lichen cluing to the damp brickwork and at far end was a pile of old chairs, broken tables and assorted cast offs. The only exit was a single padlocked gate.
'I don't like this,' I said to Holmes. 'There's something amiss.'
'Courage Watson,' said Holmes. 'We will footle about here for an hour or so then make our excuses and leave.'
Together we raised an ancient looking ladder up against the wall of the house and made half hearted efforts to get our tools in order.
'Personally,' I said, inspecting the rotting wood, 'I'm not keen to test the soundness of this ladder.'
'Watson,' said Holmes at length. 'I am minded to admit that I may have made a mistake. In the future, whenever my plans grow too outlandish, you may remind me of this. Now what do you say to turning the ladder around, leaning it against the back wall and making our escape?'
'A much better plan,' I agreed.
'And the soundness of the ladder?'
'I am prepared to risk it!'
'Excellent.'

We lifted the ladder from the house and carried it over to the far end of the yard. I agreed to go first.

'Quickly,' urged Holmes. 'I believe we have aroused some suspicion.' I stood on the highest rung and saw that there was an identical yard and house on the other side of the wall. I glanced back at Holmes then shouted in alarm.

'My dear Holmes! Behind you!'

In the far corner, from behind a lean-to shed attached to the house I was aware of something in the shadows. It was a dark, slow moving object that emerged from the darkness.

'Dear God,' I shouted. 'It's a bear!'

Holmes seized a heavy iron from the tool bag and set himself in a defensive position. Sure enough the animal lumbered forward, its head down, advancing on all fours. I could see its enormous head and loathsome claws.

'Up the ladder, Holmes,' I shouted. 'There's no time to be lost.'

My friend made a leap for the ladder and staggered up a rung or two. However the shock was too great for the antique; there was a crack and I lurched to one side clawing at the top of the wall. The ladder gave way beneath me, despatching Holmes into the yard. I was left hanging from the wall. The bear continued its slow advance; Holmes ran to the gate and shook the lock, hammering it with his iron.

'I can't hang on!' I shouted then dropped, landing heavily next to my friend. We stared in horror as the beast rose up on its hind legs.

'Well, Watson,' said Holmes gravely. 'This may very well be goodbye.'

Holmes seized a broken chair and held it, legs outwards as our last defence against the great beast.

'Not a pistol between us,' I sighed.

'Fools!' cried the bear.

The head rose to reveal the snarling, bearded face of Snitterton. There was the wild look of the devil in his eyes and in any other situation, it would have been absurd.

'You!' I shouted. He levelled a shot gun at us.

'Not a step closer or I'll blow you both to kingdom come.'

I raised my eyes to the three figures standing in the upstairs window. The impostors playing Mrs Hudson, Holmes and myself stood impassively at the window staring at us in the most unnerving fashion.

'You were fools to come here,' Snitterton growled. 'But I knew *he* could not resist.' He nodded towards Holmes. You masquerade as a detective, a vigilante, an angel of justice, but that's just a charade. Watson, I almost feel sorry for you. You are nothing but a meddler. But Holmes, you are the master of it all. Your simple friend here follows you like a lapdog. You hold yourself above the law; cooperating where it is convenient and where there is a chance to curry favour. Otherwise, you are a slave to your superhuman ego, your arrogance and your greed.' He cocked the rifle. 'Yes,' he sneered. 'Greed.' I looked over at Holmes, who was as grim faced as I had ever seen him.

'Doctor,' he said, jabbing me with the end of the rifle. 'Would it surprise you that Sherlock Holmes has known about my plan all along? The plan to reunite the eight elephants of Ranjit Singh?' I narrowed my eyes.
'If he was holding back, he had good reason,' I said.
'Never fear, Watson,' said Holmes calmly.
'Then he did not tell you what power you hold if you possess all eight? As you will soon both be dead there is nothing to be lost in telling you now. Our society, The House of the Ruby Elephant, was a front for eight common thieves. We had heard the legend of the Nizam Diamond: a stone of supreme size, 340 carats of pure starlight. Then by chance, we met a traveller at the Viceroy's Palace who had spent time at the old fort at Golconda, home of the legendary diamond vault. The fort was long since ruined. But he spoke of a hidden chamber. Inside was a safe in the shape of an elephant, impregnable in every way. But it was a safe without a combination. Instead, there are the indentations of eight elephants. Only when all eight are in place will the door to the safe spring open. On his deathbed, Singh sent the ruby elephants to the four corners of the world. Our life's work has been to bring them together.'

It seemed hopeless. He had us caught like rabbits; but for now he was absorbed in his tale. 'Chatburn was the first to find one; he bought it from a corrupt official at an exorbitant price. The man did not know the true worth of the ruby, but he could see Chatburn wanted it badly. For a time, this gave Chatburn some power among us. Then I heard of a famous dealer in Lahore who dealt only in the finest gemstones. I travelled to see him; brought him as much as could afford and promised him favour with the Viceroy. He resisted for a long time then finally gave way; he had a pair of ruby elephants. He did not know, or did not admit to knowing there were others. We bargained for two days over them. I left a poor man, but with two rubies in my pocket. The others searched; travelled all around India. Only two more were found. Peaceheart got lucky; he saw his in a bazaar; picked it up for the price of a chapatti. That left only Ignatius; the musician who stole one from a visiting prince.

'From then on, there was nothing but bitterness and rancor. We fought; we despised those who had found none; they in their turn lived in resentment. For a while, I contented myself with my work: healing the great beasts of India; taming the tigers and elephants. Then I found one of my rubies had vanished. I accused Chatburn of stealing it from me by bribing a servant to take it from my rooms. In a rage, I faced down the servant with a lion I was treating; I only meant to scare him, but the animal was in a fever, broke loose and savaged the man. I left after this under a shadow; our quest for the ruby elephants incomplete.'

'A colourful tale, Snitterton,' I snarled, 'but what is the meaning of these actors?' I pointed up at the window.

'Ah, Doctor Watson,' he smiled. 'This is a stroke worthy of Holmes himself. I have employed these impostors as an accessory to your own death. They will be seen fleeing from the property in open view. The police will find the bodies of two grubby, anonymous workmen in the back garden. Holmes you are well known enough to be recognised without any trouble, especially after your heroics with the elephant. You will be convicted of your own murder.'

'Ingenious!' congratulated Holmes. 'Now perhaps you will allow me to put forward a theory about the elephant at the Zoological Gardens. Your target was not the beast at all. It was the man riding on its back. He was an employee of the East India Company and was the only witness to your crime at the palace; he was blackmailing you. You devised a dart and impregnated it with a poison of your own devising. But your aim was not as good as your laboratory skills. You shot the elephant instead, driving it mad. It was enough poison to kill a man, but not a great beast such as Juno. Watson, you remember the wound on the elephant's flank? That was no broken branch; it was the place where the arrow hit home.'

'Impressive,' said Snitterton, 'but alas no one else will get to hear your theory. Any final questions?'

'The other ruby elephants,' I asked. 'Where are they?'

'Where are they indeed!' he exclaimed.

'For a long time I suspected Chatburn had them. I staged a truce with him; tried to take him into my confidence. But it seemed he had no others, at which point I realised he was of no further use. Then it occurred to me. Surely the Maharajah, also the owner of the infamous Koh-I-Noor, would not be so cruel as to deny his son the chance to acquire the Nizam diamond too. From that moment on, I knew it was the son who had them - the last Maharajah.'

'And what of these Archangels? Are they in your power? Are they your agents?'

'You ask too much doctor,' he said, growing tired. 'I have told all I care to.'

'If you had any sense, you would turn yourself in,' I reasoned. 'You are possessed of a brilliant mind who could still offer some useful service to your country. The Crown may take your record into account and grant some leniency.' He laughed at this suggestion.

'Perhaps in your fairy tale world, doctor. Besides, think what I stand to lose. I am so close to my goal and unimaginable wealth. Which path would you take?'

'I would choose the path that would allow me to live with my conscience and at peace with my soul.'

'Then doctor,' he said. 'We are very different men.'

'But . . .'

'Enough!' he exclaimed. 'It ends here!'

'One last thing,' said Holmes, raising a finger. 'Would you allow us a last drink?'

'A drink?' he asked.

'Yes,' said Holmes. 'We are civilised people after all. Perhaps a gin and an Indian Quinine Tonic?'

As my friend uttered these words Snitterton dropped the rifle and his eyes glazed over.

'Don't mind if I do,' he said, then reached into thin air, wrapping his hand around an invisible glass.

'Quick, Watson,' shouted Holmes, grabbing my arm, 'back through the house.' He pushed me ahead and swiftly followed.

We tore through the building while the three strange actors thundered down the stairs in pursuit. We burst through the front door while a shot rang out.

Holmes and I stumbled into the street, tripping on the loose hems of our ill-fitting work trousers. Another bullet cracked over our heads.

'Keep running!' urged Holmes.

We rounded a corner into a side street and straight into the arms of a waiting police constable.

'Not so fast,' he said, seizing us both by the collar. We both flew forward and were almost strangled by our own neckties. The constable was a giant of a fellow. Over six and half feet tall and almost as wide, he not so much resembled a policeman as a brick wall. I was still reeling from the impact with his torso.

'Constable!' I cried, 'we are in mortal danger.'

'You are now you've run into me.'

'Constable,' I persisted, 'this is no business of yours.'

'You're finely spoken for a mumper; a lovely bit of jerry talk. A more likely pair of mutchers I have never seen.'

'Constable Gibbons!' said Holmes breaking into a smile.

'Don't get familiar with me . . .' he warned.

Holmes wiped some of the dirt from his face and removed his hat.

'I don't believe it!' cried the astonished constable. 'Sherlock Holmes!'

'The very same.'

They greeted each other like old friends.

'If there was any justice in this world,' remarked Holmes, returning the dirty cap to his famous cranium, 'you would be the head of Scotland Yard by now. In my view there are too many blunderers hiding behind their desks. The real police work happens out here on the streets where the scoundrels of the earth plough their wicked furrow.'

'Please, Mr Holmes, that's enough,' the embarrassed constable returned, blushing. 'Now how may I be of service? You and your friend seem to be in an awful hurry.'

'As it happens,' said Holmes. 'The good doctor Watson here was perfectly correct. We are both about to be murdered.'

'Murdered, you say!' He glanced behind us. 'Well these murderers of yours seem to have lost interest all of a sudden.' Sure enough there was no sign of our pursuers.

'They clearly saw you, Gibbons,' laughed Holmes, 'and thought better of it. Now as you can see, we have been working incognito and I believe we are on the verge of catching London's most dangerous man. If you are quick, you will be the one who leads to the eventual arrest of Warwick Snitterton, the killer of Ignatius Wimpole and Wenceslas Chatburn.' Gibbons' eyes bulged.

Holmes scribbled down the address and pressed it into the constable's outstretched hand.

'Summon Gregson and whoever else you need,' instructed Holmes. 'Arrest anyone you find in this house.' The man nodded his assent.

'Gibbons,' cried Holmes. 'Take great care, but this is your moment!'

'You can rely on me, sir.'

'One more thing,' added Holmes. 'I see you have remarried?'

'How would you know that sir?'

'The minute indentation on your ring finger, the extra polish of your shoes and the fact that you have begun to trim the hair of your nose and ears and eyebrows. You had rather begun to let yourself go following your return to bachelor life, is that not so?'

'You could say that, sir, yes.'

'Well I rather think a sergeant's salary will come in rather useful to a newly married man, wouldn't you agree constable?'

'I couldn't agree more, sir!' he replied.

'Well, so long Gibbons,' said Holmes, 'and good luck!'

'Right you are, sir!' he replied, then jogged off, transporting his portly frame in the opposite direction.

'Now I don't know about you, Watson,' said Holmes. 'But I'm famished. What do you say to a plate of eels?'

I looked up and sure enough we were standing outside the premises of A. Grimes, one of the new pie and mash shops that seemed to be springing up all over London. If truth be told, I cared neither for eels, nor for the queer establishments in which they were served, which, with their white tiles and mirrors, more closely resembled public conveniences than respectable restaurants. However, I had to confess that the strain on the nerves supplied by the day's adventures had also given me a ravenous hunger.

Moments later we were inside the shop, cradling huge mugs of tea while the eels were coaxed into their pastries and doused in their own juices.

'Well, Holmes,' I began, leaning back in my chair. I can't wait a moment longer.'

'Give them a chance!' he said. 'We've barely sat down.'

'Don't be absurd. Not the food, the tonic water!'

'Ah,' my friend smiled. 'It had a marvellous effect did it not? I wondered myself if it would work, but I was not disappointed.'

'But ... how?'

'You will remember Mr Nicholas Kibble, the charming head keeper at the Zoological Gardens? As we were leaving he muttered a little piece of advice in my ear. You will remember that he and Snitterton were once acquainted? Well, years ago, they would regularly attend social functions together. On one particular evening, he mentioned that they had been treated to an after dinner entertainment by a hypnotist who asked for a volunteer. Being a young, plucky sort of fellow, Snitterton put himself forward and challenged the man to put him into a trance. But being a gifted practitioner of the art, the hypnotist swiftly took him into his power, using the words 'Quinine Tonic Water' as the trigger. It was a harmless trick that caused the subject to reach for an imaginary glass. Snitterton was furious to discover he had fallen so easily for the hypnotist's ruse and stormed out of the room before the man could undo the work. It subsequently became widely known that you only had to mention these three words, and the man would be thrown, temporarily, into the same trance. Such was his fearsome reputation, few dared to try this for themselves.'

'Astounding!' I cried. 'Your man Kibble saved our lives.'

'Really such a silly thing,' said Holmes glancing across at the counter, 'but useful none the less. Now here comes our lunch and not a moment too soon.'

THIRTEEN

The Admiral

Holmes emerged from a long spell in the bath. The soak appeared to have done him good; he looked a good deal less jaded than I had seen him of late and the combination of a hearty supper of Mrs Hudson's pease pudding and a good night's sleep appeared to have restored his energies. He was clad in his dressing gown, cradling a drink of his own devising in one hand and holding an old pamphlet in the other.

'Now, Watson,' said Holmes. 'What do you make of this?' He cast the publication in my direction, It was the programme from the Great Exhibition of 1851, slightly damp, presumably from Holmes having read it in the bath.

'Something of a relic,' I said. 'It's forty years old. It may even be worth something; or it would have been if it hadn't just been steamed through.'

'It's more to do with where I found it,' said Holmes, 'that is to say, in Snitterton's feather factory.'

'How curious,' I said. 'A bit of a risk, though, don't you think? Do you not think he'll miss it?'

'I left Snitterton's copy in place then purchased another from Samuel's near St Paul's. What do you make of his interest in it?' I leafed through the damp pages.

'Surely the gemstones,' I said at length, 'given the nature of his interests.'

'I concur, Watson.'

'I'm so sorry,' said Mrs Hudson dusting flour from her hands, 'I've tried to keep him outside, but he's a like a stray mongrel. The minute the door's ajar, he slips straight in.'

'Allo, Mr 'Olmes,' smiled Wiggins, the smartest urchin north of of the Thames and de facto leader of the Baker Street Irregulars. He was wearing an ill-fitting pair of black trousers fashioned at some point in the distant past for a small man rather than a boy. They were sheared off near the ankle and held up by a length of string tied haphazardly around the waist and a pair of braces. A grubby vest was partially hidden by an even grubbier grey shirt. The outfit, which gave off a pungent odour all of its own, was topped off with a raffish looking cap.

'Urgent message from Inspector Gregson,' he panted, evidently having arrived directly from the scene.

Holmes rose to his feet.

'Well, let us have it, Wiggins,' said Holmes impatiently. 'Don't just stand there wearing out Mrs Hudson's carpet.'

The boy cocked his head to one side and adjusted the angle of his hat.

'Oh I see,' continued Holmes. 'You are entitled to enjoy the comforts of our study but I am not entitled to a word of your message until I part with a shilling? I understand.'

Holmes patted his dressing gown pockets. 'Well you will excuse me Wiggins, but like most others, I am not in the habit of carrying much short change with me in the bath. Perhaps the good Dr Watson would be prepared to sub me?' I rolled my eyes and fished a shilling from my pocket. I flipped it across the room. Wiggins snatched it expertly from the air.

'There's something up in Trafalgar Square,' he explained.

'Be precise!' said Holmes indignantly.

'That is precise,' Wiggins insisted. 'There is a man at the top of Nelson's Column.'

'There has been a man has been at the top of Nelson's column since 1843!'

'Well, now there's another one, sir!' blurted Wiggins. 'They don't know if he's alive or dead. He's right up there at the top and no one's got a single idea how he got up there or how to get him down. Gregson says you need to come straight away.'

'Hellfire, Watson, this sounds like a scorcher.'

A hard, warm rain was falling on London. It darkened the stone and washed the dust from the great facades of Regent Street. The shoppers took shelter beneath the awnings of the shop fronts as we churned past in our growler, the spray hissing from our wheels. Coach and horses, mighty spires and towering buildings reflected themselves in the glistening streets.

'There is hysteria in the air, Watson,' mused Holmes, his gloved hands resting on his cane. 'The summer brings with it a peculiar kind of crime: a wrong-headed spirit which grips the criminal mind and persuades him that his scheme possesses a logic to which it cannot possibly aspire.' My friend peered out into the streets, lost in his thoughts.

We found that a sizeable crowd had mustered in Trafalgar Square. Constables in shining capes stood at even intervals holding it back. Our driver shouted our credentials and we drove through a narrow opening that took us almost up to the great column itself.
I spied Gregson in charge of the scene, issuing instructions and answering questions.

My friend and I descended from our carriage and were quickly ushered beneath police umbrellas. The rain applauded loudly while the inspector filled us in. 'Mr Holmes, Dr Watson,' Gregson nodded. 'I thought this might appeal to your bizarre tastes. We've decided he's not a jumper. In fact, if he's not just a very sound sleeper, it's quite possible he's dead already. Our men have telescopes trained on him and he hasn't moved so much as an inch in an hour. There's no evidence of a rope and so far we have no clear idea how he got there. I don't mind confessing that we are almost at a loss.' Holmes was clearly disarmed by Gregson's frank admission.
'Surely inspector,' he goaded. 'You have a theory. You always have a theory even if it is later proved to be entirely erroneous.' Gregson smiled.
'Well, I did say, we are "almost at a loss." There is an idea forming.'
'Splendid. Well then let us hear it,' Holmes invited. 'I always knew you were one of the few men of Scotland Yard possessed of an imagination.'
'One of my constables found this,' he said, producing what appeared to be the end of an arrow. The arrowhead itself was contorted by some blunt trauma. 'It is my conjecture,' Gregson postulated, 'that an arrow was fired from the upper window of a nearby building. This arrow was connected to a fine thread, which was in turn connected to a stouter rope or line. A pulley was then installed on this make-shift system. It is perfectly plausible that the body was transported along

this line to the top of the column. The first attempt was unsuccessful; the arrow rebounded from the stone and this fragment fell to the ground. The villain tried to tidy up after himself but in the darkness and in his haste, missed this vital piece of evidence. I have men making enquiries at both Canada House and the South Africa High Commission.' Holmes nodded throughout this explanation.

'Bravo, Inspector. It is an entirely credible theory but one that is alas, perfectly wrong.'

Gregson's face fell. 'Show me your evidence to the contrary,' he demanded. 'My theory is not only perfectly reasonable, it has the advantage of material proof. On what grounds do you reject it?'

Holmes took the broken arrowhead out of Gregson's hand and inspected it at close quarters.

'The first thing I would say is that this is the end of an iron railing.' He scanned the immediate area and pointed to a grassy patch adjacent to the National Gallery. 'I would suggest it came from over there. I'm sure the gallery's director, Sir Frederick would be glad of its safe return.'

'Crestfallen' would not do justice to the expression that formed on Gregson's face in those few moments. He knew he was beaten, but he fought on regardless.

'Well,' he said, gathering himself, 'let us say for a moment you are right about the railing. My theory is still entirely within the realms of possibility. There is no other way for a man to ascend the column, bearing the full dead weight of another man upon his back and without a rope. For the sake of the younger officers here, perhaps you would be so good as to provide an alternative explanation?'

'Given time,' said Holmes, 'given time. If you would just allow me to inspect the scene as carefully as you have done yourself, I would happily join you in your willingness to discount the impossible, which perhaps will leave us with the truth.'

All efforts were being made to reach the top. An enormous ladder had been fetched from somewhere and another was being lashed to it. This improvised staircase was then hoisted up against the column to create a vertiginous, bending mechanism that rose to three quarters of its height. The policemen appeared to be drawing lots to decide who would be the first to make the ascent. While they were debating, the ladder swayed and bent in the wind like legs of a drunken giraffe. Finally, a sergeant volunteered himself for the terrifying mission, and so, with a rope and hook slung over his shoulder, I watched in horror as he scaled the first ten or so rungs. The ladder undulated wildly, and for a moment he appeared to lose his balance, which drew a collective gasp from the crowd. He had only just regained his composure when the ladder suddenly buckled and he toppled into the arms of the constables below.

'What would you say to a stroll, Watson?' asked Holmes, observing this chaotic scene.
'How congenial,' I replied, and making our excuses we left the police to their public tomfoolery.
'This case certainly presents some unique features,' he mused. 'Whether this is a new case or one connected to the series of strange occurrences I am not yet sure, but from what I have seen through Inspector Gregson's binoculars, there is something curiously familiar about the man at top.'

When it came to evidence, Holmes was like a buzzard stalking its prey. If it was there, he would find it. Holmes' eyes darted left and right, looking for anything out of the ordinary. I have never forgotten his words: "you know my method. It is founded on the observation of trifles." However, today they seemed in short supply. We found nothing but the usual detritus of London – newspapers, the wrapping of a sandwich, a hairpin and an old sixpence. Holmes tapped the ground with his end of his cane then watched as the wind caught a sheet of newspaper and carried it across the paving stones. His eyes lit up.
'You've had an idea,' I said.
'An inkling,' he corrected, then strode with purpose back the way we came. In that precise, efficient way of his, he scanned the building tops at each compass point.
'There!' he cried in triumph. 'Do you see the weather vane up there on the gallery?'
'Yes,' I said, peering into the drizzle. 'It is at something of an angle.'
'Exactly right, Watson. Now look at the flag on Canada House.' I peered in the direction he indicated.

'That too; it is leaning to one side.'

'Not just one side, Watson,' shouted Holmes, 'the same side! It is as if it has been knocked or dislodged by someone or something.'

'The storm? The wind?'

'Impossible,' snorted Holmes. 'This is merely a little light summer rain.'

He strode to the very edge of the square where a man sat huddled on the ground, his back to a stone wall. He was almost entirely obscured in a pile of rags, his face dark with dirt and grease.

'Hello, my friend,' said Holmes. My friend nudged me for a shilling to give to the vagrant. 'How long have you been here?' The man opened a single eye.

'Toast your blooming eyebrows.'

'Another shilling? Very well then.' I produced another.

'What are you, one of these mutton shunters? I got every right to be here. Just as much as you.'

'Of course, you have,' my friend assured him, 'and no, I'm not a policeman.'

'Well, if you're willing to sub me a shant of bivvy, then I'll tell ya. I've been here for two days and two nights and a better spot there could not be found in all of London. I'm an old sailor, you see, and while the Admiral watches over me, no 'arm will come. Do you follow? No 'arm! Not that I'm afraid of any man alive. '

'Tell me,' asked Holmes, suddenly serious of purpose. 'Did you notice anything unusual last night?'

The man looked quizzically at Holmes, narrowing his single eye.

'Well there are sights to be had any hour of the day or night. Just yesterday evening for instance, a couple had a right collie shangles right in front of my nose.'

'I believe he means a fight,' I elucidated.

'That's right,' the man continued, 'like I said, a fight. I don't think they even knew I was here. She took the hat off his head and put her fist clean through it. He chased her right round the column.'

'Did you see anything else out of the ordinary?'

'Let me see.' He appeared to freeze mind sentence. I passed him another coin.

'Ah yes,' he said, like a clockwork toy springing back to life. 'An old man came and stood by the column for close on an hour yester-night at around eight of the clock. He just stood there and didn't say a thing. Troubled looking he was.'

'Could you describe him?'

'Of course I could. He was a bald headed fellow, sixty if he was a day, with a full dark beard. He had a dour look about him and heavy saddle bags under the eyes.'

'A remarkable description,' complemented Holmes. 'It is as if you know the man.'

'I do,' the man said plainly. 'It was the Prime Minister, the Marquis of Salisbury!'

'Upon my word!' I exclaimed.

'My guess is that he came here to think things over,' the old seadog continued. 'If he'd asked for my opinion, I would have given it to him. He's been building houses for the poor but he hasn't built one for me yet!'

'How about the night itself,' pressed Holmes. 'Did you see anything in the early hours?'

'Well this rain gave me a proper drenching, alright,' he complained, pulling his rags closer around him. 'Like a drowned rat, I was.'

Behind me, the ladder was again brought to bear against the column and the crowd emitted another theatrical gasp. I was losing patience with the man's tales.

'Perhaps we ought to leave this gentleman in peace, Holmes,' I suggested. 'He has been most illuminating, has he not?'

'Tell me,' said Holmes, raising a finger, 'one thing more.' I sighed and passed the man another shilling. It was as if I was feeding a machine in an amusement hall.

'Did you happen to see, at any point, a giant balloon?'

Not for the first time, my jaw slackened. However, the old sailor didn't skip a beat.

'A balloon you say,' he said, stroking his grizzled chin, 'a balloon.' He peered up into the sky, and rolled his single eye across the heavens as if he had at one time been the beneficiary of some theatrical training.

'Now you mention it that does sound familiar.'

'Quickly Watson, another coin!'

'I'm growing short,' I said, handing over yet another.

'Yes, a balloon!' he cried, as if in a moment of epiphany 'It was a magnificent white balloon. It appeared out of nowhere at around three in the morning. I was awoken by the hiss of its escaping gas.'

'Great heavens!' I ejaculated.

'I thought I was dreaming,' the man said in a voice filled with wonder. 'I looked up and it was as if I was staring at a huge diamond.'

'Did you not think to mention this before?' I demanded, infuriated. Holmes held up a calming hand.

'Describe what you saw,' he cajoled.

'It came in low from the west and glided east,' the sailor said, jingling the coins in his hand. 'Blow me if it didn't clip the tops of them roofs,' he added, waving his arm around vaguely.

'It clipped them!' said Holmes, hopping in triumph, 'did you hear that, Watson? It clipped them!'

'You are a strange fellow and no mistake,' the sailor said, peering at my friend.

'What else? What else?' Holmes cried.

'It passed only for a moment over the admiral but if my eye didn't deceive me, something was bundled out and left at the top with him. I'm thinking now, that this is the cause of all this benjo, am I right?'

'You most certainly are!' said Holmes. 'Anything else? Was the square deserted?'

'There was a woman on the ground,' the vagrant continued. 'A right bag of oranges, she was. She had some sort of light, as if she was signalling to them fellows in the balloon.'

'What was she wearing?'

'That's the strange thing,' he said. 'She was a white woman but she was wearing Indian type clothes. What do you call those things?'

'A sari?' I asked.

'If you say so, sir. And one thing more; I would swear blind she was carrying a violin case.'

'My dear Holmes!' I cried. 'This is too much; surely this man is describing our friend Miss Braithwaite?' Holmes appeared perfectly unruffled.

'Your single eye served you well. Your last shilling, if you please, Dr Watson.'

'How did you know it was my last?' I asked.

'Because I watched you count them this morning before you dropped them into your pocket. Since then it has been a simple matter of subtraction.'

'Or in my case,' grinned the oily man, baring his three remaining fangs, 'addition!'

Holmes whipped around and headed back towards Gregson, the crowd parting before him.

'He's never going to believe it,' I counselled, chasing hard on his heels.

'Of course he won't,' my friend agreed. 'But we cannot wait any longer to inspect the body.'

Gregson by now was attempting to personally supervise the rescue, without any noticeable result.

'Send for this man,' said Holmes, pressing a card into Gregson's hand. 'He is the finest steeple jack in London. If any man can do it, it will be him.'

While we waited, Holmes and I tumbled into the welcoming glow of The Harp, a public house a stone's throw from Charing Cross. I lined up a pair of pints and for a brief, blissful moment of serenity we supped at the nutty brown ale.

'Surely this changes everything,' I said, wiping my lips.

'Only if your mind was set in a particular direction,' sparkled Holmes. 'I'm afraid you always had more faith in Miss Braithwaite than I did. Think back on the portraits of India on her staircase; the curious connection between the Ruby Elephant and her violin teacher; the unexplained presence of Snitterton at the concert. I'm afraid Watson, that she deliberately positioned herself in our midst from the beginning.' I shook my head, while at the same time, concurring with Holmes' logic. 'Surely,' my friend added. 'it would not surprise you entirely to know that she is Snitterton's daughter.' I spluttered into my pint, succeeding in showering my friend in froth.

'I take it from that,' Holmes remarked coolly wiping beer from his face, 'that you had not yet arrived at the same conclusion.'

It was late afternoon by the time Morris Digby, the man with the best head for heights on either side of the Thames had been summoned from the spire of St Helen's and transported under police escort to Trafalgar Square. He was not a man to be hurried. He unpacked his equipment carefully, unfolding a cloth that contained his rivets, winches and pliers and brought out a small suitcase that contained several coils of ropes and the wooden boards that made up his bosun's chair.

Inspector Gregson, who had presided over the public farce for the bulk of the day, was well beyond the point of frustration.

'Can't we hurry this along?' he asked, retrieving and replacing his pocket watch without even bothering to look at the time.

'If you would prefer to ascend, Inspector,' said Digby slowly, without taking his eyes off the column, 'then be my guest.' He weighed up the column as a chef might survey his ingredients before cooking a delicious dinner. Eventually the climb began. As the offices emptied, the crowd swelled to an even greater size as the show unfolded against the skyline. He inched up, as a sloth might ascend a great tree in the great forests of South America and after ten minutes, he was half way. He had his own elaborate system of ropes and pulleys, which appeared magically from his person rather like thread from a spider. He swung a little to the left and right, dropped down a foot or so while he secured a position, before winching himself up again. He was an artist at work. Within half an hour, he was at the base of the Corinthian capital, where the column flowers outwards and five minutes later he was at the top. A hush fell upon the crowd as they waited for him to pronounce on the fate of the man.

'Dead!'

The steeplejack's shout echoed around the hushed square. A low murmur soon replaced the silence, and the crowd began to disperse. The game was up.

'Another notch on the reaper's belt,' I heard a man mutter.

'This strange summer grows stranger still,' I said to an impassive Holmes.

Presently we heard a squeaking coming from the top of the column. The bosom's chair was being gently lowered and Gregson was preparing to clamber aboard.

'We always knew you'd rise to the top, sir,' one of his constables joked. The inspector glared at him. Having safely delivered Gregson, the chair began to lower again. A note pinned to the wooden seat requested that Holmes join them.

'Well,' said Holmes, 'I think it's only fair, in the interests of the public record that you join us too, doctor.'

All of London lay below us. It was a city of spires and rooftops, towers and thoroughfares. The buildings curved and twisted as if distorted in a hall of mirrors. I don't know how much time Nelson spent in a crow's nest himself but I imagine the sensation was similar. We seem to sway in the breeze. Nelson had become a stone god pushing his way up into the clouds, his face as cold and impassive as it was when he sighted the French fleet.

'You've gone a little green, Gregson,' remarked Holmes.

'Thank you, Holmes,' said the Inspector. 'I would be grateful if we do not prolong this any longer than is strictly necessary.'

My friend and I were already one step ahead of Gregson. The dead man was the queer, bald headed fellow we had seen negotiating with Snitterton in the feather factory. Holmes gave me that steely look that told me this information was not to be shared. The body was quite rigid and lying at a haphazard angle face down at Nelson's feet.

'I say this body fell from a height,' averred Holmes

'Preposterous,' scoffed Gregson. 'Where from? The moon?'

'Close,' said Holmes. 'A balloon.' Gregson stared at him. My friend explained his theory in that clear, reasonable manner of his, showing the path that the hot balloon had taken, crushing the weather vanes and railings along the tops of the buildings. Holmes even picked up a piece of ribbon and a scattering of sand that could, conceivably have spilled from the balloon's basket. Gregson stare had turned into a look of intense irritation.

'I'm afraid I find that very hard to believe. Help me turn the body, doctor.'

We grasped the man's shoulders and with some effort (he was a portly fellow) managed to turn him onto his belly. I leapt back in horror, a dangerous business one hundred and seventy feet above the ground. His eyelids were wide open but where his eyes should have been, there were two gleaming stones.

'Are they diamonds?' I spluttered.

'No, said, Holmes, bending low over the body, 'only glass.'

'A ghoulish business,' said the steeplejack distastefully as he watched the scene unfold.

'There's something in his hand,' I said.

Rigor mortis had set in, and Gregson had to break the poor man's finger to release the small slip of paper he still clutched. The inspector uncurled the note and read the first line with some astonishment.

'To Mr Sherlock Holmes, Esq.' He stared at the note and scanned it again. 'It's for you!' he blurted.

'So it appears,' agreed Holmes. 'Read on.'

To Mr Sherlock Holmes, Esq,

The state of play at lunch

You have played a fine innings. You have managed to deny my bowlers any easy wickets. Your defensive play is ingenious and your attack has a grace that few possess. But now it is my turn to bat. I feel you have exhausted yourself at the crease. Abandon the match and return to the club house while you still can. This is your final warning.

GW

'Who is this GW?' Gregson demanded.

'I have no idea,' said Holmes.

'I should arrest you now,' the Inspector threatened. 'What exactly are you holding back?'

'I assure you,' said Holmes truthfully. 'I have to the best of my knowledge, and without consulting my notes, had any dealings with a GW.' He peered at the finger Gregson was pointing at his chest.

'Are you a cricketing man?' asked Holmes.

'When I have time, yes,' said Gregson.

'Then you will know that W.G. Grace scored two centuries in a single match against Yorkshire in the summer before last. Watson, I believe you were there.'

'I certainly was,' I confirmed. It was a magnificent match.'

'What is your point, Holmes?'

'I'm not sure I have one yet,' my friend said. 'But look at those initials, albeit the wrong way around, the cricketing theme and the use of the word 'grace' in the second line.'

'Are you implying the finest cricketer this country has yet produced has blood on his hands?'

'I have no idea,' said Holmes innocently. 'It is merely an observation. Inspector, I have a thousand enemies in London alone. Any one of them could have sent this note.'

'But how did they know you would be here to receive it?'

'Because of the extraordinary manner of its delivery. They knew you would call me for me at once.'

'I have had quite enough of this,' said Gregson, his complexion by now an even sicklier shade of green. 'If you don't mind gentlemen, I would be grateful if we could continue this discussion on terra firma.'

FOURTEEN

The Maharajah

'What are your thoughts,' I asked Holmes, laying down my copy of The Time Machine, 'on intelligent life on other planets?'

'I sometimes wonder if there is any on our own,' quipped Holmes.

The thermometer beneath the portrait of General Gordon confirmed that it was the warmest day of the year so far. The bricks of the houses opposite gleamed as if they were made from nine carat gold and despite the fact that our windows were half open, the air in our stuffy rooms at Baker Street had become so hot and heavy it was a wonder we did not have to spoon it like treacle into our mouths. I could barely think for the heat and loosened my collar.

I was constantly astonished by Holmes' ignorance of the celestial bodies. Around the time of our first adventure, he had confessed that he was ignorant of the fact that the Earth revolves around the Sun. He could not point out a single constellation and reached the grand total of four when I asked him to name the planets. I was not therefore expecting any kind of sensible response.

'Gentlemen,' said Mrs Hudson, appearing at the door with a tray of lemonade and sugar. 'I thought you might like a cooling glass of something.'

'Mrs Hudson, how thoughtful and timely; it is as if you escaped from the court of Nebuchadnezzar,' congratulated Holmes. 'In a previous life I am convinced that you attended to the needs of a great king or emperor.'

'Well I have come down in the world,' she said, raising an eyebrow and casting a disapproving look around the room.

The beverage had a powerful restorative affect on my brain, dousing some of the fires that had taken hold therein.

'Well?' I prompted Holmes, pressing the side of the glass like a cool balm against my forehead. 'What is your view of extraterrestrial life and its chances of communicating with our own?' Holmes sat forward and joined his fingers like a great general about to make his first move.

'I can only provide an answer to this question by applying the sort of

155

hard logic you find so infuriating.'

'Try me,' I invited.

'We have good reason,' he began, 'to believe that we are the very zenith of civilisation. No human society has ever reached our level of scientific advancement, our sheer pitch of reasoning, knowledge or sophistication. It has taken us two thousand million years to reach this point and what have we achieved? We have produced the paperclip. Watson, it is a great leap from a paperclip, or even a steam locomotive to producing a vehicle that can escape the clutches of gravity, pierce the iron roof of the Earth and travel to the stars. It could take another five billion years.

'Let us say, for the sake of argument, that there are a number of Earth-like bodies in the universe capable of sustaining life similar to our own. What stage are they at in their evolution? Are they still grubbing at the mouths of their caves? Have they stumbled yet on the advantages of the wheel or the means to produce fire? Are they at the paperclip stage? Let us infer from the deafening silence of the universe that none of them have gone beyond this. This means that we are the apotheosis of all extant life, which means if we wish to send an olive branch, it is incumbent on us to devise the steel dove that will deliver it.

'By the time we develop such a mechanism, it is possible that we will have exhausted the generosity of the sun and disappeared in a lightning flash and a puff of smoke. I therefore believe that while it may of course be possible that there is intelligent life in the universe, it is unlikely we will ever have the evidence to prove or disprove it either way. This is precisely why I choose not to waste energy on any matters that go beyond the realm of the Earth. There is quite enough incident in our own goldfish bowl to keep us from wondering what other fittings and furnishings can be found in the sitting room.'

I let Holmes' words die away and such was their definitive tone, it felt there was no more that could be said on the subject. Indeed it was the sort of pronouncement that might, if overheard south of the river, in all probability cause the gentlemen of the Royal Observatory in Greenwich to shake their heads in defeat, fold up their star charts and pack away their telescopes for good. It was at this moment that Holmes spotted the bird at the window.

'I say, he's a handsome devil,' Holmes remarked, pointing to a sparrow hawk that had inexplicably appeared on the sill. It stared at me with a piercing, yellow eye; its black pupil fixing me to the spot.

'It must have escaped from the gardens at Buckingham Palace,' I said. 'Shoo it away. There will be pandemonium if it gets into the room.'

'Wait,' said Holmes. 'What's that tied around its leg?'

He advanced carefully, treading softly across the room in his moccasins. Two feet away from the bird, he pounced, catching it in both hands. He detached a tiny scroll from its left leg then placed the bird back on the sill. It appeared to be entirely unfazed by its molestation.

'Well, well,' said Holmes, unfurling the message, 'it's from the Maharajah.' He handed the note to me.

Gentlemen,

You have proved yourselves highly worthy of my respect. The manner in which you conducted yourselves in Regent's Park has proved you are brave and resourceful men. I was only too glad to be of some small assistance with my rifle when you ran into difficulties. I am a modest man, but you will understand now why I am said to be fourth best shot in England.

I have returned from exile to conclude one piece of unfinished business and with this I require your assistance. I would therefore like to invite you both to my estate which has lain dormant these past years. There we will enjoy each other's company while I explain the particulars. A carriage is waiting outside which will bear you to the station. I will be only too delighted to meet you in person.

Your friend,

Maharajah Duleep Singh

'It was him!' I exclaimed.

'Naturally,' said Holmes. 'It had all the hallmarks of a test which he observed throughout. Why else would he ask us to retrieve an object he had placed there himself?'

'Astonishing.'

Holmes scribbled a reply, rolled it tightly and then with the patience of a veterinarian secured it to the foot of the sparrow hawk. At Holmes' nod, it blinked its eyes, shook out its wings then soared into the sky.

'Well,' said Holmes, gathering up his smoking paraphernalia, 'are you game for a weekend in the country?'

'Never more so,' I cried. 'London in August is a dustbowl. Good riddance to it!'

We packed within minutes and soon found ourselves inside an airy brougham heading in the direction of King's Cross Station.

'The country!' I mused, as we bowled along Bishopsgate. 'The sun setting over the fields, the balmy mists over the lakes; the cool cider served by the smiling maiden . . .'

'I fail to share your enthusiasm,' remarked Holmes. 'Every hour in the city offers a fresh strain of criminality. A decade can pass in a country village without so much as a corrupt postmaster.'

'Come, Holmes,' I urged. 'Think of it as a holiday.'

'At least,' my friend said, gazing at the sun gleaming in an office window, 'there is the prospect of progress in our case. The Maharajah I feel sure will provide some intelligence on this singular business of the ruby elephants.'

London slipped away in a blur of red brick, chimney stacks, dusty yards and windowless factories. It gave way to the fields of the Home Counties, cool marshes, long grass, lakes like pools of melted gold, crowds of willows at the edge of the water, farms and the great country houses.

'A perfect tonic, wouldn't you agree Holmes?'

'A glass of claret for me,' he replied.

He was distracted by a volume he had brought with him from 221b Baker Street.

'A remarkable man,' he murmured, looking up from his book. 'The Maharajah has been a guest of Queen Victoria since the age of 15.

He has been extended every luxury and enjoyed every trapping of the British aristocracy. He has lived in splendour in Northern Britain, in Yorkshire and finally in Elevedon, Norfolk. He has been baptised in the Church of England, taught to shoot, to appreciate art and architecture. And yet, he was a prisoner. He was forbidden to see his mother, to return to India independently lest he rallied the people of the Punjab against the British. Four years ago he left - attempting to return to his homeland - but was prevented by our government. He has converted to Sikhism and now lives in unhappy exile in Paris.'

Holmes closed the book.

'Where is that glass of wine, Watson?'

Let me find the steward,' I said and rose from my seat.

The train was roughly half full; for the most part, it was business types and gentlemen farmers, all semi-obscured by their copies of The Times and the Illustrated London News. Eventually I located the steward who promised that we would receive his prompt attention. Returning to my carriage, I encountered a tall, gaunt looking man in the corridor, distinguished by a scar across his chin and a hollow look in his eye. He pushed past me, without making eye contact.

'I say,' I said. 'What's the hurry?' He disappeared down the corridor without looking back.

A sleek black cab was waiting for us at the station, its driver a wily looking old man with uneven features. His nose swerved like a signpost over to the left and his moustache sprouted beneath like a tuft of grass.

'Are you the gentlemen that have come up to see the Maharajah?' he burred in his local dialect. Holmes nodded. 'Then you need to come alonga me.' He climbed down to help us with the luggage, glancing at the station clock. 'You have made masterous good time.' Perhaps mistaking me for Holmes' man servant he stopped and stared at me at moment. 'Well are you going to mow in with these bags, or will I be doing it all by myself?'

'My name is Doctor Watson,' I said.

'Beggin' your pardon, doctor,' he said, bowing a little too deferentially. There was something about the man I did not like.

'Thass a rare gentlemen, that Maharajah,' remarked William, the driver, who had introduced himself as we jogged along the lane.

'So I understand,' replied Holmes.

'I was mighty surprised to find he had returned. Four years he been gone; then last week, there he wuz again. I don't know what's brought him back. But he pays a tidy wage and I am obliged of it.'

Holmes nodded, distractedly. 'But he 'ain't half got a temper,' the driver said, disloyally as we turned into the drive. 'He wuz hooly raw wi me when I wuz late the other day.'

The hall was an imposing Georgian construction that had been subjected to a number of radical alterations over the years. The Maharajah had brought his own ideas to the house, rendering it in the Italian style on the outside while inside it resembled a palace in Lahore. It had strong vertical lines, a pleasing symmetry and stared out over the grounds through its forty windows. Handsome balustrades lined the ramparts.

As we drew closer we could make out a figure standing in the portico. He was extending his arms in welcome, a glass orb of yellow light above his head, giving him a saint-like aspect in the early evening dusk. It was immediately apparent that we were being met by the Maharajah himself. 'There he is,' William exclaimed in his barely comprehensible way, 'standing right there on the throshel!'

He was a handsome man of fifty, of medium height and portly build from plenty of good living. He stood straight and proud, making full use of his five and a half feet. His skin was dark and lustrous and his eyes shone with an intelligence tempered with a distant sadness. He carried himself with the nobility of his bloodline: the generations of Indian kings who came before him. His clothes were those of a conventional English aristocrat: a velvet jacket with a fine gold braid, a waistcoat, pocket watch, shirt and tie. Like my friend Holmes, he sported a deerstalker, suggesting a fondness for the outdoor life. It seemed curiously regalia for the last King of India.

'My friends, my friends!' the Maharajah exclaimed as we ascended the steps. 'I am perfectly honoured by your visit.' He shook us both warmly by the hand.

'On the contrary,' said Holmes. 'It is we who are humbled by your invitation.'

'Forgive the paucity of the welcome,' said Singh, waving a hand dismissively towards the stupendous house and grounds. 'Four years have seen the place slide almost into ruin. There was a time when fifty staff would assemble for a visit such as this. When the Prince of Wales would visit on a shooting tip, they would line the drive from the gate to the door. Now there are but a handful of us.' He clapped his hands and four men sprang from inside the door. They collected every piece of our luggage and disappeared back into the house. The Maharajah gave the driver a steely look. 'That will be all, William,' he snapped. The man, who had clearly been lingering for a tip, barely hid a scowl.

'Now, come inside, gentlemen. There is fresh tea in the pot and much to discuss.'

Walking through the door was like stepping from one continent into another. We were led into the main hall where huge arches towered over us, each decorated with smaller arches in the Indian style. The balconies were supported by stone pillars, each painted white and topped with an intricately carved stone block, as if lifted from a temple in the Punjab. Enormous patterned rugs carpeted the floor. Back copies of The Wildfowlers' Shooting Times and The Amateur Photographer lay scattered on the tabletops. Two servants arrived carrying a giant silver dish between them. On this was a silver tea pot whose contents would have quenched the thirst of twenty men.

'Your journey was without incident?' our host enquired politely.
'Entirely,' said Holmes.
'A blessing,' said the Maharajah. 'Motion and long-during action tires the sinewy vigour of the traveller.'
'Love's Labours Lost!' identified Holmes. 'You are a scholar as well as a sportsman. But sir, it is you who has travelled most these last years? You are barely a week back from Paris, I note?'
'William told you I expect.'
'He revealed when you arrived, but the country is obvious from your cologne: a scent only obtainable from a perfumier on La Rue de la Saint Croix, unless I am very much mistaken?'
The Maharajah shook his head and laughed.

'I have heard stories of your powers but it is something wonderful to witness them at first hand.' He clapped his hands again and the tea was poured with great ceremony.

'And now to business,' he said. 'You have brought the ruby elephant?'

'Of course,' said Holmes, reaching into his pocket.

'Keep it,' said the Maharajah holding up his hands. 'Keep it for now. All will be revealed.'

'Do you have the others?' I blundered.

'All in good time, doctor!' I sipped my tea, an astonishing concoction, both delicious and revitalising.

'The leaves are picked from a small valley near my home town,' he said, noting my appreciation. 'It is a like a vale of heaven.' He sighed and returned his tea cup to its saucer. 'You will know gentlemen, something of my history. I cannot pretend I have been misused. Your government and especially your Queen have given me everything I have asked for; everything except my freedom. For decades I have played at your expense. I have grown to love your fields and moors; your hills and lakes. I have dined with lords and sported with princes. But now, I only wish to return to my home. Of course, I understand why they cannot allow this. They know it would spark a revolution, a mutiny; a call for India to once more belong to its people. But all the same, this cannot stop me wishing it were so. At night I dream of the five rivers of my homeland. I see the Chenab slide past me like a stream of silver bringing the melted snows from the mountains.'

'How may we assist, you?' asked Holmes plainly.

'Gentlemen, I do not expect you to defy your Queen and be an accessory to my escape. But perhaps you can thwart the plot to steal the Nizam Diamond. You have met this man Snitterton and know him to be a monster. If I can help you apprehend him, then perhaps, just perhaps, Her Majesty will relent and allow me to return home.'

'But what of the Koh-I-Noor?' I asked.

'I will propose an exchange,' said the Maharajah. 'I believe the Nizam to be of greater value than the Koh-I-Noor. I believe that it will be in the interests of your country to accept the arrangement.' Holmes and I exchanged a look.

'The Queen is very attached to the stone,' cautioned Holmes.

'Be that as it may,' he said with a little impatience. 'But first, there is a matter of some pressing importance.' He clicked his fingers and two assistants appeared, ferrying a large item obscured by a rich purple cloth, decorated with gold braid. 'Over time I have cultivated certain interests,' he explained. He rose to his feet and approached the object. 'Would you do me the very great honour,' he asked, whipping away the cloth 'of allowing me to take your photograph?' A large, mahogany, tailboard box camera was mounted on a tripod.

'Well,' said Holmes at length. 'Unless you plan to publish the results in the gutter press, I cannot see why not. Watson, do you have any objection?'

'Certainly not,' I replied.

'Splendid!' said the Maharajah. 'Then let us proceed. You may not know, but I am a member of the Photographic Society. Of course, I am strictly an amateur but I have no doubt that the photograph will be the dominant art form of the 20th century. If you wouldn't mind standing over there, leave the rest to me.'

He arranged us by a wall with a small arched window to our left and a gaudy painting of Singh as a younger man on the right.

'That will do nicely!' he said, disappearing beneath the black hood. 'Hold very still! I can see you are both naturals at this.'

We posed until a small explosion told us the Maharajah had what he wanted.

'Perfect!' he exclaimed. 'And now, perhaps you could allow me to show you something else?'

'Lead on!' said Holmes.

We followed the Maharajah up an ornate staircase and into a darkened room lit only by a single lamp. Across an entire wall was a simply enormous painting of an Indian street scene cast in shadow. The light flickered on the ceiling to reveal elaborately decorated patterns and coving, entirely in keeping with this house of wonders.

'My friends,' he said. 'What I am about to show you has never been seen before by western eyes. It was transported in secret by my most trusted men.' We followed Singh to the far end of the room where a large safe lay against the wall. He crouched and worked at the lock until we heard a click and saw the cold, steel door swing open. He reached in and extracted a metallic object the size of a dinner plate

'My dear Holmes!' I shouted. 'It's an elephant!'

'Of course it is!' said the Maharajah. He lifted it onto an octagonal card table at the centre of the room and laid it down with great care. It was a thing of great beauty, cast in gold and studded with jewels. 'It is centuries old,' he said. 'It may not even have been opened for a hundred years.' He brought the lamp closer to reveal its detail: namely eight indentations, each in the shape of a small elephant. 'It was designed by a master craftsman,' he said. 'His artistry was only exceeded by his ingenuity. Although it is plated with gold, the structure was fashioned from one of the strongest alloys available at the time. This master then devised a mechanism that would only open when all eight animals are in place.' He reached into the pocket of his waistcoat and withdrew a small black velvet bag. Untying the cord, it opened to reveal three of the fabled ruby elephants.'

'It is too much to hope,' he asked, 'that one day we may unite them all?'

Holmes smiled one of his impossible smiles. He reached into his own pocket then scattered five more elephants like dice onto the table.

'Impossible!' whispered the Maharajah.

'Not at all,' said Holmes calmly. 'May I smoke?' he asked. Singh waved his assent, still staring at the assembled elephants before collapsing heavily into a chair. My friend sat at the table and drew a silver cigarette case from his jacket. I had not seen it before. He flipped open the lid and offered it around the group. We each took a cigarette, accepting the flame Holmes proffered.

'Watson,' my friend began. 'You are intrigued by this new cigarette case and are wondering at this very moment where I acquired it. Am I right?'

'Exactly,' I confirmed.

'The answer is in plain view.' He dropped the lid to reveal the initials: WS.

'Warwick Snitteron!' I ejaculated.

'Bullseye, Watson.'

'But how . . .'

'You remember in the yard when I succeeded in putting the man under a hypnotic spell? Well, before we made our escape, I decided to test my powers as a dipper, or pickpocket as the art is more commonly known. I thought I had struck unusually lucky with the cigarette case until I alighted on the elephants. A lucky hit, wouldn't you say?'

The Maharajah appeared to be in a state of shock. The cigarette burned away in his fingers, his mouth agape. He was utterly transfixed by the sight of all eight elephants together on the tabletop. Impressive though it was, I was still somewhat offended that Holmes had not revealed this momentous news to me before.

'Snitterton will be madder than a wounded bull after this,' I said.

'This is precisely why I held back from telling you while we were still in London. If he had succeeded in accosting you, it would have been better that you knew nothing.'

'Words fail me, Holmes,' I sighed and leant back shaking my head at the limitless guile of the great detective.

It was some time before the Maharajah felt his hand was steady enough to drop the ruby elephants into place. They fitted snugly into their golden graves and it was wondrous to think of the time that had elapsed since they were last united.

As he held the last ruby, the nobleman gave us a long, sorrowful look.

'Truly,' he said. 'I did not believe that this moment would come.' He extended his thumb and fingers around the lid and prepared to open the casket. A single bead of sweat formed on his brow.

'Wait!' I cried. They both stared at me. 'What if it's a trap?' The Maharajah lifted his hands from the treasure. 'I have heard stories of such things,' I continued, 'mechanisms to ward against grave robbers and ancient enemies. Who knows what waits for us inside? A poison? A blade? A primitive explosive?'

'Come now, Watson,' said Holmes. 'You have been reading too much of The Arabian Nights. If anyone knew of such a thing, it would be the Maharajah. Surely, if he was aware of any danger, he would have mentioned it before?'

Singh rose from his chair, put a hand to his beard and walked over to the painting.

'Doctor, you are wiser than you know,' he said, without turning around. 'As a boy, I knew of the curse of the ruby elephants. There was a curious rhyme that we chanted:

He who seeks them will not see eight
He who finds them will not see five
He who unites them will not survive'

'Superstitious nonsense!' scoffed Holmes. 'It was most probably devised by the man who made the casket.

'There is no greater deterrent than a curse,' I suggested. The Maharajah appeared agitated.

'A curse is no more superstitious than a prayer,' he mused, staring at the painting. 'And yet we do not laugh at the man praying to his God.'

'Let us say for a moment that there is some truth in it,' I said. 'What is its meaning?'

'"He who seeks them will not see eight," Holmes repeated. 'Perhaps this infers that the man who seeks the elephants will not live longer than eight years. So if we open it, there is no immediate danger. . .'

'The last line is not so vague,' I pointed out.

'Enough of this,' cried the Maharajah. He ran back to the table and dropped the final elephant into place. At once the lid sprang open and the Maharajah let out a shriek of horror.

Holmes and I rushed to his side. Singh's hands were pressed to his eyes and he shouted in pain.

'The curse!' I cried. A curious green cloud had enveloped the table.

'Dust!' exclaimed Holmes covering his mouth. 'It is nothing more that dust!'

'Dust?' repeated the Maharajah, groggily. As he spoke, the cloud began to clear. Inside the golden elephant lay the stone.'

'The Nizam!' I shouted. 'Look at its size! It's impossible!'

I was seized by the same fever that gripped me upon seeing the Koh-I-Noor. I began to laugh hysterically. 'It's absurd!' I roared. 'Holmes, it's perfectly absurd.' I began to lose my balance.

Holmes struck me smartly across the face.

'Watson!' he shouted. 'Pull yourself together, man.' In a moment of superhuman strength, Holmes seized both the Maharajah and I and dragged us to the window. He threw open the shutters and smashed the glass.

166

I awoke in the drawing room, lying on a couch of exotic design. The doors to the garden were open and a warm breeze flowed into the light filled room. I focused to find Holmes sitting next to me, offering me a glass of water.

'Drink slowly Watson,' he said. I did as he said, then sat up.

'Where is the Maharajah?' I said, glancing around the room.

'Recovering,' said Holmes. 'He had a greater dose than you.'

I rubbed the side of my face where a handsome bruise was developing.

'You have me to thank for that, Watson,' my friend confessed. 'For a moment, I thought I was losing you. Once again, if ever there is a time when I appear to have gone beyond the limits of my powers, remind me of this day. Watson, you were right to be wary and I was wrong to be so belligerent. That was no dust. It was a noxious powder of some unknown provenance that produced an hallucinogenic and ultimately asphyxiating affect. I have taken a sample to study once we are back at Baker Street. I fancy, once I have processed my results, it will make an excellent subject for a short, instructive monogram.'

'The diamond,' I murmured. The vision of that astonishing rock reappeared in my head.

'It is quite safe,' smiled Holmes, unwrapping a handkerchief. 'I seem to be collecting diamonds like a child collects pebbles from the beach.'

Two cups of strong tea restored some vigour to the system. While we waited for the Maharajah to sleep off the ill-effects, Holmes and I decided to take a constitutional.

'Another five seconds and I fear you would have both slipped away,' explained Holmes as we strolled across the grass. A deer sprang from behind a beech tree, stopped for a moment to study my friend and me, then darted into the undergrowth. 'While it wasn't a curse, the rhyme was a fair warning of what to expect. Given the formidable levels of toxicity, I am now inclined to believe that the five and the eight referred to seconds, not years.'

The sun illuminated the estate in all its glorious colour. It had been a wet summer and the grass was as green as it would be in spring.

Despite the fact the Maharajah had been away, the grounds were in excellent order.

'What do you make of the Maharajah's plans?' I asked Holmes, retrieving a scrap of blue cloth from the ground.

'I am uncertain,' Holmes admitted. 'However I am inclined to let him leave with the Nizam diamond. The Queen, I fancy, can afford to go without another foreign object in the treasury. Singh was much wronged by the British and I would not stand in his way if he wished to make a further attempt to return to India. You will remember Watson, that we owe him our lives. I have no doubt that he will make adequate compensation for our time and trouble in this matter, despite the fact that he was not our original client. It has been, would you not agree Watson, a singular case?'

'Quite. But what of Snitterton and the Koh-I-Noor?' I asked.

'Half of Scotland Yard is currently on his trail and notwithstanding Gregson's limited powers of detection, I would suggest that he will be apprehended within days rather than weeks. It was too much to hope that he would be arrested at the property we visited. I have also wired some particulars to the inspector that will make the task of finding him somewhat less onerous. As to locating the Koh-I-Noor, that is work still ahead of us.'

That evening we joined the Maharajah for a feast that defied easy description. He was dressed in full ceremonial robes. A splendid red turban covered his head while a ceremonial sword swung from a silk sash at his belt. Holmes and I sat on either side of him as his guests of honour. The rest of the party was made up of his retinue. While all appeared to be in his employ there was it seemed, a graded system of servants. Those acting as advisers were afforded privileges of the office, dining with us, while those of lower rank assumed more menial duties. All trace of the poison's effects had disappeared from the Maharajah and he spoke with gusto, lambasting the service, toasting Holmes and me, while holding forth on politics, photography and philosophy. He was more than a match for Holmes on all of these subjects.

Plate upon plate of brightly coloured food arrived at the table. Vast dishes of tandoori chicken arrived, piled high, followed by lamb rogan josh, Chicken biryani and shami kebabs. Fish courses followed, including a spectacular catfish that had been prepared in a delicate sauce.

'Lip-smacking good, isn't it?' the Maharajah said, registering my obvious enjoyment. All this was complemented by a supply of excellent wine that flowed liberally from his cellar. Judging by his spirits, I could tell that Holmes had been as good as his word and repatriated the diamond to him. We fought our way to the end of a peculiar carrot based dessert that was the only dish that had failed to make an entirely positive impression.

'So gentlemen,' the Maharajah said, drawing on a cigar. 'It appears you have solved the mystery of the ruby elephants. No doubt Dr Watson, we can look forward to a written record of the case? You have taken some notes?'

'I have jotted down one or two points,' I confessed, 'although such is the singular nature of the events that they have printed themselves, albeit in somewhat jumbled and unedited form, indelibly on my mind.'

'I have no doubt,' he remarked. 'It will surely take its place alongside your splendid account of the Study in Scarlet and the Sign of the Four.'

'The Sign of Four,' I corrected him.

'I apologise. Both are, as you say in the book trade, humdingers.'

'You are too kind,' I bowed. 'If I do write it up I hope that I will do justice to your kindness and hospitality.'

'No doubt,' said Holmes, 'it will be embellished with a great deal of the unnecessary decoration that his readers seem to enjoy. It is my own view that a simple statement of the facts will be remarkable enough in itself.'

We puffed contentedly on the Maharajah's splendid cigars.

'Of course,' said Holmes, 'it is possible that there are some events which are yet to reveal themselves which may still have a bearing on the outcome of this singular case.'

'Mr Holmes,' said the Maharajah as the stopper was removed once again from the port, 'I have one last request before you leave.'

'Name it,' my friend stated.

'In life it is rare to encounter a mind as fine as yours. Would you do me the great honour of joining me in a game of chess?'

The Maharajah led us into the main hall which been cleared as if for a dance. Along the walls orange trees sprouted from porcelain jars; chairs and couches were set back in the archways and tea things and sweetmeats were laid out on the tables.
'I thought you said chess, my dear sir,' said Holmes affably. 'Or are we to dance the tango?'
'Chess,' laughed Singh, 'just as I said.' The ornate gold doors at the far end of the hall slowly opened and a procession of masked men and women began to file in.
'A masquerade?' I asked.
'Not quite doctor,' said Singh. We watched them drift past us in their curious costumes. Some were in flowing red robes; others were in splendid royal cloaks and headdresses. Others had a curious animal-like appearance. They glided by as if in a trance, appearing neither to see or hear us, moving to pre-determined places in the hall. Presently, I noticed they were dividing into two groups. Holmes smiled and shook his head.
'Magnificent,' he said. 'Maharajah, you do nothing by halves.'

I remained mystified until the point at which all thirty two guests had formed themselves into two opposing lines, with a space of perhaps ten feet between them.
'Great Scott!' I shouted. 'Human chess!'
The two commanders met in the middle and shook hands. Holmes as the guest was elected white and made the first move, tapping his left knight and requesting that he move to the third row. The knight was a tall, thin man, his skin painted white, a small horse head mask disguising his features.
'The Queen's Gambit,' remarked the Maharajah. 'I have heard that it is growing in popularity.' Singh replied by moving his own queen pawn forward. 'It begins!' he cried.
The man, a small fellow scuttled forward. I noticed a faint grid had been marked on the floor. Holmes parried with a white pawn of his own to meet it.
Presently, the Maharajah's bishop, a tall, elegant fellow silently glided across the room, moving four spaces, until it was next to

170

Holmes' knight.

'You are in a little danger,' smiled Singh.

Holmes appeared unruffled and signaled for his knight to press ahead with the attack, sending it forward until it stood next to the Maharajah's forward pawn. Singh's bishop retreated back a space to consolidate his position. Holmes slid over to his queen, a slight, graceful woman wearing the painted mask of a goddess. He bowed theatrically before her and whispered in her ear. She stepped forward two spaces.

'Now it gets interesting, Mr Holmes!' laughed the Maharajah, lifting his cigar from an ashtray and drawing on it thoughtfully. He sent the pawn to his queen's immediate right forward a space. In reply, Holmes' queen quickstepped to the extreme right of the board.

'You have a curious mind, my dear Holmes,' he muttered, shaking his head, 'most curious.' He dispatched his knight on the king side to the third row until it stood next to Holmes' own horseman. Holmes responded instantly, sending another pawn forward from the ranks.

The Maharajah's bishop appeared to have a mind of its own and retreated back to the third rank without being asked. It seemed to be answering a nod from Singh. His initiative was not rewarded as Holmes drew first blood, taking it with his knight. The Maharajah reacted swiftly, his pawn in turn taking the knight. The pieces retreated gracefully from play. Holmes charged with another pawn, while Singh's knight surged forward with a daring attack down the centre. My friend covered this with his bishop in an effort to repel the advance.

'Knight,' called the Maharajah, 'retreat to the third rank, in front of your queen.' For a moment, nothing happened. Then Holmes' pawn let out a cry, falling to the ground, clutching its side.

'Illegal move!' shouted my friend.

'He's hurt!' cried another pawn, breaking ranks and running forward. 'Suddenly the same black knight flew towards Holmes, wielding a switchblade.

'Assassin!' I shouted and the board went into uproar, pieces flying in all directions. I pulled my revolver and took aim but such was the chaos, I could not be sure I wouldn't hit an innocent party. From the alcoves emerged a cohort of Singh's attendants, their swords drawn.

Seeing himself outmanoeuvred, the assassin turned and bolted up the stairs towards the gallery.

'After him,' shouted Singh, 'and bring me my rifle!'

While the pawn received attention the rest of us joined the pursuit. I found myself next to Holmes on the staircase.

'Who is he?' I asked.

'I believe him to be Gabriel, the Archangel. And unless I am very much mistaken, he wants the Nizam diamond.'

'Well he can't have it!' shouted Singh, on my other side, clutching his gun.

'We have him cornered,' called one of the attendants as we arrived on the landing. 'He's barred the door.'

'Then break it down!' ordered the Maharajah and together we put our shoulders behind the effort. As it crashed to the ground we saw Gabriel poring over the golden elephant, attempting to lever it open, quite impossible without the eight ruby elephants.

'Don't move!' I shouted, but it was too late. Like a vampire bat, he moved in a blur, melting from one space to another. My bullet did nothing more than dislodge a piece of plaster from the wall. Singh meanwhile discharged a round from his rifle that almost succeeded in blowing a hole in the side of the house.

'He's gone!' shouted Holmes as the smoke cleared. Sure enough, the window swung on its frame and the room was empty. Singh dived to the window and took aim, but the darkness was complete and we could do little more than listen to the sound of the man bounding like a hare into the fields.

The pawn (in fact the same man who had served us dessert earlier that evening) had escaped with a light injury. His cut was dressed and brandy was served to all.

'The world is at war,' said the Maharajah gravely, staring into the middle distance from his couch. 'It is an invisible war, conducted from the shadows. It is not a war between nations but between the forces of good and evil. At stake is everything that is fine and noble in the world.'

The next morning we took breakfast on the lawn beneath a large parasol. The strong August sun buttered the grass and two of the

Maharajah's attendants stood by, cooling us with giant fans that appeared to have once been the tail feathers of a pair of peacocks.

'Really,' I said, nodding towards the servants, feeling a little embarrassed by the attention, 'it is not necessary.' The Maharajah frowned, suggesting I had caused some offence. I said no more.

We each drained at least a pint of coffee before attacking the contents of an adventurous menu consisting of Halwa, Puri and Chanay; a dish based around a flattened bread, cooked in oil. When we had eaten our fill, Holmes laid down his fork and sat back in his chair.

'Watson,' he said, wiping his greasy fingers on a napkin, 'my dear Maharajah. There is something I have not yet shared with you. ' He reached into his pocket and produced a note. 'The ruby elephants,' he said, 'were not all I found in Snitterton's pocket. He was careless enough to leave a letter containing a message, which I believe will be of the greatest interest. The astonishing thing is that I do not think he has read it.' He laid the envelope and letter on the table.

'The envelope is almost revealing as the message itself. The postmark is Bury St Edmunds, which gives us a location, without knowing whether it has any significance beyond the place of dispatch. The handwriting on the envelope is rudimentary. Do you see there are no less than four spelling mistakes in the words:

DILIVURD BUY HAND

This would lead us to believe that either it was inscribed by an uneducated fellow or by a child, deliberately employed for the purpose. However I believe there is something ticklish in this . . . You will have noticed the odd bend of the second d? The pen was held in the right hand of a normally left handed fellow, which gives us a significant clue.'

'So much from three simple words!' exclaimed the Maharajah.

'The ink too is of singular interest,' continued Holmes. 'On first glance, it appears to be a dark blue. Closer inspection however, reveals it to be a shade of purple, which is a much rarer choice, principally used abroad. If my memory serves me, the purple is produced by the addition of an indigo paste to a gallo tannate solution, a method almost unheard of in this country.

'The letter itself is typed. It is written on a heavy stationery of a superior type produced by Jarrold and Sons up until last year. Do you see the small watermark of the J in the bottom left hand corner? They are a Norfolk based company, indicating a local connection. Watson, you will be aware that I am a minor authority on stationery and the author of a handful of monograms on the subject that are considered definitive in certain circles.'

'Yes, I said, tapping the ash from my cigarette. 'I believe you have mentioned it before.'

'I have such stationery myself,' admitted Singh, looking more closely. 'I hope that does not put me in the frame?'

'Based on the evidence alone,' said Holmes crisply, 'it tells us that the author is a person of significant means and lives locally, which puts you entirely within the frame.' Singh frowned.

'And what of the message itself? Is it Polish?' We stared at the singular type.

vpsvwil, wt xgn epby fystgsjyu xgns unmx xgn vwkk hgv epby ywrem ykyfephma jyym jy pm mey hpmwghpk rpkkysx ox mey fpwhmwhr gt mey aeswjf rwsk pm 7fj gh 7 pnrnam, w vwkk oy vypswhr mey apffewsy onmmystkx, w vwkk kypby twsam, meyh vpkl mg hykagha igknjh, xgn vwkk fpaa jy mey fpilpry phu w vwkk rwby xgn mey rsypm jgrnk, rnampbna

'It certainly appears to be Eastern European in origin, with the super abundance of the letters v and w, and initially that is where I began my enquiries. I hope you don't mind, sir, but I availed myself of your excellent library this morning before breakfast.' The Maharajah nodded his approval. 'My instinct was the same as yours; that it was perhaps Slav in root, possibly a dialect; however I found nothing to corroborate my theory. I therefore concluded it was a cipher of some description.' Singh clapped his hands and more tea was summoned.

'At first of course, it seems impossible. However there is a grammar of sorts at work, although the type is all set in a lower case. I did not know initially whether this had any significance. I then looked at the words around the numbers, which could conceivably be a date and time.

'Yes,' I cried, seeing a little sense in the code. 'Do you see the letters "pm" before the first seven? Does this tell us it is written backwards?'

'Watson,' my friend laughed gently. 'As a man of medicine, I would put my faith in no other. However in this area you are something of a novice.' I was a little taken aback by my friends' remark.

'It seems a perfectly plausible notion,' I said defensively.

'Of course it does,' agreed Holmes. 'But it also suffers from being entirely incorrect. Let us assume instead that the letters "fj" represent "pm." This gives us two letters of our alphabet. Let us make a further leap and suggest that "gh" will be the words "on." This takes us to four. Still too few to provide a breakthrough, but a positive start none the less. Let us make one more assumption, that the word "pnrnam' stands for the present month of 'August.'

'There is a single w,' pointed out the Maharajah. 'Surely an "i" or an "a"?'

'Splendid!' said Holmes. I wholly concur.' Singh flashed me a defiant look, as if we were playing a childish game of point scoring with Holmes.

'Don't lose heart, Watson,' my friend encouraged. 'What else do you see?'

'The first and last words,' I cried. 'Surely they are names!'

'Bravo!' shouted Holmes. The Maharajah looked crestfallen.

'Then it is Snitterton?' he asked, looking rather doubtful.

'Too few letters,' tutted Holmes. 'It is "Warwick." This confirms our speculation about the letter "i." Armed with this knowledge, we now have the following slightly less garbled message.' He produced a fresh piece of paper and swiftly scribbled the following:

warwick, it xou eaby pyrtormyu xous uutx xou wikk now eaby yiget ykypeants myyt my at tey hational gallyrx ox tey painting ot tey serimp girk at 7pm on 7 august i wikk oy wyaring tey aappeiry outtyrtkx, i wikk kyaby tirpt, teyn wakk to nykaons cokumn, xou wikk pass my tey packagy anu i wikk giby xou tey gryat moguk, guatabua

Holmes turned the piece of paper around and presented the fruits of his labours. 'It is tantalisingly close to a kind of sense, would you not agree?' While I continued to puzzle over the note I drummed my fingers impatiently on the breakfast table. Holmes watched them dancing on the table top with a strange curiosity. '

'Eureka, Watson!' he cried, slamming a hand down onto the table. 'You have it!' Singh and I both looked utterly baffled.

'You have an idea?' said the Maharajah?

'I have the solution,' cried Holmes. 'Quickly,' he said, turning to our host. 'Do you have a typewriter?'

'Certainly,' he confirmed. He clapped his hands yet again and a machine was produced, made by North's of London.

'The keys, the keys!' cried Holmes, rubbing his hands feverishly. He fed a clean sheet into the typewriter and started to clatter away at the keyboard. Finally the commotion ceased and my friend whipped the paper from beneath the ribbon and slid it across the table.

warwick, if you have performed your duty you will now have eight elephants meet me at the national gallery by the painting of the shrimp girl at 7pm on 7 august. i will be wearing the sapphire butterfly. i will leave first, then walk to nelson's column. you will pass me the package and I will give you the great mogul. gustavus

'My dear Holmes!' I shouted.

'How did you do it?' Singh spluttered.

'Once I had the key, it was absurdly simple. Watson here provided the vital inspiration with the dance of his fingers on an invisible keyboard. What is more, Watson was also correct when he said that the code was written backwards.'

I laid back in my chair, beaming, slowly folding one hand and then the other behind my head in a look of supreme triumph.

'This man Gustavus,' Holmes went on, 'has created a rudimentary cipher of his own devising by reversing the letters on each row of the keyboard. Therefore we begin top left of the keyboard, with "poi" representing "abc" down to the third row of letters on the bottom left with "cxz." It is an ingenious, but ultimately flawed system. The Maharajah stood up and gave my friend a low neck bow.

'Sherlock Holmes,' he said. 'I believe your skills to be unrivalled in all of the Empire. No criminal is safe while you remain alive.'

Only I would notice it, having spent innumerable hours observing his habits and mannerisms, but Holmes' eyes narrowed a fraction of an inch at this remark.

'But who or what,' I asked, 'is this great mogul?'

Singh nodded slowly. 'I believe, doctor, that he is referring to yet another diamond. The Great Mogul is a stone of nearly 800 carats. It belonged to Shah Jahan, the great Mughal Emperor. It was last owned by Nadir Shah, the ruler of Persia. When he was murdered, in the middle of the last century, all trace of it was lost.'

'Another stone!' I exclaimed. 'It is as if we are in the Valley of Diamonds.'

'And are blinded from the truth,' said the Maharajah, 'by the brilliance of their light.'

'The seventh is not until next week,' said the Maharajah. 'We have plenty of time to plan our next move.'

'I think not,' retorted Holmes, 'for if he was consistent in his methods, then the numerals would be subjected to the same treatment as the letters. This means that the rendez-vous is due to take place tomorrow, the 4th of August at 4pm. Gentlemen, we will need to return to London with all speed.'

William, the sly coachman, was waiting at the front of the house, ready to transport us back to the station.

'My heart alive!' he cried on seeing us. 'That was a short trip, Mr Holmes. Did you get what ye wanted?'

'We concluded our affairs, if that's what you mean, thank you,' I confirmed.

'I was talking to Mr Holmes,' snarled the insubordinate man.

'I would be grateful if you could take us directly to the station,' said Holmes. 'If we make good speed, we should be in time to catch the 4.15 to King's Cross.'

'Don't you worry, Mr Holmes,' William sang in his toadying manner, 'we should soon be lolloping along nicely.' We had barely passed the gates when he was off again. 'Thas a rum business that was last night. If only I could have caught those fumble fisted hoodlums, they would have got wrong off me.'

'I'm sure they would have,' said Holmes impassively. 'By the by, is that a new hat you are sporting this morning?'

'That it is,' the coachman said vainly.

'And a new cloak?'

'It is and a beauty 'ain't it? A rather fine mawkin, I make all in all, don't I?'

'A mawkin?' I queried.

'What you gentlemen might call a scarecrow.'

'Perhaps you have come into a little money of late?'

'Like I said, the Maharajah is a generous man.'

'I did not see him tip you when we arrived.'

'Must have slipped his mind.'

'You didn't perhaps take another lucrative fare?' my friend asked.

'Perhaps yesterday evening?' William did not reply and when we arrived at the station with only seconds to spare, I handed over a pair of farthings.'

'He stared at the two tiny coins in his open palm.'

'Well there's a titty-totty tip,' he complained.

'More than you deserve,' Holmes replied contemptuously.

'Go to heck, the pair of you.'

'A crook if ever I saw one,' growled Holmes as we swung our own bags onto the train.

Holmes appeared lost in thought as he gazed out of our carriage window. The sunlight burst through the rows of Scots Pines like light greeting a prisoner through the bars of his prison cell.

'What's your view on the Maharajah?' he asked.

'He strikes me as a capital fellow,' I replied.

'Trustworthy?'

'Entirely.'

'He seemed a little affronted when I asked him not to join us in London.'

'You gave him a perfectly sensible reason; that he would attract unwarranted attention.'

'And what of the paper and typewriter?'

'What of them?'

'He had stocks of the same stationery and the letter was composed on an identical typewriter.'

'How do you know?'

'Once you gave me the idea of the typewriter, of course I simply visualised the keyboard. This was enough to allow me to decipher the message. I did not need the actual typewriter to prove my theory. I wanted to see if it was a match.'

'And it was an identical match?'

'Identical.'

'The same machine?'

Holmes nodded.

'Good God,' I cried. 'Do you believe he wrote the letter?'

'It is a possibility. Did you see his face when I presented the letter in its legible form? For a fraction of a second, there was a flash of fear on his face. This was before he explained the big mogul was a diamond. Is it not possible that the great mogul may not refer to a diamond at all, but to a man?

'The Maharajah himself?'

'The very same.'

'He has made no attempt to hide the fact that he wants the diamonds,' I reasoned. 'He has saved our lives on two occasions and the entire English aristocracy can vouch for his integrity.'

'Of course, you are right, Watson,' said Holmes unconvincingly, then returned his gaze to the passing fields.

The carriage bumped along the tracks and jogged me into a light sleep. We were on the outskirts of London by the time I awoke.

'Pleasant dreams, Watson?' Holmes enquired.

'None at all,' I replied, blinking in the late evening light.

'The sign of a clear conscience,' my friend said. 'Now, let us pass a quiet evening at Baker Street ahead of tomorrow's excitement. My copy of The Strand will be awaiting my attention. '

FIFTEEN

The Rendezvous

Holmes was up unusually early the next morning. I found him at 8.30am in the sitting room, already dressed and engrossed in the folding of a sheet of red paper.

On the coffee table was a herd of no less than seven origami elephants that he had evidently just completed.

'Marvellous!' he exclaimed looking up. 'Aren't they marvellous?!' I picked one up and inspected it.

'Most ingenious; I never knew that origami was among your gifts?'

'Neither did I,' he confessed. I found a volume on the subject, The Secrets of Paper Folding, absorbed the salient points and applied them in the creation of this charming collection. 'Did you know that recreational paper-folding has only been practised in Europe since the 16th century?

'I did not.'

'Have you ever tried it yourself?'

'Well, I have been folding a copy of The Times for most of my adult life.'

'Very good Watson,' said Holmes with a thin laugh.

'Impressive though this is,' I reasoned, taking a seat opposite my friend. 'Surely there is more profitable work we can do in advance of our appointment this afternoon?'

'Such as?' he asked abruptly, apparently affronted.

'Well are we planning to go in disguise? Is there a possibility that Snitterton may attempt to make the rendezvous himself?'

Holmes completed the eighth elephant with an emphatic final crease and set it down on the table.

'My dear Watson,' he said. 'Have a little faith. Everything has been considered. What has not been revealed is the unknowable and only time can reveal the unknowable. Now what do you say in the interim to a pot of tea?'

At midday I slipped out for a bag of apples and an almond slice. I also needed to clear my head. I was still somewhat fuzzy from my encounter with the dust of the Nazim Diamond and badly needed to blow off some cobwebs. I returned a little after one o'clock to find the sitting room empty. I tried the bedrooms and called out to Mrs Hudson but the house appeared to be entirely deserted. I returned to my chair to consider my next move, idly picking up one of Holmes' paper elephants, turning it slowly to admire the handiwork. It was typical of his genius that Holmes could have mastered this difficult art so quickly and so perfectly.

Presently I noticed some ink above one of the feet. I unfolded the elephant to reveal two letters printed in block capitals: AS. I pondered these for a while. Was it an initial? I listed the cast of characters we had encountered during our most recent adventures, but none seemed to fit the bill. I was loath to spoil another of Holmes' delightful creations but by now my curiosity was aroused. I unfolded a second to reveal the letters AT. Again I struggled to think of a person who could legitimately claim the initials. It was clear that Holmes had left me a puzzle, but for what conceivable reason? I quickly unfolded the remaining elephants and laid them flat on the table. AT AS COME YOU FOUR GIRL ARE SHRIMP. It was a short message and at present made little sense. SHRIMP GIRL and FOUR were all words relating to our appointment, so I arranged these together at the end. After some trial and error, I realised I had these at the wrong end, so instead tried them at the start to produce: SHRIMP GIRL AT FOUR COME AS YOU ARE. I stared at the message, wondering at Holmes' thinking, while at the same time feeling not a little pleased that I had succeeded in unscrambling the message.

What if I had failed to find the message or deciphered this simple puzzle? Clearly Holmes had gambled that I would manage both. Respecting Holmes' wish for me not to change, I spent the remainder of the afternoon leafing distractedly through my ancient copy of the Arabian Nights, although was quite unable to concentrate. It was with some relief therefore when I finally stepped outside 221b Baker Street with my service revolver and a pair of Coxes apples in my pocket. I hailed a hansom to take me to Trafalgar Square.

As I arrived, the crowds were beginning to thin. The foyer was almost deserted as I walked out of the hot, dusty afternoon and into the cool, quiet of the National Gallery itself. The stone was as cold as the walls of a crypt. I took a moment to compose myself, entirely unsure what to do or who I was likely to meet. What possible advantage did Holmes believe he was creating by leaving me the cryptic note and denying me any sort of briefing? It seemed deliberately obscure. Above all, I was arriving empty handed. Whoever else was arriving at 4pm was expecting to be greeted by all eight ruby elephants. I felt instinctively for my revolver, but instead felt the wrong pocket. Inside was a small paper packet I had no memory of leaving, twisted shut. It was of roughly the same weight and appearance as a bag of humbugs. Was this a leftover from our encounter with Peaceheart, the mad confectioner? It seemed conceivable. I glanced at my watch. Five minutes to four. I was beginning to perspire. I was also quite conscious that I was now beginning to look suspicious. Just as an attendant began to advance in my direction, I strode purposefully towards a Turner painting and gave my best impersonation of a man genuinely interested in the man's work.

At two minutes to the hour, I realised there was no more time for procrastination. With an appalling sense of foreboding, I headed towards Room 35 and whatever fate lay waiting for me there. Sure enough, a figure was standing in front of the painting, perfectly still, with his hands joined behind his back. He wore a long purple coat and black boots. His hair was long and brown. I stopped in my tracks. Then, compelled by a sense of duty to my friend Sherlock Holmes, I pushed myself forward, feeling my heart thumping against my chest like a prisoner against the wall of his cell. As I approached, the figure slowly turned.
'Macintosh!' I shouted, with indescribable relief.
'My dear, Dr Watson! Whatever are you doing here?'
'I have half an hour to kill,' I explained quickly, 'and thought I would visit my favourite painting. Or fake, I should say. But what about you? What possible interest would you have in this copy?' His skin was sallow and dark rings circled his eyes. He was perspiring freely and dabbed at his forehead with a silk handkerchief.'
'Well,' he said. 'You know I was in the habit of visiting this

painting. Old habits die hard.' I inspected his features at close range.
'If I was to give a medical opinion,' I said. 'I would suggest that you would be better off in bed this afternoon. You are not well, Macintosh.'
'Merely self inflicted,' he said, brushing aside my concern. '"This evening's folly, tomorrow's regret," if you take my meaning?'
'Quite. Well, a little less indulgence would serve us all well,' I laughed. I glanced at my pocket watch. It was three minutes past four.
'Meeting someone?' asked Abercrombie.
'Oh, no I don't think so.'
'You look a little flustered yourself, Watson,' noted Abercrombie.
'Not at all.'
'Are you sure you are not here to meet someone?' he asked again.
'It's absurd really,' I said. 'We had a note, suggesting that someone would appear at 4pm.
'For what reason?'
'An exchange. For a pocketful of trinkets, we were hoping to take receipt of an exceedingly large diamond.'
'Quite a bargain,' said Macintosh. 'And were you here to make the exchange yourself?'
'Well,' I said, feeling there was no need to hold back, 'since the strange disappearance of Sherlock Holmes this morning, yes I am.'
'Then I suggest we make our way to Nelson's Column and conduct our business there.' I was dumbfounded.
'There is a small problem,' I muttered.
'Don't tell me here, dear boy,' he returned. 'There are eyes everywhere. Let us venture abroad.'

Macintosh strolled on ahead. An owlish looking attendant, who I felt had been watching me from the very moment I stepped inside, peered at me intently. He appeared to shake his head slightly, as if to warn me against following the critic. The entire business seemed wrong-headed and utterly confusing. I peered around in the vain hope that I would see Holmes leaning against the wall, smiling that confounded smile of his, about to tell me the whole thing was a practical joke. Holmes had a peculiar sense of humour and it struck me that it was entirely plausible that he would involve a harmless fellow like Macintosh in such a caper. The more I thought about this, the more convinced I became that this was the truth of the matter.

I stepped into a pool of sunlight and felt its reassuring warmth on my skin. Across the square, I could see Macintosh standing alone, leaning on his cane, staring directly at me. It was a little unnerving. A moment later I joined him.

'Did Holmes put you up to this?' I asked.

'You mentioned a problem,' he said, ignoring my question.

'Yes,' I replied, my blood running cold once more. 'I don't have the ruby elephants.'

He pressed his lips together and stared at me.

'Of course you do,' he said.

'I'm afraid I don't.'

'Getting cold feet, Watson?'

'Not at all,' I said.

'Then what's that inside your pocket, besides your revolver?' I felt for the package.

'Pineapple cubes,' I said, pulling out the paper bag. 'Would you care for one?' I twisted it open and extended the bag to Abercrombie. He peered inside, his face bathed in a faint reddish glow.

'Splendid!' he said, breaking into a smile. I glanced in myself to find eight ruby elephants at the bottom of the bag. He peered at my astonished expression.

'You are either one of the world greatest actors, doctor, or one of its biggest fools. I know not which.' I was still too surprised to speak. A beggar sidled up to us.

'Got any tin for me?' he croaked, baring his three teeth. 'Two pucker gents like you must be weighed down with it. If either of you went overboard, you'd drop to the bottom of the sea before someone could say Davy Jones' Locker! Let me lighten the loads on your pockets. Weak seams these modern breeches have. Very weak!'

'Shoo,' said Macintosh, taking a step away from the man.

'Yes, would you mind?' I asked.

'Very well,' he muttered, 'but don't say I didn't warn you!'

'Tell me, doctor,' said Macintosh, casting his eyes around for further interruptions. 'When did you decide to betray Sherlock Holmes?' A large bird flew past my ear and settled on the head of one of the lions.

'I beg your pardon?' I spluttered.

'Demanding wife, is it? Snitterton pays well, doesn't he?'

'I have no idea,' I said.

'Self denial is simply a method by which a man arrest his progress,' intoned Macintosh. 'A friend of mine said much the same thing. Shall we get on with it then?' He reached into his pocket and pulled out a thin envelope.

'Rather lean for a diamond,' I remarked.

'This,' he said, waving the envelope, 'is the Great Mogul.'

'How would I know?'

'That is not my concern.' He looked agitated and was now sweating profusely.

'Macintosh,' I said, raising my voice a little, 'I could not possibly surrender the ruby elephants for a piece of paper. You would make me a laughing stock.'

'Doctor,' he warned. 'You are drawing unwanted attention.' Sure enough, several passers had noticed the fractious nature of our exchange. The beggar too was skulking within earshot. Macintosh's eyes looked horribly bloodshot, beyond the worst hangover I had ever seen. I levelled with the man.

'Do they have you in their power?' For a moment he said nothing.

'Just give me the rubies,' he said sullenly.

At that moment, I heard a shriek and a flock of pigeons scattered into the sky.

A black shadow swept across the square; a sparrow hawk plucked the envelope from Macintosh's hands and shot into the air.

'No!' Macintosh cried, extending an outstretched hand.

A smartly dressed city gent brushed against him.

'Do you mind?' the businessman asked brusquely and carried on his way. The beggar reappeared beside me.

'Go away!' I shouted.

'It is I - Holmes,' he whispered, gripping my arm. 'We must leave now; we are in grave danger. There is no time to be lost.' My head reeled as I suddenly recognised the man beneath the grimy façade.

'Macintosh,' my friend urged, 'you must come with us.'

The critic's expression was one of infinite sadness.

185

'I'm afraid that won't be possible, my dear friends.'

'Why ever not?' I cried. Macintosh smiled thinly then fell forward. A silver helmed dagger protruded from his back and I saw a black stain expanding across his lilac cape.

'Heaven help us,' I cried, but Holmes was already pulling me away. We tore across the square.

'Murder!' shouted a newspaper vendor. 'Stop those men!' We bolted for our lives, Holmes proving himself quite the most athletic beggar to have plied his trade in the nation's capital. We took off down Pall Mall and then into Whitcomb Street where a carriage was waiting for us.

'Inside!' my friend cried.

The driver, a huge fellow in a dark cape shook out the reins, let out a cry and away we flew.

Holmes was pale. He slumped against the side of the carriage, holding his head.

'Suffice to say,' he said gravely, 'that did not go according to plan.' I felt my pocket.

'The ruby elephants,' I moaned, 'they're gone. It must have been Macintosh's assailant. Confound it, all Holmes.'

My friend reached into his own pocket and mechanically passed me the paper bag. I took the liberty of picking your pocket first,' he said grimly.

'But why send me alone?'

'I would have been too conspicuous. Whoever was sent would never have dealt with me. It had to be you, Watson, and you had to appear entirely honest and straightforward.'

'Then who are we dealing with. That bird. Didn't the Maharajah send us a note via similar means? He can't have had anything to do with this, surely.' Holmes did not reply. 'There are forces at work, Watson, which we have yet to fully understand. There are conspiracies upon conspiracies.'

'Poor Macintosh,' I said, shaking my head.

'The piteous fool was doomed from the moment he made a pact with the devil,' said Holmes. 'I believe he was living beyond his means and was an especially weak target. He needed the money. It was either that or blackmail. They knew we would trust him.'

'And then they planned to murder him?'

'His assailant had two targets,' muttered Holmes grimly. 'Both Macintosh and Snitterton. Our veterinarian was prudent enough to send a stooge.' Holmes leaned his head out of the carriage.

'Thank you Mycroft,' he said. 'Here will do.'

SIXTEEN

The Archangels

The next day was as fine and bright as a new penny. The disasters of the last twenty four hours seemed somehow distant, as if they had befallen perfect strangers or were something we had read about in the newspapers.

At breakfast there was no sign of Holmes. By nine thirty he had still not made an appearance and the door to his bedroom remained firmly shut. Had he finally succumbed to his fatigue after a prolonged spell of excitement? I peered out of the window. Poor Macintosh! What was to be done? Surely the police would need to speak to us. But then how much should we tell them? I felt that Holmes must be formulating a plan.

Sunlight streamed into our rooms at 221b Baker Street, illuminating the unholy mess that my friend insisted on leaving behind him. For a military man, tidiness is next to godliness and judged by this Holmes was the devil himself. The ashtray was spilling over; his papers were spread out on the rug at the foot of his armchair in a haphazard order known only to the great detective and no fewer than ten books were left open on the tables and armrests, each with its own idiosyncratic book mark: a white goose feather; a spoke from a bicycle and a single strand of red hair.

I felt there was vital work to do. But what? The day could not go to waste. After feasting on eggs, perfectly poached by Mrs Hudson, I was suddenly taken with the notion of visiting our friend Juno at London Zoo. I was intrigued to discover whether the elephant had returned to more docile habits. It was she, after all, who had begun this odd train of events.

I passed Mrs Hudson at the door. 'Would you be so good,' I asked her, 'to let Holmes know I have gone to the zoo? The Elephant House, to be precise.'
'Of course,' she said. She was clutching a large bouquet of flowers.

'How lovely,' I said. 'Do you have an admirer?' She blushed. 'They've just arrived, Doctor. No name.'
'How odd. Well, if I were you, I would accept them in good faith. I will be back at around one o'clock.'

I walked briskly along the pavement, tapping my cane to a tune and rhythm of my own making, when presently I got the sensation I was being followed. I turned briskly and looked back at the sea of bowlers, bonnets and Homburgs hoping to catch the sneak. The pedestrians swam past me like so many fish.

I set off again at marching pace, weaving through the crowd and crossing the road in an attempt to drop my pursuer. I even stopped to tie my shoelace thinking that if I went out of sight I would lose him. Still, when I set off once again, I got the distinct feeling he was back on my tail. It occurred to me of course that this was an irrational paranoia. Turning, I could not identify a single one of the four million Londoners with any malign intent. But when I walked, I could hear a pair of footsteps echoing my own. It was clearly someone highly trained, skilled in the art of concealment and subterfuge. Naturally, this brought Holmes to mind. Was this a prank of his? Was he testing me again? What would Holmes himself do to evade such a pursuer? Up ahead I saw Whittington's, the gentleman's hatter. That was when I hit upon the notion of a disguise. It was the perfect Holmesian solution. I sidled up to the entrance then slipped inside.

Only slowly did my eyes acclimatise to the gloom. I knew Mr Pettiman, the owner, slightly, and he bowed when I entered.
'Dr Watson,' he began in his own charming way, 'to what do we owe this pleasure? A new bowler for the autumn, perhaps?' He was a large, portly man with ruddy cheeks and a flattened nose, suggesting a much earlier career as a boxer.
'I was in fact thinking of something entirely different.'
'A radical!' Pettiman applauded. 'So many gentleman of a certain age become stuck in their ways. Only a few of us have the capacity for change.'
'I was thinking perhaps of a top hat.'

Pettiman winced momentarily, and held up his fingers in a gesture of exaggerated delicacy.

'Would you not consider that something of a backward step, doctor?'

'Perhaps you're right,' I said. I glanced behind me, once again feeling an uncomfortable presence. Then I hit upon it.

'The deerstalker,' I said. 'Would you have any?'

'Surely, Dr Watson that is the exclusive domain of Mr Holmes. It is a hat he has made all his own these recent years, would you not agree?'

'Then I confess,' I said quickly, 'it is a surprise present for him. The other has become somewhat dog-eared and I fear, in his fondness for it, he has become blind to its demerits.'

'What a friend he has in you!' Mr Pettiman exclaimed.

I heard the doorbell and slipped towards the back of the shop.

'Mr Pettiman,' I confessed. 'I have an inkling I am being followed. Would you be so good as to invent a white lie for me while I retire to your store room?' He gave me a wink and I disappeared behind a large green curtain concealing the entrance to the back room.

The customer spoke in a hushed tone and I didn't catch the exact nature of his enquiry. Mr Pettiman's response however was plain enough:

'No,' he affirmed in his powerful baritone, 'it's been entirely quiet all day in fact. It's this infernal sunshine. How can a man sell a hat without a drop of rain? I have a mind to switch to selling parasols.'

I parted the curtain a half inch and peered through. It was a tall, thin man in tight fitting black suit and waistcoat, a tall black hat in his hand and a monocle affixed to one eye. His face was just as thin, white and drawn almost to a ghostly degree and his nose was that of a sparrow hawk. It could only be one of the Archangels, although which one, I could not make out. He nodded in a slow and rather sinister fashion then left the shop.

'I am most obliged,' I said, remerging. 'From the moment I set foot outside 221b Baker Street, I have had the feeling I was being followed. At least now I know I am not losing my mind.'

'A strange fellow indeed,' mused Pettiman. 'But say what you like about him, he is the owner of a magnificent hat.'

Mr Pettiman took a dim view of me trying on the deerstalker. I confessed that in reality I planned to use it as a disguise.

'While of course I understand the parlous circumstances you find yourself in,' he cautioned, 'you must be aware how easy it is to put a hat out of shape.' I declined the hat box and pressed it down on my head.

'Dr Watson,' said Pettiman in a low, cautioning voice, 'I sincerely hope you resolve your current difficulties and return for a fitting of your own. A man's choice of hat is no mere trifle. It defines a man in every sense. I am not the first to say that you can tell a man's character by the way he wears his hat.' I nodded and thanked him for his consideration.

Stepping out of the back of the shop, I negotiated my way along an alley and past a pair of cats scrapping over some discarded bones. At the corner I passed another man, also dressed in a long black coat with a black topper. He was sitting on a bench holding a black cane, topped with a globe of gold or brass. I had no doubt that this was the Archangel. I pulled the brim of the hat lower on my face and hurriedly crossed the street. How had he so quickly worked his way around to the back? There was no adjoining road for a hundred yards and even then he would have had to take a long detour around the houses. It seemed nothing short of wizardry.

I hurried around another corner and I believed I heard once again the sound of footsteps echoing my own. How I wished Holmes was with me! He would have engineered an ingenious escape. As things stood there was nothing else to do except put myself into the care of a policeman before it was too late. But even if I could make it back to Baker Street, would that not bring dangers of its own? It would be like letting the lion in through the front door.

At the corner of Devonshire Place my prayers appeared to be answered. There, in all the sombre finery of his office, was a police constable ambling at that dignified pace that chills the heart of every scoundrel and blackguard in London. His hands were folded behind him, his truncheon in one of them. Occasionally irritated by their pedantry, I confess I rarely been so relieved to see a policeman.

'Constable!' I called. The man turned slowly and eyed me with immediate suspicion. He was thinner than most and had an intelligent sparkle and keenness in his expression that surprised me.

'My name is Dr John Watson of Baker Street and I believe I am being followed.'

'I see,' he said thoughtfully.

'That hat you're sporting sir,' he said in a slow, measured tone. 'Is it one you normally wear?'

'It's new,' I said quickly, glancing back along the street.

'How new?' he asked.

'Whatever do you mean?' I demanded. 'I bought it today as it happens, but how can this be of any consequence?'

'Just that it looks rather ill-fitting, sir,' he went on. 'If it's new, I would consider returning it for something closer to your size.'

'Well, thank you for your advice Constable,' I said, 'but if it's all the same to you, I would be grateful if you would escort me back to Baker Street.

'I wonder,' he said, after a pause. 'Whether you have your receipt with you?'

'My receipt?'

'Yes, sir.'

'No I do not, and what's more,' I warned him, 'I don't much like your insinuation.'

'I am not a magistrate, Dr Watson,' he said, narrowing his eyes at me in a most uncomfortable manner. 'But I can tell you that we take a dim view of petty larceny. Now would you like to tell me where you acquired this hat here of yours or am going to have to invite you to explain yourself down at the police station?'

'I obtained this hat perfectly lawfully at Pettiman's on Marylebone Road,' I said, quite red about the gills. 'Now if you don't mind, constable, I believe that my life is be in immediate danger. Would you mind if we discussed this further in a hansom on route to Baker Street?'

'All in good time, sir,' he said. 'Now tell me,' he said. 'What would you think if a perfect stranger appeared before you dressed as Sherlock Holmes and asking to be taken to Baker Street?'

I stared at him dumbfounded.

'Why, I am Holmes' closest friend,' I protested. 'I live at the same address.'

'Of course you do, sir,' he said, peering along the street himself.

As we were speaking, the tall, gaunt man with pale face and topper swept past us, fixing me with a deadly stare as he went. His eyes were those of the devil himself, black and fathomless.

'Constable,' I exclaimed. 'That's the man! Arrest him!'

'On what possible charge?' the infuriating fellow asked.

'This is preposterous!' I shouted. 'If you cannot help me, then I insist on making my own way home.' I bustled past him, before feeling his heavy hand on my shoulder.

'Not so fast, Doctor,' he said. 'I think before we progress further, a visit to Mr Pettiman's is in order.' I stared at him in disbelief.

'Please,' I said, 'I am asking you as a law abiding citizen, either take me into custody or allow me to go on my way. My sincere belief is that if we remain here, both of our lives are in danger.' The constable gave me a rum look.

'I am afraid Dr Watson, that some of this sunshine may have gone to your head. 'You are beginning to sound like a fantasist.'

It was too late. At that moment, a brougham swept past, its driver flailing his whip, pitched forward like one of the four horse men of the apocalypse. I saw the policeman topple to the ground in front of me, still with the same expression of mild amusement on his face, his throat perfectly slit. I reached for my own, for a moment wondering whether I had suffered the same fate. I spun around in terror, looking for an escape, but the carriage had already turned and was bearing down on me at a thunderous pace. The driver, shrouded by a hood, had the look of the reaper himself, his features buried in darkness. At the last moment I saw a sabre appear, flashing brilliant silver in the morning sunlight.

I awoke in a room that was perfectly dark. In fact, I could not say whether it was a room or not. I felt my head and neck, which gave some small comfort that I was not mortally wounded, or even dead, but I could not say for sure whether there was any blood or injury. I was in no pain and I was not bound or gagged. I considered for a moment that this was some sort of purgatory. I walked a few paces, feeling in front of me with my hands like a blinded man, but felt nothing. I touch the floor which was cold, smooth and slightly damp, like that of a cellar.

'Where am I?' I heard my own voice echo and die away. I tried again: 'Who are you?'

I heard my voice reverberate with no answer except its own, decaying to nothing. I stumbled forward in one direction and then another and finally fell to my knees.

'Stand up, Dr Watson,' came a voice. 'This is the hour of your testing.' It was a voice as calm as it was commanding.

'Look here,' I warned. 'Half of Scotland Yard will be bearing down on you within in a few minutes. You mark my words.' There was no answer. I listened for any sound that might orientate me: horses, carriages, people, but heard nothing that might give away my location.

'Let us bring an end to this nonsense,' I said, collecting my wits and dusting down my trousers. 'There is a right and a wrong way to do business, no matter how dark your dealings. What is it you want?'

'You know what we want,' the voice pressed.

'Quite frankly,' I said, beginning to lose patience, 'I don't. If you name your terms we can discuss this sensibly. And for pity's sake light a lamp.'

'There is no need for that here.'

There was something about the voice that was cold, but familiar.

'Have we met?' I demanded. 'Are you the man who followed me?'

There was no answer.

'Tell me your name at least,' I asked.

'My name,' he said, 'is Michael.'

''What are you?' I demanded. Feeling emboldened. 'A forger? A thief. A blackmailer?'

'I am Michael, the Archangel.'

I struggled for breath. I saw the policeman once again fall to the ground. I saw the blood on the pavement. I felt my hand once again rise to my throat. I shouted in terror.

There was a light, in the form of a single flame, at one end of the room. From the other side, I heard another voice.

'I am Raphael,' it announced and another torch was lit.

Then behind me, another: 'Uriel.' And at the fourth point of the compass: 'I am Gabriel.' I was at the centre of the four flames. In the flickering light I could now make out the figures of four men, almost identical in form. Tall, thin, pale of face, each with a top hat, a burning torch in one hand and a cane in the other.

I had by now the small comfort of knowing at least that these were mortal men of flesh and blood. But I could not fathom what they wanted with me.

'The Archangels,' I began bravely. 'Were they not guardians of all that is good? Were they not the enemies of evil?'

'Good and evil,' said Michael, in his sinister way, 'are relative constructs. Every man believes in his own just and good cause. What one man sees as abhorrent, to another is a noble act. We all have our obligations and motivations. And we have good reason to believe that you know something to our advantage. What do you know, Dr Watson, of the mountain of light?'

I was stunned into silence. Eventually, I essayed an answer.

'Is it the Biblical home of the Archangels?'

'Come now, Doctor,' said the man announcing himself as Raphael. He stepped into the light, 'now is not the time for games.'

I stared at him, recognising him as the constable I had met on the street, who I had left for dead in a pool of blood.

'But . . . ' I stammered.

'Yes, we are sometimes a little theatrical,' he admitted. 'But today you are centre stage, doctor. We are but the producers of this drama. This is your moment to shine.'

'Where am I?' I repeated.

'That is of no consequence,' uttered Uriel, immediately sounding less patient than the others.

I reached for my pocket watch and in an instant felt a hand at my throat.

Michael had leapt with the speed of a devil, throwing his torch to Raphael, who caught it in a free hand.

'My watch,' I gasped, 'I was only looking for the time.' The grip loosened a little.

'We know you are a military man, Doctor,' continued Raphael. 'We have already taken your service revolver into safekeeping.'

'The time,' I said more defiantly, 'I just wanted to know the time.'

'In here it is always night,' said Raphael. 'That is all you need to know.'

'Then you are vampires, not angels,' I said, by now, ceasing to care what became of me. 'May God have mercy on you.'

'Be that as it may,' said Michael, 'but now to our question. The Mountain of Light. Tell us what you know.'

'I know nothing!' I shouted. 'You talk in riddles. What are you, a secret police?'

'We are police of a kind; guardians of a kind too.'

'Of what?'

'If you will not speak of the Mountain of Light,' persisted Michael, 'then what of the Ruby Elephants? The ones that you were to give to Macintosh.'

'What do you know of Macintosh? Did one of you kill him?'

'He is of no concern to us now.'

I felt the heat of the flames scorch my skin then stared at the ground, thinking of Holmes. What a fool he would think me for getting into this fix.

'Come now, doctor. It is but the work of a moment. Tell us about the Ruby Elephants.'

'Very well,' I spluttered, 'but keep those flames back. I am no use to you dead.'

Michael nodded and they stepped back together in an odd synchronicity.

'The Ruby Elephant, I believe is a society of men. They met in the Punjab on the business of her Majesty's Government and the East India Company. They have all now returned to England.

'Where do they meet?' hissed Uriel.

'In London!'

A flame flashed through the air and stung my face. I felt a blinding pain in my eyes and I dropped to my knees.

'Do not insult us, doctor!' he screamed. 'Where do they meet?'

'I do not know!' I felt a boot in my ribs.

'Perhaps,' said Michael more calmly. 'You believe you are protecting someone. You are not. If it is question of trust, then we act for the very highest authority, I assure you.'

A thousand thoughts tumbled through my mind. Who was I protecting? Holmes? Surely not. The Maharajah? I barely knew him. Would I endanger his life if I revealed his whereabouts? Almost certainly. Did I wish to die to protect him? It did not seem fair... Uriel stepped forward again, his boot approaching as I lay on the stone floor. I noticed a pair of silver angels on the buckle of his boot as it swung back. There was the sound of shattering glass.

A caped figure flew through the air and the world was splintered into a thousand shards of light. There was shouting, a gunshot, then the whip and flash of the drawing of swords. A second shot was fired and for the second time that day, I believed myself to be a ghost.
'Watson!' a clear, commanding voice called through the gloom.
'My dear Holmes!' I exclaimed. He threw a revolver through the air and catching it cleanly, I felt its cold, comforting weight in my hand.
'Behind me,' he instructed. 'These ghouls have poor manners and would not hesitate to slit our throats.' I stumbled to his side, my eyes still streaming from the smoke and flames.
At the far end of the room the Archangels gathered themselves into a knot, their sabres drawn and eyes gleaming likes demons.
'I fear we shall not hold them off for long,' he warned, glancing up at the broken window behind him. Presently I noticed a stout rope hanging down.
'Up and away, Watson,' Holmes said. I wasted no time throwing myself on the line, keen not to spend a moment longer in this bear pit. I pulled myself up then turned to cover my friend's escape.
'Holmes!' I cried, 'now you.' I fired a volley into the darkness and heard the shots riccochet around the walls as Holmes swarmed up the rope. In the darkness I saw the Archangels swoop upon us like a murder of crows.

We emerged into a shabby looking street. At a glance I guessed it was Hackney and judging by the faint blues, orange and purples colouring the darkness, that it was dawn. A carriage rumbled past, laden with bags of coal and a dishevelled looking old woman trudged past with a consignment of the first editions.
'Look alive, Watson,' said Holmes, sprinting up to me. 'These men will stop at nothing until we are ghosts.' We dashed down a narrow

street, hurdling a bollard that obstructed our end of the thoroughfare, and tore past a row of tatty houses. Already we could hear the clatter of boots behind us as the Archangels gave chase. Holmes' stride began to lengthen, covering the ground like a cheetah. As a sprinter, he was technically superb. Presently, we turned a corner and found ourselves in a cul-de-sac. Holmes stopped on a pin and I had to do everything in my power to avoid a collision.

'Over the wall, Watson,' he urged and in a single bound he was up and over. I followed with less finesse.

'Holmes,' I said, 'I fear we are trapped.'

'There is always a way,' said Holmes.

We were in the small back yard of what appeared to be a keen sportsman. Beside the neatly potted plants and vegetable patch was a selection of gymnastic apparatus: dumbbells, a pommel horse and a set of parallel bars. My friend nodded, his bright eyes darting about the yard, finally alighting on the lean-to against the wall of the house. He dashed over, threw open the door and shouted in triumph.

'I knew it!' he cried. The open door revealed a pair of bicycles, each with vastly different sized wheels. Relevant to each other, one wheel was the size of a penny, the other, a farthing. 'One would have been miraculous,' cried Holmes. 'Two is a thing of serendipity. This, Watson, is the moment of our salvation. With a favourable wind behind them these machines can reach thirty miles per hour.'

'Have you ever ridden one, Holmes?' I cautioned. 'I have heard ghastly stories of young men coming a cropper on such things. Young Horatio Carr, the son of the MP almost broke his neck on one the other Sunday on the Brighton Road.'

'In the wrong hands, Watson, a child's hobbyhorse is a dangerous thing. Just do what I do.'

In the street outside, I heard the skirmishing of feet against the gravel as the Archangels reached the other side of the wall. Holmes and I silently wheeled our machines to the gate and waited for our moment. My friend pressed his ear to the wooded panel and held a finger to his lips.

'Now,' cried Holmes and kicked open the door to the yard at the same time propelling himself and his bicycle through the gateway. I followed at speed.

'Look down, you gods,' intoned Holmes as we scrambled up the step and into the saddle, 'and on this couple drop a blessed crown!' Holmes ascended like an angel into his saddle. I on the other hand had never fancied myself as a cyclist and that opinion remains unchanged. I still don't hold that it is an appropriate or dignified way for a gentleman to transport himself. I planted a foot on the peg just above the back wheel and only by some miracle found myself up and in the seat.

The fiends were upon us immediately. To see them in daylight rendered them almost absurd. All of them dressed in their identical black suits, three quarter length coats, dark, round spectacles, black top hats and canes. They were like four undertakers on a day out. Yet there was nothing comical in their expressions. They wanted only our murder. They were tightly drilled and to a man in the most perfect physical condition; each was as lithe as a panther and kept up with us with ease.

'This way!' shouted Holmes, pointing forwards like a cavalry officer. We turned into Burma Road, a wide, perfectly straight road with handsome houses on either side, and reached a terrifying speed. Still the Archangels were at our heels. 'Don't slow down!' yelled Holmes, as he took the corner into Clissold Crescent. I felt a cold rush of air at my left ear and saw a black cane land in the street ahead of me; a blade was fixed like a bayonet to one end. Another narrowly passed me on the right and I doubled my efforts at the pedals. At any moment I expected to feel a knife in my back. I followed Holmes into the bend and swerved at a most foolhardy angle, almost colliding with a hansom coming the other way. A boy on the corner whistled his appreciation and Holmes did not disappoint, lifting his hat in acknowledgement. The madness continued down Stoke Newington Church Street and then onto Green Lanes which was teeming with traffic. Somehow we managed to weave a path through the carriages and only at Newington Green did I feel that we had managed to put some safe distance between us and our pursuers. For a terrifying moment I lost sight of Holmes and was only able to breathe again when I saw him dismount at the red brick archway of

199

the new headquarters of the China Inland Mission.

My own dismount only narrowly managed to avoid coinciding with my early death. I hit the curb and flew forwards over the handlebars, landing in the forgiving earth of the freshly planted flowerbeds. Holmes watched this with his arms folded, an expression of high amusement on his gaunt and usually rather severe face. It took a moment to recover my dignity but eventually even I had to admit that the situation was not without a comic dimension.

We recovered our senses at The Edinburgh, a public house on the corner of Newington Green.
'Do you think it's quite safe to stay in the area?' I cautioned.
'In here, certainly, Watson,' he said, 'and besides, I don't think your nerves could stand another journey without something to settle them first.'
By some freak of chance, Holmes was on familiar terms with the publican, a former boxer, a fact confirmed by his handsomely broken nose.
'I won't be the last to say you are a loss to the fancy,' the gnarly landlord growled, dropping two tumblers onto the bar and filling them to the brim with some noxious liquor. 'If you wanted a return to the ring, of course I could arrange that for you.'
'I shall bear that in mind, Charlie,' Holmes twinkled. 'Now to be on the safe side, do you have a back room where my friend and I can discuss some private business?'
'Of course, Mr 'Olmes,' and if you are in any sort of trouble, 'I should be only too happy to organise some local muscle to help you out. Not that you need it with that fearsome right hook of yours.'
'You are too kind, my friend,' beamed Holmes as we were led into a dingy little room with a table and two chairs. 'And you'd better let us have two more of these, if you don't mind,' Holmes added, nodding at the drinks.
I drained my glass in a single gulp and stared into it as if some truth would be revealed.
'What can I say?' I began.
'You don't have to say anything at all,' said Holmes. 'No doubt they would have taken me too if I was strolling in broad daylight. It is not

a question of what you did or didn't do. It would have made no difference to the outcome. These are not the common or garden criminals we are used to. These are men of a quite different order.' I knew he was right.

'Nonetheless,' I faltered. 'Not many men would have attempted so daring a rescue.' I looked up at Holmes and caught his eye.

'Come now, Watson,' he said, 'you know I am not one for sentiment. You would have done the same for me.' I nodded.

'But there is just one question,' Holmes put in. 'Why were you wearing my hat?'

I felt the top of my head, realising the deerstalker must have blown away in the excitement.

'Now let me see,' proceeded Holmes, without waiting for an answer, laying his flat hands on the table. 'You were heading towards the zoo. That much I divined from Mrs Hudson. You crossed the road after Allsop Place and headed into Pettiman's. You managed to pick up a little of red paint on your trouser, do you see? It's from the freshly painted pillar box that stands on the corner of Allsop Place. By this point you realised you were being followed. Am I working along the right lines?'

'Perfectly,' I said, stinging my lips with the invigorating liquid from my second glass.

'Here you attempted a disguise.'

'Exactly,' I confirmed.

'I admire the idea, my dear Watson, but the execution was poor, very poor. If they knew who you were, then naturally they would know of your association with me.' I admitted readily to my muddled thinking. 'I would not presume to think of myself as the greater prize,' Holmes went on, 'but I am afraid to say that your choice of impersonation was somewhat wayward.'

'Enough, Holmes,' I laughed. 'I have admitted my folly.'

'You escaped through the back of the shop and down to Bingham Place, where you stopped and conducted an interview.'

'A policeman,' I said. 'At least I thought it was.'

'An imposter?' asked Holmes.

'Right again.'

'It is an old trick. In my experience the keenest villains are drawn to the theatrical arts.'

'But how did you know that was the spot of my abduction?'

'Take a look at the sole of your shoe,' he said.

A red stain was impressed there.

'Blood!' I cried.

'Paint,' corrected Holmes. 'Not only did you brush against the pillar box, you stepped into a great pool of paint that had been left behind by the careless workman.'

'Then his negligence did me a great service.'

'Quite so,' said Holmes,

'But what then?' After they abducted me, how could you possibly know our destination?'

'Because my friend, by this time, I was only a few yards behind you. I rose late that morning but on learning you had ventured out, was immediately concerned for your safety. I knew Baker Street was being watched. I followed your trail and only when I reached Pettiman's did I discover the trouble you were in. A few moments later and I would have either saved you from your ordeal altogether, or would have fallen into the same trap. In any event, I commandeered a hansom and pursued you. I lost you in traffic and it was only after exhaustive enquiries and the sharing of the best part of a pound among the drivers that I traced the address in Hackney.'

'Well I am most grateful.'

'We must be on our guard,' said Holmes. 'These men are a new breed. No one is safe until they are locked inside those fine new buildings at Wormwood Scrubs. I have already sent word to Mrs Hudson to leave for her sister's house in Margate. Baker Street for now is a death trap. But alas, that is exactly where we need to go.'

'You are incorrigible Holmes,' I said. 'But a hansom, I insist. No more bicycles.'

My friend was true to his word and half an hour later we were making good speed down the Essex Road. However, somewhere past the Angel, Holmes called out a series of complicated instructions to our driver and our route home became rather less familiar. The driver took us through one narrow thoroughfare to another until I was quite lost.

'I thought we were heading to Baker Street?' I said, puzzled.

'My dear Watson, we are,' he reassured me. 'However, I just have one or two items to collect first.'

'From whom?' I asked.

'Myself.'

Unwilling to expand on this enigmatic answer, I folded my arms and watched as one district folded into the next and huge houses emerged and disappeared. It struck me how desperate we are to make our mark on the world, to create our own great monuments of bricks and mortar. I peered in at the afternoonified front parlours and thought of Mary and the quiet and orderly life we ought to be leading.

'Here!' shouted Holmes and leapt out of the carriage.

We scurried up a gloomy alleyway between two large houses until we arrived at a set of damp stone steps. These in turn led up to a flat balcony thickly lined with moss and lichen, set against a solid brick wall. There was a single windowless door. It seemed to me a place for the worst kind of back street dealing and skullduggery and I baulked at the prospect of meeting whatever low life lurked behind it. Holmes peered at the door intensely, as if trying to open it by sheer force of will, then suddenly, as if remembering something vital, he returned to the steps, lifted a loose slab and retrieved a rusting key. I was intrigued all the more.

'I almost forgot my own hiding place,' he admitted, turning the lock and disappearing inside. 'Well don't let your shadow grow cold Watson, come on in.'

I stepped into the darkness while Holmes fussed with the lamp. There was a smell to the place that was eerily familiar; a combination of tobacco, sulphuric acid, musty books and papers, cinnamon and leather.

'Why, Holmes,' I began. 'This place smells almost exactly like...' The room flooded with light.

'Home?' my friend asked, looking entirely delighted with himself.

It was an astonishing scene. Before me, was a perfect recreation of our sitting room in Baker Street including our two chairs, our coffee table, our fireplace, even many of our books. The same wallpaper covered the walls; the same mirror adorned the wall. For a moment, I caught sight of myself walking in through another door.

'Great George's Ghost, Holmes!' I exclaimed. 'What is the meaning of this?'

'My dear Watson,' said Holmes, retrieving his stash of tobacco from his Persian slipper. 'Surely I have told you before that I have five dens hidden about the city.'

'But,' I marvelled, 'it is the same in every detail!'

'Well if it's good enough for Baker Street, it's good enough for here.' He primed a pipe and busied himself in its ignition. He vanished in a triumphant cloud of smoke. 'After all, Watson,' he continued through the fog, 'the idea is to feel entirely at home.' He collapsed into his armchair and I followed suit.

'Now,' Holmes began, 'we find ourselves in one of our most singular adventures facing perhaps our most formidable adversaries. I have a theory developing but there are several components which remain elusive. It is as if we are assembling a large jigsaw puzzle on a table. We have the outer edges; we have formed one or two scenes in the interior but it is too early to guess at the overall picture. Do you follow?'

'Quite,' I said, drawing on a cigarette.

'We know some of the key players: Snitterton, Miss Braithwaite and the mysterious Gustavus. We have joined enough pieces to get a clear picture of Snitterton and Miss Braithwaite and to know something of their characters. To my mind, they are equally dangerous. It is too early to say which of these is the principal danger or whether there is a higher power at work. We know they want the ruby elephants and ultimately the diamonds, but what is the extent of their ambitions? Where will they stop?'

'And what of these Archangels? Are they in Snitterton's power, or do they belong to another case entirely?'

'I applaud the question but I cannot yet give you an answer. As you know I dislike speculation. That is the business of the London Stock Exchange. We have a choice: either wait for the facts to reveal themselves or seek out them out for ourselves.'

The one key feature these parallel rooms lacked was Mrs Hudson. After our exertions, a bowl of her delicious stewed prawns or curried eggs would have worked wonders on our constitutions. As it was, Holmes and I had to make do with a tin of hard biscuits and a half pint of a passable claret that my friend had kept in reserve for an eventuality such as this. Fortified, Holmes went about collecting various items. From a drawer, he retrieved an identical copy of his Webley Bulldog revolver, which he unwrapped from an oily cloth. He filled the barrel then handed it to me. I also saw him find a cane and riding crop.

'If we find these Archangels enjoying tea in our front parlour,' he warned, 'then we at least ought to be ready for them.'

Miraculously, there was hot water and while Holmes busied himself with some papers, I ran a bath. An hour later and wearing a fresh collar courtesy of my friend's standby wardrobe, we were ready.

SEVENTEEN

The Castle

We were on our guard as we swept into Baker Street, but were not prepared for the sight of our front door left wide open to the street.

'It doesn't look promising, Holmes,' I remarked. 'Do you think we ought to call Gregson?'

'Not yet,' my friend said, his eyes darting up at the first floor window. We approached with caution.

'Of course it's possible,' I suggested, 'that Mrs Hudson simply forgot to close the door behind her?'

'Impossible,' said Holmes. 'She is scrupulous in that respect. No I'm afraid we have had some uninvited visitors.' Both of us reflected glumly on our respective possessions and what may or may not have been taken.

Holmes cocked his pistol and led the way up the stairs, treading softly and avoiding the fifth step and its incurable creak. The scene was as bad as we feared. Just as Holmes' facsimile rooms were reassuringly familiar, our Baker Street original was now an alien landscape. Our chairs had been upended; the mirror was broken and our books and papers were scattered across the floor. Holmes immediately checked his emerald tie pin and Persian slipper, both of which were safe in their hiding place in the coal scuttle. I looked over my own things and while disordered, curiously nothing was missing.

'They were looking for something specific,' I put in.

'Plainly,' said Holmes. 'But there is something else. I believe they were surprised.'

'By whom?' Holmes knelt down and retrieved a single hair pin from the rug.

'I have a terrible suspicion,' said Holmes gravely, 'that Mrs Hudson either did not receive my warning to leave for her sisters,' or chose to ignore it.'

'Great heavens!' I shouted. 'Then we must call Gregson. There is no time to be lost.'

'Calm yourself, Watson,' my friend warned. 'Do we really want their clumsy boots all over the evidence? Let me at least examine it first.'

This was a development neither of us had foreseen. Ordinarily Mrs Hudson was spared the perils that routinely faced Holmes and me in our adventures. We had previously thought of 221b Baker Street as a haven of safety; a refuge from the madness of the world. While neither of us spoke of it, we both knew that a terrible weight of responsibility lay upon our shoulders.

Holmes was like a hound following a scent. He stepped carefully towards the door, knelt down and retrieved another small item; a few steps further and he had found another.

'Oh, bravo, Mrs Hudson!' my friend exclaimed.

'What is it, Holmes?'

'She has left us a trail. These hair pins have been deliberately placed; they are guiding us somewhere, Watson. I have long suspected that Mrs Hudson was a student of my methods. This is the proof!' My friend was feverish in his excitement.

'Another!' he cried as he descended the stairs, 'and another!' However towards the bottom of the staircase, the trail went cold.

'Perhaps she simply ran out,' I suggested.

'Unimaginable,' said Holmes. 'She uses twenty at least at any one time.' For a moment we stood, desolate on those famous steps thinking of the consequence of our actions.

'My, my, Watson,' Holmes began, 'look at this.' He pointed at the portrait of Queen Victoria that hung from the wall directly above the place where he had found the last hair pin. He then lifted a single diamond stud earring from the floor. 'This is the final clue.'

'What can it possibly mean?'

Holmes peered at Her Majesty with a look of the greatest concentration. If I had been closer it is possible I would have heard the very whirring of his brain.

'Watson,' he said. 'What say you to a pot of tea? I suspect this will be a three pipe problem.'

Holmes made the necessary preparations. He righted his armchair, plumped a pillow and brought sufficient quantities of loose shag tobacco to within arm's reach to sustain him in his contemplation. Before him lay the portrait of the Queen and the single, stray piece of jewellery. I watched my friend as he gazed at the items, biting on his pipe, until, in the manner of a fakir, his eyes glazed over and he was lost to all other things in the world. For him, all that existed was the problem.

After clearing up in a rather rudimentary fashion, restoring a picture to the wall here, adjusting a rug there, I retired to my room with my copy of The Time Machine. Yet reading was impossible. Instead I stared out of the window thinking of Mrs Hudson and the dreadful state of affairs in which we found ourselves. Waiting seemed intolerable and every ounce of common sense told me to interrupt Holmes, call in Scotland Yard and put the whole matter in their hands. It was no longer a theoretical game of cat and mouse.

Before I had even time to finish the thought, Holmes burst in. It had been barely five minutes since I had left him.
'It's absurdly simple,' he said. 'They are using Mrs Hudson to gain access to the Queen.'
'Mrs Hudson?!' I repeated in disbelief. 'Although she is a woman of some standing, I somehow feel she would be unable to make such an introduction.'
'Not to the Queen herself; of course not,' my friend explained, 'but indirectly. You remember two months ago she received a guest from out of London; an old friend. She entertained her for three days. You remember. We were half starved. I made us supper one evening.'
'Yes,' I remember that, I said, 'your beef was inedible.'
'Of course it was,' my friend agreed. 'But I recall overhearing a conversation while I was retrieving a tin of pineapple from the pantry. It was gossip of a particular sort - the transgressions of a footman and a chambermaid. It was obvious that she was employed in some domestic capacity at one of the royal palaces.'
'But which one?'
'I have no idea.'
'Where would she be in residence at this time of the year?'
'I am afraid Watson, that in order for us to progress the case we will need to invade a little of Mrs Hudson' privacy. I suggest that we begin with her diary, which should provide us with the name of her acquaintance.'

'I feel Holmes, that in the circumstances, she would forgive the transgression.'

The diary was found easily enough; it was a small red volume, with a black band, containing the minutia of her daily life. Inside, on a date in early June, we discovered the name Lydia Woodbridge, which revived a memory of an introduction Mrs Hudson had made some time back. Her friend was a stout, practical looking woman with a relentlessly cheerful disposition and a penchant for pear drops, which gave the house a distinctive ether-like fragrance for the duration of her stay. We were just as fortunate to find a note that revealed the time her train arrived in London and which terminus: the three o'clock train from Windsor, arriving at Waterloo at 4pm.

'There it is, Watson,' my friend said, clapping the diary shut. 'They are bound for Windsor Castle.'

An hour later, we were rattling through the Berkshire countryside in a first class carriage.

'It is safe to assume Watson, that they will have at least a four hour head start on us, which means they are likely to have caught the 10 o'clock train. Of course it is possible that they took a less direct route, or indeed that Mrs Hudson is still in London. However my instinct tells me that once they had her in their possession, they would proceed directly to the castle.'

'But what do they want?'

'I believe they wish to steal an item of immense value from the Queen's household.'

'Is it possible they mean harm to the Queen herself?'

'That is entirely possible, which is why I have arranged for an inspector from the Windsor constabulary to meet us at the station. He has already sent his men ahead to the castle.'

'Great heavens, Holmes. How did you relay this message so quickly?'

'I asked Wiggins to send a telegram to Gregson.'

The ancient trees and fields of England flashed past. Meadows shone a luminous green and sheep grazed in their sleepy pastures. It did not seem conceivable that our own Mrs Hudson was now implicated, albeit involuntarily, in a plot against the Queen. The quiet villages, the bustling towns, the farmers trudging with their beasts in the fields were all unaware of the threat to the crown.

As we pulled in, I leaned out of the window and saw a deputation waiting for us at the station. Gregson himself was on the platform with a small party of local men.

'You made extraordinary speed, Gregson,' Holmes congratulated, stepping down from the carriage.

'I was fortunate to be on the right side of London and came directly.' He leaned a little closer and lowered his voice: 'I sincerely hope that the business is as serious as you have outlined. There will be considerable embarrassment if this proves to be a wild goose chase. The Queen herself has been moved to a place of safety.'

'What could be safer than the greatest castle in all of England?' asked Holmes.

'What indeed, Sherlock?' rumbled a familiar voice.

We turned and were met with the astonishing sight of Mycroft Holmes standing just behind us on the platform.

'Are we the last ones at the party?' I asked.

'So it would seem,' said Gregson.

'Sherlock,' said Mycroft gruffly, 'what were you thinking endangering Mrs Hudson like that?'

'I sent a message for her to go to her sisters,' replied Holmes, rather crossly, 'which she ignored.' He did not enjoy being challenged, least of all in public and especially by his own brother.

'You may be wondering, Sherlock, how I got here so quickly.' Sherlock smiled.

'Hair pins?' he asked.

'Precisely,' yawned Mycroft. 'I was just passing Baker Street...'

'Mycroft,' my friend interrupted, 'you hardly ever pass Baker Street!'

'I was merely planning a social call,' Mycroft explained, 'when I saw the door ajar. I found the same scene as you and of course followed the same trail left by Mrs Hudson.'

'You make quite a pair,' said Gregson. 'I should like to have met your father.' Mycroft and Sherlock exchanged a look. 'Why is it neither of you gave your talents to the police force? If we had you

210

two at Scotland Yard there would not be a single criminal at large in all of London.'

'Are we not of service enough?' asked my friend a little hurt.

'Gentlemen,' I cried, 'we must find Mrs Hudson!'

'Yes, of course,' said Mycroft, chastened.

We made our way to a pair of carriages that were waiting to take us to the castle.

'You could at least,' whispered Holmes to his brother, 'have shut the front door.'

As the afternoon turned to evening, the castle rose up like a kingdom in the clouds. The brickwork blushed a magnificent shade of puce.

'Has Miss Woodbridge been found?' asked Holmes.

'Not as far as we know,' said Gregson. 'She was in the kitchens this morning but has not been seen since.'

'A rather worrying sign,' I ventured.

'Not really,' said Gregson. 'One of her duties is to compile the royal menus, which necessitates a great deal of research around the castle. Such is the enormity of the place, if she became engrossed in a particular volume, she may not be seen for several hours.'

We entered through the Henry VII Gateway and were driven towards the Round Tower. It seemed stupendous that we were here at all.

'We must begin in the kitchen,' said Holmes. 'I believe that is where they would have gained access most easily and least conspicuously.'

We were met by a rake-thin official from the Royal Household, Horace Ampleforth, wearing a wig of tightly curled brown hair who informed us at length of his title and role. I cannot now precisely recall this, but it may have been possible that he was Master of the Royal Candlesticks. He greeted us curtly, rattled off a list of things we were not permitted to do, then led the way to the kitchens. His head was raised at an angle no lower than forty five degrees, which produced the effect of his nose pointing like a small arrow into the air. It seemed astonishing that he was able to navigate his way across the courtyard without falling over.

The doors swung open to the Great Kitchen, a magnificent, steaming hall with high wooden roof beams, ornate stone windows and the black head of a stag peering down on the cooks. Along the stone walls was a gleaming collection of copper pots. One of the staff stepped forward from the fog, an emaciated woman with crimson cheeks who looked herself as if she was in need of feeding.

'Have you found her?' she demanded, rubbing her thin, red-raw fingers together. There was an intoxicating smell of roasting meat in the air and we could barely hear for the clash of knives, clatter of spoons and the bubbling of a score of saucepans.

'Not yet, madam,' said Gregson. 'But we are doing everything we can. These gentlemen are here to assist.'

Mycroft peered over her shoulder, his eyes gleaming at the delicious dishes being prepared.

'We have a banquet for 160 this evening,' the cook went on, 'and we barely have a recipe to work from. We have resorted to my roast hare, tripe and onions, cider jelly and apricot charlotte. Beyond that, we are at sixes and nines. If Mrs Woodbridge is not found, we shall be serving bread, butter and bow wow mutton to the King of Denmark.'

'When did you see her last?' asked Holmes.

'This morning at eleven,' she sighed, repeating herself. 'She said she was going to the royal library.'

'Was anyone with her?' my friend pressed.

'A woman. I sincerely hope it was the supplier of the grouse we have been waiting for.'

'Brown hair, five foot six?'

'Yes, that's her.'

'Did either appear flummoxed in any way?'

'Flummoxed, sir? We are all flummoxed here, from the moment we wake to the moment we collapse. There is not a moment of peace on God's Earth.'

'Thank you,' said Holmes. 'Rest assured, we shall find her.'

'If you don't, it will not be me walking into St George's Hall empty handed.'

We made our way with all speed to the library, led on by the supercilious royal staffer. His legs moved with astonishing swiftness, while the upper half of his body remained almost perfectly still. Mycroft was suffering with the pace, while Sherlock hopped like a sprite as we neared our destination. All about us was sensational opulence; great chandeliers hung down like baubles of light and the works of the old masters gazed on.

The library was a place of unexpected light. Sunshine streamed in through the tall, elegant windows and reflected on the white stucco ceiling. Holmes gazed out of the window to the spires of Eton College beyond, the birthing pool for so many of our prime ministers and men of state.

'I fear,' he said, 'despite the great learning contained within these walls, my friend, our answer does not lie here.' He peered at his shadow cast against the floor. 'Tell me,' he asked Ampleforth, 'is Mrs Woodbridge trusted within the household?'

'Implicitly,' he confirmed. 'In fact, I would go further. In my opinion her lobster cutlets and marbled blancmange are valued by the Queen more highly than half her fortune. This has given her a special place in the Queen's affections, perhaps second only to the Munshi, her faithful Indian companion.'

'Which of the Queen's jewels are held here?'

'The royal collection is too vast to contain in a single sentence, nor is it curated in a single location.'

'Let me put it another way,' said Holmes. 'What jewels are closest to the Queen's heart?'

'Again, that is an impossible question.'

'I applaud your need for precision,' laughed Holmes. 'Please let me be more direct. Which is her favourite diamond and her favourite ruby?'

'Then that is perfectly simple: the diamond known as the Koh-I-Noor, and let us not speak of that, and the Timur Ruby, now known to be a spinel. In fact I happen to know that the Timur Ruby necklace has been laid out in readiness for this evening's state banquet. The Queen is planning to wear it; or rather she was planning to wear it. As things stand, an international incident appears inevitable. We already have Christian IX of Denmark demanding an explanation. We have confined him and Queen Louise to their rooms.'

'Are all of the exits to the castle being watched?' asked Mycroft.

'Of course,' said Gregson, 'even the Hundred Steps. We have men at every gate.'

'Then our answer lies in the Queen's Private Apartment. I believe our villains may still be within the castle walls.' We bustled across more lawns and courtyards.

'This is all highly irregular,' complained Ampleforth.

We spiralled up another set of stairs until we stood in front of the door to the Queen's Royal Bedchamber. The equerry stepped forward and knocked three times on the door. While we waited for a response, the Holmes brothers occupied themselves with the study of some minute indentations on the carpet immediately in front of the door.

'I would say four men of average build,' said Holmes. 'One is walking with the aid of a cane.'

'Nonsense, Sherlock,' tutted Mycroft. 'It is two men, one walking with a cane and two women.' We stared at the perfectly ordinary looking carpet. To my eyes, there was simply nothing there.

'Well whoever was in here has since departed' muttered Holmes. 'Do you have a key, Ampleforth?'

'To the Queen's Royal Bedchamber? Are you quite mad?'

'Then we have no choice but to force the door.' The man looked aghast.

'I won't stand for it,' he shouted. 'You would swing for less.'

'Then we will have to take that chance. Mycroft, would you be so good as to lend me your shoulder?' Ampleforth threw himself in front of the door.

'You will have to get past me first,' Ampleforth said defiantly, folding his arms. Just then we heard what sounded like muffled cries from inside the room.

'Heavens!' shouted Ampleforth, his ear to the wood. He thumped his fist against the door. 'Lady Catherine, is that you?' The sounds grew louder.

'Who is it?' Gregson demanded.

'Lady Catherine Crebble, The Mistress of the Bedchamber,' said Ampleforth. 'She must have stayed behind when Her Majesty was taken to safety.'

Gregson cupped his hands and called through the wood: 'Can you unlock the door?' he asked.

'If she could, I believe she would have done so my now,' reasoned Holmes. My friend produced one of the hairpins he had retrieved from the staircase at 221b Baker Street.

'Ampleforth,' he said, dropping to one knee and fiddling with the lock, 'let me see if I can spare you the gallows.'

'Why,' he said haughtily, 'You are little more than a common cracksman. It is you I should hand over to Scotland Yard.'

'I am Scotland Yard,' said Gregson. 'Get a move on, Holmes.'

There was a click and all at once we tumbled through the door: Holmes first, followed by Gregson, Ampleforth, myself and finally Mycroft, who collapsed heavily upon us all. It took some time to extricate ourselves from each other's limbs. Ampleforth adjusted his toupée.

'Lady Catherine!' he cried again and ran towards the woman who was gagged and bound to a chair at the centre of the room. She was a handsome, formidable woman of forty five. Her flame-coloured hair was swept up in a mass of curls and she held up her head in defiance. Ampleforth fumbled with the gag and finally succeeded in removing it.

'Unhand me!' the woman cried.

'Are you hurt?' he fussed.

'That is no concern of yours,' she fired back. 'Now loosen these bonds and be quick about it.' Gregson stepped forward and slit the ropes with his pocket knife. Lady Catherine rose imperiously to her feet.

'A half an hour ago and you would have been of some assistance. Now you are merely a troupe of fools.'

'Please tell us exactly what happened,' instructed Gregson, drawing a notebook from his pocket.

'Give me one good reason?' she asked, folding her arms. 'For all I know, you are part of the same rabid mob. I would be mad to trust another man so long as I live.' She turned her face away.

'The taller man entered the room first,' said Holmes, surveying the room.

'Followed by Mrs Hudson,' continued Mycroft.

'Then Miss Woodbridge, followed by the second man,' my friend concluded.

'Mrs Woodbridge made an attempt to burst free,' Mycroft said, 'and then ran towards the bed. She banged her leg against the bed frame and dropped this.' He stooped and picked up a bracelet.

'The taller man took a bite from an apple,' said Holmes, with a surprised tone. He picked up the remains of an apple from the bowl and examined the tooth marks. 'He should see a good dentist when all this is over.'

'He then asked you,' said Mycroft calmly, 'where you had hidden the rubies.'

Lady Catherine peered at him with a deep suspicion, tempered with a growing astonishment.

'You told him that he would have to kill you first,' said Holmes. A smile grew on his face. 'Then I do believe that they turned you upside down and shook you.' The woman's mouth widened a little.

'An outrage!' she cried. 'It was an outrage and every word you have said is true.' She clenched her fist and raised it quivering to her mouth.

'I don't know who you are but you are late. You are too late! Our dear Queen may be safe, but her precious Timur Ruby is lost! It is lost! She will never forgive me. I hid it as best I could and would have defended it until the last, but now, it is gone. She will be inconsolable.'

'But what of the two women?' asked Gregson, somewhat dumbfounded himself. His pencil hovered above his pad and I noticed he had not yet written a single word. Lady Catherine gestured towards the window.

'They bound me, then opened the window. For all I know, they are still on the roof. Mrs Woodbridge I know. She was brave, so very brave. She told them they would feel a stretch upon their necks before the month is out. The other woman I did not know. But she was even finer. She told them that there was a man who would find them. This man, she said, was like no other who had ever lived. He had a nose like a beagle; a mind like Aristotle; the body of one who had conditioned himself to withstand any assault. He could live for days without food; spend a week without sleep. His senses, she said, were as honed as those of a spider. She told them that they had only days to live.' My friend listened to this description with the keenest

216

of interest.

'Would you mind,' asked Mycroft, 'if I finished this apple?'

Gregson ran to the window and threw open the shutters.

'Not a trace,' he said, peering around. And yet the roof is sheer. No one could climb down from here.'

'Perhaps they had ropes,' asked Ampleforth.

'Well if they did, I did not see them,' said Lady Catherine.

'But what did you hear?' asked Holmes. She paused.

'It was the sound,' she said slowly, 'like the breath of a dragon.'

Holmes and I stared at each other.

'A balloon!' we shouted.

EIGHTEEN

The Scarred Man

We returned to Baker Street to consider our position. Scotland Yard had committed everything to the case and the Queen herself had declared that the safe return of Mrs Hudson and Mrs Woodbridge was the national priority. She said nothing of the Timur Ruby or Koh-I-Noor, but the implication was there that any inspector returning empty handed would find his career severely limited. I was all for joining the search ourselves. Holmes however was convinced that the best policy was to stay at home. 'If they want something,' he reasoned, 'they will know where to find us.' Sure enough, half an hour later there was a knock at the door. I re-entered the sitting room clutching a card.

'It appears to be an entirely new case,' I said, somewhat crestfallen. 'A gentleman has travelled from Suffolk. He has an injury to his face and I have told him he should see his own doctor rather than call here. He then told me that he needs to see you at all costs.'

'Did you catch his name?

'A Thomas Featherstone,' I said, glancing at the card. 'He is the manager of the Hixstead Estate.'

'Well, we have a doctor in the house and he can tell me his business while you look him over. Why not let him in?' I cast a disapproving eye around the room, still in some disarray. 'Really Holmes, we should make some effort in here.'

The man was a tall, broad fellow of fifty with thick brown hair with a widow's peak and ruddy cheeks. His teeth were widely spaced like yellow pegs and he had an unusually long chin, giving him something of a Mr Punch demeanour. A livid scar ran across his face diagonally from his chin to his forehead. His suit was of heavy tweed, expensively made, but which had seen some wear.

'You have had an argument with a riding crop,' I see, said Holmes. 'Please take a seat and my friend, Dr Watson, will be only too glad to take a look.' The man brushed this offer aside.

'Then a cigarette?' He accepted one without comment and sat down on the couch. Holmes and I exchanged a look.

'Please state the particulars of the case, Mr Featherstone, leaving out no detail.'

'My master is Gustavus Wyndham,' he began. 'Perhaps you have heard of him?' My friend suppressed a smile.

'The diamond magnate?'

'The very same,' confirmed Featherstone. 'It is two years since we returned from Kimberley, on the Cape Colony. Wyndham made spectacular gains from his stake in the diamond mines. His company extracted no less than 200kg of diamonds from the Big Hole. He was a hard man, but fair in his own way, and paid his employees well, myself included. He was often to be seen at the Big Hole himself, swinging his pick with the other men, and earned their respect by working the same hours as them, drinking from the same canteens and sharing his bread and cheese. He built accommodation for his workers and provided schools for their children.

'As time wore on, however, I believe that he began to tire of the business. It was all too easy. There were months when the diamonds came out of the ground as easily as flint. But he never found a diamond in size or brilliance to match the Eureka or the Star of South Africa. Increasingly, he flew into rages, chastising his managers for failing to find the diamond that would make him truly great.

"How is it," he asked them, "that children have found the greatest diamonds on Earth, and yet my managers, some of the most well paid men in Africa, bring me pebbles and stones?" He would throw them out, then turn over the tables. He stopped visiting the mines. The schools fell into disrepair. He slashed the wages and the families began to despair.

'One by one, he fired the managers and the men began to leave of their own accord to work for Rhodes or Rudd, more constant employers, or even to take up on their own. Only I stayed by his side, hoping he would see sense and bring us back to a more business-like footing. One morning I went to the office and found it closed. This was unprecedented. Even in the darkest days, Gustavus Wyndham was always the first in without fail. Then a boy came running up to me, saying that he had seen him heading to the hole with a cart laden with dynamite. I rode over as quickly as I could, but had not reached it when I heard a huge explosion. It was as if there was an earthquake. A cloud of rock and ash rose high above the mine and when I arrived, I believed he was dead. His face was bloodied beyond recognition. If it had not been so early in the day, I believe many men would have died. As it was two other miners were injured. One lost a leg.

'After this, there was no future for him in Africa. De Beers was formed and they squeezed us out. Few would do business with us. As for Wyndham himself, although he survived, he was blind from the day of the accident. It was many days before I could get any sense out of him, but it was clear that he had taken it upon himself to find the diamond he was dreaming of. After he paid hefty compensation to the injured men, he sold up at a greatly reduced price and we returned to England in ignominy. Despite his setbacks, Wyndham was still in possession of a considerable fortune. He acquired a magnificent house and estate from a Suffolk Earl who had squandered his own wealth. He shed most of the staff and shut up an entire wing of the house. He continued to employ me to manage the estate and keep the world away from him. He is generally a sullen man, but prone to fits of great excitement followed by rage and then depression. He still talks of finding the diamond.'

'A fascinating story,' noted Holmes who had been listening intently, his fingers joined together. 'But none of this explains how you found the butler dead in his office.' Featherstone rose to his feet in astonishment.
'What else do you know?' Featherstone demanded. 'How do you know this much?'
'Simplicity itself,' said Holmes. 'You have two identical sets of keys in your pockets. Each is heavy, and ordinarily no man would carry both. I therefore surmised that you are holding another man's keys. From what you have told us about the house and estate, it would be the butler who held the other set. You also have the butler's accounts book in your pocket. I have seen this type of stationery a hundred times in the great houses of England and no butler who values his position would ever let it out of his sight. My third clue was your un-ironed shirt. The household is in disarray.'

'But still this could not explain how you know the man is dead?'

'It was your own grim face which told me this. I know the look of a man who is confronted with a dead body and who harbours a terrible secret.' Featherstone hung his head and shook it a number of times, as if hoping to wake from a nightmare.

'You found the body did you not,' continued Holmes 'and confronted Wyndham. His reply is written across your face.'

'Mr Holmes,' said Featherstone slowly, 'I have heard talk of your methods and your powers of deduction, but it is another thing to witness them at first hand.'

My friend beamed, and only I knew how much he enjoyed the flattery despite his protestations to the contrary.

'Nonsense,' said Holmes. 'It is a simple matter of observation. If the evidence is before you, the only work left to do is put it in a comprehensible order. And as my brother Mycroft knows, having the information is only half the struggle. It is the practical application of the knowledge where the difference can be made.'

Holmes drew thoughtfully on his cigar.

'Tell us exactly how you found the butler.'

'He was in his office, as you say, at his desk and slumped in his chair. My first thought was that the man's heart had given way. And yet he was an active man who walked five miles a day. He was not yet sixty and had not missed a day's work in two years.'

'Was there anything on the desk?' pressed Holmes. 'Any paper that might give a clue to what may have precipitated this collapse?'

'There were papers everywhere,' said Featherstone. 'Which was entirely out of character. Mr Brillington was perhaps the most ordered man I have ever encountered. All of the papers were all of a domestic nature. Nothing remotely out of the ordinary. I did however find this at his feet.' Featherstone reached into his pocket and retrieved a single monocle. 'He did not wear one,' said Featherstone. In fact, to my knowledge, the only man who affected a monocle, despite his blindness was Mr Wyndham himself. I confronted Wyndham and asked him straight out what he knew. It was then I received this lash across my face. For a man with no sight, he had a deadly aim. For all I know, the matter has a simple explanation. But that is not perhaps how it will look to the police. That is why I came to you.'

'Your case certainly has features of interest,' said Holmes. 'Is everything as you left it?'

'Exactly,' said Featherstone.

'And what of Wyndham himself?'

'After the altercation he returned to his room and locked the door, I believe overcome with remorse. I have endured similar behaviour in the past. The pattern is that he leaves me a gift of sorts and the matter will not be discussed again. No doubt he will assume that I will deal with the incident and protect him as I have always done. He has his own kitchen annex and is entirely self sufficient.'

'Just a few more questions,' said Holmes.

'Of course.'

'Mr Brillington; does he have a family?'

'He is a bachelor with few close friends.'

'And the other staff?'

'There is only the gardener, the stable boy and I. None of these others live in the house itself.'

'That certainly buys us some time,' said Holmes.

'Then you will take the case?' asked Featherstone, sitting forward with an earnest look about him.

'Naturally,' said Holmes. 'But one thing more. Have you seen Wyndham associate with any unfamiliar men, four to be precise?'

Featherstone glanced at me then looked back at Holmes.

'No,' he said, not entirely convincingly, in my view. Holmes glanced at his pocket watch.

'Gentlemen,' he announced, we still have time to catch the four o'clock train to Bury St Edmunds. Watson, there is a chance we will miss the last service back to London, so pack what you need for a trip to the country and let us be ready in ten minutes.'

We had no trouble finding a growler and soon found ourselves bumping down Marylebone Road towards King's Cross. Presently, we swerved from the main road and darted down a side alley, into another and like so many occasions, within the space of ten minutes of leaving Baker Street, I had entirely lost my bearings.

'There is an expert I wish to consult briefly,' Holmes said by of explanation. The carriage slowed and Holmes let himself out.

We were standing outside Crabtree's shop. I had never seen it before and did not even recognise the street. The walls were painted black, the window was also blackened and across the door was the legend, in a minute superscription: Crabtree's Lenses. Holmes pushed open the door to the accompaniment of a single ting from a tiny bell. As we entered the grotto, I felt as a child might, stepping into a house of wonders. All about me was shimmering glass: a thousand monocles hung suspended from the ceiling with gas light glinting from each one. They winked and glistened as they slowly revolved this way and that, never quite catching the light in the same way. It was as if we had walked into a rainstorm and the rain had stopped in mid air.

As the breeze blew through the open door, several hundred of these monocles began to chime together. And it was in this sweet cacophony that our small, bespectacled friend appeared on the other side of the counter. He was barely tall enough to see over the top, but on seeing the towering figure of Holmes his small eyes lit up.
'Mr dear Mr Holmes,' said Crabtree, lifting his counter slightly and walking beneath it into the shop. 'What a pleasant and unexpected surprise.' He was clearly never more comfortable than on home soil.
'There is talk,' he said, addressing Featherstone, 'of the monocle falling out of fashion. However I can see that you are gentleman of impeccable taste. That much is evidenced by your choice of Mr Sherlock Holmes as your friend.'
'Crabtree,' said Holmes, 'there is none other like you in all of London. Your single minded dedication to your craft, to the art and science of the single lens is a credit to you. There is nothing you do not know about the monocle.' Crabtree blushed and bowed low, so as almost to disappear. 'We have come on an urgent matter,' said Holmes, moving to business. 'Mr Featherstone, if you would be so kind as to produce the monocle you found in the butler's parlour.' The man placed it in Crabtree's outstretched palm. He received it as solemnly as a communion host. The optician bustled to his counter and searching with his hand on the surface felt for a magnifying glass. He let his two monocles dangle on their cords.
'Gold,' Crabtree muttered. 'Not more than five years old. Not English.' He squinted and continued to mumble to himself. 'A darker

lens than you would find here. South African I would say.'

'Excellent,' said Holmes. 'You are worth your weight in gold sovereigns.'

'Then I would be only too happy to accept them,' Crabtree said, returning the monocle to Featherstone and rubbing his hands together. 'You know how much I love an adventure, Mr Holmes,' he added. 'Could you not give an inkling of what's afoot?'

'Alas, not yet my dear Crabtree,' sighed Holmes. 'You find us at the very crux of our case. We are heading to Bury St Edmunds on the four o'clock train to settle a matter that may have far reaching consequences.'

'And you could not use my powers once again on your adventure? I would only be too happy to join you and provide what service I can. You will know how quiet it can become in a specialist trade such as mine and in a backstreet such as this.' He looked a little crestfallen, peering around the walls of his shop. The monocle trade, I do not mind admitting, can at times become, well, rather monotonous.'

'Your services rendered so far have acquitted you well enough,' said Holmes. 'I have no doubt that if ever the day comes when Dr Watson chooses to chronicle the case, he will not forget you in his account.'

NINETEEN

The Man with the Diamond Eyes

It is difficult now to recall my precise feelings as we sped once again into the east on the 4.24pm from King's Cross. Although I could not know it at the time, it felt that we were nearing the end of our adventure, perhaps even all of our adventures together. We were rushing towards some final fate; good or ill.

I reflected on my role in this singular drama. In many ways, I had simply been carried on successive waves of events: dropped by one and picked up again by another. At times I had plunged beneath the surface, tumbled helplessly on the ocean floor, only for my companion, Sherlock Holmes of 221b Baker Street, to seize my collar and haul me back up again. How much Holmes himself was carried on the same waves and how much of the course he steered himself was impossible to say. The difference was how he faced them. While I went under, he appeared to ride effortlessly above the swell, gaining a view of the sea all around us. He seemed to know where each new wave would form, when it would reach its zenith, and how it would break before it reached the shore. His was an extraordinary gift of observation enhanced by intuition, and even, though he would never care to admit it, a little clairvoyance. Foresight, instinct; call it what you will, but at times it seemed my companion was possessed of superhuman powers. He was a man who might, if he had wished, have had anything he wanted, had he not been consumed by the art and science of crime, its detection and punishment. He pursued each case with the doggedness of a scientist determined to solve a seemingly impossible problem. Whether he did this simply to amuse his overactive mind, or was compelled by some inner moral compass, I do not believe I will ever discover. However, the radiance of his mind was beyond doubt. It had a tremendous, almost physical presence. It was like a glow of a lighthouse in a storm. When all was lost, Holmes shone brightest.

We had a compartment to ourselves. Holmes and I sat opposite each other at the window with Featherstone next to me, his arms folded, staring straight ahead. As was his habit on such journeys, Holmes spent most of his time with his nose in The Times until we were well into the Essex countryside.

'The youth are rising in the north,' my friend remarked looking up from his paper. 'Have you heard of this disturbing trend of scuttling?' I shook my head. 'Gangs of young men, alienated by their work, are at war with each other. They give themselves exotic names such as the Bengal Tigers and the Angel Meadow Lads. They take to the streets and attack each other with the heavy buckles of their belts. There appears to be little good reason beyond boredom and lack of purpose.'

'They should box, for heaven's sake,' I put in, 'or try a walk in the hills. Then there is a mountain of exciting literature.'

'Not everyone spends their leisure time like you,' Holmes said. 'But regardless, these gangs are the breeding ground for a new criminal class. You mark my words, gentleman. This needs to be stopped or the country is at risk of collapse.'

The station at Bury St Edmunds was a fine, mid-century, red brick building. Two magnificent towers flanked the tracks. It seemed a wonderful thing that such embellishment could be found at a simple country station. As we pulled in, the sky darkened and a thin rain began to fall.

We found a hansom easily enough and took off through the bustling streets until the town was left behind. We drove through a forest, catching the occasional flash of a deer through the trees. We came then into a pretty village, each house set well apart from the next with colourful gardens. Finally we reached the imposing black gates of the Hixstead Estate, bolted shut. On either side of the gate were stone columns, each topped with a stone pineapple: a touch of the exotic. Featherstone dropped down and unlocked the gates himself, waving us through, before securing them again. He rejoined us on the other side. As we made our way down the drive, all trace of summer seemed to vanish from the land. We passed one dead tree after another, each twisted in horrible fashion, or else split by lightning. A bird of prey roosted in the upper branches of a dead beech tree while a few desultory sheep nibbled at the thin grass.

'The estate,' Featherstone admitted, 'has fallen into some disrepair.' We felt it better not to concur. 'Just a word of warning, gentlemen: do not expect a warm welcome from Wyndham.'

The house was an extraordinary construction: an octagonal tower adorned with a frieze of stone carvings of classical inspiration. To this folly, a wing had been added at each side. Every window was shuttered and the place gave the impression of being entirely deserted. Foliage grew freely between the brickwork and an unmistakable air of neglect hung about the place.'
'If you don't mind,' our driver said, casting his eyes up at the grim facade, 'I will take my leave of you now.' Featherstone fetched the stable boy who was loitering by a wall and handed him the keys to gate, with instructions to return after he had let the man out of the grounds.

We entered by a side door and immediately the house announced itself as a dismal place. The smell of damp hung in the air and notwithstanding the month, it was bitterly cold. Many of the statues and sideboards were covered, as if the house had been shut up for the season. Featherstone led the way down the corridor, holding a dim lamp ahead of us.

Presently, we found ourselves in a large drawing room. A coffee pot and cup lay unwashed on the table, showing signs of recent habitation but in every other respect it was more like a museum of curiosities than a room in a house. Even in the poor light, my eyes leapt from one extraordinary object to another. A large chandelier hung from the ceiling and Featherstone fiddled with a mechanism that eventually succeeding in illuminating it. In its glow we gazed about the chamber in much the same way as grave robbers may once have gazed upon the chambers of the great pharaohs. On the wall were two clocks, one showing London time, the other, South African. Examination of the second hands showed that both were running backwards. In a glass cabinet was a stuffed pigeon, distinguished from the mundane in that it had two heads. In another cabinet was a ghoulishly misshaped skeleton, purporting to be that of a mer-man.

'A regular house of horrors!' remarked Holmes. 'But pray, Featherstone, take us to the true horror: the scene of the crime.' We filed out and followed him down another dimly lit corridor.

'The paintings, Holmes,' I remarked, stopping suddenly, 'look at the paintings!'

Along the walls were canvasses, housed in heavy gilt frames. Beneath each was the name of the work and the artist. But it was the paintings themselves that astonished. Each one had been painted perfectly black.

'A singular business,' murmured Holmes. 'And yet one that has a perfectly simple explanation. I believe that Wyndham thinks that if he cannot see these great paintings, then no one shall. The world is as blind to them as he is. Am I right.'

'Perfectly correct, Mr Holmes.' said Featherstone, shaking his head.
We finally arrived at the butler's office.

'I must prepare you gentlemen, for an unwelcome sight.'

'I assure you,' said Holmes, 'we have seen worse.'

Featherstone pushed open the door and held up the lamp. The butler was slumped forward, his arms hanging down straight and apelike, his knuckles almost brushing the floor. But his head, which rested on the desk, was turned to us, his eyes and mouth wide open. His face had a horrific white pallor, as if he had died in a moment of appalling shock.

'This,' said Featherstone, 'is exactly as I found him. I would say he was surprised.'

'An understatement,' pronounced Holmes. 'Could we have a little more light in here?' he requested. Featherstone fiddled with the gas and the room was filled with a pale, yellow light.

Holmes stepped nimbly over several of the papers scattered across the floor. He lifted one carefully between thumb and forefinger and showed it to the man.

'What does this relate to?' he asked.

'Nothing more than household accounts,' said Featherstone, glancing at the sheet. He scrutinised it rather more carefully. 'It is a bill for laundry.'

'The candidates for this person who surprised him,' suggested Holmes, 'are rather few in number are they not? The stable boy, the gardener or Mr Wyndham himself. Besides you, of course.'

'Generally speaking,' the manager went on, 'the gardener and the boy are not permitted inside the house and they do not have a key.'

'Then my list becomes shorter still.'

'There is a wound to his head,' Featherstone pointed out.

Holmes peered carefully at the butler's body. 'He is a large man. I suppose it is possible that he fainted and struck his head against the table. But there would be hardly enough force to kill him.' My friend continued his inspection. 'There is a tear in the back of the man's jacket,' Holmes observed. 'He is an otherwise impeccably turned out fellow. How could that have happened?'

'I have no idea,' said Featherstone.

'I can't imagine,' my friend continued, 'that this is something he overlooked when he dressed this morning.' My friend peered at the small rip in the fabric and carefully lifted the flap of material. The white shirt beneath was also torn and a section of the man's skin was revealed, a horrible purplish red colour.'

'What is your theory, Featherstone?'

'I believe that Mr Gustavus Wyndham, sadly, has finally taken leave of his senses and murdered this poor man. It could have been done on a whim, over some trifling task left unfinished. As I have already said, he has a fiendish temper and I found his monocle beside the body.'

'I see,' said Holmes. 'Well I think it is time we met this friend of yours.'

We returned along the corridor towards the drawing room. Holmes appeared to drag his heels a little, which was unlike him, and followed at the back of the group. As we re-entered the chamber, I marvelled again at the bizarre paraphernalia that filled the shelves and sideboards. An ashtray fashioned from the upturned shell of an armadillo contained a collection of coloured birds' eggs. A stuffed badger stood on hind legs in the corner, thoughtfully smoking a pipe. It was both unpleasant and tasteless. The air was still and thick with dust and I felt a terrible urge for fresh air. Preoccupied as I was, therefore, I had entirely failed to notice the man sitting in the armchair bent over a draughts board. I could not see his face, but it was immediately clear from his hair and demeanour that this was the same blind millionaire we had met at Lords Cricket Ground. He did not look up from his game.

'Welcome,' said Gustavus Wyndham. 'Tell me, do any of you play draughts?'

'On occasion,' my friend replied, joining us.

'Then take a seat.' It was only at the second glance that I saw that each of the pieces was a diamond; on one side pure white stones, on the other, brown.

Holmes pinched his trousers at the knee and dropped into the empty chair opposite the man.

'Your move,' said our host. He touched a hand to the gold rim of his dark tinted spectacles.

Holmes, playing black, analysed his position, then moved a piece.

'I am here at the invitation of your employee, Mr Featherstone.'

'Is that so?' asked Wyndham.

'What do you think, Tom? Can he beat me?'

'Impossible to say,' Featherstone replied.

'I have come to provide an opinion on the matter of your butler, Mr Billington.'

'A very fussy man, wouldn't you say, Tom?'

'If you say so Wyndham,' muttered Featherstone.

'Well I do say so.'

'Tell me,' asked my friend. 'How is it you can play draughts, despite your handicap?' Wyndham did not reply, instead continuing to scrutinise the board. Presently, he raised his head and removed his glasses.

'You see, Mr Holmes,' he said, calmly. 'I don't see it as a handicap.'

I was aghast. It was not the fact that this man was injured. It was the embellishment he had made to his damaged face. In the hollow of his scarred eye sockets, Gustavus Wyndham wore a pair of large diamonds. Holmes appeared unruffled.

'What can you tell me about the butler?' asked Holmes.

'That the man is a fool. That he cannot make a decent gin and tonic. What else do you want to know?'

'I want to know how he died.'

Wyndham returned a hand to his knee.

'Tom,' he said, slowly. 'Is this true?'

230

'We found the body,' Featherstone answered.

'When did you find it?' Wyndham demanded, rising to his feet. 'Why was I not informed? Perhaps this is why fresh clothes did not appear this morning and the reason he has been ignoring my bell all day. What is the meaning of this?'

'I thought perhaps you would like to explain,' said Featherstone folding his arms. 'Mr Holmes has seen what I have seen and the evidence appears conclusive.' Wyndham appeared genuinely shaken.

'The man was a fool, yes,' he murmured, 'but a well meaning one.' Featherstone sloshed some brandy into a glass.

'Drink this,' he said, planting it in Wyndham's hand.

'Do you mean to say,' the older man said, 'a murderer has been at large in my house and no one has had the decency to tell me?'

'I think we can dispense with the play acting, can't we?' said Featherstone. 'Of all your talents, I was unaware that amateur dramatics was among them.'

'Let us suppose for a moment,' said Holmes, interrupting. 'That Mr Wyndham did not murder his butler.'

'May I ask why?' asked Featherstone. 'The evidence is clear.'

'On the contrary,' suggested Holmes. 'For one, I do not believe that the butler died in his study. The tear in his jacket and shirt revealed a singular detail: the presence of Livor Mortis in the body, which my friend, Dr Watson has confirmed. This peculiar state is characterised by a discolouration of the corpse resulting from the settling of red blood cells. For example, if a body is found on its back, you would find that the back has turned a distasteful red and purple colour. The front of the body would be comparatively pale. If he had died slumped forward, then the discolouration would be found on his front rather than on his back.'

The manager glared at Holmes, biting the lower part of his lip. I saw his fists slowly clench, then unclench as if he was making an attempt to restrain himself. 'It occurred to me,' continued Holmes, 'that the butler died in another location in the house and was transported here by some means. We have already identified that Mr Brillington is a large man by any ordinary standard and that carrying him would have been difficult for the murderer. We therefore deduce that he was dragged. Along the corridor I found a loose tack protruding from the carpet. Snagged to it, I found this piece of black cloth. I have not yet had an opportunity to test my theory, but I am certain that it will correspond to the missing section of the butler's tail coat.'

'I don't care what you found or where he died,' growled Featherstone. 'All I know is that Wyndham here is responsible.'

'Featherstone,' the old man declared, 'you can consider yourself fired.' His associate laughed. 'I haven't worked for you since we returned from Africa.'

'Whatever do you mean?'

'You heard me,' snarled Featherstone.

'Gentlemen,' said Wyndham, 'if you are the police, I would be grateful if you escort Mr Featherstone from my house.'

'And leave you here alone, blind? As helpless as a child?'

An atmosphere of violence gripped the room; Featherstone was an intimidating presence but I still believed that if he lost control my friend and I would be able to contain him.

'It is my supposition, Featherstone,' asserted Holmes, 'that you have Mr Wyndham here in your power. As his business associate, you have access to his funds and have imprisoned him here in his own home under the delusion that you are still his employee.'

'You know nothing, Holmes,' growled Featherstone.

'I believe that Mr Brillington stumbled upon a piece of incriminating evidence. Was it a transaction? Was it a conversation? You had no option but to dispose of him. I believe a coroner would confirm that a blunt blow to the head was the cause of death. I'm afraid Featherstone, you have simply invited us to here to witness your own confession. It is clear to me that you intend to frame your former employer for the murder of his butler and steal his fortune. That whiplash across your face was not administered by Wyndham at all. It was the butler's last desperate act as he tried to defend himself. Even if we didn't hear it on your lips, the evidence tells the same story.' Featherstone folded his arms.

'None of you will leave Hixstead alive,' he said calmly. He pulled a revolver from his pocket before I had time to draw my own.

'That's enough,' I said, finally losing my temper. 'That's enough!' I could barely believe the voice was my own. 'We have half of

Scotland Yard on the way, if they're not already at your front gate. Gregson is one of the Yard's most brilliant men. You didn't think we would be foolish enough to accompany you here without an insurance policy?' I astonished myself with this piece of improvisation.

'You're bluffing,' said Featherstone. 'I've got you covered too, Holmes. Drop your weapon.'

Without taking his eyes from us, he strolled to the door and pulled a chain, connected to some remote part of the house. We heard the distant chime of a bell.

'We have dined very well of late, incidentally,' Featherstone said. 'We have acquired two splendid cooks who have raised the standards considerably. The curried lamb and Apricot Charlotte are particular favourites.'

'Mrs Hudson?' I cried. 'You have Mrs Hudson here!'

Four men appeared in the doorway, brooding silently in the shadows. One of them, Raphael, held his arm in a sling; no doubt the victim of the Maharajah's splendid aim.

'Dr Watson,' said Michael. 'I had a feeling we would meet again.'

'We were only beginning to get to know each other,' added Uriel. 'Before you disappeared in the middle of the evening. Still, that is of no consequence now.'

Gabriel fixed my friend with an icy stare. 'I see that you play draughts as well as chess, Mr Holmes.'

'Well,' said Featherstone, 'this is a touching reunion.'

Suddenly we heard the sound of a violin. My friend listened to a bar or two with the keenest interest.

'It appears we have a houseful,' said Holmes. 'Unless I am very much mistaken, that it the sound of Miss Penelope Braithwaite playing a 1724 Stradivarius.'

'You must be referring to my charming fiancée,' said Featherstone. 'Perhaps I should ask her to join us? He moved to the door and called for her:

'Penelope, we have some old friends for dinner. Would you care to join us?'

Ms Braithwaite appeared in the doorway, still holding the priceless instrument, smiling serenely.

'Dr Watson, Sherlock Holmes. What a pleasant surprise.' She looked as sensational as ever; in a flowing red gown, daringly low cut, her hair trussed in her customary turban. All of this was as nothing beside the necklace that hung about her neck; at its centre was the Timor Ruby. 'You must be feeling a little envious, Mr Holmes. The violin has a beautiful tone, would you not agree?'

'Quite wonderful,' said my friend.

'What seems more wonderful,' said Miss Braithwaite, 'is that London's greatest detective not only failed to discover the killer of my teacher, but also failed to notice that I was engaged to the same man who arranged it. How much time did I spend in Baker Street, listening to your muddled thoughts on the affair? I'm afraid your reputation lies in tatters, Mr Holmes.'

I thought for a moment. Was it true? Was this part of Holmes' scheme; how much did he know? I knew better than to doubt my friend, but the cards certainly seemed stacked against him.

'Well,' said Holmes. 'We appear to be in the lion's den, Watson. Miss Braithwaite, it disappoints me beyond measure that you are wrapped up in all of this. For you, the motivation was quite simple: an obsession with the Stradivarius. Each week, you could not bear to see it being played by your teacher Ignatius Wimpole. Finally you spoke to your father, Warwick Snitterton and demanded that he secure it for you, at any cost. He introduced you to his associate, Featherstone here, and you developed a further interest. How congenial. Featherstone was only too happy to oblige with the disposal of poor Ignatius. He even involved poor Peaceheart, the weak minded confectioner, to deflect attention away from himself. I must confess you threw me there. I believed Peaceheart acted alone. Snitterton knew that Peaceheart feared him and that he would never turn you in if caught. And all along, Featherstone was obsessed with the diamonds. Watson, would it surprise you to know that Featherstone is also a member of the Order of the Sapphire Butterfly?'

'It had occurred to me,' I said.

'Together, they hatched their plan to secure the Koh-I-Noor and the Nizam diamond, as well as the Timur Ruby. Quite a list. Not a little greedy, Featherstone?'

234

'Not especially.'

'As part of the Order of the Sapphire Butterfly, Snitterton was already on the trail of the Nizam. Eight elephants and it would have been his. He told his other associates that once it was found, the stone would be cut and the spoils divided. But they would never live to receive their share. But there was more than one rival. You knew the Maharajah wanted it too.'

'Tom, what is the meaning of this?' muttered Wyndham. 'Is this the truth.'

'Every word of it. And we have almost succeeded too,' laughed Featherstone. 'You already know that we stole the Koh-I-Noor from the Queen herself at the Royal Albert Hall. You are the expert in these matters, Holmes, but surely this would rank as one of the most audacious robberies of our age? Gabriel, take a bow. Then there was the matter of the Timur Ruby. That was all too easy. Your own Mrs Hudson took us through the gates of Windsor Castle with her association with Mrs Woodbridge. I would almost go as far as to say they were accessories to the crime. Just think of the headline: "Holmes' Housekeeper Implicated in Crown Jewel Theft." You would never have another case so long as you live! But now, that is of course, merely academic.

'That only leaves the Nazim diamond. I am aware that we did not succeed in taking the rubies from you. Macintosh bungled his work and got what he deserved. As we speak Snitterton is paying the Maharajah a visit and I have full confidence that he will return with the stone. Like you, gentlemen, the Maharajah has been a meddlesome distraction. Within a week, I will have every jewel re-cut and on the European market. They will be lost without a trace.'

'You will never get away with this,' I warned.

'The simple fact of the matter, doctor,' he said, 'is that I already have. You have already seen our rather fine collection of art; the National Gallery was foolish enough to allow us to steal a painting a night for almost a month. Naturally Wyndham has bankrolled the operation and he believed we were stealing the paintings for him. The truth of the matter is that the black paint will make them easier to smuggle out of the country. Now, enough of me. Raphael, would you be good enough to fetch the two ladies?' The Archangel slipped away.

'What of our plans, Tom?' cried Wyndham.

'What of them?'

'You told me you would give me the Koh-I-Noor; that it would be mine . . . that I would hold a star in the palm of my hand.'

'Change of plan,' snapped Featherstone.

'Oh, Mr Holmes!' cried Mrs Hudson as she appeared in the doorway. 'Doctor Watson!'

She was a good deal changed from the formidable woman we knew so well. Her eyes were rheumy with worry and fatigue; her skin had lost its ruddy glow. Mrs Woodbridge, who leaned upon her shoulder looked worse still.

'I told them you would come for us,' Mrs Hudson said in defiance.

'Some rescue!' Featherstone scoffed.

'Don't move, any of you.'

In the other doorway stood none other than our dear friend, Crabtree. He cut an extraordinary figure. Dressed in his own interpretation of an English country gentleman, he wore an ill-fitting tweed suit, checked shirt and yellow tie. Naturally, he also sported his patent pair of matching monocles. In his hands he brandished quite the oldest rifle I had ever seen.

'And about time too, Crabtree!' exclaimed Holmes. 'What took you?' I knew that my friend was bluffing; even Crabtree looked confused by this statement.

'Good God, man!' Featherstone exclaimed. 'When was that gun last used, the Napoleonic wars?' Crabtree glanced down at the ancient weapon.

'As a matter of fact,' he said, 'it was. It was last used in anger by my grandfather at Tolosa.'

'Is this the best you could do, Holmes?'

'You have no idea what you're dealing with, Featherstone,' he retorted. 'Crabtree here is one of the most feared men in London. The Baker rifle he is holding could take a man down at 300 yards. In his jacket pocket he has a pair of Webley Self Extracting Revolvers. You don't stand a chance. And Scotland Yard is right behind him.'

Crabtree was just about holding his nerve.

'So what's your plan, Crabtree?' asked Featherstone.

'I'll do the talking,' returned the optician smartly. 'Move over there by the badger with the pipe and keep your hands where I can see them.'

Remarkably, Featherstone did as he was told. 'You too,' he cried, seeing one of the Archangels going for his pistol. 'And you, missy,' he nodded to Penelope.

'Excellent work, Crabtree,' complemented Holmes as my friend and I slid over to his side. We pulled our own weapons and the tables it appeared, had entirely turned. The next few moments represented something of a blur. In fact it is difficult to reconstruct the order of events without recourse to a little creative licence, given my own memory of them is now confused by the repeated telling.

There was an enormous explosion following by a thick cloud of smoke. Presently pieces of stuffed badger began to rain down on our heads and the bowl of the animal's pipe I saw clip Featherstone on the forehead. At the same time, several more shots were fired.

'Downstairs!' shouted Holmes and we bolted through the door and down the corridor. We arrived at a huge sweeping staircase with wide marble steps; a musty red carpet running down the middle. Below us we saw what I immediately realised must be the gardener wielding a fearsome hunting rifle. 'Upstairs,' shouted Holmes. 'Go up!' We raced up the stairs, a giant dome of glass above us. 'There must be an exit from the roof,' my friend shouted. Crabtree was struggling to keep up, his shorter legs working twice as hard as our own. His two monocles swung like pendulums. 'What on Earth are you doing here?' I demanded.

'I followed you to the station,' he panted. 'I caught the 4.24, the same as you!'

'You must have lost your mind!' I yelled. 'These men are monsters.'

'But it's jolly exciting!' he returned.

A shot rang past me and cracked straight through the glass roof, a tiny shower of shards falling behind us. Far below now was the chessboard patterned floor and at the centre, a pond of electric eels, the water fizzing and crackling with an ethereal blue light in the gloom.

We found ourselves in a room at the very top of the house, which was lined with glass cabinets. These in turned were filled with ornate glass jars, punch bowls and exotic pots of all descriptions. At the far end was one of the most stupendous sights I had ever seen: a magnificent throne, seemingly made from solid gold and embedded with gems of every kind. It was rectangular in shape, with a golden canopy supported on twelve gold pillars, each studded with rows of pearls and embedded with rubies. Most remarkably, peacocks of gold and sapphires roosted on the top of the canopy and in pairs at the top of each column.

'Well, well,' murmured Holmes, stopping short and breaking into a bemused smile. 'Unless I am very much mistaken this is the lost Peacock Throne, the seat of the ancient Mughal emperors of India.'

Crabtree stumbled into the room a way behind and gawped.

'Now that's what I call an armchair!' he exclaimed.

'Not much good to us now,' I muttered.

'To the roof!' shouted Holmes.

A side door took us out onto a narrow terrace and into a strong breeze. The afternoon was slowly fading and the evening was beginning to mine the first diamonds from the night.

'We seem to spend half our time on rooftops,' I complained.

'The situation, I grant, may seem perilous,' my friend began, 'and I appreciate that you have all endured a spell of some discomfort. However, I promise that we are entering the endgame and that a solution to the present crisis will present itself. "Out of this nettle, danger, we pluck this flower, safety." As sure as night follows day, there will be another way down.'

I took Mrs Hudson's hand, while Crabtree did the same for Mrs Woodbridge. Standing a full foot shorter than her, however, it appeared the lady was caretaking him. In this manner, we followed Holmes around the perimeter of the octagonal roof, as if participating in some elaborate dance.

We were not alone for long. From the same door, the Archangels followed, scuttling after us like black beetles. We could see the glint of the blades attached to their canes and already they were taking pot shots at us across the roof, shattering pane after pane in the glass dome. Ducking beneath the shelter of a balustrade, we finally found a defensive position. Holmes and I pulled our revolvers and made an inventory of our ammunition.

'It is hopeless,' I whispered beneath my breath.

'At first glance, it would seem our position is weak,' agreed Holmes. 'However, we have three shots a piece. Enough to take care of each of these villains, with one left over for sport.' It was an optimistic assessment. Mrs Hudson crouched with clenched fists.

'Let them have it, doctor!' she urged. 'They deserve nothing more than a supper of lead this evening.'

'Hear, hear,' said Mrs Woodbridge. 'A fussy lot they are, too. Last night they turned their noses up at my marbled blancmanche. The cheek of it!' Holmes pressed a finger to his lips.

'A challenge!' he shouted. A shot rang out, followed by another, then the firing ceased.

'If you are men of any honour,' Holmes cried. 'Then you will let these women go. What's more, I challenge each of you in turn to single handed combat. That is, without firearms. I will give you a minute to consider my proposition.'

'As you wish, Holmes,' returned a voice at last. It belonged to Michael. 'A foolish notion, but it will provide us with some amusement. I shall be the first to challenge you - and the last.'

'Then step forward with your hands clear and I shall do the same.'

'If there is foul play,' warned Michael, 'my friends will make short work of you.'

'Sherlock Holmes does not break his promises,' he said, giving us a little wink.

Holmes stepped forward and I saw the Archangel emerge from the shadows. They both stepped forward onto the glass dome, edging along the steel seams that held the panes together. The glass was already pockmarked with holes from our previous exchanges and it seemed the whole thing would give at any time.

'You are agents of evil,' pronounced Holmes, balancing himself beautifully, his arms outstretched like a tightrope walker.

'We are merely mercenaries,' said Michael. 'Morality does not enter into it. You are simply an impediment to a financial goal.'

'You talk like a city banker!' remarked Holmes.

'Who knows who we used to be?'

Soon they stood facing each other at the very top of the dome. From a distance they appeared like two stone gods, silhouetted against the sky. Then it began.

Michael lunged, striking Holmes with a blow to the solar plexus. In the same moment, my friend drew back, absorbing little of its intended force, then parried with a jab that immediately hit home. Michael barely flinched, instead ducking low and sweeping his foot in an attempt to knock Holmes off balance. He almost succeeded. Holmes hopped over the foot and chopped at Michael's neck from above with the side of his hand.

'Heaven's alive, doctor!' cried Mrs Hudson. 'Wherever are the police?'

'They will be here directly,' I assured her, with little conviction.

Holmes was employing much the same technique I had seen before; the mysterious art of Bartitsu, that exotic but effective combination of the eastern martial arts with the best of the British Fancy, that is to say, the boxing ring. Michael recovered swiftly and leapt up, for a moment entirely clear of the dome, landing on a steel seam, perhaps four feet from Holmes. He reassumed his attacking pose then lurched forward with both fists in a hammer blow. With the reactions of a man half his age, Holmes stepped sideways and watched dispassionately as Michael mistimed his landing and crashed directly through a pane of glass. His horrifying scream filled the night sky. Below we could see the outline of his body in the pool of water, the shadows of the electric eels snapping at his immobile form.

'Another!' shouted Holmes. At that moment, he was a gladiator, an ancient champion of justice.

The Archangels however had reconsidered their position. The firing resumed and Holmes darted back to the safety of the balustrades.

'Smart work,' I muttered.

'Merely perfunctory,' he replied. 'I knew they would not see it through. Still, it has bought us a little time.' He retrieved a cigarette from the silver case and a lick of flame brought it to life. 'Now when

did you say Gregson will here?' I stared at him in disbelief.
'He's not coming,' I said. 'I made it up.'
'As I suspected; a remarkable fib, Watson, splendidly told. Then we require another plan. I suggest you stay here while I investigate our exit options.' As it turned out, we were overtaken by events.

A huge white object appeared like a new moon from behind a cloud. A burst of flame illuminated it, filling it entirely with light.
'The balloon!' I exclaimed. Until now, it had been nothing but supposition, but here was the evidence, right before our eyes.
'Holmes,' I gasped, 'you were right!'

I caught a glimpse of Featherstone in the basket, his face fixed in an expression of devilish glee. In his hand, he appeared to holding one of the stars from Orion's Belt. It gleamed brighter than anything else in the night sky.
'Can you see it, Holmes?' he shouted. 'It's only the Koh-I-Noor!'
For a moment, everything stopped; even the Archangels looked transfixed by the moonlight gleaming through the stone.
'Take a good look,' Featherstone cried. 'It will be the last you ever see of it. Give my regards to Wyndham.' At his side, we saw Miss Braithwaite, still wearing the ruby necklace, disappearing into a life of untold riches and unknown brutality. As the balloon slowly rose, Holmes and I trained our revolvers at the basket, but we both knew the barrels were empty. Crabtree's muzzle-loading musket had already expelled its single shot and we watched helplessly as the diamond, the fiend and his mistress all slipped from our grasp.

There was the sound of a horse's hooves. At first, it was a faint drumming, like fingers on a tabletop, then it grew louder, more insistent until the clatter was unmistakable. We turned and in the darkness made out the flash of a white stallion galloping up the drive.
'Here comes the cavalry!' cried Mrs Woodbridge.
'Lord save us!' exclaimed Mrs Hudson.
I glanced at Holmes, who wore a non-committal look. As ever it was impossible to discern whether this was part of some master scheme of his, or just another quirk of fate.

'Whoever this rider is,' I remarked, 'he is alone.' Sure enough our cavalry was a small one; as the single rider approached I saw he was wearing a turban; a purple cape trailing behind him. He held the reigns in one hand and in the other gripped his rifle. He stood up in his saddle: 'By the five rivers!' he cried.

A single shot rang out and Featherstone dropped like a mannequin from the basket. Miss Braithwaite screamed. Still a hundred yards away and the rider had hit his mark.

'A remarkable shot!' I cried.

'It can only be the Maharajah,' declared Holmes. 'You will recall he is the fourth best shot in England. But look alive; the balloon is running away with itself.' Sure enough, the contraption had begun to veer and lurch, throwing the unscrupulous Miss Braithwaite from one side of the basket to the other. She had no control over it. The balloon was drifting above the house and we saw her only opportunity. In an instant Holmes was on his feet.

'Jump!' he shouted to her. 'You must jump!' We saw her face blanch as she peered down on us, at the shattered panes of glass beneath and the dead Archangel far below.

'Never!' she cried.

'It is your only chance,' I called. The balloon drifted not six feet above us and all at once she tumbled into our arms, narrowly avoiding the same fate as Michael.

'The diamond!' she screamed, reaching up at the abandoned balloon.

'A simple thank you would suffice,' remarked Holmes.

'The Stradivarius!' she wept.

'Now that it is a shame,' agreed Holmes. Lightened of its load, we watched the balloon sail up and over the trees. Presently we saw the three remaining Archangels fleeing into the fields on the backs of three black stallions.

'They must believe the police are here,' my friend laughed. 'Watson, I do believe your remarkable piece of fiction has saved the day. Crabtree once again looked crestfallen. 'Not forgetting,' added Holmes, 'the remarkable valour of our friend here.'

The Maharajah brought his horse to a halt directly below us and bowed low.

'Bravo!' Holmes called down from the roof.

'What of the diamond?' Singh asked. We pointed in the direction of the balloon. 'Then it is my destiny to follow it,' he returned.

'We understand,' replied Holmes. But wait, what of Snitterton?'

'In the hands of the law,' he explained. 'His attack was rendered harmless by the very simple administration of an Indian Quinine Tonic.' Holmes smiled broadly.

'His Achilles' Heel!'

'My associates have promised to deliver him to Scotland Yard.'

'We are once again in your debt, Maharajah,' said Holmes.

'Farewell, my friends,' he cried. 'I fear this will be the last time we meet, but your kindness will never be forgotten.' With that, he turned his steed, snapped the reins and galloped away down the long drive.

'I wonder,' said Holmes, as we made our way back into the house, 'if there is any tea to be had? I feel we could all benefit from a pot of Lipton and a slice of fruit pie.' We stepped carefully over the broken glass and down the steps to the upper chamber.

'Good lord, Holmes,' I shouted as we entered the room. 'Look over there.' Slumped on the Peacock Throne was the lifeless body of Gustavus Wyndham, his diamond eyes staring into nothing. He had been shot through the heart.

We pulled open the front doors of Hixstead Hall and were met almost immediately by the man Mrs Hudson identified as the gardener. His face was pale with fear.

'He's nothing but a coward,' she dismissed.

'And he has no idea how to grow tomatoes,' added Mrs Woodbridge.

'Summon the local inspector,' Holmes told him, 'and they may look more favourably on your case. Attempt to flee and things will not go well for you.' We left him running down the drive in the direction of the village.

'Now,' said Holmes. 'What do you say to that pot of tea?'

'A splendid idea,' I agreed, and we proceeded to the kitchen.

TWENTY

The Gift

What have I learned these long years in Holmes' shadow? Surely it is that there is no finer way to spend an afternoon than with a good blend of tobacco and an equally well chosen blend of tea. Perhaps I have also learned that there is no black and white when it comes to the workings of the human soul. The more dealings I have had with men of Scotland Yard and those of the criminal world, the less sure I am of the difference between them. I have witnessed the same qualities in the best inspectors as I have seen in the most notorious of thieves. There is the same delight in their control of each turn of events, the thrill of the chase, the prospect of glory and the pursuit of the prize. Above all, in the best of them, there is a sheer joy in the way they play the game. If the prize was nothing more than a handful of dust or sack of straw, it seems, they would still play with the same vigour.

Holmes himself, I have said on more than one occasion, would have made quite the most fearsome adversary the world could ever face. To watch him break a safe with the same ease you and I open our front door or to slip away into the shadows pursued by twenty men is to recognise his talent for the dark arts. When the coin is thrown that puts a soul on the side of good or on the side of evil, it has equal chance of falling on either. An additional turn of the coin in the air and Holmes would have been the leader of a criminal dynasty and Featherstone, the staunchest ally of Scotland Yard.

I am sometimes asked what keeps me returning to the door of 221b Baker Street. When I have a beautiful, intelligent wife at home, a medical practice that delivers a steady if unspectacular income, why do I continue to put myself into harm's way? The answer is simple; Baker Street is a place where adventures begin. It is a place where the speckled shell of ordinary life breaks away to reveal the bizarre workings beneath. It is a portal into another world. The seventeen steps occasionally lead down to the gates of hell; they also lead up to the doors of paradise, as they did when they led me into the path of

Mary Morstan. I have no compunction in admitting that I am a man of limited scope and abilities with no greater than usual charisma; adventure would not normally find me. Without my excursions with Holmes, life would be safer, more regular and more peaceable. It would also be intolerably dull. But if I am pressed, there is another reason that drives me along Baker Street and that is Sherlock Holmes himself. Like the man who becomes obsessed with a great work of art, I am compelled by his company. Each day, I marvel afresh at the glint and gleam of his mind; at the way he looks at the world. I imagine it is like the workers who spent time with Leonardo or Michelangelo. Just to watch them work, to listen to the workings of their minds as one tiny cog meshes with another, is to lose oneself in a world of wonderment.

These are the consolations for dwelling in the life-draining fog of tobacco smoke, the insufferable mess; for enduring the tiresome mood swings and the infernal air of superiority. And yet there is something else too. I return to Baker Street for his friendship; it is hard won, it is testing in the extreme; at times it is barely reciprocated and yet Sherlock Holmes is the dearest friend I have ever had.

Two days later and Holmes and I were in familiar positions, lounging in leather chairs at 221b Baker Street. Mrs Hudson was recuperating with her sister at the coast and once more we were fending for ourselves. The next day Mary would return from Bath, entirely oblivious of our escapades.
'Time for another pipe before Gregson arrives?' asked Holmes.
'I'm afraid not,' I said. 'I think I hear him now.'

Soon enough the tow-headed Gregson was in our midst, rattling off his questions, some of which would never be fully answered.
'It's been a damnable affair,' he said, turning his hat slowly in his hands. 'Naturally, we are grateful for the return of the Timur Ruby. But the loss of the Koh-I-Noor is a dent on the reputation of Scotland Yard from which we may never fully recover. To have it stolen before us renders us fools in the eyes of the public.' He glanced out of the window. 'Lestrade has taken a leave of absence,' he added, not

wholly without pleasure. 'I'm afraid he's taken it rather personally.' Holmes, who I believe held Lestrade in higher regard than the self-serving Gregson, narrowed his eyes at this remark.

'Then there is the body count,' Gregson went on. 'Not inconsiderable, even by your standards; and three of these so called Archangels are still at large.'

'A regrettable lapse,' agreed Holmes. 'But I'm certain that you have your best men on it.'

'Naturally,' said Gregson. He tapped his fingers lightly on the top of his hat.

'I cannot help but feel, Holmes,' he ventured, a little accusingly. 'That there is more to this business than meets the eye.'

'In what sense?'

'Well, we have Miss Braithwaite in custody as you know. She talks of this Maharajah and believes he has escaped to the continent with the diamond. We happen to know of your visit to his estate. You understand that your special status would afford you no protection if it was discovered that you have abetted him in any way?'

'We would never seek any special treatment,' Holmes replied calmly. 'There is a single law and each one of us is subject to it.'

'Still... ' said Gregson.

Holmes rose to his feet with an air of finality. The interview was over.

'The case, I believe, is closed,' he said, shaking the man's hand. 'You have work to do, a ruby to return and three villains to locate. Then there must be a mountain of paperwork awaiting you.' Gregson nodded, still clearly unsatisfied with the answers he had received.

'Perhaps,' suggested Holmes, 'this will help?' He held up a single bent wire and placed it in the Inspector's hand. 'It will revolutionise the world of work. It is called: the paperclip.' Gregson stared at the tiny object and then back at our stony faces.

'Gentlemen,' he said briskly, then put the paperclip in his pocket and returned the hat to his head.

We waited until the door was firmly closed before uttering a word.

'Now,' said Holmes with a smile. 'I have been saving a 1865 port for a moment such as this. Would you make it worth opening the bottle?'

'Certainly,' I replied. He retrieved the vintage from the cabinet along with a pair of glasses.

'There is just one small errand we need to run in the morning,' he said, toasting my health.

'Oh, yes?' I asked.

'We have a diamond to return to Her Majesty the Queen.' I stared at him, dumbfounded.

'You will recall our audience at the Royal Albert Hall,' he said with a dry laugh, 'when she was good enough to let us hold the Koh-I-Noor?' I nodded. 'Well I took the opportunity to switch it with the perfect replica made by our friend Mr Wilberforce. When I asked you to keep my opera glasses safe, you were in fact, in possession of the world's most famous diamond.' He leaned over and picked up the case from the mantelpiece where it had remained since I placed it there. He unbuckled the leather strap and rolled the diamond into his palm.

'Quite a pebble!' he chortled and sipped at his port.

'And the Maharajah?'

'Duleep Singh, who succeeded in capturing our runaway balloon, will go to his grave believing he is in possession of his birthright and in all likelihood, will never know the truth.' I shook my head.

There was another knock at the door.

'Who is it this time?' I demanded returning my glass to the table. I trotted down the seventeen steps and was met by a tradesman at the door.

'A delivery for Mr Holmes,' the man said. I signed for the parcel and returned with it upstairs.

'Anything important?' enquired Holmes.

'No idea,' I replied, handing it to him.

He carefully untied the string and threw off the brown paper.

Inside was a violin case. A moment later he held in his hands a 1724 Stradivarius and a card inscribed in purple ink:

A gift for Mr Sherlock Holmes, a prince amongst men, from Duleep Singh, last Maharajah of the Sikh Empire.

There was an envelope too, one I recognised from my encounter with Macintosh in Trafalgar Square. My friend slit it open with a silver paper knife and peered inside. It was a photograph; the portrait of Sherlock Holmes and me taken by Singh himself at his house. At the bottom, beneath the image of my friend, Maharajah had written: *The Great Mogul*.

'But what is the meaning of this?' I asked.

But Holmes was absorbed by his violin. He applied a little resin, picked up the instrument, drew back the bow, closed his eyes and began to play.

Acknowledgements

To Sir Arthur Conan Doyle and to the creator of the invaluable website www.victorianlondon.org

I would also like to thank Simon Hetherington for his expert advice and for sharing his knowledge and passion for all things Sherlock Holmes. All mistakes that remain of course, are all my own. Thank you to my publisher, Steve Emecz and to Bob Gibson for the terrific cover design.

The game of chess played by Holmes and the Maharajah was inspired by a real match from 1890 between Francis Joseph Lee and Joseph Henry Blackburne.

Love and thanks to Maria, Polly, Noah and Martha, my friends and family.

Also from MX Publishing

MX Publishing is the world's largest specialist Sherlock Holmes publisher, with over a hundred titles and fifty authors creating the latest in Sherlock Holmes fiction and non-fiction.

From traditional short stories and novels to travel guides and quiz books, MX Publishing cater for all Holmes fans.

The collection includes leading titles such as *Benedict Cumberbatch In Transition* and *The Norwood Author* which won the 2011 Howlett Award (Sherlock Holmes Book of the Year).

MX Publishing also has one of the largest communities of Holmes fans on Facebook with regular contributions from dozens of authors.

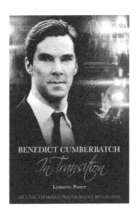

www.mxpublishing.com

251

Also from MX Publishing

Our bestselling short story collections 'Lost Stories of Sherlock
Holmes', 'The Outstanding Mysteries of Sherlock Holmes',
'Untold Adventures of Sherlock Holmes' (and the sequel
'Studies in Legacy') and 'Sherlock Holmes in Pursuit'.

Also From MX Publishing

The Amateur Executioner

London, 1920: Boston-bred Enoch Hale, working as a reporter for the Central Press Syndicate, arrives on the scene shortly after a music hall escape artist is found hanging from the ceiling in his dressing room. What at first appears to be a suicide turns out to be murder . . .

The Enoch Hale and Sherlock Holmes series continues with *The Poisoned Penman* and concludes with *The Egyptian Curse*.

This series brings together two of the most prolific Sherlock Holmes writers of their era – Dan Andriacco and Kieran McMullen.

Also from MX Publishing

"Phil Growick's, *'The Secret Journal of Dr Watson'*, is an adventure which takes place in the latter part of Holmes and Watson's lives. They are entrusted by HM Government (although not officially) and the King no less to undertake a rescue mission to save the Romanovs, Russia's Royal family from a grisly end at the hand of the Bolsheviks. There is a wealth of detail in the story but not so much as would detract us from the enjoyment of the story. Espionage, counter-espionage, the ace of spies himself, double-agents, double-crossers...all these flit across the pages in a realistic and exciting way. All the characters are extremely well-drawn and Mr Growick, most importantly, does not falter with a very good ear for Holmesian dialogue indeed. Highly recommended. A five-star effort."
The Baker Street Society

The characters return in the sequel *'The Revenge of Sherlock Holmes'*.

Lightning Source UK Ltd.
Milton Keynes UK
UKOW06f0601070316

269730UK00001B/33/P